The New Girl

BILLIE CARVER #2

ZELMER WILSON

BLACK SPRINGS PRESS

Also by Zelmer Wilson

For my mother
Myra Jean Wilson
(1944-2025)
in loving memory

"Once again, I find myself in a familiar role, much to my irritation. I am the new girl, and while you might think I would relish this chance to reinvent myself, I miss being known as the bad girl of Beacon Hill."

Josephine Carter, in a letter to her younger brother Jacob, dated September 26, 1924

Blurbs

"Author Zelmer Wilson created a wonderful coming-of-age story of a charismatic yet hesitant girl. Billie is a fascinating character. She is determined, sympathetic, and relatable. I loved how the author made sure Billie's identity never changed. She was tested in many ways at times, but she always handled it with grace...She is complicated, written to perfection, and a joy to read." by Rabia Tanveer for Reader's Favorite (5 star review)

"The New Girl is a coming-of-age tale that follows a young woman's journey of self-discovery as she learns to embrace her family legacy. It's a beautiful story about acclimating oneself to a culture and place so different from the one the protagonist grew up in. Our heroine, Billie, is an intelligent woman who lights up the setting every time she features on the page...At its core, it's a heartwarming slice-of-life drama." by Pikasho Deka for Reader's Favorite (5 star review)

"Set in the nineties, The New Girl describes a cultured, "upper crust" world that, for a young, attractive, outgoing, biracial woman from the South, would have seemed daunting. Author Zelmer Wilson does a superb job of character portrayals and filling out the differing motivations, prejudices, and self-seeking actions of the many people Billie comes across...This is a gentle but satisfying read, and it is one I highly recommend" by Grant Leishman for Reader's Favorite (5 star review)

"The New Girl by Zelmer Wilson is the second book in the Billie Carver series, but it absolutely reads as a standalone... The story has a lot of moving pieces; little things that slowly build...Overall, this is an excellent, tightly written read. Very highly recommended" by Jamie Michele for Reader's Favorite (5 star review)

Chapter One

Billie Carver found herself in a unique position when she arrived in Boston the day after Labor Day, in September of 1990, having discovered that she had been born there, not in New Orleans, where she had lived most of her life. She belonged to not one, but three different communities: the African-American, the LGBT, and the Upper Crust.

Billie's mixed heritage, a result of her white father and black mother, left her feeling like she didn't fully belong in either the white or black world. This struggle was a constant in her life, often leading to misunderstandings and accusations from both black girls and boys. They would often hold her having a white father against her, accusing her of not being black enough or acting white.

The LGBT community, a new chapter in Billie's life, welcomed her with open arms. It was a community she had only recently embraced, accepting her bisexuality the summer after her graduation. Her first love with another girl had opened her eyes to a world of acceptance and understanding. While she was eager to explore this community, she was also hesitant to dive into another relationship, still healing from her past experiences.

Another new community for Billie was the Upper Crust one. Growing up middle-class, she had no idea about the importance of her father's family and their influence in Boston. It was a shock when her paternal grandmother reached out to her, revealing the truth about her father and her parents' marriage.

Billie had already met her older half-brother, Truman, but didn't know him well. She had talked with him enough the two times she had been in Boston before she moved there to know that he loved their grandmother and wanted to get to know her, not rejecting the idea of having her as his younger sister.

Billie's relationship with Truman, along with her relationship with Josephine, would help her adjust to living in Boston, away from her mother, her stepfather, and her best friend. And Truman would become her guide, helping her become familiar with the Upper Crust community.

***

Truman had just walked into his tiny studio apartment in South Boston. The phone was ringing, so he answered it. He picked it up, frowning. *I hope it isn't anyone from work.* "Hello," he said. "I hope whoever is calling has good news because I'm tired, and I'm not in the mood for any kind of bullshit."

"Hello, Truman," an elderly woman said. "It is I, your grandmother."

Truman smiled. *Well, I would know that voice anywhere.* "Hi, Josephine," he said, remembering she didn't like to be called grandmother or any other variation. He glanced at his watch. "We just talked the other day, so what's on your mind?"

Josephine chuckled. "I know we talked the other day," she said. "I am not getting senile yet." She sighed. "Do I have to remind you what today is?"

Truman glanced at the calendar hanging on the wall by the phone. *Well, shit, I didn't write anything down for today.* "Yeah, I guess you do have to remind me about today."

Josephine sighed again. "Today is the day Billie is coming home," she said. "She called me this morning, right before she left New York City."

Truman slapped his forehead and chuckled. "Yeah, that's right," he said. "I'm sorry I didn't write it down on my calendar." *I was sure I wouldn't forget, but I was wrong.*

"I told you to write it down," Josephine said. "I am sure she would love to see you when she arrives."

Truman grinned. "Well, I would love to see her again," he said. He shook his head and chuckled. "I don't know how you convinced her to come here." *I wasn't sure Billie would accept Josephine's offer.*

"I did not have to convince her," Josephine said. "Would you like to have dinner with us this evening?"

Well, that's an easy question. "I sure would love to have dinner with you and Billie," Truman said. He glanced at his watch. "Dinner at the usual time, seven o'clock?"

"Of course, Truman," Josephine said. "We will be expecting you."

"And I'll be there," Truman said. "I'll see you at seven. Goodbye, Josephine." *I'm glad she asked Billie to move here. I'm looking forward to getting to know Billie better.*

"Goodbye, Truman," Josephine said. She then hung up the phone.

***

An hour later, Truman left his apartment and traveled from South Boston to Josephine's house in Beacon Hill, the part of Boston where the old-money families, the Upper Crust, lived. Truman could have lived there if he had wanted to, but unlike his peers, he saw being a member of the Upper Crust as more of a burden than a privilege.

Truman spotted the Louisiana license plate. He couldn't help but smile. "I'm surprised she didn't fly here instead of driving," he said. "But then again, if I had this car, I wouldn't want to leave it in New Orleans."

Truman approached the front door and knocked, even though he knew Josephine had always told him he didn't have to knock. His mother had raised him to knock before entering any house he didn't live in, even if that house belonged to a family member like Josephine.

Truman was about to knock again when the front door opened. "Well, hey there," he said. "I guess you made good time getting here, didn't you, Billie?" *Sometimes, life will give you the last thing you ever wanted or needed. I never thought I wanted a younger sister until I met her.*

Billie smiled and nodded. "I sure did," she said. "So, are you just going to stand there, or are you going to give me a hug?"

Oh, that's right. Billie's an affectionate person. "I guess I can give you a hug," Truman said. He hugged Billie, his arms going around her shoulders.

Billie chuckled. "Well, I'm glad to see you, too," she said. She untangled herself from Truman and took a step back from him. "Josephine's expecting us to join her."

Did I hug her too tightly or for too long? "Well, we shouldn't leave her waiting," Truman said. "Show me the way."

Truman followed Billie to the dining room, where Josephine waited for them.

"You were right, Josephine," Billie said, sitting at the dining room table on Josephine's right. "He was right on time."

Truman's punctuality was one of his few virtues, and he took pride in it. "You said dinner was at seven, so here I am, only a few minutes past seven." He pointed at his watch. *Despite my resistance when I was younger, my mother did her best to turn me into a gentleman.*

Josephine smiled. "I am glad to see your mother raised you right," she said. She shook her head and cleared her throat. "How is your mother?"

Oh, yeah, the two of them don't talk to each other. Truman shrugged his shoulders. "She's about the same," he said. "She spends too much time gossiping while neglecting her health."

Josephine frowned and nodded. "I would say I am surprised to hear that, but I am not," she said. She sighed. "I do not think your mother has ever gotten over losing your father."

Truman nodded. "I think you're right about that, Josephine," he said. *Now, I'm not sure what Josephine means when she says that my father died or when he left my mother to be with Billie's mother when she says that my mother hasn't gotten over losing him.* He sighed. "I'm afraid her drinking has gotten worse since I graduated from Columbia."

Josephine nodded. "I noticed that too," she said. She cleared her throat. "I am sorry, Billie, for not including you in our conversation."

Billie smiled. "It's okay," she said. "I'm enjoying listening to y'all make small talk."

I wouldn't call gossiping about my mother and her drinking problem making small talk, but I'll cut Billie some slack. Truman cleared his throat. "So, is dinner ready or not?"

Josephine nodded and rang the dinner bell.

Their dinner was served as the cook and the maid emerged from the kitchen and entered the dining room.

***

An hour later, dinner was over. Truman sat in the parlor with Billie and Josephine.

Josephine smiled. "If either of you wants to smoke a cigarette, go ahead," she said. "I may not be allowed to smoke anymore, but that does not mean you cannot smoke."

Billie chuckled. "Okay, you don't have to twist my arm," she said. She took out a cigarette and lit it. "What about you, Truman?"

Truman grinned. "I guess I'll join you and have a smoke," he said. *Well, it will be harder for me to quit with Billie around.* "Are you sure you don't mind us smoking in front of you, Josephine?"

"I am sure," Josephine said. She cleared her throat. "I do not wish to continue the conversation we were having before dinner."

Good, because I don't feel like talking about my mother anymore. "Well, why don't we find another subject to discuss?" *Let's include Billie this time.* "So, Billie, tell us about New Orleans."

Billie smiled. "Well, what do you want to know?"

She seems a little guarded. "Tell us what it was like growing up there," Truman said. He shook his head and chuckled. "Willie has told me many stories about growing up there." *I wish he would embrace me as his brother like Billie seems to have, but I guess I have to settle for just being his friend.*

"I'm sure he has," Billie said. She shook her head and chuckled. "I've got plenty of stories I could tell about my life in New Orleans and growing up there."

"But you don't want to tell them, do you?" Truman took a drag off his cigarette. "What would you rather talk about, Billie?" *I might be wrong, but she seems troubled. I think I see sadness in her beautiful brown eyes.*

Billie smiled. "Well, I would rather learn more about Boston," she said. "I was born here, but don't know anything about it."

Josephine nodded in approval. "We can change that," she said. She looked over at Truman. "You understand why Billie would want to talk about Boston more than she would New Orleans, do you not, Truman?"

Truman chuckled. "Yeah, I guess I do," he said. He then shrugged his shoulders. *I was looking forward to hearing Billie's stories, but I guess I will have to wait for another time.* "What do you want to know, Billie?" *I don't think I've ever talked about Boston with anyone else before.*

"I know what Billie should know," Josephine said. She reached out and took one of Billie's hands. "My dear Billie, you are now part of the so-called Upper Crust."

Billie frowned. "What do you mean, Josephine?"

Josephine sighed and shook her head. "I know that your family in New Orleans was a middle-class family, but here in Boston, you are a member of the upper class."

Billie nodded. "Yeah, I remember you mentioning that before," she said. "So, tell me about the Upper Crust families."

I never had to ask Josephine about my place among the Upper Crust. Truman shook his head and chuckled. *My mother made sure I knew how important our family was in Boston.*

Josephine cleared her throat. "There are seven main families of the Upper Crust," she said. "They are the Carvers, the Carters, the Adams, the Jacksons, the Dubois family, the Robinsons, and the Wilsons."

Billie grinned. "What about the Kennedys?" She chuckled. "I thought they were a big deal here in Boston."

Josephine smiled. "They are a big deal, but they are not part of the old money families of Boston," she said. "I must caution you, Billie, not to expect a warm welcome from anyone from the other families since you are new here and mixed."

"I'll help you, Billie, however I can," Truman said. "I'm sure Billie will charm them."

Billie smiled. "They may not accept me, but they won't be able to ignore me."

Josephine frowned. "I admire your confidence, Billie," she said. She sighed and shook her head. "I have to deal with the other families all my life, and while I have dealt with all kinds of people, I have never met anyone quite as backstabbing and vicious as them."

Truman nodded. *Josephine knows what she's talking about. I've heard the stories about her, how she used to be an absolute hell raiser when she was younger, before she settled down and married.* "Josephine's right," he said. "I've grown up with them, and none are my friends."

Billie chuckled. "Well, I'm not looking to make any new friends," she said. She took a drag off her cigarette. "And I'm not sure I even want to be part of this world."

Josephine nodded. "It is your choice, Billie," she said. "Is there any reason you may not want to be part of it?"

Truman chuckled. *I didn't know there was a choice. I've always been told I belonged there, even when I didn't feel like I did.* "Maybe she feels like she doesn't want to have to prove herself," he said. "Or maybe she doesn't feel like she belongs here, either in our family or in Boston."

Billie frowned. "You don't know me well enough even to guess how I feel, Truman," she said. She shook her head and cleared her throat. "Sorry, I know you weren't trying to upset me."

Truman chuckled. *Yeah, I was trying to upset you, Billie.* "You should know that it isn't going to be easy," he said. "Josephine's right, they're going to give you a hard time." He sighed and shook his head. "They're not going to care that you're a Carver."

Billie smiled. "But I am," she said. "And I won't pretend I'm not just because it makes other people uncomfortable."

***

Eight weeks after Billie arrived in Boston, it was Halloween. The country club to which all the Upper Crust families belonged was having its usual Halloween party.

Billie would meet two of her three rivals at the country club. One was Jasmine Carter, a quiet but observant girl who often found herself in the shadows. The other was Bridget Jackson, a confident and outspoken girl unafraid to voice her opinions.

Bridget had coffee with her parents at their favorite cafe a few hours before the Halloween party started.

"So, I hope you picked out a costume for the party," her mother said. "We can't go because your father's doctor has said he can't drink anymore, so we need you to go for us."

Bridget sighed. "Do I have to, Mother?" *It's good that I still have the costume I wore last year. Shit, I think my mother knows I still have it, so I can't lie to her and tell her I can't go because I don't have a costume. The weight of my parents' expectations is heavy, and I can't bear to disappoint them. I feel the weight of their expectations pressing down on me, making it hard to breathe.*

Her mother frowned. "Yes, Bridget, you have to go," she said. "We need you there to represent our family."

Bridget tried to argue with her mother for another twenty minutes, but her mother wouldn't change her mind.

"Okay," Bridget said, holding up her hands. "I'll go to the stupid costume party." *One of the drawbacks to being an only child is that your parents expect you always to obey them, and you can't escape their attention. I feel like I'm in a cage, unable to make my own choices. The walls of their expectations are closing in on me, leaving me no room to breathe.*

Bridget departed company with her parents before they could ask her to do anything else. She returned to her apartment and dug out her Halloween costume from the previous year from her closet.

***

Jasmine Carter arrived at the country club. She had only come to the annual Halloween party because she knew she was expected to attend and that if she didn't, her peers would notice her absence.

Jasmine sighed and shook her head. *Every year, I tell myself the same thing: I won't go to this stupid party, and I still find myself going by myself most of the time.*

Jasmine always went to the Halloween party because she didn't want to disappoint her mother, the most important person in her life, whom she always tried to please.

You're privileged, her mother would tell her often, and with privilege comes duty. Jasmine frowned. *Sometimes, I wonder if I would have been better off being raised by my father's family instead of by my mother and being the only black girl in a white family.*

Jasmine had once said so to her mother, only a few years before, when she was a rebellious teenager. She had expected her mother to snap back at her, but her mother started crying and ran out of the room. Jasmine promised she would never say anything like that to her mother again.

Since that day, Jasmine had become a good girl, doing everything her mother expected, including attending parties at the country club. However, her awkward, shy personality made her struggle to engage in social activities.

Another thing that Jasmine often wished for was to be born white. She didn't believe her life would be easier in most ways, but she did think it would be easier for her to make friends. It was always frustrating to be the only black girl, knowing her peers would never fully accept her.

Chapter Two

J asmine walked into the country club and made her way to the bar. She found an empty stool and sat on it. She looked around for the bartender and waved to get his attention.

"Good evening, Miss Carter," the bartender said. "Would you like your usual?"

Jasmine nodded. "I'm sure I would," she said. She took out a cigarette and lit it. She looked around, noting who was there and what costume they were wearing. "I see that the usual crowd showed up."

The bartender chuckled. "Well, you know, any excuse to get drunk," he said. He then handed Jasmine her drink. "Here you go, Miss Carter."

"Thanks," Jasmine said. She took a sip and grinned. "I've told you before, but you make the best scotch and soda." *I wish I could say more to him. He's cute and charming, but he's a bartender. My mother wouldn't allow me to date a guy like him.*

The bartender smiled at Jasmine and nodded. "Yeah, you've told me before," he said. "I noticed you're not wearing a costume."

"For most people, Halloween is the one day a year they allow themselves to dress up and wear a mask," Jasmine said. She sighed and shook her head. "I wear a mask all the time." *Okay, cool it. He doesn't need or want to hear about your problems.*

The bartender nodded and gave Jasmine an understanding smile. "I know what you mean, Miss Carter," he said. "Do me a favor and try to have a good time."

Jasmine smiled back. "I'm not making any promises, but I'll try to have a good time," she said. *I'm not sure if he's just being nice or if he is flirting with me.* She looked over her shoulder and frowned. "The usual couples are here."

The bartender nodded. "You're right about that," he said. He then chuckled and grinned. "Well, it looks like your favorite person just showed up."

How does he know who my favorite person is? Did I tell him, or could he tell by watching my face? Jasmine turned around and smiled. "Well, I'm glad I came here," she said. "Truman Carver is the best-looking man in Boston, and I don't want to live anywhere else." *And I see he's not alone, which isn't surprising.* "Hey, Truman." She waved at him, hoping he would see her and come over to see her.

Truman looked around until he saw Jasmine sitting at the bar. He smiled and walked to her, the young lady following him. "Hey, Jasmine," he said. "I wasn't sure you would be here."

Now, why would he say something like that? "You know me," Jasmine said. "If there's a party here, I won't miss it."

Truman chuckled. "Every party I've ever seen you at, you're always sitting by yourself and watching everyone else," he said. "Anyway, how's your mother doing?"

Jasmine smiled. *Truman's one of the few people who always asks me about my mother, which is another reason why I've got a crush on him.* "She's doing well; thanks for asking," she said. *Okay, so enough of the polite talk.* "Aren't you going to introduce me to your friend, Truman?"

"She's not my friend," Truman said. He chuckled and grinned. "Jasmine Carter, I want you to meet Billie Carver, my little sister."

Jasmine frowned. "What do you mean, little sister?" She shook her head. "I've known you all my life, and this is the first time you've mentioned having a younger sister." *Is he playing some joke on me?*

"Well, I hadn't mentioned having a younger sister before because I didn't know I had one until a few months ago," Truman said. "Billie's my half-sister, and until this last September, she has lived in New Orleans with her mother."

"I moved here because our grandmother asked me to live with her," Billie said. She offered Jasmine her hand to shake. "It's nice to meet you, Jasmine."

Jasmine shook Billie's hand. "Yeah, same here," she said. *She's gorgeous and has the brightest smile I've ever seen.* "I've met Truman's mother, and you don't look like her." *I think I remember my mother telling me once that Truman's father died when Truman was only five.*

"We had the same father but different mothers," Billie said. "And yes, my mother's black, in case you were wondering."

"You see, Jasmine, Billie's like you," Truman said. "She's the product of an interracial relationship, too."

I'm sure that's the only thing I have in common with her. Jasmine shook her head. "There are many people my age who are products of an interracial relationship," she said. "In the Sixties, there were a lot of white people getting with black people."

Truman chuckled and grinned. "Yeah, you're right about that," he said. He cleared his throat, glancing over at Billie. "We came here to have a few drinks, and I was going to introduce Billie around and let the other members have a chance to meet her."

Jasmine nodded. "Sounds like a good plan," she said. *Good luck with anyone here accepting her. I've lived here my whole life, and they still treat me like an outsider.* "Well, I won't keep you from doing that any longer."

Truman looked over at Billie, who nodded. "Say, why don't you join us, Jasmine?"

Jasmine hesitated. *I didn't come here to socialize but to drink instead.* "Okay, I would love to join you two," she said. *I can't pass up a chance to sit with Truman and talk to him.* She stood up, getting off the stool. "Let's go."

The three of them left the bar and went to a nearby table. Truman sat at one end of the table, Billie sat on his right, and Jasmine sat on his left.

Billie looked around, smiling. "This place reminds me of the country club back in New Orleans," she said. She chuckled and grinned. "I guess all country clubs are the same, for the most part."

Jasmine nodded. *No one asked you, country girl.* "So, Truman," she said, giving Truman her complete attention. "I noticed you haven't been around lately."

Truman shrugged. "I've been busy at work," he said. "I'm a junior associate there, and they expect me to work long hours every week."

Billie smiled. "Well, you're the one who wanted to be a lawyer," she said. "Josephine told me you wanted to be a journalist when you were younger."

Truman laughed. "I did until I found out that lawyers get paid much more than journalists," he said. "And I realized I wanted to be more like our father."

Jasmine nodded. "Oh, yeah, I remember my mother telling me your father was some civil rights lawyer," she said. "Was she right about him?"

Billie nodded. "Your mother was right about our father," she said. "If our father hadn't been a civil rights lawyer, he wouldn't have met my mother."

***

Bridget arrived at the country club and parked near the front entrance. She looked at herself in the rearview mirror and adjusted her costume.

Bridget hadn't gotten rid of her Halloween costume because she admired the person she dressed as, though she wouldn't admit it to anyone. And that person was the German cabaret singer Lisbeth Reinhart.

Bridget left the parking lot and entered the country club. She went straight to the bar, not even bothering to look around for an empty table. She found an empty stool and sat down, feeling like an outsider in a sea of people. The chatter and laughter around her only served to highlight her loneliness.

The bartender walked over to her and smiled. "Well, good evening, Miss Jackson," he said. "I was wondering if you would show up."

Bridget chuckled. "Well, my parents forced me to come," she said. "Hopefully, no one will notice I'm wearing the same costume I did last year." *He's the only person I enjoy talking to, even if he flirts with me.*

The bartender grinned and chuckled. "I'm sure some people will notice, but I doubt they'll say anything about it," he said. "Anyway, would you like your usual?"

Bridget nodded. "I sure would," she said. "There's no way I'm staying sober."

"Okay, Miss Jackson," the bartender said. "Just remember not to overdo it."

Bridget chuckled. "I'll try not to overdo it," she said. She turned around on her stool and looked around. *Okay, so who showed up, and who's not here?* She searched for a familiar or friendly face while waiting for her drink.

Bridget smiled. *Now, I didn't expect to see him here.*

"Here you go, Miss Jackson," the bartender said, handing Bridget her drink. "If you need anything else, I'll be around."

"Thanks," Bridget said. *Maybe he knows how long he's been here and who the young lady sitting with him is, because I don't know her.* "Tell me, how long has Truman Carver been here?"

The bartender chuckled. "Mister Carver showed up about ten minutes ago," he said. "He managed to talk Miss Carter into joining him and his guest."

Bridget nodded. *I saw Jasmine sitting with him, which didn't surprise me. Truman might be the only one who doesn't know about her crush on him.*

Bridget took out a cigarette and lit it. "Well, I see some people didn't bother getting a costume," she said. She shook her head and chuckled. *Why even bother coming here for a Halloween party if you won't wear a costume?*

"Well, if I were you, I wouldn't say anything to Miss Carter about not wearing a costume or a mask," the bartender said. "I pointed it out to her, and she made a strange remark."

Bridget laughed and grinned. "Miss Carter always makes strange remarks," she said. *I haven't figured out that young lady yet. She comes to every party here but always sits by herself. I don't think she has any friends.* "She's a strange young lady."

The bartender shrugged his shoulders. "Maybe so, but she's always polite and leaves good tips," he said. He smiled. "I'd rather deal with her than with most people here."

"I hope you're not talking about me," Bridget said. "I'm polite and leave good tips, too." *I know what he means. Most of the people, the country club members, aren't worth a shit.*

"Of course, I wasn't speaking about you, Miss Jackson," the bartender said, blushing. "You're one of my favorite members."

Bridget smiled. "I hope so," she said. *Okay, I can stop teasing him.* "Otherwise, I might have to sit at a table instead of here, at the bar." *I'll stop now.*

***

Rebecca Dubois arrived at the country club in a taxi. Unlike Bridget or Jasmine, she didn't become a rival; instead, she became one of the two friends Billie made while living in Boston.

"Here you go, miss," the taxi driver said, looking over his shoulder at Rebecca. "Okay, I have to ask. Who are you dressed up as again?"

Rebecca chuckled. "I'm the Dominican dancer, Bella Cuevas," she said. *I think he heard me the first time I told him. He's just looking for any excuse to talk to me some more before I get out of his taxi.* She shrugged her shoulders. "She was famous a long time ago."

The taxi driver grinned. "If you say so, miss," he said. "I like it, even if I don't know who that is."

Rebecca glanced at the meter and handed the taxi driver a twenty. "Thanks for the ride," she said. *Well, I've had worse taxi drivers to deal with before.* She got out of the taxi and closed the door.

"Thanks for the tip," the taxi driver said. "And I hope you have a good time at your Halloween party."

Rebecca waved at the taxi driver, and the taxi drove away. *Well, the fare wasn't cheap, but since I plan on drinking tonight, I'd rather pay for a taxi instead of getting caught drinking and driving.*

Rebecca took out a cigarette and lit it while looking around the parking lot. *Okay, let's see who showed up. Well, it seems like the usual crowd is here.* She smiled. *Hey, I know that car. I hope she's holding because I'd love some powder.*

Rebecca walked to the front entrance. On her way there, she passed some other cars she recognized, though she wasn't quite as excited about seeing them. *I see Jasmine's here. I'd be willing to bet that she's sitting by herself at the bar. Why does she come to parties when it's clear that she doesn't enjoy them?* Rebecca couldn't help but feel a twinge of pity for Jasmine, who always seemed to be a loner at these events.

Rebecca left the parking lot after she finished her cigarette and entered the country club. She looked around, noting who was there and who wasn't. She smiled when she looked over at the bar. *There she is, sitting at the bar.*

Rebecca made her way to the bar, and as she got closer, the conversation between the bartender and Bridget became clearer.

"I hope so," Bridget said. "Otherwise, I might have to sit elsewhere instead of at the bar."

***

"Why don't you leave him alone, Bridget?"

I know that voice. Bridget glanced over her shoulder. *Of course, it's her.* "Good evening, Rebecca," she said. "Are you here just to bother me, or do you want something?"

Rebecca grinned and chuckled. "Why can't I do both?"

She seems pleased to see me. "I guess you could do both," Bridget said. *Okay, it's time to snap back at her.* "I'm surprised to see you by yourself. I didn't think you could go anywhere without one of your followers."

Rebecca sighed. "I've told you before, I don't have any followers," she said. She chuckled. "I can't help, I have many admirers."

Bridget shrugged her shoulders. "You can call them whatever you want to," she said.

"I didn't come here to debate with you," Rebecca said. She leaned closer to Bridget, closing the distance between them. "Are you holding or not?"

Of course, that's why she walked over here and started talking to me. "Lucky for you, I am," Bridget said. *I doubt my parents would approve of me being the main supplier of cocaine to all their friends' children.* She stood up, leaving the stool. "Let's go to the ladies' room and talk privately about it."

Rebecca nodded. "Sounds like a good idea to me," she said. She pointed over her shoulder at the table where Truman was sitting. "But before that, why don't we go over there and say hi?"

Bridget frowned. "Do you want to go over there because you want to say hi to Truman or because Jasmine's sitting over there, and you want to give her a hard time?" *She likes teasing poor Jasmine, not because she doesn't like her, but because I think she's trying to get Jasmine out of her shell.* "Can't you tell she's uncomfortable enough, sitting at the same table with Truman and someone she doesn't know?"

Rebecca chuckled. "Maybe a little of both," she said. "Jasmine needs to be able to find a way to be comfortable around people she doesn't know."

Bridget shook her head. "Does she know that you've adopted her?" *I would tell Jasmine, but I don't think she would believe me.* "She's not your little sister; you don't have to look out for her."

Rebecca smiled. "Someone has to look out for her," she said. She looked around, sighing. "I know how the others here can treat someone they decide doesn't belong here."

Bridget nodded. "I'm sure you do," she said. *Rebecca's lucky, in a way. I don't know what's worse: being treated like you don't belong here, or feeling like you don't belong.*

"Here's your drink, Miss Dubois," the bartender said, handing Rebecca her drink.

Bridget frowned. "Did you order a drink?" *I didn't hear her order a drink. Did I miss something?*

Rebecca nodded. "I did, but I didn't say anything," she said. She smiled at the bartender. "I didn't have to say anything. He looked at me, and I nodded."

Bridget chuckled. "Well, I guess that's why he's the bartender here," she said. *So, I guess he flirts with all the ladies here.*

"Anyway, enough stalling," Rebecca said. "Let's go over there and say hi to Truman." She leaned closer to Bridget. "Don't you want to find out who he's with?"

Bridget chuckled and nodded. "I'll admit, I'm curious about who she is," she said. *I still don't want to say hi to Truman, even though he's one of the few men I'm attracted to, preferring to admire him from afar. If I talk to him, I risk saying or doing something that could embarrass me or him.*

"Well, let's go find out," Rebecca said. She picked up her drink from the bar and gestured for Bridget to follow her.

Bridget and Rebecca walked away from the bar. They went to the table where Truman, Jasmine, and the young lady they didn't know were sitting.

Truman smiled. "Hi, Rebecca," he said. He nodded at Bridget. "I like your costume, Bridget."

Bridget smiled back at Truman. "Thanks, I'm glad you like it," she said. *Okay, don't say anything else.* She looked over at Jasmine, who was staring at her drink. "Hi, Jasmine." *I won't tease her like Rebecca does.*

Jasmine looked up. "Hi, Bridget," she said. She chuckled and shook her head. "Didn't you wear that costume last year?"

Bridget nodded. "You're right, I did," she said. "I'm afraid I forgot about this party and didn't have time to get a new one." She leaned closer to Jasmine. "What's your excuse for not wearing one this year?"

Jasmine blushed. "I have to use the ladies' room," she said, standing up.

Bridget leaned closer to Rebecca. "We should wait a few minutes before we go to the ladies' room," she said.

Jasmine's not coming back here. Rebecca shook her head. "Let's go now," she said. She looked over at Truman and smiled. "I'll be right back. I need to talk with Bridget about something." *I don't know if he's a fan of the powder. From what I've heard about him, he keeps himself out of trouble.*

Truman nodded. "Okay, we will be here."

Chapter Three

J asmine arrived at the ladies' room and pushed open the door. She went to the sink and washed her face. *Okay, pull yourself together. You're not acting like the young lady your mother raised you to be. My mother would be disappointed in me for being so rude to Billie.* "She's the most beautiful woman I've ever seen," she said, looking at her reflection in the mirror. "And she's charming, too." *Okay, here's what you're going to do. You're going to dry your face off and go back out there. You sit with them and be polite to Billie.*

***

Rebecca and Bridget walked away and went to the ladies' room. They didn't see Jasmine, but one of the stalls was occupied; the door closed.

"Okay, let's get down to business," Bridget said. "How much do you want?"

Rebecca held up two fingers. "I know she can hear us, so let's not make it too obvious," she said. She pulled out a wad of bills from her bra. "How much?"

"The usual price," Bridget said, holding out her hand.

Rebecca peeled off a few bills and handed them to Bridget. "It's your turn now," she said, holding out her hand. *She better not short me any of it, like last time.*

Bridget nodded and removed two small baggies of cocaine from underneath her bra. "Here you go," she said, handing them to Rebecca. She started to count the money that Rebecca had just given her.

Rebecca took two small bumps and put the rest away, slipping the two tied-up small baggies of cocaine in her bra underneath it. "Say, why don't you go back with me?"

Bridget shook her head. "Billie makes me nervous," she said. She sighed and shook her head. "I don't know why, but she does."

Rebecca nodded. *I saw the way Billie looked at Bridget. I guess it didn't even occur to her that Billie might be attracted to her.* "I like your costume," she said. "Have you always been a fan of Lisbeth Reinhart?"

Bridget sighed. "You can go now," she said. "We don't have to make small talk."

She doesn't think much of me. "I need to wash my face first," Rebecca said. She touched her nose. "I have to make sure nothing is showing." *I'm sure it's not a secret that I love the powder, but I need to be discreet.*

Bridget nodded. She walked away without saying another word and left the ladies' room.

The stall door opened, and Jasmine walked out. She went to the sink and started washing her hands.

I know her answer, but I should ask her anyway. "Would you like a bump, Jasmine?" *The poor girl needs someone to look out for her.*

Jasmine shook her head. "I don't need any of that shit," she said. "I prefer just to drink."

Rebecca shrugged her shoulders. "Okay, well, see you later," she said. *I'm sure she won't return to join Truman and Billie.*

***

Rebecca left the ladies' room and returned to the table where Truman and Billie sat. She sat down next to Truman and across the table from Billie.

Billie looked past the table. "So, are Jasmine and Bridget not coming back?"

Well, at least she remembered their names. "Jasmine's still in the ladies' room, washing her hands, while I'm sure Bridget went back to sitting at the bar," she said. She turned around in her chair and pointed at the bar. "Bridget's back at the bar." She chuckled and grinned. "She's giving the bartender a hard time." She took a sip of her vodka tonic. "So, did you move here, Billie, or are you just visiting?"

"I moved here about eight weeks ago," Billie said. She smiled. "I was born here, but haven't lived here since I was a baby."

***

Three days later, Rebecca found herself at the nearest branch of the Boston Public Library in Beacon Hill, not far from her house.

I should be Christmas shopping since I still have plenty of gifts to buy. Rebecca sighed and shook her head. *I'm just not in the mood to do any Christmas shopping.* She rubbed her forehead. *I'm just getting over Halloween. Today's the first day I don't feel hungover.*

Rebecca parked her car in an empty parking space near the front door. She glanced at her watch. *Let's see, it's Saturday, so the library won't be open all day. I think it closes at noon, and it's only ten o'clock now, so I've got plenty of time to go in and look around for almost two hours.*

Rebecca got out of her car and walked over to the front door. *I've got time to smoke a cigarette.* She took one out and lit it, looking around the parking lot. *Not many people here today, which doesn't surprise me.* She chuckled and grinned. *This library might be in one of the wealthiest parts of Boston, but I don't think it's ever busy on the weekend.*

Rebecca smoked her cigarette, deciding what book she would look for in the library. *One good thing about no longer being in school is that I only read books I want to read instead of having to read books I've been assigned to read.* She chuckled. *But then again, some of the books I was forced to read ended up being the ones I loved the most. It's funny how life works out sometimes.*

***

Rebecca took one last drag off her cigarette and threw it on the ground. She smashed it out with the heel of her boot. *Okay, try not to stay here too long. You'll go in there and look around for maybe an hour.*

Rebecca shook her head, grinning. She walked into the library, pushing the front door open. She went to the fiction/literature section, hoping that Henry Young's newest novel was there. *They should have a few copies. I hope they do, anyway.* She smiled at seeing three copies of his novel, The Distance Between.

Rebecca pulled one of the copies off the shelf and looked at the front cover. *Now, this is a great cover. I don't understand the title, which doesn't match the front cover, but I like it. It makes me want to read this book.*

Rebecca opened the book and flipped through it. She stopped on the dedication page and frowned. *Well, it looks like he dedicated this book to the same young lady he did in his last book I read, The Girl with the Broken Smile.*

"Thanks for everything. I couldn't have written this book without your help," Rebecca said, reading the dedication out loud. "And her name's Bobbie Lamont." *Now, who in the world is Bobbie Lamont? I know she's not an author because I've searched for her name and can't find it anywhere.* "Who's Bobbie Lamont? And how in the hell does she know Henry Young?"

"Oh, that's a long story," Billie said, stepping out from the other end of the bookshelf. She grinned and chuckled. "Hi, Rebecca. I didn't think I would run into anyone I knew here."

Rebecca closed the book and walked over to Billie. "Hi, Billie," she said. *She might be one of the few people I wouldn't mind running into today. I enjoyed my conversation with her on Halloween, only three days ago.*

Billie smiled and pointed at the book Rebecca was holding. "Well, I'm glad to find out that you've got good taste in books," she said. "Henry Young is one of my favorite authors."

Rebecca smiled. "He's one of my favorite authors, too," she said. She sighed and shook her head. "I don't know many people I can talk about books and authors with." *Being an avid reader doesn't win you any popularity points among the people I grew up with here in Boston.*

Billie smiled. "Well, now you do," she said. She chuckled and shook her head. "I may not be the bookworm my best friend is, but I do love to read."

Billie sure is gorgeous, no matter what she wears. She's a heartbreaker, even just wearing jeans and a long-sleeved blouse. "Your best friend sounds interesting."

Billie smiled and nodded. "I think she is," she said. She sighed. "I need to remember to call her later today."

Does Billie's best friend live here in Boston, or does she live somewhere else? "I've always wanted to meet him," Rebecca said.

Billie seems upset, so maybe we should talk about something else.
"Have you ever met him, Billie?"

Billie nodded and grinned. "Oh, yeah, I've met him," she said.
"Six years ago, in New Orleans, my best friend and I cut class to
go to his book reading."

Rebecca grinned back at Billie. "Six years ago? I think I know
which one of his books you're talking about," she said. *Let's see,
six years ago, Henry Young's book was Someone to Love.* "It was
his first book that I read and loved."

Billie nodded. "It's a good one," she said. She grinned. "Now,
you may not believe this, but I kind of know him, too."

Rebecca squinted at Billie. *Is she being straight with me or
trying to pull a fast one?* "Oh, you know him," she said. "That's
quite a big claim to make, Billie." *So far, Billie doesn't seem to be
a person who tells wild stories about herself. She hardly talks about
herself, though she didn't hesitate to answer any of the questions I
asked her three days ago.*

Billie nodded and grinned. "You're right about that," she
said. She then shrugged her shoulders. "I'm not saying I'm best
friends with him or anything like that."

So, what is she saying? "You'll understand if I'm not sure
you're telling me the truth," Rebecca said. "So, I hope you won't
mind if I ask you a few questions."

Billie shook her head. "I don't mind answering any question
you might have for me," she said. She grinned at Rebecca. "Ask
me anything you want."

***

Rebecca questioned Billie for almost ten minutes, still standing,
both of them, in the fiction/literature section of the library. As
she had done three days before, Billie didn't hesitate to answer
any of Rebecca's questions, proving to Rebecca that she was
honest with her about knowing Henry Young.

"Do you want to go outside for a quick smoke?"

Billie smiled. "So, I guess I've proven to you that I know Henry Young," she said. "I'll join you outside for a quick smoke."

Rebecca smiled back at Billie. "I need to check this out before we leave," she said. *I'm not leaving here without this book.* "If you want to, you can go ahead and go outside. I'll be out there in a few minutes."

Billie nodded. "I'll see you in a few minutes," she said. She turned around and walked away from Rebecca.

Rebecca went to the checkout counter. She smiled at the librarian behind the counter. "Hello," she said. "I'd like to check this book out." She handed the book to the librarian.

The librarian nodded in approval. "You picked a good one," she said. "I've read it three times myself."

Rebecca smiled. "Well, my mother always said if you want to find a good book to read, ask a librarian," she said. *Of course, she was also a librarian, so she had a high opinion of librarians.*

The librarian smiled. "Your mother sounds like a smart woman," she said. She handed the book back to Rebecca. "There you go, miss. Be sure to bring it back in two weeks."

Rebecca giggled. "To be honest with you, ma'am," she said. "If this book is as good as his last one, I'll be back in about three or four days."

Rebecca joined Billie outside the library.

Rebecca took out a cigarette and lit it. "I want to ask you something," she said. She took a drag off her cigarette. "You've convinced me that you somewhat know Henry Young." *Maybe she knows who Bobbie Lamont is and how or why Henry has dedicated three of his last four novels. She opened the book and pointed at the dedication.* "Do you know who Bobbie Lamont is?"

Billie smiled. "I do know who she is," she said. "She's my best friend." She chuckled and shook her head. "Bobbie met him at the same book reading I did, and she has an unusual relationship with him, one I don't even understand."

***

The second time Jasmine ran into Billie happened three weeks later.

Jasmine was at her favorite bookstore, Adams Used Books. She went there often whenever she wanted to browse through books or escape her house and her mother.

Jasmine sighed and shook her head. The approaching Thanksgiving only deepened her profound sense of isolation. She had never found solace in the holiday, but it took her a long time to understand the root of her discomfort.

Jasmine entered the bookstore and recognized the young lady standing behind the cash register. *Oh, no, I hope she doesn't try to talk to me. I never know what to say to her.*

The young lady nodded and gave Jasmine a guarded look. "You haven't been by in a few days," she said. "Are you doing some last-minute book shopping?"

Jasmine shook her head. "The only person I buy books for is myself," she said. "I'm the only reader in my family." *Why am I telling her this about myself? I tell myself every time I come here not to talk to her, but every time, I find myself talking to her instead of just walking by and not saying a word.*

The young lady nodded. "I know what you mean," she said. "I'm the only reader in my family, too." She grinned. "The only person I can talk to about books is my best friend."

Jasmine nodded. *I wish that I had a best friend.* "Well, if I need anything, I'll let you know," she said. She pointed towards the bookshelves. "I'm going to look at some books now."

"Okay, Jasmine," the young lady said. "I'll be here if you need any help."

"Thanks, Sadie," Jasmine said, reading the young lady's name off her name tag. She turned and walked away.

Jasmine went to her favorite section of the bookstore: the fiction and literature shelves. She frowned as she started looking at the books. She always looked for books by her favorite authors, Millie Harlow, known for her intricate character development, and Isabel Mathews, whose writing style resonated deeply with Jasmine, particularly her use of vivid imagery and complex narratives.

Jasmine found no new book by Millie Harlow, so she left the fiction and literature section.

Jasmine went to the biography section and started looking for any new books by Isabel Mathews. She sighed and shook her head. So far, no new books. They have five copies of the memoir she wrote about thirteen years ago, *Savage Daughter*. It was her first bestseller, but it wasn't her only book. *One day, I might find a copy of her first book, although I doubt it, since it wasn't a bestseller and only a limited number of copies were printed.*

"I wish she would write more books," Jasmine said, almost whispering, not wanting to draw attention to herself. She looked around, frowning. *I need to be more careful about talking to myself when I'm out in public.*

Jasmine knew why Isabel Mathews didn't write more books. Isabel wasn't a full-time author like Millie Harlow. Instead, she was a literature professor, which meant she either didn't have the free time or the need to write more. I write to learn, Jasmine remembered Isabel saying once in an interview.

Jasmine chuckled. *I guess Isabel isn't driven to write like other authors. She writes when she wants and about what interests her.* She sighed, running her fingers over the five copies of Isabel's memoir. *Still, I wish she would write more books. It's hard waiting for her to write a new book when I never know when she will write another one.*

"Well, hey there, Jasmine," a familiar voice said.

Jasmine frowned. *I know that voice.* She looked over her shoulder and saw Billie walking towards her. *She's the last person I want to see today or any other day.*

Jasmine turned around and started walking away when Billie stopped her by grabbing her elbow. She frowned. "Hey, do you mind?"

Billie let go of Jasmine's elbow. "I would like to talk to you, Jasmine," she said. "I think we got off on the wrong foot the other day." She sighed and shook her head. "I wasn't trying to hurt your feelings, but I'm sure I did."

Jasmine frowned and shook her head. "You didn't say anything that I haven't heard a million times by now," she said. *I don't even remember what she said. I do remember feeling uncomfortable around her.*

"Well, I'm sorry," Billie said. She sighed and shook her head. "I'm still trying to figure out my place here." She chuckled and grinned. "Back home, I knew who I was and where I belonged."

"Well, good luck figuring out who you are and if you belong here," Jasmine said. She sighed and rubbed the bridge of her nose. "I've been living here my whole life and still don't know if I belong here or even who I am." *Why am I telling her this stuff about myself? I should give her a nod and walk past her.*

Billie nodded. "You may not believe me, but I understand what you mean," she said. "My best friend is the one person who could always help me understand myself." She smiled. "One of the good things about having a best friend for most of your life is that you can count on them to keep you grounded."

Jasmine shrugged her shoulders. "Well, you might be right about that, but I wouldn't know," she said. "I don't have a best friend or any friends."

Billie's brows furrowed in disbelief. "You can't be serious," she said. "You're telling me that you don't have any friends?"

Jasmine nodded. "I've always been a loner," she said. "So, I wouldn't worry about what you said to me the other day because we won't be friends." *I appreciate her telling me she was sorry for what she said, even if I don't remember what it was.*

Billie frowned, surprised. "I'm sorry you think that," she said. "I plan on living here in Boston for a few years and want to make new friends."

"Well, good luck with that," Jasmine said. She sighed. "I learned long ago that I shouldn't have any friends." *My life's just easier that way.*

Billie put her hands on Jasmine's shoulders. "I think that's the saddest thing I've ever heard," she said. "Everyone should have at least one friend."

Jasmine shrugged her shoulders. *I don't want her pity.* "It's better for me not to have friends," she said. *I don't think she's going to be satisfied with that answer.*

Billie shook her head. "I know it's none of my business, Jasmine, but I don't accept that," she said. She frowned. "From what I've heard about you, you're a lovely young lady."

Who told her that? Jasmine shook her head. "I'm glad you heard that about me," she said. *I guess I have a better reputation than I thought I did.* "I've had friends before, and they're why I don't have friends now."

"If you don't mind, I'd like to hear more," Billie said. She reached out and took one of Jasmine's hands. "I want to know your story."

I don't think anyone has ever asked me to tell them my story. "Okay, Billie," Jasmine said. "I don't know why I'm about to tell you this, but since you asked, my story is one of constant betrayal and hurt feelings, my feelings most of the time."

"I'm sorry to hear that," Billie said. "Please, go on and continue, Jasmine. How did those who you thought were your friends hurt you?"

Jasmine sighed. "They hurt me the same way people always hurt others," she said. *Billie doesn't need to know anything more.* "They lied to me, used me, and made my life miserable."

Billie nodded. "I'm confused," she said. "I was sure you had friends."

Jasmine shook her head. "If you heard that, you heard wrong," she said. She sighed. "Like I said, I don't have any friends." *Are there people out there who are calling themselves my friends? If so, who are they? I need them to stop lying.*

Billie shook her head. "I didn't hear anything," she said. "I was just under the impression you were friends with Rebecca." She pointed at the young lady behind the cash register. "And her, too. I think her name's Sadie."

"Rebecca's not my friend," Jasmine said. "She sometimes acts like my big sister, but we're not friends."

Chapter Four

When Billie moved to Boston, she already knew some people. She knew four people, and they were her family. Besides Josephine (her grandmother) and Truman (her older half-brother), Billie's other family members were her older brother, Willie Baldwin, and her younger half-sister, Nina Carson. Their relationship was not always smooth, especially between Willie and Billie, and this dynamic would change the most during the years Billie lived in Boston.

***

Two days before Thanksgiving, Willie was sitting in his small studio apartment, reading his favorite novel by Millie Harlow for the second or third time, when the phone rang.

Willie sighed and shook his head. I could just let it ring and not answer it. He reached over and answered the phone, picking it up. "Hello," he said. "This is the Baldwin house."

"I thought I raised you right, young man," a familiar voice said.

Willie sat up straight. *Shit, it's Mama.* "Oh, hi, Mom," he said. His mother's voice was the only thing that could make him pay attention. "How are you? How's Franklin doing?"

"Oh, Franklin's doing fine," his mother said. "I think he's enjoying not having children around more than I am."

Willie nodded, not surprised. "I would think you'd be glad to have the house to yourself after all these years," he said. He chuckled. "I remember how crazy we would drive you." *Mom has been married to Franklin for twenty years, I think.*

His mother laughed. "Well, the reason y'all drove me crazy is because I love y'all," she said. She cleared her throat. "I called you, Willie, even though you haven't asked me yet, because I wanted to remind you that Billie also lives in Boston."

Willie chuckled. "Oh, yeah, I remember you mentioned that she might be moving here," he said. "So, I guess she's living with that old white lady?" *I shouldn't be surprised. If Billie lived here in Boston, she would be closer to her white best friend, that Bobbie chick. I'll never understand their friendship.*

"That old white lady is your grandmother," his mother said. She sighed. "I'm not having that discussion right now. Since all my children are in Boston, I would like y'all to spend Thanksgiving together."

Willie chuckled and shook his head. "Did you forget that we don't get along, Mom?" *I may have the same mother as Nina and Billie, but we're as different as we can be, even though we're related.*

His mother sighed. "Well, none of y'all are kids anymore," she said. "The three of y'all need to find a way to get along because I won't be around forever."

Willie sighed. "I wish you wouldn't say things like that," he said. *I hope she doesn't remind me of my promise to her the last time we talked, only a few weeks before.*

"You haven't even talked to Nina, have you?"

"Well, no, I haven't, Mama," Willie said. *Shit, she's not going to believe any excuse I try to tell her.* "Honestly, I haven't seen or talked to either of them, Nina or Billie, since I left New Orleans a few months ago."

"Well, the three of y'all might have lived in the same house and not talked to each other, but now, things are different," his mother said. "I would worry about y'all a little less if I knew y'all were looking out for each other."

Willie sighed and shook his head. "I can't promise we'll start getting along now, just because the three of us all live here," he said. *So, what can I promise her? She's worried about us, and I need to say something, so maybe she'll worry a little less.*

"If I have to, I'll jump on a plane and fly up there myself," his mother said. "Do I need to do that, Willie? Do I need to give y'all an ass whipping?"

Willie chuckled, not because he found what his mother said funny, but because he knew she was serious. "No, Mama, you don't have to do that," he said. He sighed. *If I make a promise to her, I need to keep it. But how can I force myself to spend time with them when I don't even know them?* "I promise I will celebrate Thanksgiving with Nina and Billie."

"Thank you, Willie," his mother said. "I'm going to call you on Thanksgiving now."

Willie nodded. *I know what she's saying to me. She's going to call me, and if she doesn't hear either Billie or Nina in the background or she can't talk to them because they're not there, she'll come up here, all the way from New Orleans, and kick my ass.* "I'll talk to you on Thanksgiving, Mama," he said. "Now, go spend some time with Franklin."

"Boy, don't even think about telling me what to do," his mother said, chuckling. "Be good, Willie."

"I'll try to be, Mom," Willie said. "I'll talk to you again soon." He hung up the phone before he could say anything else. *It's hard for me to tell her that I love her.*

Willie leaned back, frowning. *Okay, so I have to talk to both Nina and Billie. I've got Nina's phone number, but I don't have Billie's phone number.* He took out a cigarette and lit it. *And I don't have the white lady's phone number either. So, what do I do? How can I contact Billie?*

***

Willie smoked his cigarette and thought about finding Billie's phone number or, even better, where she was so he could talk to her face to face. He snapped his fingers and grinned. He picked up the phone and dialed Truman's number.

The phone rang three times before Truman picked it up.

"Hey, Truman, it's me, Willie," he said. *I need to get to the point of why I'm calling him quickly so that he doesn't think I called him because I've changed my mind about our relationship. We might be half-brothers, but I prefer him to be my friend.* "You wouldn't happen to know either Billie's phone number or where she might be right now?"

"Well, I don't think she has a phone number," Truman said. "I think she just uses Josephine's phone when she makes a call."

Willie sighed. "Do you know where she might be right now? I need to talk to her." *Come on, Truman, don't make this difficult for me or yourself.*

"From what Josephine's told me, Billie doesn't leave the house often," Truman said. "But when she does, she either goes to the library or the used bookstore."

Willie chuckled. *She hasn't changed at all.* "Okay, thanks," he said. "Do you know which used bookstore she goes to? There's a lot of used books around here."

"Billie goes to the one in Beacon Hill," Truman said. "I think it's called Adams Used Books."

"Okay, thanks," Willie said. "I'll talk to you again later." He hung up the phone before Truman could say anything. *Okay, so how am I going to approach her? We haven't always gotten along.* He chuckled and shook his head. *The truth is, we drive each other crazy.* He shrugged his shoulders. *I made a promise, so I'd better try to keep it.*

***

Fifteen minutes later, Willie parked his car outside of Adams Used Books. *I'm lucky I already know where this bookstore is and didn't have to drive around to look for it. Driving in this part of Boston, Beacon Hill, always makes me nervous.*

Willie grinned. *I'd know that car anywhere.* He shook his head and laughed. *Of course, Billie drove up here from New Orleans instead of flying or taking the bus, like I did the first time I came up here.*

Willie got out of his car and walked over to the front entrance. He stopped, frowning. *Okay, I still haven't decided what to say to her.* He took out a cigarette and lit it. *I had better smoke a quick cigarette and think.*

***

Willie finished his cigarette about five minutes later. Well, I will have to be straight with her and tell her about my phone call with our mother. He threw his cigarette on the ground and smashed it flat. He then took a few steps, grabbed the door handle, and pulled the door open.

Willie walked into the bookstore and started looking for Billie. *I'm glad I came here first instead of the library. Maybe, since I'm already here, I should look for some new books to read.* He grinned. *I can't buy books with Billie around because I can't have her find out that I love to read like she does, not after all the shit I used to give her for being a bookworm.*

Willie found Billie, which wasn't hard since the bookstore wasn't that big, and to his surprise, she was talking to Jasmine. He chuckled and shook his head. *I didn't know that they knew each other.*

Willie walked up to Billie and Jasmine. He cleared his throat to get their attention.

Billie frowned and looked over Jasmine's shoulder. "Oh, hi, Willie," she said. "I was wondering when I would run into you." She chuckled and shook her head. "I didn't think it would happen at a bookstore."

Willie shrugged his shoulders. "Well, we used to live in the same house and would go days without seeing each other," he said. *Okay, remember why you wanted to talk to her.* "I need to talk to you, Billie."

Billie sighed and shook her head. "It must be serious then," she said. She looked over at Jasmine. "I'm sorry, Jasmine, but we will have to continue our conversation another time."

Jasmine nodded while glancing over her shoulder at Willie. "Okay," she said. She leaned closer to Billie. "I didn't know he was your other brother."

Billie chuckled and nodded. "Well, now you do," she said. "We'll talk again soon."

Jasmine nodded again, this time with a hopeful smile. She walked past Willie, glancing over at him but not saying anything.

"I see you've been making new friends," Willie said. *And here I was, sure she had forgotten how to make friends. After all, she's been friends with that Bobbie chick since they were kids.*

Billie chuckled and shrugged her shoulders. "I wouldn't say I'm friends with Jasmine," she said. "I met her at the country club almost three weeks ago."

"Oh, Truman took you to the country club," Willie said. *He seems more thrilled about being her brother than I've ever felt.* "What did you think of it?"

"Of course, he took me," Billie said. "Unlike you, he's proud to be my older brother." She then grinned and rolled her eyes. "I've been to a country club before, and it seemed about the same as the one back home in New Orleans."

Willie cleared his throat. "Anyway, I talked to Mom today, and she wants us to have Thanksgiving dinner together," he said. "All three of us, including Nina."

Billie frowned. "Nina's living here now, just like us?"

***

Billie's relationship with her younger half-sister, Nina, was different from the one she had with her older brother, Willie, before she moved to Boston and when the three of them were still living at home, with their mother and her husband, Nina's father, in New Orleans. Nina looked up to Billie and wanted to be like her older sister. Billie barely paid any attention to Nina, too busy with her own life and dealing with her own problems.

***

Two days before Thanksgiving, Willie had surprised Nina when he came by her dorm room. The door was open, but he still knocked on it before entering her dorm room.

"Oh, hi, Willie," Nina said. "I've been wondering if you would ever drop by." *So, it only took about three weeks of my calling him almost every day for him to visit me.*

Willie nodded. "I know you've been calling me, wanting me to come by and see you," he said. "Thanksgiving is only two days away."

Nina chuckled. "Yeah, I know," she said. *So, he didn't come by because I've been calling him, but because of another reason.* "So, do you want to tell me something?"

"I do," Willie said. He smiled. "I talked to Mom just a few hours ago, and she wants us all to have Thanksgiving together."

Nina smiled. "All of us? That's including Billie, right?" *Good job, Mama. Please leave it to you to be the one who gets us to spend time together.* "I remember Mama telling me that Billie was moving here."

Willie nodded. "She did," he said. He shrugged his shoulders. "I just talked to her, maybe twenty minutes ago, and told her about our mother's wishes." He sighed. "I invited her to join us for Thanksgiving. It's up to her now. I did all I could do."

***

On Thanksgiving, Nina found herself at Willie's apartment. The phone rang when she stood in the kitchen, preparing their Thanksgiving dinner.

Nina frowned. *I'm not sure if I should answer the phone or not.* She looked for Willie and saw him standing on the patio, smoking a cigarette and leaning against the railing. She chuckled and shook her head. *I guess he can't hear the phone out there.*

Maybe that's Billie calling. Jasmine shrugged her shoulders. *Or perhaps it's not, but I won't know until I pick up the phone.* She stepped over to the phone hanging on the wall near the refrigerator and picked it up.

"Hello, you've reached Willie's apartment," Nina said. "He can't come to the phone right now. You can call back later, or I can take a message from you for him." *I don't know how Willie answers his phone, but I remember how Mama taught us to answer the phone. She believed in having good manners over the phone.*

"Is that my baby girl, I hear?"

Nina smiled. *Oh, good, it's Mama.* "Yeah, Mama, it's me," she said. "Willie's out on the patio smoking a cigarette, but I can get him if you want to talk to him."

"I talked to him two days ago," her mother said. "I haven't talked to you in almost a month."

Nina sighed and shook her head. "I know I promised you that I would call you every week, and I'm sorry I haven't called you in a month," she said. "I've been busy with school and everything." *I hope she believes me and doesn't challenge me.*

Her mother chuckled. "I'm sure you're busy with school," she said. "I'm glad you're at Willie's apartment with him."

"Well, he said you wanted us to celebrate Thanksgiving together," Nina said. *So, she will ask me about Billie now.* "I've been cooking all day." *I'm glad I used to help Mama in the kitchen.* She smiled. *And I bet Willie's glad too.*

"I knew I could depend on my little helper," her mother said. "Now, what about Billie? Is she there or on her way there?"

Nina sighed. *I knew she would ask me about Billie.* "I don't know, Mama," she said. "Willie said he talked to her two days ago and told her you wanted us to be together for Thanksgiving."

"So, is she coming or not?"

Nina shrugged her shoulders. "I don't know, Mama," she said. "And I don't think Willie knows either." She glanced at her watch. "She might be on her way here."

Her mother sighed. "Of course, Billie would be the one who would defy my wishes," she said. "I hoped she might do it if I wasn't the one who asked her."

Nina cleared her throat. "Now, come on, Mama," she said. "Billie's not a rebellious teenager anymore." *I once heard Mama tell Papa that Billie was more trouble than Willie, and Papa agreed with her.*

Her mother laughed. "Thank God for that," she said. "I know Billie moved up there because she wanted to get to know

Josephine and her older half-brother, Truman, but I hope she won't forget that you and Willie are still her family, too."

"I'm sure Billie hasn't forgotten that, Mama," Nina said. "Willie said he did talk to her, which means she didn't walk away when he approached her." *I don't know what he said to her since he didn't tell me, and I didn't ask him either.*

Her mother chuckled. "Well, I see that living up in Boston hasn't changed you yet, my little optimistic girl," she said. She sighed. "I wish I could be like you, Nina, and believe Billie was on her way there."

Nina glanced at her watch. "Well, it's not dinner time yet," she said. She shrugged her shoulders. "And maybe she's having a hard time finding Willie's apartment." She shook her head and chuckled. "I had a hard time finding it, even with Willie's directions." *If I know Billie, she probably bought a few maps of Boston and never goes anywhere without them in her car.*

"You've always defended her," her mother said. "Willie always thought the worst of her, while you always saw her best side."

Nina chuckled. "Well, of course I did," she said. "Billie's my big sister, and I've always wanted to be like her." *I never told Billie that, but maybe I didn't have to tell her. I wasn't even sure if she was paying attention to me, though she was usually too busy hanging out with her best friend to notice me or my friends.*

"I know, Nina," her mother said. She sighed. "When she does get there, would you tell her to call me?" She chuckled. "And would you please call me tomorrow?"

"I promise I will call you tomorrow, Mama," Nina said. *I need to keep this promise. I can't let her down again.* "I need to get back to cooking, so is there anything else you want to tell me or ask me?"

"I'll let you get back to cooking," her mother said. "I'll talk to you again tomorrow."

"Yeah, tomorrow, Mama," Nina said. She hung up the phone, chuckling. *I hope I have some good news to tell her the next time I talk to her, which will be tomorrow.* She checked on the food. She adjusted the burners and turned the stove off.

***

Nina left the kitchen and went to the patio, wanting to talk to Willie. She pushed the sliding door open and stepped out on the patio.

Willie looked over his shoulder and smiled. "So, how's the cooking going?"

Nina chuckled. "We're lucky that I used to help Mama with her cooking," she said. "Otherwise, we would have to go out to eat or crash someone else's Thanksgiving dinner." *I'm glad we didn't have to do either one of those bad options.* "To answer your question, everything's cooking, and dinner will be ready soon."

Willie glanced at his watch and nodded. "That's good," he said. He took a drag off his cigarette and looked away from Nina.

I should tell him about Mama calling. "The phone rang, and I answered it," Nina said. She chuckled and shook her head. "Don't worry, it wasn't one of your girlfriends calling you." *I didn't know he had so many girlfriends until the other day, when I called him and a strange woman answered his phone.*

Willie chuckled and grinned. "I told you already, Nina," he said. "I don't have girlfriends. I'm not in high school." He took a drag off his cigarette. "I have lady friends."

Nina shook her head and laughed. "You can call them whatever you want to, Willie," she said. *Okay, tell him now.* "Mama called, and she asked me about Billie."

Willie sighed and shook his head. "I'm not surprised she called," he said. "What did you tell her?"

"I told her what you told me," Nina said. "You invited her to join us for Thanksgiving."

Willie frowned and squinted at Nina. "I did invite Billie to join us for Thanksgiving," he said. "Mom asked me to do it, so I did." He shrugged his shoulders. "Now, I can't make Billie join us if she doesn't want to celebrate Thanksgiving with us."

"She'll join us," Nina said. "After all, we're her family." *I can't admit to Willie that I'm worried about Billie coming. We might both feel disconnected from her, but I want to feel connected to her, but he doesn't. I've always noticed the tension between them, and I don't know why it's like that with them.*

Willie shook his head. "We're not her family anymore, Nina," he said. He finished his cigarette, taking one last drag off it. He tossed it off the patio, frowning. "Billie's got a new family now."

Nina frowned. *How can he say something like that?* "Do you mean Truman and Grandma Josephine?" *Mama said that Willie couldn't or wouldn't accept them as family.* "They're not her new family but part of our family now."

"Truman is only a friend," Willie said. He shook his head. "And Josephine isn't my grandmother. The only grandmother I have is Grandma Lucy."

Nina sighed. "That's the thing about family, Willie," she said. "You don't get to choose your family." *I'm surprised he didn't mention that I'm unrelated to Josephine, unlike him or Billie. She's their grandmother, not mine.*

Willie chuckled and nodded. "I know, Nina," he said.

Chapter Five

A few minutes later, someone knocked on the door. Willie was on the phone with his friend Drew. He looked over at Nina and pointed at the door. "Find out who's knocking on the door."

Nina nodded and left the kitchen. She approached the door and looked through the peephole before opening it. She grinned and nodded. *I knew she would come.* She opened the door and took a few steps back.

"We were wondering when you would show up," Nina said.

Billie smiled back at Nina. 'Well, I had to bake this pie," she said. "We might live in Boston now, but it isn't Thanksgiving without some pumpkin pie."

Billie would find herself with not one but two love interests in her first three years in Boston. The first one she would meet on Thanksgiving was because of her older brother, Willie.

***

As Billie arrived at Willie's cozy apartment with a freshly baked pumpkin pie, the inviting aroma of the pie filled the air. Meanwhile, Willie was on the phone, pacing back and forth, talking to his friend Drew Anderson.

"Look, you shouldn't be spending Thanksgiving alone," Willie said. "Why don't you just call your folks and apologize to them?"

"I don't have anything to apologize for, Willie," Drew said. "I'm not the one who insulted my girlfriend; they did." *I knew it was a mistake to bring her with me even before we got there. I had even told her so, but she wouldn't listen. She didn't think I was serious about her because I hadn't introduced her to them.*

Willie sighed. "You knew your folks weren't going to be happy with you bringing a white girl home with you for Labor Day," he said. "From what you've told me about them, they're old-fashioned like mine are and don't approve of black men dating white women."

Why is he telling me this? Doesn't he think that I already know that about my parents? Drew sighed and shook his head. "Yeah, I know," he said. "They don't realize it's 1990, not 1970." He chuckled. "Besides, you're one to talk. How many white chicks have you banged, anyway, Willie?"

Willie laughed. "Yeah, you're right, I've banged my share of white women," he said. "But you know what I've never done? I've never taken any of them home to meet my parents."

Drew sighed and nodded. "Yeah, you're right," he said. "It wasn't my idea, and I told her they wouldn't like her." *She didn't believe me. She convinced me she could win them over with her charm, but she was wrong. For all their talk about not judging another person by the color of their skin, they couldn't see past her being white.*

"Hey, it doesn't matter anymore," Willie said. "She's the one who ended it, not you."

"Yeah, I know," Drew said, his voice tinged with regret. "She ended it because she couldn't deal with them not liking her." *She told me we didn't have a future because of them, and I couldn't argue with her.*

Willie cleared his throat. "Let's get back to what I was saying," he said. "You don't have to be alone today. You should come over and have Thanksgiving with me."

Drew frowned. "I thought you said your mom wanted you to celebrate today with your sisters," he said. He shook his head. "I don't want to crash your celebration." *I appreciate the thought behind his offer, but I don't need to be that guy; I am only there because I have nowhere to go.*

Willie chuckled. "You wouldn't be crashing it," he said. "I'm inviting you, and there's a difference."

"Oh, I guess you're right," Drew said. *I have to be sure he's serious about me coming over there.* "Are you sure it will be okay? You don't think your sisters will mind me being there, do you?"

"I know Nina won't mind," Willie said. "She's a real sweet girl and will be thrilled to meet you since I don't introduce any of my friends to her."

Drew grinned. *Yeah, and I know why you don't do that.* "Well, what about your other sister?" *I think he said her name was Billie.*

"I'm not even sure she's going to show up," Willie said. "Besides, this dinner is happening at my apartment, which means I'm the one who's in charge of inviting other people, not anyone else."

"Okay," Drew said. *Well, I can sit here and spend Thanksgiving when you're supposed to spend it with your friends or family, or I can go to Willie's apartment and spend it with him and his sisters.* "You win, Willie. I'll spend Thanksgiving with you and your sisters."

"Okay," Willie said. "Well, I'll see you when you get here."

***

Drew hung up the phone and got dressed. He had almost left his apartment, having just opened the front door, and was about to leave when his phone rang again. He frowned. *Is Willie calling me back? Or maybe it's my parents, and they're calling me because they want to see me.* He turned around and went to the phone. He answered it, picking it up.

"Hey, Drew, it's me again," Willie said. "I don't believe it, but my other sister, Billie, just showed up."

Drew sighed. "So, I guess I'm no longer invited to join you to celebrate Thanksgiving?" *For some reason, I don't think Willie expected his other sister, Billie, to show up. After all, why else would he invite me?*

Willie chuckled. "You're still invited," he said. "I'll admit that I didn't expect Billie to show up when I invited you to join Nina and me for Thanksgiving."

So, I was right. "You've talked about Nina a lot more than you have your sister, Billie," Drew said. "Why's that, Willie?" *I didn't even know he had another sister until the other day when he mentioned she also lived in Boston. I should've pressed him for more details.*

Willie sighed. "I don't have much to say about Billie," he said. He chuckled. "To say we aren't close is to put it in the best way possible. I irritate her, and she drives me crazy."

"I would say that I understand, but I don't at all," Drew said. "I'm an only child." *Sometimes, after hearing some of Willie's stories about his sisters, I'm glad I don't have any siblings. But then, other times, when my parents are giving me a hard time, most of the time about dating white girls, I wish I had either a brother or a sister who could come to my defense or do something to take the heat off me.*

Willie laughed. "You don't know how lucky you are," he said. "Anyway, you're still invited, so get your ass over here."

Drew grinned. "Okay, I will," he said. "Should I bring anything, like dessert?" *So, I will get to meet Willie's other sister, the one he doesn't like talking about.*

"Yeah, it would be great if you brought some dessert," Willie said. "I think we're good on all the other food most people eat today."

"Okay, I'm on my way," Drew said. He hung up the phone. He retrieved the sweet potato pie he had bought the day before and left his apartment.

Well, I'm glad I live in the same part of Boston as Willie. Drew smiled. *I remember how my parents freaked out when I told them where I decided to live. They couldn't understand why I wanted to live in Roxbury when I could afford to live in Beacon Hill if I wanted to, which I didn't.*

***

Drew arrived at Willie's apartment about ten minutes later. He parked his car in the parking lot behind the building, walked through the front entrance, and climbed three flights of stairs. He knocked on the door while holding the sweet potato pie in his other hand.

The door opened. "Well, there, Drew," Nina, Willie's youngest sister, said while smiling. "Willie said that he had invited you to join us."

Drew smiled back at Nina. "He did, and now I'm here," he said. He handed the pie to Nina. "And I brought some dessert, too." *I remember Willie telling me that Nina was his half-sister, and they had the same mother but different fathers.*

"Oh, good, you brought sweet potato pie," Nina said. "Maybe now Willie will stop bitching about not having any pie he likes to eat."

I need to catch up on what's been going on. "What do you mean, Nina?" Willie stepped inside Willie's apartment and turned around to look at Nina. "Did I miss something?"

Nina chuckled and nodded. "Willie doesn't pass up a chance to give our other sister a hard time," she said. "She brought pumpkin pie, and Willie's been giving her shit about it for the last ten minutes."

Drew laughed and grinned. "Let me guess," he said. "He told her only white people eat pumpkin pie for Thanksgiving." *I've heard his opinion on this matter before; only I was the one he was giving a hard time.* "Where is he, anyway?"

Nina closed the door and pointed towards the patio. "He's out there, smoking a cigarette," she said. She grinned. "She's out there, too, if you want to meet her."

"Well, I'm looking forward to finally meeting the mysterious other sister," Drew said. "It was nice seeing you, Nina." *I remember Willie being thrilled when he learned that Nina was attending college here.*

Nina walked over to Drew and hugged him. "I'm glad Willie invited you," she said. "Maybe he'll behave himself because you're here."

Drew shook his head and grinned. "I doubt that," he said. "He says what he wants to say and does what he wants to do."

Nina nodded. "You're right about that," she said. "Anyway, they're out on the patio."

Drew turned around and went to the patio. He had been to Willie's apartment before, so he knew the layout. Before he opened the sliding door, he looked out the glass door and saw Willie smoking a cigarette while talking to an attractive black woman.

Drew opened the sliding door and stepped out on the patio.

Willie glanced over his shoulder and smiled. "Good, you're here," he said. He walked over to Drew, and they shook hands. "Thanks for coming, Drew."

Drew nodded and grinned. "Well, thanks for inviting me," he said. *Okay, so are you going to introduce me to your other sister?* He cleared his throat and gave Willie a questioning look.

Willie chuckled. "Oh, yeah, where are my manners?" He turned his attention to the young black woman standing next to him. "Well, you've already met my two other friends, Malcolm and Truman." He pointed at Drew. "This is my other friend, Drew. We became friends at Columbia."

The woman smiled at Drew and offered her hand to him. "I've heard a few stories about you," she said. "You're the one who managed to keep my troublesome older brother from getting kicked out a few times. I'm Billie, by the way."

Drew shook Billie's hand. "You're the mysterious other sister Willie hasn't ever mentioned," he said, chuckling while glancing at Willie. *I can tell that she's related to Nina.*

Willie grinned and shook his head. "Dinner should be ready soon," he said. He left the patio, leaving Drew alone with Billie.

"I think we have enough time for a quick smoke," Billie said. She smiled at Drew. "Do you want to join me?"

Drew nodded. "Sure," he said. He took out a cigarette and lit it. "So, is this your first time in Boston?" *Since he left us alone, Willie must want me to talk to her.*

Billie shook her head. She took out a cigarette and lit it before she answered Drew's question. "The first time I was here was a few months ago, during the summer," she said.

***

A little over a month later, it was Christmas.

Truman stood up. "Well, Mom, I've got to go," he said. "I enjoyed spending time with you." *I hope she believes me. Sometimes, it isn't easy being her son.*

His mother sighed. "Yes, you don't want to keep Josephine waiting," she said. "I would rather you have Christmas dinner with me instead of her, Truman."

Truman sighed. *Okay, so now she will lay a guilt trip on me.* "I know you would, Mom," he said. "But I promised Josephine I would have dinner with her and Billie."

His mother nodded. "Oh, yes, of course, she's having dinner with her," she said. "If your grandfather were still alive,

Josephine wouldn't be having Christmas dinner with your father's Negro daughter."

Truman sighed and shook his head. "I've told you before, Mom, not to say that word," he said. "They're not called Negros anymore." *I wish she would find a way to forgive my father for leaving us and marrying Billie's and Willie's mother.*

His mother shrugged her shoulders. "I don't care what the correct name to call them is, Truman," she said. "My point is, your grandfather wouldn't even consider accepting your father's illegitimate children as part of his family."

I know she's right. "Well, Grandpa Bill was born in the 19th century," Truman said. "This is the 20th century, and things are different now." *In many ways, it's not different enough. We still have a long way to go, but we have come so far in my lifetime.* "And Billie isn't illegitimate. My father married her mother before Billie was born."

His mother shook her head and waved her hands dismissively. "Well, your father's other son was illegitimate," she said. She took a sip of her wine. "Your father was still married to me when he got that Negro woman pregnant."

Truman sighed. "Yeah, I know," he said. *I hope that one day, she'll be able to forgive my father for having two children with another woman and for leaving us to be with that other woman.* "I'll call you tonight."

Truman left his mother's house without saying another word.

***

Truman's mother lived in the same part of Boston, Beacon Hill, as his grandmother, Josephine. It took him less than ten minutes to drive from his mother's house, the same house he had spent his childhood in and lived in until he left for college.

Truman parked his car in the driveway behind Billie's car. He exited his car and retrieved the Christmas gifts he had bought for Josephine and Billie from the trunk. He then walked to the front door.

Truman knocked on the door using his elbow, his hands holding the gifts he had bought for Josephine and Billie. His conversation with his mother just before he left her house still bothered him.

I wish I could make her understand that just because she doesn't want to have a relationship with Josephine, that doesn't mean I shouldn't have a relationship with her. I also wish she would forgive Josephine for encouraging my father to follow his heart and be with Billie's and Willie's mother.

The front door opened.

"Hey, Truman," Billie said, smiling at him. "I was wondering when you were going to show up."

Truman chuckled. "Well, you don't have to wonder any-more," he said. "I'm here." *I'm glad Billie seems willing to accept me as her older brother. I tried with Willie, but he didn't want me to be his brother. I don't know why, and when I asked him about it, he just changed the subject.*

"Well, I'm glad you're here," Billie said. She pointed at the gifts Truman was holding. "Are those gifts I see you holding?"

Truman nodded. "There's nothing wrong with your eye-sight," he said. *I love her Southern accent. I've noticed that her accent is different from Willie's accent. I know they grew up in the same house, so why do they sound so different?*

"I know you didn't drive over here just to stand outside the door," Billie said. She took a few steps back and welcomed Truman into the house. "Come on in now."

Truman grinned. "Well, lead the way, Miss Carver," he said. *Billie seems to be making herself at home. I know she doesn't leave the house often, only going to the store when she needs cigarettes or the nearby library branch.*

Truman followed Billie into the house. She closed the front door, and he followed her to the parlor, where their grandmother was waiting for them, sitting on a red Victorian couch and smoking a cigarette.

Truman stopped Billie by grabbing her elbow. "I thought her doctor said that she couldn't smoke anymore," he said, frowning. *I hoped that her recent health scare would have convinced her to quit smoking.*

Billie sighed. "Yeah, he did," she said. She shrugged her shoulders. "I remind her every time I catch her smoking a cigarette."

Truman nodded. "I do the same thing," he said. He sighed and shook his head. "I see she doesn't want to listen to either of us." *I don't remember her smoking when I was a kid. It was only after Grandpa Bill died that I could remember her smoking.*

Truman and Billie walked into the parlor.

Josephine smiled. "My two favorite people," she said. She took a drag off her cigarette. "Is there something wrong, Truman? Why are you giving me that disappointed look?"

"I'm disappointed you're smoking a cigarette, Josephine," Truman said. He looked over at Billie, who nodded. "You know that you don't need to be smoking, not with your health problems." *She's one stubborn old lady.*

Josephine sighed and shook her head. "The only health problem I have is I am eighty-something years old," she said, holding up her hands in surrender. "But to make you two happy, I will put it out."

Billie looked over at Truman. "I think we can sit down now," she said. She punched him in the shoulder. "You can put those things down."

Truman sat down on the other couch, the modern blue one, and placed the Christmas gifts on the coffee table between them. "So, did I make it in time for some Christmas dinner?"

Josephine smiled. "You did, Truman," she said. She glanced at her watch. "Dinner should be ready in about thirty minutes."

Truman smiled. "Well, good," he said. He pointed at the gifts sitting on the coffee table. "Do you want to open those now or after dinner?" *This will be the first time I've spent Christmas with her, and it won't just be the two of us for a long time. After Grandpa Bill died, she stopped going to family gatherings.*

"I think we can wait to open them until after dinner," Josephine said. She smoothed out her skirt. "So, how is your mother?"

Truman sighed. "She's about the same," he said. "Thank you for asking." *I don't know how Josephine feels about my mother. She's never said anything negative about her around me, and I appreciate her for being that way.*

Josephine sighed and nodded. "I know she is still bitter towards me," she said. "I understand she feels I betrayed her, in some sense." She shook her head. "But enough about that." She smiled at Truman. "How are you, Truman?"

Truman shrugged his shoulders. "I'm okay," he said. *I'm glad she changed the subject. I don't want to talk about my mother with her.* "I've been working some long work days at the firm."

Josephine chuckled and shook her head. "I have not seen or talked to you since Thanksgiving, Truman," she said. "I need to hear more than just that you have been working long hours at the firm."

"I'd like to hear more about your work at the firm," Billie said. She smiled. "Josephine says that you work at one of the best law firms in New England."

Truman chuckled and grinned. "Well, I do," he said. *The last thing I want to discuss is my work at the firm. It's just not that exciting.* "I don't want to even think about work right now, let alone talk about it."

Billie rolled her eyes. "Well, you're no fun," she said. "So, since you don't want to talk about your work at the firm, what do you want to talk about, Truman?"

Truman smiled. *Now, that's an easy question to answer.* "Well, why don't we talk about what's been going on with you, Billie?"

He chuckled and looked over at Josephine. "I know everyone I know is talking about Billie, trying to figure her out."

Billie grinned and chuckled. "What do you mean, everyone?" She looked over at Josephine. "Truman took me to the Halloween party at the country club and introduced me to a few people."

Josephine smiled and nodded. "Yes, I remember, Billie," she said. "Truman also told me about it." She chuckled. "He believes that you made a strong impression on the people he introduced you to, especially Rebecca Dubois."

Billie shrugged her shoulders. "Maybe I did," she said. She smiled. "I did run into her a few days later, at the library."

Truman smiled. *Of course, Billie ran into Rebecca at the library.* "Have you run into anyone else?"

Billie chuckled. "I did," she said. "I ran into Jasmine at a bookstore."

Josephine smiled. "Of course you did," she said. "Did you apologize to her?"

Billie nodded. "I did," she said. She sighed and frowned. "I found out that she doesn't have any friends." She shook her head. "I don't understand how that could be true."

Truman shrugged his shoulders. "I don't know why either," he said. "Jasmine's a lovely young lady." *I don't think Billie knows that we're related to Jasmine. I'm surprised that Josephine hasn't already told her.*

Billie smiled. "I think so too," she said.

Chapter Six

T ruman was right. Billie had only been living in Boston for three months, but by the time New Year's Eve arrived, everyone in the Upper Crust world was talking about her. The nasty rumors came from Bridget, while all the positive talk came from Rebecca.

On New Year's Eve, Billie would meet her third rival, Sadie Zimmerman, and cross paths with two other young ladies. One would fall in love with her, and the other would become a close friend.

Sadie's best friend and roommate, Iris Mathews, would become friends with Billie.

***

Iris sat at her desk in her cozy office, the soft glow of the desk lamp illuminating the room as she finished writing the article her editor had assigned her, her fingers dancing over the keyboard.

Her office phone rang, and Iris answered it. "Good evening. You've reached Iris Mathews' desk. How may I help you?" She glanced at her watch. *There's only one person who would be calling me right now.*

"Hey, Iris," Sadie said. "I'm almost done here at the bookstore."

Iris smiled. *I knew it was her.* "Well, you should be, considering it's almost nine o'clock, and it's New Year's Eve, too," she said. She put the phone between her shoulder and neck, cradling it while she went back to typing. *I'm almost done.*

Sadie chuckled. "I know it's New Year's Eve," she said. "So, are we going out tonight?" *I hope she says yes because I need to go out and have fun tonight.*

"I don't see any reason why we shouldn't go out tonight," Iris said. "We're both single ladies who have worked hard for the last few months." *I'm so glad that Sadie has calmed down. When we moved here, I immediately found a job, while she took her time. I didn't say anything at first, knowing what kind of person Sadie was, but when she hadn't found a job after almost two months, I put my foot down and gave her a piece of my mind. Luckily for her and our friendship, she listened and got her job at the bookstore the next day. I know she doesn't want to work forever, but it's good enough for now.*

"Good, I'm glad I don't have to talk you into going out," Sadie said. "There's only one place I want to go to tonight." She chuckled. "I'm not in the mood to hop from one bar to another."

Iris grinned. "Well, good, because I'm not in the mood to bar hop either," she said. "So, do you know where you want to go?" *I'm just teasing her. Sadie's a creature of habit, and once she decides that she likes a bar, that's the only bar she wants to go to and drink in. So, I'm sure I know what she's about to say.*

Sadie laughed. "There's only one bar I want to go to tonight," she said. "I'm surprised you would even ask me. I thought we were best friends."

Iris giggled. "Of course, we're best friends," she said. *I should stop teasing her.* "So, you want us to go to Capote's, right?" *It wasn't easy finding a bar we both liked. We might be best friends, but we're different in many ways.*

Sadie chuckled. "Well, that's our favorite bar," she said. *I sometimes wonder if we're one of the few who know that the bar is named after the infamous gay author Truman Capote.*

"Yes, it is," Iris said. She looked over what she had typed so far. "I'm not quite done yet." *She's not going to be happy to hear that.* "Why don't I meet you at the bar?"

Sadie bit her bottom lip. "I'd rather we go there together," she said. She sighed and shook her head. "But I understand you're on a deadline." *Sometimes, I wish Iris had a regular job, like me, and not be a journalist. It would make going out with her easier if her work schedule were more like mine.* "Do you have any idea how soon you'll be done? You know that I don't like going out by myself."

"I know," Iris said. *Despite my best efforts, she remains determined to be antisocial.* "I'm sure I'll be done in about forty minutes. So, why don't I meet you there?"

"Well, I'm not crazy about meeting you there," Sadie said. She sighed. "But since I don't want to wait for you at the apartment, meeting you there isn't the worst idea I've ever heard."

"It's settled then," Iris said. "I'll finish here while you wait to clock out and then go home to change clothes. After that, you'll go to Capote's and wait for me there." *Unlike Sadie, I don't have to go home to change clothes. I don't have any outfits just for going out.*

"Okay," Sadie said. "Well, I'll see you at Capote's."

"I'll be there as soon as I can," Iris said. "Goodbye, Sadie." She hung up her office phone and went back to typing. She lost herself in the steady hum of her black IBM Selectric II typewriter, her fingers flying over the keys and her eyes never looking down.

***

Iris finished writing her article about ten minutes later. She removed the paper from her typewriter, gathered the other pages, and stood up. She grabbed her things and went to her editor's office to drop off her article.

Iris left the building and went to her car, a cherry red 1988 Ford Mustang GT, parked nearby. She got in and drove away.

Iris lit a cigarette, her mind not on joining Sadie at Capote's but on the article she had just finished writing. *When my editor gave me the assignment to write an article about the differences between being gay here and being gay back home in Nashville. I've only been living here, with Sadie, for about two years now, and I still feel like I just moved here. Boston still doesn't feel like home, not yet.*

But you didn't feel at home in Nashville either, Iris.

Iris smiled. Whenever troubled or something bothered her, she would think of Sadie and talk to her. *I felt uncomfortable back home because I had to hide who I was, and you know that, Sadie.*

You never had to hide who you were with me.

Iris smiled. *And that's why we became best friends, Sadie. We were just two little weirdos who got lucky and found each other.* She sighed and shook her head. *But we're not in Nashville anymore. It's okay for us to have other friends.*

I don't want any more friends, Iris. You're enough for me.

Iris frowned. *It always comes back to this. Don't you remember why we left Nashville and moved here to Boston?*

I moved here because you did, Iris. I couldn't stay in Nashville without you.

***

Sadie clocked out and left the bookstore, waving at the owner as she walked by his office.

Sadie went by the apartment she shared with Iris to change out of her work clothes. She went to her bedroom and undressed, dropping her clothes on the floor. *I need to pick those up before I leave. They need to be in the hamper, not on the floor.* She went to her closet and opened it. *Okay, so what should I wear?*

It took Sadie almost ten minutes to pick out her outfit. She put it on and examined herself in the mirror. *This outfit is good enough to get the kind of attention I want to get tonight.*

Oh, it looks good enough to me.

Sadie smiled, hearing her best friend, Iris's, voice in her head. They had known each other and had been best friends for most of their lives, starting in the second grade.

Whenever Sadie wanted to, she could talk, in a way, to Iris in her mind. *Thanks, Iris.* She sighed and shook her head. *The real question is whether my outfit is good enough to catch the attention of a stranger.*

Oh, that's right. It's New Year's Eve, and you hope to have a one-night stand tonight, right?

Sadie grinned and nodded. *Of course, I am. I hope it will happen every New Year's Eve for the last four years.* She frowned. *It hasn't happened yet.*

It may happen this year.

I hope so. Sadie shook her head. *So far, it does seem easier to be myself here. I don't have to pretend to like guys here.*

You didn't have to pretend to like guys back home in Nashville.

Sadie chuckled. *Maybe you didn't have to, Iris. I did, and you know why I did it, too. Growing up black is hard enough, especially in the South, but it's even more complicated if you're also gay.*

It wasn't easy for me to be gay, Sadie. I didn't tell my parents until we left Nashville and came to Boston.

Sadie nodded. *I remember being there with you.* She sighed. *But your parents still talk to you, don't they? Do you think mine would if they knew the truth about me?*

I don't think you're giving them enough credit. They love you.

Sadie shook her head. *They may love me, but they don't know me. And I don't think they would love the real me if they ever found out. Anyway, that's enough about that. I will have a good time tonight with you, even if I don't hook up with a stranger.*

***

Sadie left her bedroom and the apartment she shared with Iris. She glanced at her watch and frowned. *I hope Iris isn't still at her office and is on her way to Capote's. I don't want to get there only to find out she isn't there yet.*

Don't worry, Sadie. You know I'll be there when I can.

Sadie nodded. *Yeah, I know. And you also know that I hate going there by myself.* She shook her head and frowned. *The saddest thing in the world is a person sitting alone at a bar. It bothers other people, too.*

You don't care what other people think or how they feel, Sadie.

Sadie grinned. *You're right, Iris. I don't care most of the time, but I don't want other people's pity. I'd rather be disliked.*

Sadie entered her faded blue Nissan Sentra and left their apartment building. While she drove to the bar, she continued the conversation she had in her mind with Iris's voice. *I hope you're there when I get there.* She frowned, her hands gripping the steering wheel.

I didn't promise you when I would be there, Sadie. I told you that I would be there as soon as I could. I'm a journalist, remember?

Sadie nodded and sighed. *Yeah, I remember. You're lucky, Iris. You've known what you wanted to do with your life since we were teenagers.* She shook her head. *I'm still trying to figure my life out.*

***

Sadie arrived at the bar twenty minutes later. The neon lights of the bar sign reflected off the wet pavement, casting a colorful glow. She was lucky enough to find a parking space near the front entrance. She parked, the sound of her car door closing echoing in the quiet street, and glanced at her watch again.

It had been about thirty minutes since Sadie last spoke to Iris. She couldn't help but wonder if Iris was on her way or perhaps wrapping up her work, maybe even finishing an article.

Sadie's friendship with Iris was a steadfast anchor in her life. They had been through thick and thin together, from navigating their identities to supporting each other's career choices. She couldn't change her skin color, she wouldn't deny her sexuality, and she wouldn't give up her friendship with Iris. She didn't know who she was if she didn't have Iris. Their bond was the most significant relationship in her life.

Sadie walked into the bar and looked around, hoping to see Iris. *Well, shit. Iris still isn't here.* She frowned, her heart sinking a little. She spotted Rebecca Dubois sitting at a table near the bar. Rebecca wasn't alone; sitting next to her was someone Sadie had heard about and had seen around but hadn't met yet.

So, Rebecca's here.

Of course, she's here, Iris. It's New Year's Eve, and if Rebecca didn't at least drop in for a few minutes before midnight, she would lose her gay card. Sadie chuckled, pleased by her joke.

So, now you're in a good mood, Sadie?

Sadie shook her head. *I will be once you get here, Iris. Now, is there anywhere to sit and wait for you to arrive?*

Why don't you sit at the bar?

No, I'm not sitting at the bar, Iris. Only losers sit at the bar.

Now, that's a harsh thing to say, Sadie. We've sat at the bar plenty of times. Are we losers?

Sadie smiled and shook her head. *No, Iris, we're not losers. We're misfits, and there's a significant difference.*

Oh, how so? What's the difference, Sadie?

Losers are failures who have tried to fit in and succeed in this world but don't, and they don't blame the world for rejecting them. Misfits, on the other hand, may succeed but don't try to fit in, rejecting the world and having no need for its approval.

Okay, I see your point, Sadie. What would you call a misfit who doesn't want to be friends with other misfits and prefers to have only one friend?

Sadie sighed. *Let's not have this argument again, okay? I don't need to have any other friends besides you. You're enough for me.*

Did it ever occur to you that I might like to have more friends? If I hadn't, I would have stayed in Nashville.

"Hey, come over here, Sadie."

We know that voice, don't we, Sadie?

Sadie sighed and nodded. *Yes, we do, Iris. I was hoping that Rebecca didn't see me walk into the bar.*

Well, don't be rude now, Sadie. Go over there and say hi.

Okay, I will. Sometimes, I wish I hadn't been raised to be a polite Southern lady. Sadie walked over to the table where Rebecca was sitting. "Hi, Rebecca," she said. "You're here early." *Should I say hi to Billie or wait for Rebecca to introduce her to me?*

Rebecca chuckled and nodded. "I decided not to bar-hop this year," she said. She looked over at Billie and smiled. "And I wanted to bring her here."

Sadie nodded. "You haven't seen Iris, have you?" She looked around, frowning. "She promised me that she would meet me here." *Shit, maybe I should sit at the bar. I'll be able to see her as soon as she gets here.*

"Oh, I'm sorry. Where are my manners?" Rebecca got Sadie's attention. "Sadie, I would like you to meet Billie Carver."

Billie smiled at Sadie and offered her hand to her. "It's nice to meet you, Sadie," she said. "You work at the bookstore, don't you?"

Sadie nodded and shook Billie's hand. *So, she did notice me.* "Yeah, I do," she said. "You're becoming one of our regulars." *Her accent's Southern, though I can't tell from which part of the South she's from.*

Billie nodded. "I love bookstores," she said. "Some of my best memories are walking around in a bookstore and looking at books with my best friend Bobbie."

Rebecca pointed at the empty chair next to her. "Why don't you join us, Sadie?"

Sadie shook her head. "I'm waiting for Iris," she said. She glanced at her watch and frowned. "She promised to meet me here after she finished her assignment."

"You could sit with us while you wait for your best friend," Billie said. She shrugged her shoulders. "There might be enough time for us to talk to each other and maybe even get to know each other."

Sadie chuckled and sat at the table beside Rebecca and across from Billie.

***

It took Iris almost thirty minutes to drive from her workplace to Capote's because of holiday traffic. She spotted Sadie's car when she arrived at Capote's and smiled. *I hope she hasn't been waiting here long for me.* She found an empty parking space nearby and parked her car.

Iris walked away from her car and entered the bar. She looked around for Sadie and saw her sitting at a table near the bar with Rebecca Dubois and someone Iris didn't know.

Iris smiled. *I don't know how Rebecca convinced Sadie to sit with her and her friend, but I will find out.* She walked over to them and pointed at her watch. "I said I would be here in forty minutes, and here I am," she said. "I thought you would be waiting for me at the bar, Sadie."

Sadie's voice was filled with relief as she greeted Iris. "You know how I hate sitting at the bar alone," she said. "How did your article turn out?"

Iris smiled. "It turned out fine," she said. "I'm sure my editor's going to love it." *He loves almost everything I write, but he doesn't hesitate to let me know when I write something that isn't my best. He pushes me to become a better journalist and writer.*

Rebecca cleared her throat while smiling.

Sadie shook her head. "I guess I should be polite," she said. "The two young ladies at the table here, where I've been sitting while waiting for you, are Rebecca Dubois and Billie Carver."

Iris smiled and nodded. "Good job, Sadie," she said. She looked over at Rebecca. "So, how have you been, Rebecca? You still turning heads at the country club?" *I'm just teasing her. I'm sure she turns heads there, even though I've never been to the country club, not being from the right family, because I've seen her turn heads here.*

Rebecca smiled back at Iris. "Oh, you know I do," she said. "Just like you turn heads here, Iris."

Sadie frowned. "Do you know her, Iris?"

Iris nodded. "We met a few months ago at a party," she said. She shrugged her shoulders. "I meant to tell you about it, but I forgot." *I didn't tell her on purpose. I didn't want her to think I had made a new friend.*

Sadie squinted at Iris. "If you say so, Iris," she said. "What about her? Do you know her, too?"

Iris shook her head. "No, I don't know Billie, though I've been hearing some stories about her," she said. She turned her attention to Billie and smiled at her. "It's nice to meet you, Billie." She offered her hand to Billie to shake.

"Yeah, same here," Billie said. She took Iris's hand, and they shook hands.

Iris sat at the table next to Sadie. She took out a cigarette and lit it, looking around. "Well, the usual crowd's here," she said. *It has been too long since the last time I've had to make small talk. I'm out of practice.* She looked over at Billie. "So, what do you think of this place?"

Billie chuckled. "It's nice," she said. "This isn't the first time I've been to a gay bar or the first gay bar I've ever been to before."

Iris grinned. "Oh, is that right?" *Well, she's not shy. I wonder how accurate the stories I've heard about her are.* "What other gay bars have you been to, Billie?"

"Well, I've only been to one other gay bar," Billie said. She smiled and looked around some more. "I'd say this one is a little more upscale."

Sadie frowned. "Thanks," she said. "I'm glad you approve."

Iris sighed. *Something about Billie irritates her, but I don't know.* She took one of Sadie's hands and leaned closer to her. "You behave yourself," she said. "There's no need to be rude to her."

"So, does anyone here know why the owner named the bar after Truman Capote, the author?" Billie took a drag off her cigarette and smiled at Rebecca. "I was sure that Rebecca was teasing me when she told me where we were going," she said. "But after I thought about it, it seems only fitting that a gay bar be named after one of America's most famous gay authors."

I'm impressed. Iris grinned at Billie. "I don't know why the owner named his bar after Truman Capote," she said. She shrugged her shoulders. "I've always wanted to ask him, ever since the first time Sadie and I came here, but so far, I haven't gotten the chance to talk to him and ask him about it."

"Maybe the owner's a fan of Truman Capote," Sadie said. She pointed out some posters hanging on some of the walls. "All the posters are front covers from Capote's books or pictures of him."

Billie nodded. "You might be right, Sadie," she said.

Billie is the only other person I've met, after Rebecca, who guessed that the bar was named after the author Truman Capote. Iris smiled. "I think Sadie's right," she said. She looked around and nodded. "Only a fan would both name his bar after Truman Capote and decorate the walls with posters of him and his books."

***

Sadie had hoped that Iris's arrival at Capote's would alleviate her discomfort sitting with Rebecca and her new friend, Billie.

I could stand up and leave. Sadie sighed and shook her head. *No, I can't do that. I came here tonight to celebrate New Year's Eve with my best friend, and that's what I'm going to do, even if I have to sit with two other women, one who makes me uncomfortable for some reason and the other one who reminds me too much of the girls back home, in Nashville who always made me feel like I didn't belong anywhere.*

Chapter Seven

Around the same time Iris arrived at Capote's, the other young lady Billie would meet that night, New Year's Eve, sat in the break room in the back of the bar, near the stockroom, and smoked a cigarette. The break room was a small, dimly lit space with a few chairs, a table, and a window that offered a view of the bustling bar. Her name was Georgia Stern, and like Billie, Iris, and Sadie, she was also Southern, her hometown being Fayetteville, Arkansas.

Georgia sat in the breakroom and smoked a cigarette. *I was sitting in bed reading only an hour ago, and now I'm here on my day off from work. I should've let the phone ring instead of picking it up.*

Georgia was about to light another cigarette when the owner entered the break room.

"So is where you've been hiding," the owner said. "When I asked you to work tonight, I meant for you to be out there, taking care of our customers, not sitting in the break room, smoking a cigarette."

Georgia frowned. "I've been busting my ass for three hours ever since I got here," she said. She held up her cigarette. "Let me smoke one more, and I'll be good for the rest of the night." *Come on, man. Let me smoke one more.*

The owner glanced at his watch and shook his head. "Sorry, I need you out there, doing your job," he said. "It's getting closer to midnight, and more people are showing up, so no, you can't have another cigarette."

Most of the time, I would argue with him because he knows how hard I work. Georgia sighed and shook her head. *But this isn't a typical night; it's New Year's Eve.* She put her cigarette back up in the pack and shoved her lighter back in the left front pocket of her jeans. "Okay," she said. "You win, boss. I'll go back to work."

The owner chuckled. "Thanks, Georgia," he said. "Four women are sitting in your section; the last time I looked, none had drinks."

Georgia frowned. "Which table are they sitting in?" *I took care of all my customers before I came back here.* "The last time I checked, before I came back here to smoke a quick cigarette, all of my customers were fine."

The owner shook his head. "Well, the four women need drinks," he said. "So, if you don't mind, go out there and take care of them, okay?"

Georgia nodded. "I'll take care of them," she said. "I'll do my job."

The owner chuckled. "Thanks, I would appreciate it if you could do that," he said. He turned around and was about to leave the break room when he glanced over his shoulder at Georgia. "I'll see you out there, Georgia."

Georgia nodded and stood up. She waited for the owner to leave the break room, not wanting him to think she was following him. She left the break room and went to her section.

Georgia looked around her section, searching for a table with four women. *He must be referring to that table.* One of the tables near the bar, which had been empty when Georgia went to the break room for a quick smoke break, had four women sitting at it. And she knew three of the four women; they were her regular customers, and she had a good relationship with them.

Georgia smiled. *Well, three of my favorite regulars are here.* She glanced at her watch and chuckled. *I'm surprised to see them here so early. I wouldn't think they would even be there until it was closer to midnight. But here they are, and I know what they like to drink. Well, I'd better go over there and find out if they're ready to start drinking.*

Georgia walked over to the table. "Good evening, ladies," she said. "I hope you're ready to start having some fun." *These four ladies are the least likely four women to share a table. I know two of them are friends, but I'm not familiar with the other two. One of them I know is Rebecca, and she's my favorite regular. She's a good tipper and knows how to behave herself.*

Rebecca grinned. "Oh, yeah, I'd say we're ready to have fun," she said. She shrugged her shoulders. "In my opinion, anyway."

"Hi, Georgia," Iris said, smiling. "I'm glad you're our waitress."

Georgia smiled back at Iris. "Thanks, Iris," she said. "Are you ready to order something to drink?" *I need to say hi to her friend.* "Hey, Sadie. I'm glad to see you again."

"Thanks," Sadie said. "I'm ready to order a drink."

Iris shook her head and chuckled. "Hey, wait your turn," she said. She looked over at Georgia. "I'll have my usual, Georgia."

"Same here," Sadie said, giving Iris an irritated look.

Georgia looked over at Rebecca. "What about you, Rebecca? Do you want your usual?" *Is she brave enough to try something new tonight, or will she stick to her usual drink?*

Rebecca smiled. "I think I'll stick to my usual scotch and soda," she said. "What about you, Billie? What would you like to drink?"

Okay, her name's Billie. "I would ask you if you would like your usual, but since this is the first time I've seen you here, I don't know what your usual drink is," Georgia said, smiling at

Billie. *She's gorgeous. I could lose myself in her beautiful brown eyes.*

"That's true," Billie said. "Most of the time, I drink a vodka tonic." She glanced over at Rebecca. "I know you said you would buy my first drink, and I'm okay with you doing that." She shook her head and chuckled. "I'll buy the second round, okay?"

"Okay," Rebecca said. She cleared her throat. "I'm sorry, Georgia. I'm being rude." She pointed at Billie. "Georgia, I would like you to meet Billie Carver. She just moved back here a few months ago."

What did Rebecca mean by saying that she had moved back here? Georgia grinned and waved at Billie. "Welcome to Boston, Billie," she said. "I hope you're making yourself at home here." *You need to stop flirting with her and get her order.* "Would you like a vodka tonic?"

Billie nodded. "I would love one," she said. She took one last drag off her cigarette and put it out. "I think that's everyone."

Oh, shit, did she notice that I've been staring at her? Georgia shook her head and cleared her throat. "You're right," she said. "Before I go and get your drinks, I want to say, welcome to Capote's, Billie."

Billie smiled. "Thanks, Georgia," she said. She chuckled. "Is that your real name or some sort of nickname?"

If anyone else had asked me that, I would have been pissed off, but I can tell that she's teasing me a little. And I like it. "It's my real name," Georgia said. "Do you want to hear something funny about it?"

Billie nodded. "I sure would, Georgia," she said. "What's funny about your name?"

I can't believe I'm about to tell her the story behind my first name. "Well, you would think I was named Georgia because I was born there, but I wasn't," she said. "Instead, I was born in Arkansas."

Billie nodded and laughed. "That's funny," she said. "So, why did your parents name you Georgia if you weren't born there?"

Sadie sighed. "Oh, for Christ's sake," she said. "Who cares why her parents named her Georgia?" She shook her head. "I don't mean to be rude, but please, I want my drink now."

Georgia shrugged her shoulders. "She's right," she said. She looked over at Billie and smiled. "I promise I will tell you why another time." She turned around and was about to walk away when she glanced over her shoulder at Billie. "I also promise that you'll enjoy yourself tonight. This place gets wild on New Year's Eve." *Okay, it's time for you to do your job.*

Billie grinned. "I'm going to remember you said that, Georgia," she said.

Billie might be flirting with me. Georgia nodded. "You do that, Billie," she said. She left the table and went to the bar to get their drinks. She glanced over her shoulder and caught Billie watching her walk away.

***

A few minutes later, Georgia returned to the table, carrying their drinks on a tray. She placed the tray on the table and handed their drinks to them. "Well, I'm back," she said. "And I brought your drinks with me."

Sadie sighed. "Thank God," she said. "I'm so ready to start drinking."

Iris chuckled and shook her head. "I think we're all ready for you to start drinking," she said. "Thanks, Georgia."

Georgia kept a close eye on their table, ensuring they didn't have to wait too long to get another round of drinks. She noticed that Sadie seemed uncomfortable, shifting around in her chair while giving her friend Iris an annoyed look.

***

As the old year drew to a close, the group found themselves in mixed emotions, fueled by the passing hours and the many drinks they had consumed.

Rebecca grinned and looked around the table. "It's almost midnight," she said. "Is anyone here going to get a midnight kiss?"

Iris held up her hands and chuckled. "Don't look at me, Rebecca," she said. "If you want a kiss at midnight, you'll have to get it from someone else." She reached out and took one of Sadie's hands. "I'm going to kiss my best friend at midnight like always."

Sitting at their table beside Billie, Georgia glanced at her and smiled. "I'd like a kiss at midnight," she said. She shrugged her shoulders. "But I'll be okay if I don't get one."

***

A minute later, it was midnight and the start of a new year.

Iris kissed Sadie and smiled at her. "Love you, best friend," she said. "You're stuck with me for another year."

The atmosphere shifted when, to everyone's surprise, Billie kissed Georgia, a moment that left the group in a state of pleasant shock, adding an unexpected twist to the New Year's celebration.

Sadie leaned closer to Iris. "Am I wrong, or did Billie just kiss Georgia? I didn't know she was gay," she said. She then gave Iris a stern look. "Did you know?"

"It appears Billie's like us," Iris said, smiling. She chuckled and shook her head. "If she's not gay, she has to be bisexual. It's not surprising."

Sadie frowned and shook her head. "Well, I'm surprised," she said. She chuckled. "I thought I had better radar for other gay women." She couldn't believe she hadn't seen it coming. Most of the time, she could tell when another woman was like her and Iris. But Billie had managed to surprise her. She shook her head, trying to understand why she hadn't picked up on it.

Iris giggled. "I don't think Rebecca would have brought her here if Billie were straight," she said. She grinned and shrugged her shoulders. "But then again, Rebecca might have brought Billie here anyway."

Feeling a sudden urge for solitude, Sadie stood up, pushing her chair back. "If y'all will excuse me, I'm going to the ladies' room," she said. "I need to freshen up a little."

"I'll go with you," Iris said, sensing the tension between them. She picked up her pack of cigarettes and looked in it. "I need to buy another pack of smokes." She looked over at Georgia. "Did the owner ever fix the cigarette machine by the ladies' room?"

Georgia nodded. "He had to fix it," she said. "Most of the customers and about half of the waitresses smoke."

Sadie shook her head. "Don't come with me, Iris," she said. "I'm just going to use the ladies' room. I don't need you to come with me." *Please hear the tone in my voice. I'm using my wanting-to-be-alone tone.*

Okay, she's serious about going to the ladies' room alone. Iris held up her hands in surrender. "Okay," she said. She glanced at her watch. "If you're not back in five minutes, I'll be there after you."

Sadie chuckled and nodded. "Okay, I'll keep that in mind," she said. She looked over at Rebecca and nodded. "Remember, the next round's on me." She didn't say anything to Billie or Georgia for different reasons. She turned around and walked away from the table.

Sadie walked away from the table, not looking back. She made her way through the crowd, walking past people dancing together, standing too close to each other, and talking to each other. Their hands moved around, using hand gestures to make up for the fact that they couldn't hear anything another person said to them, the music too loud to have any meaningful conversation.

***

Sadie arrived at the ladies' room. She pushed the door open and stepped inside. She found an empty stall, entered it, closed the stall door, and sat on the toilet after pulling up her skirt.

Sadie reached into her bra and pulled out the joint she had rolled earlier that day. She lit it and closed her eyes while taking a long drag off it.

Most of the time, I know it's a bad idea to mix booze with weed. You have to do it the right way because if you don't do it the right way, you'll end up having a bad night, throwing up most of your night in the bathroom or restroom.

Sadie knew the right way, and while she already had a few drinks, she wasn't drunk, only a little tipsy. She hoped that by smoking the joint she had rolled earlier that day, before she had gone to work, her nerves would settle.

***

Iris's brow furrowed with concern. *Something was bothering Sadie.* She decided to give her friend a few minutes alone in the restroom, but if she didn't return soon, Iris would go after her.

Billie cleared her throat. "So, tell me, Iris. Is Sadie okay?"

"I think so," Iris said. She then shrugged her shoulders. "But I'm sure something is bothering her." *I could lie to Billie and tell her there's nothing wrong with Sadie, but I won't because it's clear to Billie that something's bothering her.* "And she's not good at being social."

Billie smiled. "My best friend isn't good at being social either," she said. She chuckled and shook her head. "Bobbie has gotten better at it, however. She's not as shy as she was when we were younger."

Iris sighed. "I wish I could say the same thing about Sadie," she said. She chuckled. "We've been living here for three years, and she still hasn't made any new friends."

"Sadie doesn't seem to like me," Billie said. She shrugged her shoulders. "But I know that not everyone's going to like me." She frowned. "I'm not looking to make any enemies."

Iris shook her head and chuckled. "I don't think Sadie sees you as her enemy, Billie," she said. "I think it's more likely she doesn't know what to think about you." She shrugged her shoulders. "Or maybe you're right; she just doesn't like you."

Billie frowned. "Is there anything I could do to make it easier for Sadie to like me?"

Iris shook her head. "I wouldn't try to get Sadie to like you if I were you," she said. She shrugged her shoulders. "I don't know why Sadie wouldn't like you, so all I can tell you is don't worry about it." *It's almost impossible to change her mind once Sadie decides that she doesn't like someone or something.*

Billie nodded. "Okay," she said. She took out a cigarette and lit it. She looked over at Georgia and smiled at her. "Well, so far, you've been right, Georgia."

Georgia smiled back at Billie. "Oh, what have I been right about, Billie?"

Billie reached out and took one of Georgia's hands. "I'm having a good time and enjoying myself," she said. She glanced over at Rebecca. "Thanks for bringing me here."

Rebecca grinned. "You're welcome, Billie," she said.

Iris glanced at her watch. *Okay, so far, Sadie's been gone for almost five minutes. I'll give her a few more minutes and check in with her if she doesn't return. Let's find out some more about*

Billie. She cleared her throat. "So, tell me, Billie, where are you from?" She grinned. "I can tell by your accent that you're not from around here."

"Well, you're both right and wrong," Billie said. "I was born here but didn't grow up here."

Iris chuckled. "You don't get an accent from where you're born but from where you're raised and your friends," she said. "So, I know you've got a Southern accent of some kind, but I don't know it."

Billie grinned and chuckled. "I've lived most of my life in New Orleans, Louisiana," she said. "I don't have the typical Louisiana accent." She shrugged her shoulders. "I didn't realize until I moved here in September that I sound a lot like my best friend." She shook her head and laughed. "Now I know why my older brother always told me that I have the accent of a white Southern girl."

Iris smiled. "You don't sound like a white girl to me," she said. "I'm from Nashville, Tennessee, and so is Sadie." *I knew that Billie was from the South.*

Billie nodded. "I thought I heard a little Southern twang in your voice," she said. She took a drag off her cigarette. "So, how long have you been friends with Sadie?"

Iris smiled. *One of my favorite subjects to talk about is my friendship with Sadie.* "We've been best friends for most of our lives, starting in the second or third grade."

Billie smiled and nodded. "That's great," she said. "I've been best friends with Bobbie since the first grade." She sighed and took a drag off her cigarette. "She's living in New York City now, and I haven't seen her in almost four months."

Iris shook her head. "I couldn't even imagine not seeing or talking to Sadie every day," she said. She smiled. "I would still be living in Nashville without her encouraging me to follow my dream of being a journalist." *And I don't know if I would have left if I didn't know that Sadie was coming with me.*

Chapter Eight

I ris talked to Billie for about another five minutes. She
glanced at her watch and shook her head. *Okay, I guess I'm
going to have to go after her.* She stood up, pushing her chair
back. "I'll be right back," she said. "I need another pack of
smokes."

Rebecca smiled and nodded. "And you're going to make sure
Sadie's okay," she said.

Iris left the table and went to the ladies' room.

***

Sadie smoked her joint for almost five minutes, savoring each
drag off it, hoping that she would be stoned soon, not wanting
to be only tipsy.

So, this is why you left the table.

Sadie sighed and nodded. *Yeah, this is why.* She chuckled. *I'm
glad I could convince you not to come with me. Otherwise, I would
have had to share this with you.*

And you didn't want to do that?

Sadie shook her head. *No, I didn't, Iris. I rolled this joint just for myself, not to share it with you.*

I thought we shared everything, Sadie.

Sadie grinned. *No, not everything, Iris. There are some things that I don't want to share with you.*

The door to the ladies' room opened, and footsteps approached the stall.

Sadie put out her joint, knocking the cherry off it and dropping it into the toilet. *I don't want to be caught with this.*

Sadie hoped the other person was another woman. The woman stopped in front of the stall where Sadie was and knocked on the door, making Sadie jump. The loud banging echoed in the ladies' room.

Sadie frowned. "Hey, this stall's occupied," she said. *Can't you see that the stall door is closed? That means there's someone in here.* "Find another stall."

The other person laughed and knocked on the stall door again.

Sadie grinned. *I would know that laugh anywhere.* She stood up, got off the toilet, and pulled her skirt down. She then opened the stall door and left the stall.

Iris sighed and shook her head. "So, this is why you left the table," she said. *She didn't want to share it with me.*

Sadie walked past Iris and went to the sink, where she began washing her hands.

Iris frowned. "I told you that I would come after you if you didn't come back in five minutes," she said. She pointed at her watch. "You've been in here for almost ten minutes now."

Sadie shrugged her shoulders. "I told you I had to use the ladies' room," she said. *Sometimes, Iris acts more like a jealous girlfriend than she does a best friend.* "I didn't say how long I would be in here."

Iris chuckled. "No, you didn't," she said. She sighed and shook her head. "I would ask you why you've been here longer than five minutes, but I don't have to."

Sadie looked into the mirror hanging over the sink. Iris was standing right behind her. "Oh, and why's that?" *So, now you're going to interrogate me?*

Iris grinned and waved her hand in front of her face. "I know you've smoked a joint because you reek of marijuana," she said. "I didn't know you had any on you."

Sadie shrugged her shoulders. "Why would you? We haven't seen each other all day," she said. "I was still asleep when you left for work this morning, remember?" *We don't spend as much free time together as we used to when we were younger and still in school.*

Iris nodded. "I remember," she said. She sighed and shook her head. "I know something's bothering you, and I want to know what it is, Sadie."

Sadie sighed. *Of course, she noticed that something was bothering me.* "Why are you only asking me now when I've been uncomfortable for most of the night?"

Iris sighed. "I'm only asking you now because this is the first chance I've had to do so," she said. "I didn't think you would want to talk about what's bothering you in front of Rebecca and Billie."

I'm glad she did notice. Sadie nodded. "You're right about that," she said. *I could tell her the truth or lie to her, but I don't want to lie.* "I'll tell you what's been bothering me." She shook her head. "I don't know what to think of Billie." She finished washing her hands and started drying them off. "I didn't know that she was gay, and I can't decide if she's a stuck-up snob or not."

Iris shook her head. "I think you should just talk to her," she said. She shrugged her shoulders. "I think Billie's interesting, and I want to get to know her better." *Come on, Sadie, why don't you lower your guard and try to be open to someone besides me?*

Sadie sighed and shook her head. *I don't want to get to know Billie. Not at all.*

Iris and Sadie left the ladies' room and returned to the table. "Billie's Southern, just like us," she said. "She's from Louisiana."

Sadie only nodded while giving Billie an uneasy look.

***

A few hours later, Billie finished her drink and stood up. Sadie and Iris had already left an hour before, leaving Georgia alone with Billie and Rebecca.

Rebecca also stood up. "So, are you ready to go, Billie?"

Billie nodded. "Yeah, I am," she said. She looked over at Georgia and smiled. "I had fun tonight, Georgia."

Georgia smiled back at Billie. "Good, I'm glad you did," she said. She reached into her pocket and pulled out a small piece of paper. "Here's my phone number. Why don't you give me a call sometime? Maybe we can hang out." She gave Billie the paper with her phone number written on it.

Billie folded the paper and slipped it underneath her bra. "I just might do that," she said. She stepped up to Georgia and hugged her. "You're a good kisser."

It just feels right, holding her in my arms. And she smells so good, a mixture of jasmine, whiskey, and cigarette smoke. "So are you, Billie," Georgia said, smiling. *Oh, yeah, she's going to call me.*

***

Sadie followed Iris into her bedroom. Iris sat down on her bed and took off her shoes. "Wow, what a crazy night," she said, grinning. "I'm glad we went to Capote's."

Sadie sighed and nodded. "Yeah, me too," she said. She frowned. "You seemed to take a liking to that Billie girl." *Most of the time, I don't worry about Iris making another friend because while she's more outgoing than I am, she has a natural distrust of other people.*

Iris nodded. "She was easy to talk to, Sadie," she said. She chuckled. "She only said enough to keep the conversation going, without revealing much of herself."

Sadie shook her head. "There's something about her that I don't like," she said. "We shouldn't hang out with her." *Now the matter's settled.* She turned around and went to Iris's bedroom door. "I'm going to crash now. I'll see you in the morning or whenever I wake up." And then, without another word, she left Iris's bedroom.

***

Georgia's heart raced with anticipation three days later as the phone rang, her every hope pinned on it being Billie.

"Hello?" *Please, let it be Billie and not some bill collector.*

"Hey, Georgia, it's me."

Georgia couldn't help but smile. "Hey, Billie," she said. "I was starting to think you might not call."

Billie chuckled. "I'm sorry I haven't called you sooner," she said. "I've been busy the last few days."

Georgia nodded, trying to mask her disappointment. "Oh, I see," she said. "How have you been?" She found it surprisingly difficult to flirt over the phone.

"I've been good," Billie said. She sighed. "I'm looking for a job right now, and so far, I haven't found anything I like or can do."

"I'm sure you'll find something," Georgia said. "So, you were born here but haven't lived here since you were a baby, right?"

After their long conversation, Georgia was filled with a re-newed, buoyant hope. She was confident that Billie's feelings for her were more than friendship.

***

Billie started spending Friday and Saturday nights at Capote's, but always came with Rebecca.

When Georgia realized Valentine's Day was approaching, she decided to take the night off from work and spend it with Billie. A few days before, she approached Billie.

Georgia cleared her throat. "So, do you have any plans for Valentine's Day, Billie?"

Billie and Rebecca had come in a few hours before, and while Georgia wasn't their waitress, she checked in on them, using any opportunity to talk to Billie.

Billie chuckled. "Oh, yeah, Bobbie's favorite holiday," she said. She shrugged her shoulders. "I haven't made any plans, Georgia. I'm not the making plans type."

Georgia frowned. *Okay, I wasn't expecting to hear that.* "So, you don't know if you're going out or staying home on Valen-tine's Day?" *Is she not picking up on the fact that I might be asking her out?*

Billie grinned. "I like doing both," she said. "If I stay home, I can write a short story or hang out with my grandmother, Josephine."

"And if you go out, you'll be with me," Rebecca said, smiling.

"Well, you're the only friend I've made so far," Billie said. She blushed. "And you, too, Georgia." She shook her head. "I'm sorry about that."

So, it could be a good thing that Billie doesn't consider me to be her friend. Georgia laughed. "It's okay," she said. "If you en-joyed New Year's Eve here, you should come here on Valentine's Day, Billie."

Rebecca shook her head. "Yeah, it's great to come here for Valentine's Day if you're with someone," she said. "But if you're single, this place is too much, with hearts, teddy bears, and roses everywhere."

Georgia frowned. "Okay, where do you think Billie should go to celebrate Valentine's Day?" *I thought that Rebecca liked coming here. And now, she's talking shit about it.*

Rebecca grinned. "Well, I don't think she's gone to Jackson's Jukebox yet," she said. "Now, there's a great place to go to on Valentine's Day."

Georgia frowned. "I've heard it's a great bar," she said. *It's also not a gay bar.* She shrugged her shoulders. "I've never been there myself, but it's one of Boston's oldest bars."

Rebecca chuckled. "I've been there," she said. She looked over at Billie and grinned. "It's a great place just to drink and dance your ass off."

Billie nodded. "It sounds like a great bar," she said. "But what about Valentine's Day? What's it like on that night?"

Rebecca shrugged her shoulders and smiled. "To be honest, I don't know," she said. "I've never gone there on Valentine's Day."

Billie chuckled. "I like the name," she said. She nodded. "Yeah, let's go there on Valentine's Day instead of here."

Georgia sighed. *I can't help but feel that Rebecca's trying to prevent anything from happening between Billie and me.* "I hope you have a good time, Billie," she said. She frowned and stared at Rebecca. "I know you would have a good time here, even if it's Valentine's Day." *I know what you're doing, Rebecca. I don't know if you're trying to stop anything from happening between Billie and me because you want to get with her or because you don't like me.*

"Hey, I've got an idea," Billie said. "Why don't you come with us, Georgia?"

Georgia smiled. "I'd love to, Billie," she said. She looked over at Rebecca and smirked. "I'll see y'all there." *What do you think about that, Rebecca? Billie wants to spend Valentine's Day with me.*

***

A few days later, it was Valentine's Day. Georgia arrived at Jackson's Jukebox first, beating Billie and Rebecca there. She sat in a booth within view of the front entrance.

Billie and Rebecca arrived ten minutes later.

Billie smiled. "Hey, there's Georgia," she said. She waved and walked over to her. "I hope you haven't been waiting long for us."

Georgia chuckled and shook her head. "I've only been here for about ten minutes," she said. She held out her hands. "I haven't even gotten a drink yet." *I'm glad they showed up.*

Rebecca joined them in the booth and sat across from them on the other side. "I'm surprised you knew where this place was, Georgia," she said. "This isn't your part of town, is it?"

Georgia stared at Rebecca. *I know what you're saying, Rebecca.* "Like I said the other day, I've heard of this place," she said. *And yeah, I know I'm one of the few white people here, but I don't care.*

Billie looked around and smiled. "This place looks old," she said. She chuckled. "I feel like I've stepped back in time or something."

Georgia nodded and smiled. "I know what you mean, Billie," she said. "I've been to a few thrift stores, and based on what I see, the tables, the chairs, and this booth, I feel like we've stepped back into either the Sixties or the Seventies." *Okay, Rebecca, what are you going to say about that?*

"Well, I guess it's a good thing we're in the Nineties," Rebecca said. "Twenty or thirty years ago, the three of us wouldn't sit together."

"You're right, Rebecca," Billie said. "But we are sitting together, and it's the Nineties, not the Sixties or the Seventies."

Georgia sighed. *Okay, listen to Billie. You have to get along with Rebecca because, like it or not, she's Billie's friend.* "So, tell us about this place, Rebecca," she said. *I'm sure she knows everything about this place. I know that I don't know anything about it.*

Rebecca smiled. "Well, I know it's been around since 1944," she said. She looked over at Billie. "It was named after the jazz musician Jackson Baldwin."

Billie grinned. "This bar was named after Jackson Baldwin?"

Rebecca nodded. "Yeah, that's what I've been told," she said. She pointed at a picture hanging on the wall near them. "I think that's him right there."

Billie nodded. "Yeah, that's him all right," she said. She smiled. "That's my grandfather."

Chapter Nine

The next time Billie hung out with Rebecca and Georgia was at the country club almost two months later, on Easter Sunday.

Bridget was sitting at one of the tables on the patio with Jasmine and Rebecca. She sighed and shook her head. *I'd rather be anywhere else, but since my parents couldn't come, I have to be here.* She took out a cigarette and lit it.

"Are you okay, Bridget?"

Bridget took a drag off her cigarette and nodded. "Yeah, I'm okay," she said. "Don't I look like I'm okay?" *I don't know why you're asking. It's not like we're friends or anything like that.*

Rebecca shrugged her shoulders. "You look like you don't want to be here," she said. "If you want to go, you should go."

I can't do that. Bridget sighed and shook her head. "I'm here because I'm expected to be here," she said. *It's time to change the subject.* She pointed at the other chairs. "What's the deal with the two empty chairs?"

Rebecca smiled. "Two more people are joining us," she said. She glanced at her watch and frowned. "And they're late."

Bridget sighed. *You're just telling me now, Rebecca.* "So, two more people will join us," she said. "Are you going to tell me who they are, or will you make me guess, Rebecca?"

"It would be fun, making you guess who I invited to join us," Rebecca said. "But something tells me you're not in the mood to play a game like that." She chuckled and grinned. "Am I right, Bridget?"

Bridget scowled at Rebecca. "You know you're right, Rebecca," she said. "I'll ask you again. Who's late to join us?"

Rebecca smiled and chuckled. "Billie will be joining us soon," she said. "And she's bringing a friend."

Bridget shook her head. *I know why she didn't tell me Billie was coming.*

Jasmine cleared her throat to get Bridget's attention.

Bridget looked over at Jasmine. *Does she have something to say?* "Is there something on your mind, Jasmine?" *She's been sitting there, not saying anything, for the last twenty minutes. She frowned. I don't think Jasmine has said anything since she arrived at the table and took her seat.*

Jasmine nodded. "There is something on my mind, Bridget," she said. She frowned and glanced over at Rebecca. "I wasn't told that Billie would join us or that she was invited to Easter Sunday lunch."

I wasn't told either, Jasmine. "Well, good job, Rebecca," Bridget said. "You've managed to irritate both Jasmine and me." *I don't have much in common with Jasmine. I'm sure we have nothing in common except that we are both members of the country club.*

Rebecca shrugged her shoulders. "I wasn't trying to irritate either of you," she said. "The fact is, Billie's a member here." She chuckled. "I didn't invite her to Easter Sunday lunch. I invited her to join us, the three of us, for lunch."

Bridget frowned. "Now, you're just splitting hairs, Rebecca," she said. *I know what she means. Since Billie's a member here because of her grandmother, she was already invited to the Easter Sunday lunch.* "Why did you invite her to have lunch with us?"

Rebecca smiled. "I invited Billie for the same reason I invited you, Bridget," she said. She looked over at Jasmine and smiled. "And you too, Jasmine."

Okay, now she's got me curious. Bridget took out a cigarette and lit it. "I don't believe you," she said. "I'm sure you invited Billie because you are friends."

Rebecca chuckled. "Are you saying we're not friends, Bridget?"

Bridget nodded. "You know we're not," she said. *She's messing with me, and I don't know why.* "And Jasmine's not your friend, either."

Jasmine shook her head. "I can speak for myself," she said. She sighed. "I'm starting to regret accepting your invitation, Rebecca."

Bridget nodded. *I feel the same way, Jasmine.*

Rebecca shrugged her shoulders. "I was surprised when you accepted my invitation, Jasmine," she said. She chuckled and grinned while looking over at Bridget. "I expected you would accept my invitation, Bridget."

Oh, you did, did you? Bridget frowned. "And why would you expect me to accept your invitation?" *Sometimes, I think Rebecca tries to be my friend, no matter how rude I am.*

Rebecca smiled. "Well, I knew you would be here anyway, and I know I'm one of the few members you can tolerate," she said. She glanced over at Jasmine. "And I'm sure that she's the other one."

Well, shit, she's right. Bridget sighed. *But I'm not going to admit that to her. I'll never hear the end of it if I do.* "If you say so," she said. She frowned and shook her head. "But why did you invite Billie to join us?" *The only reason why I'm asking her again is that Rebecca didn't answer my question the first time I asked her.*

Rebecca sighed. "You're not going to let me avoid answering that question, are you, Bridget?"

Bridget shook her head. "I'm not, so answer my question," she said. *Okay, show her that you're serious.* "Answer me now, or I'm leaving."

"You were right, Bridget. I invited Billie to join us because I considered her my friend," Rebecca said. She shrugged her shoulders. "I know you don't like her, but I would appreciate it if you were polite with her."

Bridget shook her head. "I never said that I didn't like her," she said. She chuckled and smiled. "I rarely give her any thought." *I'm not lying to her. Well, maybe I am a little. I try not to think about Billie; it is more accurate.*

Rebecca shook her head and gave Bridget a disbelieving look. "I've heard some of the gossip about Billie going around here," she said. "And I'm sure you're the source of some of the rumors about Billie."

Bridget shook her head. "I don't gossip or spread rumors," she said. *How in the hell did Rebecca figure out that I've been spreading gossip about Billie and started a few rumors about her?*

Rebecca clicked her tongue and slowly nodded. "Okay," she said. "If you say so, Bridget." She leaned across the table towards Bridget. "Jasmine doesn't like Billie either, but I doubt she would stoop so low to spread gossip or start a rumor about Billie."

"I wouldn't do either one," Jasmine said. She sighed and shook her head. "I know what it's like to be the target of a malicious rumor."

"I know," Rebecca said. She glanced over at Bridget. "That's why I know you didn't start rumors or spread gossip about Billie."

Bridget scowled at Rebecca. "I should leave right now," she said. "I've slapped the shit out of rude bitches for saying less than that, Rebecca." *For someone who's barely a member here,*

*only showing up a few times a month, Rebecca knows a lot more
than I thought she did.*

Rebecca gave Bridget a stern look. "Go ahead and try something like that," she said. "I promise you that you'll have a red
imprint of my hand on your face for a couple of days at least."

***

Ten minutes later, Billie arrived with a guest.

Bridget frowned. *I know Billie's guest. I think she's a waitress
at Capote's.* She looked over at Jasmine and saw her puzzled
smile. *Oh, good, Jasmine doesn't know who that is, though I'm
sure Rebecca knows.*

Billie smiled at Rebecca. "Hey, I'm sorry we're late," she said.
She pointed at her guest. "Everyone, this is Georgia." She smiled
and laughed. "I know you already know Rebecca here, Georgia,
but let me introduce the two other ladies. The white girl sitting
next to Rebecca is Bridget, and the other is Jasmine."

"Hello, Georgia," Jasmine said. "Why don't you and Billie go
ahead and join us?"

Billie smiled. "Thanks, Jasmine," she said. She chuckled. "We
were planning on doing that anyway."

Oh, shit. Bridget frowned and shook her head. *Rebecca knew
that Billie was bringing Georgia with her. The two worlds I live
in, which I've tried to keep separate, are crashing together. I never
wanted this to happen. If they're a couple, I'll find a way to separate them.*

***

Almost eight weeks later, the night before the start of Memorial
Day weekend, Bridget called Jasmine.

"Hello, you've reached the Carter residence," Jasmine said, using her mother's polite greeting. "How may I help you?" *I hope it's not an obscene phone call. Those creep me out, and I don't know what to say.*

"Hey, Jasmine, it's me, Bridget," she said.

"Oh, hi, Bridget," Jasmine said, frowning. *Why did she call me?*

"Look, I need to talk to you," Bridget said. "Can you meet me at Jackson's Jukebox tomorrow night, say around eight?"

"You barely speak to me whenever we're at the country club, and now you want me to meet you at a bar?" Jasmine and Bridget had never been close; their interactions were mostly limited to polite nods and forced smiles at the country club.

Bridget sighed. "I know you and I aren't friends," she said. "So, I'm not asking you to meet me because I'm trying to be-friend you."

Jasmine chuckled. "You're a smooth talker, Bridget," she said. "Every time I wonder why we aren't friends, you say something like that." *I'm being nice. I can't think of any reason why I would be friends with her.*

Bridget chuckled. "Yeah, I guess I'm a little too blunt for you," she said. "I want to talk to you about Billie. We have to do something about her."

Okay, so now she's got me curious. "She bothers you, too?"

"Yeah, she does," Bridget said. "I'm sure my reasons are different from your reasons."

Well, why not? "Okay, I'll meet you there tomorrow night," Jasmine said. "I'll see you there at eight o'clock." She hung up the phone before Bridget said anything.

***

The next day, Jasmine sat in a booth near the bar at Jackson's Jukebox, waiting for Bridget to join her. She took a drag off her cigarette and sipped her whiskey, glancing at her watch.

Jasmine had finished her cigarette and was about to get another whiskey when Bridget arrived five minutes later. She sat down across from Jasmine.

Bridget smiled at Jasmine. "Thanks for meeting me here." She looked around. "I've heard about this place but never been here before."

Of course, you haven't been here before. They play soul music here, and you don't have one. "I'm surprised you even knew about this place," Jasmine said. "This isn't exactly your scene, is it?"

Bridget frowned. "What are you trying to say, Jasmine?"

Jasmine's response was sharp. "You know what I'm saying, Bridget. And I know you're full of shit, so you can drop the tough bitch act." She shook her head, a wry grin on her face. "I'm not buying it."

Bridget pointed at the empty whiskey glass. "How many of those have you had, Jasmine?" She shook her head. "You're lucky that I know you well enough to know how reckless you get with your mouth after you've had a few drinks."

Jasmine grinned, took out another cigarette, and lit it. "I might become reckless after I've had a few, but I'm not a liar," she said. *I know what she's trying to say, but I don't care. She might be right; I get careless about what I say and to whom.* "So, will you tell me why we're sitting here?"

Bridget frowned. "I already told you why, Jasmine," she said. "We're here because I want to talk to you about Billie."

Jasmine nodded. "Okay, so let's talk about her," she said. She took a drag off her cigarette. "Why are we meeting here? Why not at the country club?" *I knew she wouldn't do anything if I talked shit to her.*

Bridget shook her head. "I don't want anyone at the country club, especially Rebecca or Billie, overhearing what I'm going to say to you about Billie," she said. She shrugged her shoulders. "I didn't think you'd mind meeting me here."

Jasmine laughed. "Oh, I don't mind meeting you here," she said. "I'm surprised you didn't want us to meet at Capote's." *Yeah, I've heard about that bar, Bridget. And I also know that you would like to go there.*

Bridget narrowed her eyes. "I didn't think you would be comfortable there," she said. "After all, Capote's isn't your scene."

Jasmine nodded, her chuckle holding a hint of defiance. "You don't know what is or isn't my scene, Bridget," she said. "We're not friends, remember?"

Bridget sighed and held up her hands. "Okay, I think we got off on the wrong foot somehow," she said. She cleared her throat. "Let's get back to why I wanted to talk to you." She took out a cigarette and lit it. "We need to do something about Billie."

Jasmine grinned. "Haven't you done enough?" She sipped her whiskey. *I don't know what her issue with Billie is, and most of the time, I wouldn't care, but I'm curious. I want to know why she wanted to talk to me about Billie.*

Bridget frowned. "I haven't done anything," she said. She chuckled. "Okay, maybe I started rumors about Billie and have been gossiping about her."

Jasmine nodded. *So, Rebecca was right.* "Is that why you wanted to talk to me about Billie? Did you want to admit to someone that you've been bad-mouthing Billie at the country club?"

Bridget shook her head. "Do you remember the woman Billie brought with her?"

Jasmine nodded. "I do remember her," she said. *Can we get to the point, Bridget?* She frowned. "What's so special about her?"

Bridget waved her hands. "She's not important," she said. "I don't know if you picked up on it, but I'm sure Billie brought her girlfriend to the country club." She tapped her fingers on the table. "I was hoping that you would help me find a way of getting Billie's membership at the country club revoked."

Jasmine nodded. *So, I'm not the only one who doesn't like Billie being a country club member.* "And here I thought I was the only one who didn't want to see Billie at the country club anymore," she said. *I could ask Bridget why she didn't like Billie or why Billie bringing her girlfriend to the country club upset her, but it doesn't matter to me.* "How would we do that? Can we get Billie's membership revoked?"

Bridget shrugged her shoulders. "I have no idea," she said. She frowned. "I was hoping that maybe you knew how we could get her membership revoked."

Jasmine laughed. "Why would I know?" She sipped her whiskey and frowned. *I'm going to need another refill.* "I've not even tried to get anyone kicked out of the country club before."

Bridget nodded. "Neither have I," she said. She sighed and frowned. "I don't even know where to start."

Jasmine stood up. "I need a refill," she said. "I'm going to the bar to get it. Why don't you do some thinking while I'm gone?" She took a step and turned around. "Do you want a drink, Bridget?" *I may not like her, but I won't be rude to her.*

Bridget smiled. "I sure would love a drink," she said. She pointed at Jasmine's glass. "I'll have what you're drinking."

"Okay," Jasmine said. She held out her hand. "I need money for your drink." *I'm not buying you a drink, Bridget.*

Bridget sighed and pulled out a twenty from her purse. "Here you go," she said, handing Jasmine the twenty. She frowned. "Be sure to bring back my change."

***

Jasmine returned to the booth. "Here's your drink," she said, handing Bridget her drink. "And here's your change." She gave

Bridget her change. She sat back down in the booth. "Any thoughts?"

Before Bridget could answer Jasmine, the front door opened, and the last person Jasmine or Bridget wanted to see, the same person they were talking about, walked into the bar. It was Billie, and she walked over to them.

"Good, you're together, so I won't have to repeat myself," Billie said. "I don't know or even care what y'all's problem is with me. Y'all aren't getting rid of me, and I'm not going anywhere."

Bridget frowned. "How did you know we would be here?"

"Rebecca overheard you talking over the phone to Jasmine last night," Billie said. She chuckled. "The next time you're trying to be sneaky, look around when using a pay phone." She turned around and walked away.

Chapter Ten

B ridget cleared her throat and shook her head. "I'm sorry, Jasmine," she said. "I didn't know that anyone had over-heard me talking over the phone to you."

"You called me on a pay phone?" Jasmine chuckled and sipped her whiskey. "Well, now I know why you almost yelled at me." *I won't mention that Bridget also sounded like she had had a few drinks.*

"I still want her gone," Bridget said. "I don't care what she says or what she does. She doesn't belong at the country club."

Jasmine chuckled. "You don't like her, do you?" *If I didn't know better, I would think that Bridget has a crush on Billie. She's obsessed with her.* She shook her head. "Never mind. You don't have to answer me."

Bridget scowled at Jasmine. "You don't like her either," she said. She sipped her whiskey. "And don't try to tell me anything different. Don't forget, I was there, sitting at the same table on Easter Sunday lunch."

I haven't forgotten. "You don't have to remind me," Jasmine said. She sipped her whiskey and glanced at the front door. "Do you think she's gone?"

Bridget nodded. "Yeah, she's gone," she said. She shook her head. "I'll give her credit for one thing. She's not afraid to stick up for herself."

Bridget's right. "If you had been more careful when you called me last night, Rebecca wouldn't have overheard you and told Billie," Jasmine said. *I'm not going to let you forget that you screwed up.* "Now, Billie knows that we're plotting against her." *I don't know how popular Billie is with the other country club members.* She sighed. *I do know that I'm not popular.* She chuckled. *And I don't think Bridget is, either.*

Bridget squinted at Jasmine. "What's so funny?"

Jasmine shook her head. "Nothing," she said. *I should ask her why she doesn't like Billie.* "Before we figure out how to remove Billie from the country club, I have to ask you something."

Bridget nodded. "Okay," she said. "Go ahead, Jasmine. You can ask me whatever you want to." She grinned. "You should know that just because you ask me a question doesn't mean I'll answer it."

Jasmine chuckled. "Okay, fair enough," she said. She sipped her whiskey. *I think she'll answer my question.* She shrugged her shoulders. *Then again, she may not answer it.* "Why don't you like Billie?"

Bridget tilted her head. She shook her head, took out a cigarette, and lit it. "I don't see why you need to know that, Jasmine," she said. She took a drag off her cigarette. "I know you don't like her, but the difference between me and you is that I don't care why you don't like her."

Jasmine shrugged her shoulders. "No, I guess you wouldn't," she said. "Do you care at all about other people?" *I know why I don't have any friends, but I've always wondered why Bridget didn't. She seems to be more outgoing than I am.*

Bridget sighed. "I do, Jasmine," she said. She shook her head. "That's my problem."

Jasmine frowned, puzzled. "I don't understand," she said. "Are you saying that you care too much about other people?"

Bridget's full of surprises. I don't know her at all. The only thing I know for sure is that she doesn't like Billie and doesn't appreciate Billie bringing her girlfriend to the country club.

"I didn't ask you to meet me here to discuss my feelings about others," Bridget said, her hand slamming down on the table. "I want Billie out of the country club. Are you going to help me with that, Jasmine?"

Jasmine nodded. "I'll help you," she said. *I'm glad she doesn't care about why I don't like Billie. I don't think I could explain to her why I don't like Billie. She wouldn't understand.*

Bridget stood up. "We'll meet again soon," she said. She then walked away.

Jasmine shrugged her shoulders. *I don't think we came up with any ideas.* She sighed and shook her head. *I'll finish this drink, and then I'll go home.*

***

Jasmine was lost in thought the following morning as she had breakfast with her mother. She furrowed her brow as she picked at her scrambled eggs, her mind a whirlwind of conflicting thoughts.

Her mother frowned. "What's on your mind, sweetheart?"

Jasmine sighed. *I didn't want to ask her, but she might know.* "How would you get another person's country club membership canceled or revoked?"

"I don't know," her mother said. She shrugged her shoulders. "I can't remember the last time someone lost their membership at the country club." She reached across the kitchen table and took one of Jasmine's hands. "Did someone tell you that they would get your membership canceled or revoked?"

Of course, she thinks I'm the victim. Jasmine shook her head. "No, Mama," she said. *I have to be careful in what I say to her.*

"There's someone that I want to get their membership either canceled or revoked."

Her mother shook her head. "Oh, Jasmine," she said. "Why would you want to do something like that?"

Okay, so what do I tell her? I can't tell her the whole truth. "There's a new member who I don't think belongs there, at the country club," Jasmine said. "She might be a member, but doesn't belong at the country club." *I'm sure that many other people feel the same way about me.*

Her mother nodded and stood up. She left the kitchen and returned a few minutes later, carrying a leather-bound book. She sat back down at the kitchen table and handed the book to Jasmine. "This is the membership rule book," she said. "The only way any member can lose their membership, either by canceling or being revoked, is if they've broken a rule."

Jasmine smiled. "Thanks, Mama," she said, opening the book and glancing through it.

***

Jasmine finished eating her breakfast and called Bridget. She smiled. *It's a good thing I remember her phone number.*

The phone rang four times before it was answered.

"Yeah, this is Bridget," she said. "Who's calling me on a Sunday morning?"

Jasmine chuckled. *What's wrong, Bridget? Did you spend last night drinking at Capote's, and now you're hungover?* "It's me, Jasmine," she said. "I think I might have found a way to get Billie's membership revoked or canceled." She glanced at the book.

"Well, go ahead and tell me," Bridget said. "I haven't come up with any idea how to do it."

"I've got a better idea," Jasmine said. *We need to discuss revoking Billie's membership in person rather than over the phone.*

"Why don't you meet me at the country club? We can sit out on the patio."

Bridget sighed. "I'd rather you just tell me now," she said. "But I guess I need to leave the house, so I'll meet you at the country club. What time do you want to meet?"

I should give her enough time to sober up and clean up. "What don't we meet around three in the afternoon?" Jasmine giggled. "Does that work for you, Bridget?"

"Yeah, sure," Bridget said. "I'll see you at three."

***

A few hours later, Jasmine sat at a table on the country club's patio, smoking a cigarette and sipping coffee. She glanced at her watch and shook her head. *When we talked earlier, I made it clear to Bridget what time I wanted to meet her at the country club.*

Bridget arrived at the country club at five past three. She walked through the club to the patio and spotted Jasmine sitting at one of the tables. She walked over to the table and sat down across from Jasmine.

Jasmine frowned and pointed at her watch. "You're late, Bridget," she said. "I told you to meet me here at three, not at five past three." *I should've known she'd be late.*

Bridget shrugged her shoulders. "I'm not known for being on time," she said. She pointed at the book on the table. "What's that, Jasmine?"

Jasmine smiled. "This is the membership rule book," she said. "I'm sure that if we look through it, we'll find something to help us get Billie's membership revoked."

Bridget shook her head and chuckled. "I don't think it will take both of us to look through it," she said. She stood up, pushing her chair back. "You do it. I've come up with my own plan regarding Billie."

Jasmine frowned. "What do you mean, you've got your plans regarding Billie?" *I thought we were doing this together.* "What are your plans, Bridget?"

Bridget grinned. "My plans regarding Billie don't include you," she said. She leaned forward, her hands resting on the table. "You look through that rule book and find us a reason to get Billie's membership revoked." She straightened back up. "I'm going to the bar to get something to drink."

So, I'm on my own, looking through the rule book. "Okay," Jasmine said. "I'll be right here, waiting for you to return."

Bridget shook her head and laughed. "Well, you can do that if you want to, Jasmine," she said. She grinned. "I wouldn't count on me coming back if I were you." She turned around and walked away.

Jasmine, left alone, felt surprised at Bridget's departure. She couldn't help but worry about Bridget's possible drinking problem, unable to go a day without a drink.

***

Bridget went to the bar and sat on an empty stool.

The bartender walked over to her. "Good afternoon, Miss Jackson," he said. "Would you like your usual drink?"

"Yeah, I would," Bridget said, nodding. She took out a cigarette and lit it. She looked around. "It's kind of dead today, isn't it?" She glanced at her watch and chuckled. *So, that's why there's hardly anyone here. Everyone's still at church.*

The bartender nodded. "It'll get busy soon enough," he said. He made Bridget's drink and handed it to her. "There you go, Miss Jackson. I'm sure you'll enjoy it."

"I'm sure I will, too," Bridget said. She took a sip and closed her eyes, shivering in delight. She glanced over her shoulder towards the patio, where Jasmine waited. *I don't see the point in talking to her anymore. I'll let her read that rule book to find a reason to revoke Billie's membership. It's a waste of time. If there were any reason Billie shouldn't have been made a member here, she wouldn't have become a member.* She shook her head. *Jasmine's plan isn't going to work.*

Bridget left the country club ten minutes later, after finishing her drink. *I don't think Jasmine's plan will work, but I'll give it a chance.*

***

Twenty minutes later, Jasmine shook her head and sighed. *I don't think Bridget's coming back.* She looked at the rule book. *Well, there's no point in staying here.* She looked around, frowning. *I don't want anyone to see me reading this, especially not Rebecca or Billie. It might be better for me to leave and go home so that I can read it in the privacy of my bedroom.*

Jasmine stood up, finished her coffee, grabbed the rule book, and left the patio. She did her best to avoid talking to anyone or looking at them. She left the country club, went to the parking lot, got into her car, and drove away.

***

Jasmine arrived home thirty minutes later, having made a quick stop at a gas station for a pack of cigarettes. She walked past her mother in the parlor.

"Where have you been, sweetheart?"

"I've been out, Mama," Jasmine said. "I'll be in my room." She went to her bedroom, sat on her bed, and read the rule book.

Jasmine frowned. *I don't know who wrote this book, but I wouldn't call the author a good writer, whoever they were.*

"Are you okay, sweetheart?"

Jasmine looked up. Her mother was standing in the hallway outside of her bedroom, frowning. "Yes, Mama," she said, closing the rule book. "I'm okay." *I wish I could be honest with her and tell her everything, but I can't because I already know she wouldn't understand.*

Her mother sighed. "I wish you would talk to me," she said. She walked over to Jasmine's bed and sat next to her. "You've been down in the dumps since you graduated last June."

Jasmine sighed and nodded. *So, Mama did notice.* "It's been a bit of an adjustment, living back home," she said. *I never intended to come back when I left for college. I could outrun my problems by moving out of here and attending college on the other side of the country, but my problems followed me.*

Her mother put her hands on Jasmine's shoulders. "I know it has been, sweetheart," she said. She smiled. "I missed you when you were away, and I'm glad you're back home with me."

Jasmine nodded. "Me too, Mama," she said. She cleared her throat. "If you don't mind, I need to read this book, and I can't do it with you hovering over me."

Her mother nodded and stood up, getting off Jasmine's bed. "Okay, sweetheart," she said. "Dinner will be ready around six."

***

It took Jasmine almost two hours to read the six-hundred-page rule book, and she had nearly given up when she decided to look through it again, not wanting to give up until she was sure she hadn't overlooked anything.

Then, Jasmine discovered a rule she had never heard of before. She read the rule three times, unable to understand why or how it was still a rule and still in the rule book.

I can't believe this rule.

Jasmine spent the rest of the day in a daze, unable to stop thinking about the rule she had read.

Why is this rule still in the book?

Jasmine was quiet during dinner. She picked at her food, not listening to her mother.

Her mother frowned. "Are you okay, sweetheart?"

"Yes, Mama," Jasmine said. She sighed and shook her head. *I want to ask her if she knew about this rule, but I don't think either answer would satisfy me.* "Have you ever read the rule book?"

Her mother shook her head and chuckled. "Oh, goodness no," she said. "I doubt anyone has read that boring thing in a long time."

"I think you're right about that," Jasmine said. She frowned. "Well, I have, and now I wish I hadn't, Mama."

Her mother nodded. "Knowledge can be a burden, sweetheart," she said. She pointed at the rule book on the table before Jasmine. "So, did you find what you were looking for?"

Jasmine clicked her tongue. "I'm not sure, Mama," she said. *What do I do now?*

***

The following day, Memorial Day, Jasmine was back at the country club, sitting on the patio, smoking a cigarette, and staring at the rule book on the table before her.

I don't know what to do. Jasmine sighed and shook her head. *I wish I had a friend, someone I could talk to, because I need advice on how to proceed with my plan. I'm not sure if I could use this strange old rule to get Billie's membership revoked.*

"Well, there you are, Jasmine."

I know that voice. Jasmine frowned and looked up. Rebecca and Billie were walking towards her. They stopped when they reached the table.

"Are you here by yourself?"

Jasmine nodded. "My mother didn't feel like coming," she said. "I'm not surprised to see you two together." *I've never seen one without the other.*

Billie chuckled. "Well, I haven't made many friends here at the country club," she said. She looked over at Rebecca and grinned. "Except for Rebecca here."

Rebecca grinned back at Billie. "Oh, thanks, Billie," she said. "I think you're okay, too." She turned her attention back to Jasmine. "Can we join you, Jasmine? Or would you rather sit here by yourself?"

Jasmine sighed. *I could use some company, even if it's them.* She pointed at the empty chairs. "I could use some company," she said.

Rebecca and Billie sat down across from Jasmine.

Rebecca took out a cigarette and lit it. "So, how have you been, Jasmine?" She took a drag off her cigarette. "I haven't seen you since Easter Sunday. Where have you been hiding?"

Jasmine shook her head. "I haven't been hiding," she said. *Okay, I need to shift the focus away from me.* She looked over at Billie. "Where's your guest, Billie?" *I don't know if Bridget was right and Billie's guest was her girlfriend, but unlike Bridget, I don't care if that Georgia woman is or isn't Billie's girlfriend.*

Billie chuckled and shook her head while glancing over at Rebecca. "Georgia didn't enjoy herself the last time she was here," she said. She sighed. "She later told me she felt out of place, like she didn't belong here."

Rebecca reached out and grabbed one of Billie's hands. "I'm sorry she felt that way," she said. She sighed and shook her head. "This place isn't welcoming to new faces."

Billie nodded. "Yeah, I know what you mean," she said. She frowned and pointed at the rule book. "What's that, Jasmine?"

Jasmine picked up the rule book and showed it to Rebecca and Billie. "This is the membership rule book," she said. "I read it last night and found an old rule I don't know how to feel about." She opened the rule book and showed the rule to Rebecca and Billie.

Rebecca shook her head. "I'm not surprised it's in there," she said. She frowned. "You do realize, Jasmine, that if the board tried to enforce that rule, none of us would be allowed to be members?"

***

A few weeks passed, and Bridget realized, even though she hadn't heard back from Jasmine, that Jasmine's plan hadn't worked because Billie was still a member of the country club.

Bridget called Jasmine.

"So, I guess your plan didn't work, did it, Jasmine?"

Jasmine sighed. "No, Bridget, it didn't," she said. "I did find a rule that Billie's guilty of breaking."

Bridget frowned. "Then why is she still a member?"

"It's a racist rule that prohibits any black people from becoming members," Jasmine said. "Rebecca pointed out that if the board tried to enforce it, not only would Billie lose her membership, but also Rebecca and me."

Bridget chuckled. "Why are you surprised to find a racist rule, Jasmine?" *I'm not surprised.* "Don't you know how old the country club is?" *The only thing surprising is that the rule is still in the book.*

Jasmine sighed. "Yes, I know," she said. "I failed, Bridget. I couldn't find a reason to get Billie's membership revoked."

"Yeah, you did," Bridget said. *There's no point in talking to her anymore.* "Well, I'll see you around the country club." She then hung up the phone.

Bridget was about to leave her bedroom when her phone rang. She frowned. *Okay, either someone else is calling me, which is possible since I have to drive to New York City to pick up some more powder, or Jasmine's calling me back.* She picked up her phone.

"Hello?"

"Why did you hang up on me, Bridget?"

Bridget shook her head and sighed. *Of course, it's Jasmine calling me back.* "Well, I thought our conversation was over, Jasmine," she said. "Is there anything else for us to talk about?"

"Yes, there is," Jasmine said. "You never told me your plan regarding Billie."

"I didn't tell you because my plan doesn't involve you," Bridget said. *I don't know why Jasmine's asking about my plan. Does she still dislike Billie?* "My plan has nothing to do with Billie's membership at the country club."

Jasmine chuckled. "You don't want to tell me your plan regarding Billie, do you?"

"No, I don't," Bridget said. *She's a smart girl.* "I can live with her being a country club member." *I won't like it, but Billie won't be the only member I don't like.*

"We both are going to have to, Bridget," Jasmine said. She sighed. "Billie was right when she told us that she wasn't going anywhere, and we weren't going to get rid of her."

"You may have given up, but I haven't, Jasmine," Bridget said. "Now, I'm hanging up the phone. I've got an errand to run, so don't call me back again." She hung up the phone and left her bedroom.

***

Bridget wasn't entirely honest with Jasmine, but didn't lie to her either. She did have an errand to run of sorts. She needed a drink and drove to Capote's.

So, what's my next move with Billie? Bridget nodded, a sly grin forming on her lips. *I have to find a way to disrupt Billie's relationship with Georgie. But how?* She shook her head. *I may not know how yet, but I'll figure it out. I refuse to let Billie live her life openly while I can't live mine the way I want to.*

Bridget arrived at Capote's and parked her car. She walked in, looked around, and spotted an empty stool at the bar. She went to it and sat down.

A few minutes went by before the bartender approached her. She nodded at Bridget and made her a whiskey soda.

"Thanks," Bridget said, accepting her whiskey soda from the bartender. She looked around, noticing the small size of the crowd. "Where's everyone at?"

The bartender shrugged her shoulders. "Well, they're not here," she said. "So, are you stopping by for a quick drink?"

Bridget nodded. "I am," she said. "I'm making my monthly trip down to New York City." *I don't have to tell her why I'm going there.* She held out her hand. "Do you want any powder?"

The bartender chuckled and nodded. "Of course I do," she said. She reached into her pockets and pulled out a wad of bills. "Same price as last time?"

Bridget nodded. "How much do you need?" *If my parents didn't have a stranglehold on my trust fund, watching every cent of it, I wouldn't have to sell cocaine.*

"The same amount," the bartender said. She handed Bridget a handful of hundred-dollar bills. "When will I get it?"

"Tomorrow," Bridget said. She folded the hundred bills and stashed them underneath her bra. She finished her drink, downing it. "Is Georgia around?" *Since I don't know how to reach Billie, I'll have to talk to her girlfriend instead.*

The bartender nodded. "I think she's taking a break," she said. "I can get her for you if that's what you want."

Bridget smiled and nodded. "Thanks, I would appreciate it if you did," she said. She glanced at her watch. *I've got time for one more drink before I go.* "But before you do that, could you get me another whiskey soda?"

The bartender nodded. She made Bridget another whiskey soda and then left the bar.

Bridget sipped her whiskey soda and waited for Georgia. *I'm counting on her to be curious enough to want to find out why I asked for her.*

Georgia approached Bridget. "I was told you asked for me," she said, resting her elbows on the bar. She looked around and frowned. "Are you here by yourself?"

Bridget nodded. "I'd like to apologize for being rude to you at the country club," she said. "I'd also like to apologize to Billie, but I haven't seen her since Easter Sunday." *I bet Jasmine knows how to get in touch with Billie.* She chuckled. *If I had included her in my plans, she might have been able to help me.*

Georgia nodded. "Thanks," she said. "I'll tell Billie the next time I see her."

"I've got a better idea," Bridget said. "The next big holiday is the Fourth of July, and there's always a big party at the country club." *Okay, I've got to be convincing.* "Why don't you and Billie join me there to celebrate?"

"I don't think that's a good idea," Georgia said, shaking her head. "To be honest with you, I didn't feel comfortable the last time I was there at the country club."

"I understand, and I don't blame you for being reluctant to return to the country club," Bridget said. She reached out and patted one of Georgia's hands. "I promise you'll have a better time than you did on Easter Sunday." *I hope she believes me.*

Chapter Eleven

T he Fourth of July arrived. Bridget was waiting for Billie and Georgia to join her at the country club. She pulled out her pocket notebook and went over her notes. Since convincing Georgia, she had found out anything she could about Billie and Georgia. She had asked around, but while learning a lot about Georgia, she hadn't learned much about Billie. Billie, it seemed, was still a mystery.

***

Bridget was reviewing her notes for a third time when Billie and Georgia arrived at the country club. They joined Bridget outside on the patio.

Billie sat across from Bridget while Georgia sat next to her.

"Thanks for inviting us," Georgia said. She looked around and smiled. "This place goes all out to celebrate the Fourth of July."

Bridget smiled and nodded. "I told you that the Fourth is a big holiday around here," she said. *She seems happy to be here.*

What about Billie? She turned her attention towards Billie. "Is this your first Fourth of July here, in Boston?"

Billie nodded. "It is, Bridget," she said. "Rebecca cautioned me about accepting your invitation."

Of course, she did. "Well, Rebecca may not like me, but she doesn't mind buying powder from me," Bridget said. She chuckled and shook her head. "I'm surprised she didn't join you and Georgia."

"Oh, she wanted to," Billie said. "But I talked her out of it."

Bridget smiled. "And how did you do that, Billie?" She shook her head. "From my experience with her, Rebecca doesn't change her mind easily." *It's better that she didn't come. I'm going to have a hard time convincing Billie that I have good intentions.*

Billie shook her head and chuckled. "Oh, I didn't change her mind," she said. She took out a cigarette and lit it. "I was just able to reassure her that she didn't have to worry about me because I can handle myself."

So, you're not scared of me? Bridget frowned. "What was Rebecca's concern?" She held up her hands. "Did she think I would do something to you and Georgia here? At the country club?"

Billie shook her head. "Rebecca knows you well enough to know that you're too much of a coward to do anything unsavory here," she said. She took a drag off her cigarette, her eyes not leaving Bridget. "And from what I've heard about you, I'd say that you're not a coward, so to speak, but that you know the value of discretion."

Bridget leaned back in her chair and crossed her arms over her chest. *Who has Billie been talking to about me? Jasmine?* "I would say thanks, but I'm sure you just gave me a backhanded compliment," she said. "So, if you want to insult me, do me the courtesy of doing it directly." *Do you think I can't handle what you say to me, Billie? You're new to this world, but I've lived in it my whole life.*

Billie laughed. "I wasn't trying to insult you," she said. "I thought that you had thicker skin, Bridget." She leaned towards Bridget. "You're not the first stuck-up snob I've dealt with."

Bridget shook her head and chuckled. "I'm sure you have, Billie," she said. *So, she's not afraid to snap back.* "I've been surrounded by stuck-up snobs my whole life." *I'm starting to understand why she's friends with Rebecca.*

Billie shook her head. "I believe you, Bridget," she said. She took a drag off her cigarette while giving Bridget a questioning look. "I'm sure you had a tough childhood, growing up in Boston while in one of the old-money families."

Bridget clicked her tongue. "There you go again, Billie," she said. "You have no idea how tough or not my childhood was here." *Hold on a minute. I need to stop doing this with her.* She held up her hands. "Listen, I didn't invite the two of you to join me here because I wanted to argue with you, Billie."

"I'm glad you said that, Bridget," Billie said. "Rebecca asked me why you had invited Georgia and me to join you here, and I didn't know what to say to her."

"So, you accepted my invitation even though you didn't understand why I had invited you and Georgia?" Bridget chuckled and shook her head. "I've got a question for you, Billie. Why did you accept my invitation?" *I'm willing to bet that she did because she was curious.*

Billie shrugged her shoulders. "I'm not sure, to be honest with you," she said. She smiled and glanced over at Georgia. "She was determined to convince me we should accept your invitation."

Okay, it's time to set the trap. Bridget reached out and took one of Billie's hands. "I know I didn't make the best first impression on you," she said. "I'd like us to be friends, Billie." *Now, let's see if she buys it.*

"Wait, I'm confused now," Georgia said. She looked over at Billie, frowning. "I thought that you and Bridget were friends."

Billie shook her head and chuckled. "No, we're not friends," she said. She turned her attention back to Bridget. "I've been under the impression since we met on Halloween almost a year ago that you didn't want to be friends with me, Bridget."

Bridget sighed and nodded. "I'll admit that I hadn't wanted to be friends with you when we first met," she said. *I have to be careful in what I say to her. Billie seems good at reading other people. She's not easy to fool.*

Billie shrugged her shoulders. "The only person who seemed to want to be friends with me was Rebecca," she said. She chuckled. "You and Jasmine weren't welcoming or friendly."

Bridget nodded. "I'm sorry about that," she said. *Okay, so how will I convince Billie that I want to be friends with her now?*

"I'm sorry, Billie," Georgia said. "I wouldn't have accepted Bridget's invitation if I had known that y'all weren't friends."

Billie grinned. "It's okay, Georgia," she said. "I didn't think you knew anyway."

Georgia stood up, pushing her chair back. "I think that we should leave," she said. "The only reason I accepted your invitation, Bridget, was because I thought you were friends with Billie."

Okay, if I don't do something, they might leave. Bridget held out her hands. "I'm sorry, Georgia, that I allowed you to believe I was friends with Billie," she said. "And honestly, if you had asked me about it, I would have lied to you."

Georgia shook her head. "Let's go, Billie," she said. "I don't see any point in staying here since she's not your friend."

Billie reached out and took Georgia's hand. "Please sit back down, Georgia," she said. She looked over at Bridget. "I don't want to leave, not yet."

Georgia frowned, confused. "Why not, Billie?"

"I believe in giving people second chances," Billie said. "So, tell me, Bridget, why didn't you like me when we first met?"

Billie has proven that I can't lie to her, but I can't tell her the truth. So, what do I say to her? Maybe instead of lying to her or being completely honest with her, I should tell her enough truth so that she will believe me. "I didn't know what to make of you when we first met," Bridget said. She sighed and shook her head. "And I don't make new friends easily."

Billie nodded. "I understand why you wouldn't know what to think of me, Bridget," she said. "I have a feeling that you've never left New England." She grinned and leaned back in her chair. "Am I right?"

Bridget chuckled and shook her head. "No, you're not right, Billie," she said. "Every month, I drive to New York City and spend a few days there." *Billie doesn't need to know that the only reason I go there is to buy cocaine. And sometimes I go shopping while I'm there.*

Billie smiled and laughed. "Okay, so I was wrong about that," she said. "But I'd be willing to bet you've never been to the South."

Georgia chuckled and nodded. "Yeah, I think you're right, Billie," she said. "And I'm sure Bridget hasn't ever had grits or biscuits with gravy."

Bridget shook her head. "You're both right," she said. "I've never been to the South or have eaten either grits or biscuits with gravy." *I'm not sure I understand what Billie's trying to tell me.*

Billie gave Bridget a strange look. "I want to ask you something, Bridget, and I want you to be honest," she said. "You always seem uncomfortable around me. Why's that?"

Bridget sighed. *Shit, she would ask me that.* She shrugged her shoulders. *Well, let's be honest with her.* "I envy you, Billie, for being able to live your life openly," she said. "I don't know how you can live in the two different worlds of the Upper Crust and the other one."

Billie shrugged her shoulders. "I refuse to hide who I am from anyone," she said. "You should stop trying to fit in, Bridget, and find where you belong."

Bridget frowned. *That's easy for you to say, Billie. Why do you get to do that, live freely, when I can't?*

***

Bridget, Billie, and Georgia left the country club a few hours later.

Before they left, it had been awkward, with the three of them either trying to make small talk and failing or enduring uncomfortable silence.

Bridget stood up. "It might just be me, but I'm feeling a bit restless," she said. "I think we should change the scenery."

"Like where, Bridget?" Billie sipped her coffee and looked around. "Everyone else seems to be having a good time."

Bridget chuckled. "I'm sure everyone else here has been drinking since noon," she said. *If I weren't sitting with them, I would be drinking too.* "And I would like to drink, but I'd rather do it elsewhere."

Billie squinted at Bridget. "Why don't you want to stay here, Bridget?" She shook her head. "Are you afraid that someone might see you sitting with us?"

Bridget, with a nonchalant smile, dismissed Billie's assumption. "I couldn't care less about the opinions of the other members."

"I'm up for leaving," Georgia said. She looked over at Billie and smiled. "Come on, Billie, let's go somewhere else. Anywhere has got to be better than this place."

"I think we should go to a bar," Bridget said. *I see there's no way I can implement my plan at the country club.* "What do you think, Billie? Why don't you and Georgia go with me to a bar and have a few drinks?"

Billie nodded. "I don't think it's a bad idea," she said. "Where do you want to go, Bridget?"

Bridget shrugged her shoulders. "It doesn't matter to me, Billie," she said. She looked over at Georgia. "What do you think? Where do you want to go, Georgia?" *I don't care which bar we go to, though I doubt Billie thinks that.*

"Let's go to Capote's," Billie said. She smiled. "I know we all enjoy going there."

"I'm fine with Capote's," Bridget said. She frowned. "What about you, Georgia? Are you okay with going there?" *Does she mind hanging out there when she's not working?*

Georgia nodded. "I enjoy hanging out there even when I'm not working," she said. "It's one of the few places I can be myself."

Bridget, with a sly smile, made her intentions clear. "So, it's settled," she said. "Let's head to Capote's." *I can't help but anticipate what the evening might bring, especially with Georgia.*

Billie stood up. "Okay, we'll meet you there, Bridget," she said. She glanced over at Georgia. "Let's go, Georgia."

Georgia smiled and stood up. "Okay, Billie," she said. She reached out and took Billie's hand. She looked over at Bridget. "We'll see you soon, Bridget."

***

Bridget, Billie, and Georgia arrived at Capote's around the same time. Billie and Georgia shared a taxi while Bridget drove her car from the country club to Capote's.

They walked in together.

Billie looked over at Bridget. "It's kind of crowded today," she said. "It seems many people decided to come here today to celebrate the Fourth."

"Maybe they didn't want to stay home today," Georgia said. She sighed. "The Fourth is a family holiday; maybe they can't be with their families."

Bridget nodded. *Georgia's right.* She looked around and smiled. "Let's sit over there," she said, pointing at her favorite booth near the front entrance, but out of sight.

Georgia nodded and grinned. "You always sit there, Bridget," she said. She looked over at Billie. "We call that booth the posh booth."

Billie chuckled. "Why do y'all call it the posh booth, Georgia?"

"Well, because if Bridget isn't sitting there, you and Rebecca are sitting there," Georgia said. "And everyone here knows all of y'all are from Beacon Hill."

They went to the booth and sat, with Billie across from Bridget and Georgia beside her.

I don't know if I like it when Georgia and her coworkers call my favorite booth the posh booth. Bridget cleared her throat. "I'd like to buy the first round," she said. "Is that okay with you, Billie?"

Billie nodded. "Sure, it's okay with me," she said. She smiled and looked over at Georgia. "Is it okay with you?"

Georgia grinned and nodded. "It's fine with me," she said.

Bridget looked around for a waitress. She smiled when she spotted one walking by them. She raised her hand and snapped her fingers. "Hey, over here," she said. *Too bad Georgia isn't working tonight. She's the only waitress here who's worth anything.*

The waitress came over to them. She smiled at Georgia. "Hey, girl," she said. "I was wondering where you were."

Georgia smiled back. "Yeah, I've been spending the day with Billie," she said. "Have y'all been busy tonight?"

The waitress shrugged her shoulders. "Busy enough that I'm glad I traded shifts with you," she said. She looked over at Billie and smiled. "It's good to see you again, Billie."

Does everyone like Billie except for me? Bridget cleared her throat. "Are we done talking or not? I'm thirsty and want a drink," she said. "I'll have a whiskey soda." She pointed at Billie and Georgia. "And put their drinks on my bill."

"I'll have a vodka tonic, please," Billie said. She grinned. "In other words, I'll have my usual."

"I'll have the same," Georgia said.

"Okay, that's one whiskey soda and two vodka tonics," the waitress said, writing down their order. "I'll be right back with your drinks."

***

Billie waited until their waitress walked away. She frowned and leaned over the table. "I'd like to suggest that you drop the Upper Crust attitude and be more polite to our waitress," she said. "We're not at the country club."

Georgia sighed and shook her head while putting her hand on Billie's shoulder. "It's okay, Billie," she said. "Bridget wasn't that rude to her."

Bridget blushed and sighed. *I didn't know I had what Billie called an upper-crust attitude. I also didn't think I had been rude to our waitress. I've said a lot worse to the bartender at the country club.* She cleared her throat. "I'll try to do better next time," she said.

***

A few hours later, they were all feeling good. They were beyond just tipsy, but they weren't fall-down drunk yet, but they were on their way there.

"So, how long have you been coming here, Bridget?"

Okay, so we're talking again, Billie. Bridget chuckled and shrugged her shoulders. "Sometimes, it feels like I've been coming here my whole life," she said. "I don't have to worry about guys flirting with me when I'm here."

Georgia grinned and giggled. "Maybe so, Bridget, but you don't seem able to handle other women flirting with you," she said. She turned her attention to Billie. "I remember the first time I saw her sitting at the bar." She shook her head. "She was all dressed up, and I don't think she paid for a drink all night."

Bridget blushed. *I don't remember seeing her that night.* "I didn't pay for any of my drinks," she said. She looked over at Billie, who was giving her an amused look. "There had been a charity ball at the country club. That's why I was dressed up." *I'm still waiting for my opportunity to break up Billie and Georgia. I figure all it will take will be for me to kiss one of them. And I'm going to kiss Georgia. She's the weakest link between the two of them.*

Billie cleared her throat. "If y'all will excuse me," she said, standing up. "I have to use the ladies' room. I'll be right back."

Bridget smiled. *This is my chance.* She waited until Billie had walked away and was out of sight. She got closer to Georgia.

Georgia frowned. "What are you doing, Bridget?"

Bridget reached out and kissed Georgia, hoping that Billie would see her kissing Georgia.

Billie did, but she didn't react the way Bridget thought she would, not getting mad. Instead, Billie shook her head and chuckled. "I knew it," she said.

Bridget frowned. *What did Billie mean by that remark? Did she suspect that I was up to something?* She shook her head and cleared her throat. "I don't think I heard you right, Billie," she said. "Did you just say I knew it?"

Billie nodded. "Yeah, I did, Bridget," she said. She took out a cigarette and lit it, her eyes not leaving Bridget's. "Rebecca was right about you."

Georgia sighed and shook her head. "I think you've worn out your welcome, Bridget," she said. "You should leave."

What did Rebecca say to Billie? Had she warned Billie not to trust me, that I was up to something? Bridget picked up her drink and stood up, pushing her chair back. "Well, I hope you two have a good night," she said. *There's no point in staying. I didn't get the reaction I thought I would get by kissing Georgia.* "I'll see you two later."

Bridget turned around and walked away. *I thought I could break up Georgia and Billie by kissing Georgia, but I was wrong. Billie didn't seem to be mad in any way.*

Bridget didn't go home. Instead, she sat at the bar within view of Billie and Georgia's table. *Let's see if any fireworks start now that I'm gone.* She shook her head and chuckled. *Billie has to be mad. I don't believe her being okay with her girlfriend kissing another woman.*

***

Bridget watched Billie and Georgia for almost an hour. She had expected them to either leave or for one of them to stand up and leave. She didn't care which one left, though if it had been Billie, Bridget would have waited until Billie was gone, and then she would have walked back over to Georgia. But neither of them left; after a few minutes of awkward silence, they started holding each other's hands and talking.

Bridget wasn't close enough to overhear their conversation, much to her frustration. She sighed and shook her head, frowning. *I might as well go home.* She stood up and left the bar. She went home and tried to devise another plan.

Chapter Twelve

Ten days later, Iris was at her desk, writing a review of Henry Young's newest novel, which had been published the year before, when her work phone rang. She reached out and picked it up.

"Hello, you've reached Iris Mathews' desk," she said. "How may I help you?" She frowned and glanced at her watch. *I don't expect anyone to call me.*

"Hey, Iris, it's me, Rebecca," she said. "I wanted to let you know I'm not sure I'll be taking Billie out for her birthday."

Something must have happened. "Oh, and why's that, Rebecca?" Iris leaned back in her chair and propped her feet on her desk. "What's going on?" *My journalistic instincts are telling me that she isn't being entirely forthcoming.*

Rebecca sighed. "I'll tell you what's going on, Iris," she said. "I just found out today that something happened on the Fourth."

Rebecca knows how to tell a story. "Okay, stop teasing me," Iris said. "Just tell me what happened."

Rebecca chuckled. "I'm sorry about that," she said. "I love telling a good story; believe me, what I'm about to tell you is good." She cleared her throat. "Billie and Georgia celebrated the Fourth with Bridget, first at the country club and then at Capote's."

"Okay," Iris said. *I wonder why Rebecca wasn't with them.* "What happened, Rebecca?" *I don't know who Bridget is, but I won't ask her. Well, maybe I'll ask her later.*

"Billie went to the ladies' room, and when she returned to the booth where they were sitting, Bridget was kissing Georgia," Rebecca said. She sighed. "I don't think Billie feels she can trust anyone except for maybe me."

Iris sighed. "I don't blame Billie for feeling that way," she said. "You have to be careful who you let be around your girlfriend." *So, Bridget was pretending to be Billie's friend.*

"I don't want what happened to ruin her birthday," Rebecca said. She sighed. "What do you think, Iris? Should I try to convince Billie to go out still and celebrate her birthday, or should I drop it?"

Iris shook her head. "You need to take Billie out for her birthday, especially after what happened on the Fourth," she said. "I would suggest that maybe her girlfriend doesn't come with us." *I'm betting that I'm still invited to join her and Billie. I hope I'm right.*

"I think you're right, Iris," Rebecca said. "I'm about to go and pick Billie up. We're going out for drinks. I promise to convince her to go out and celebrate her birthday. And I promise I'll let you know what Billie decides."

"Thanks, Rebecca," Iris said. "I would appreciate it if you did that." *If anyone can convince Billie to go out and celebrate her birthday, it will be Rebecca.*

***

Rebecca did let Iris know, and a few days later, Iris found herself waiting for Billie and Rebecca. It was only a few hours before

Rebecca called and told her that they, she and Billie, would be having drinks at Jackson's Jukebox.

Iris was on her second drink when Rebecca and Billie finally arrived.

Billie smiled. "Hey, Iris," she said. She looked over at Rebecca, who was grinning at her. "I hope this is the surprise you were talking about, Rebecca."

Rebecca nodded. "I told you that you would like it," she said. "Now, let's join Iris."

Billie and Rebecca joined Iris at the bar, sitting next to her.

"Have you been waiting long, Iris?"

Iris shook her head. "I've been here about ten minutes," she said. She grinned and held up her drink. "I'm on my second Jack & Coke." *I'm glad I dressed up. Rebecca and Billie are wearing summer dresses, and I would've looked foolish if I had shown up in jeans and a T-shirt.*

Rebecca grinned. "So, have you been doing any reading lately?"

Iris chuckled. "I have, Rebecca," she said. She looked over at Billie and smiled. "Rebecca told me that you write short stories." *Now, let's see how she reacts. Will she be humble about being a writer, or will she take pride in it?*

Billie laughed. "I think Rebecca has told everyone I'm a writer," she said. She shrugged her shoulders. "I've written a few stories, that's all. It isn't a big deal."

***

Rebecca and Iris started talking about Billie's short stories while Billie only listened, sipping her vodka tonic.

Iris cleared her throat. *Okay, that's enough talking about Billie and her stories.* She looked over at Billie. "Thanks for meeting me here, Billie," she said. "I like this bar. It has a good atmosphere."

Billie smiled. "You're lucky that I enjoy working here and don't mind spending my free time here," she said. She looked over at Rebecca. "And you're lucky that I like Iris and don't mind hanging out with her." She frowned. "I do have a question."

"Okay," Iris said. Billie looks serious. "What's on your mind, Billie?"

"Well, I'm sure all three of us aren't straight," Billie said. "So, I'm wondering why we're here instead of at Capote's."

Iris chuckled. 'It wasn't my idea to meet here," she said. *I didn't think to question Rebecca about why we were hanging out with Billie here.* She pointed at Rebecca. "She's the one who picked this place, not me."

Rebecca shrugged her shoulders. "I didn't think you wanted to go to Capote's," she said. "Isn't Georgia working tonight?"

Billie nodded. "She is working tonight," she said. She sighed and shook her head. "She's unhappy that I won't let her take the night off and that I didn't want to spend my birthday with her."

Iris nodded. "I heard that Georgia's the jealous type," she said. *I've had to deal with jealous girlfriends before.* "I'm guessing that Rebecca felt it would be better for everyone if we went somewhere else."

Billie sighed and nodded. She looked over at Rebecca and frowned. "How much do you know about my relationship with Georgia, Iris?"

Billie isn't happy with Rebecca for discussing her relationship with Georgia with me. Iris shrugged her shoulders. She chuckled and grinned. "I didn't even know y'all were together until Rebecca told me a few weeks ago."

Rebecca held up her hands. "You didn't tell me that I couldn't tell anyone else," she said. "I only told Iris because she wanted to know what was happening with you."

Iris reached out and took one of Billie's hands. "If you don't want to talk about Georgia or your relationship with her, we don't have to, Billie," she said. "We're here to have fun, not be your therapist." *And I would like to get to know you better.*

Billie nodded. "I'd rather we didn't talk about my relationship with Georgia," she said. "I'd like to pretend for tonight that I'm single and have a simple romantic life." She took a sip of her vodka tonic and then a drag off her cigarette.

"Okay," Iris said. She smiled. "Have you been interviewed yet, Billie?" *It's time to get to know Billie. The best way to do that is to interview her as if I were writing her profile.*

Billie shook her head and grinned. "No, I haven't been interviewed yet," she said. "I've only written a few stories, so I'm not important enough for anyone to want to interview me."

"Well, maybe you're not important enough now, but that could change," Iris said. "I'm sure you will be important enough to be interviewed one day." *Come on, Billie. You don't have to be cautious with me. There's no ill intent or bad intentions here.*

"Okay, I guess you're right," Billie said. She leaned back in her chair and gave Iris her full attention. "Let's start this practice interview."

"Okay," Iris said. She cleared her throat. *Now, take it easy on Billie. Begin with some easy questions and then progress to more challenging ones.* "Tell me where you're from, Billie?"

Billie chuckled. "Well, in case you can't tell by my accent, I'm from the South," she said. "And until recently, I've lived most of my life in New Orleans, Louisiana."

Iris nodded. "And where did you go to college?" *I already knew Billie was from New Orleans. I'm guessing she went to college based on her personality and how she speaks.*

"I graduated from Tulane University last June," Billie said. She grinned. "I was almost the valedictorian, but my best friend beat me; her GPA was only a few points higher."

Iris smiled. "Tulane University? I'm impressed," she said. "I went to Vanderbilt and graduated back in June of 1988." *I know that sometimes, the best way to get someone else to reveal things about themselves is to reveal things about yourself to them.*

Billie smiled. "So, you're from Nashville, Tennessee," she said. "I've always wanted to go there."

Rebecca cleared her throat, interrupting Iris's interview with Billie. She smiled when she had Iris's and Billie's attention. "I'll get the next round," she said. She waved at the bartender to get his attention.

Billie frowned. "Iris bought the first round," she said. "I thought I would get the next round."

Rebecca grinned and shook her head. "It's your birthday," she said. "And that means you don't buy any drinks tonight." She looked over at Iris. "Isn't that right, Iris?"

Iris nodded. *I like the way Rebecca thinks.* "That's right," she said. She smiled at Billie. "The least we can do to celebrate your birthday is buy you drinks all night." *Maybe next year, I'll buy Billie a present for her birthday.*

***

The bartender brought them another round of drinks. Rebecca took a long sip of her drink, like Billie, she loved vodka tonics—and stood up, getting off her bar stool. "I have to use the ladies' room," she said. She waved her finger at Billie and Iris. "Now, you two behave yourself while I'm gone."

Iris frowned. "What do you mean, Rebecca?" *I feel like she's teasing one of us, but I'm unsure who- Billie or me.*

Rebecca chuckled and shook her head. "It doesn't matter," she said. "You two play nice while I'm gone." She turned around and walked away.

Iris waited until Rebecca was out of sight and then looked at Billie. "Do you know what Rebecca meant by that remark?"

Billie shrugged her shoulders. "I'm not sure, Iris," she said. She shook her head and cleared her throat. "I'd like to ask you a few questions if you don't mind."

Iris smiled. "I don't mind at all," she said. "Go ahead and ask me anything, Billie." *I have no idea what Billie's about to ask me.*

"Tell me about your friendship with Sadie," Billie said. "Rebecca has told me that y'all are friends."

Iris chuckled. *This wouldn't be the first time I've had to explain my friendship with Sadie.* "It's kind of a long story," she said. She shrugged her shoulders. "I don't even know where to start."

***

Iris, Rebecca, and Billie spent a few hours at Jackson's Jukebox.

The night was still young, and the trio was not ready for it to end. "So, any plans besides drinking here?" Iris asked, careful not to overstep as she hadn't organized the get-together.

Rebecca chuckled. "What do you mean, Iris?" She nudged Billie in the ribs. "Didn't you tell me that Southern ladies know how to have a good time and can out-drink any New England ladies?"

Billie grinned and nodded. "I did, Rebecca," she said. "I don't think Iris was saying that she was ready to go home or that she had drunk enough."

Iris laughed. "I'm not ready to stop drinking," she said. *Rebecca's half right. I'm ready to leave this bar and crash at home.* "But I'd like to continue this, whatever you call it, somewhere else."

"Well, I'm not ready to go home," Billie said. She sighed and shook her head. "And I don't want to bother Josephine."

Rebecca chuckled and shook her head. "I don't want to go home either," she said. She looked over at Iris. "Where do you suggest we go, Iris?"

What's the best way for me to suggest that we go back to my apartment? "Well, I do not live far from here," Iris said. "Drinking there'd be cheaper than going to another bar." *Okay, let's see how they will react to my suggestion.*

Billie glanced over at Rebecca and gave her a questioning look.

Rebecca smiled and shrugged her shoulders. "She's right," she said. "It would be cheaper to keep drinking at her apartment than go to another bar."

Billie nodded. "That's true," she said. She frowned. "But what about your friend Sadie? Is she at home, Iris?"

Okay, I understand why Billie might hesitate to agree to go back to the apartment I share with Sadie. "She might be home," Iris said. She reached out and took one of Billie's hands. "I promise she won't bother you or say anything ugly."

Billie nodded in agreement. "Let's head to your place, Iris," she said, rising from her seat.

Rebecca chuckled. "I guess it's settled," she said. She stood up and waved at the bartender. "We'd better pay our bill before we leave."

The bartender walked over to Rebecca. "How can I help you?"

"I'm paying for our tab," Rebecca said. She pulled out a twenty and handed it to the bartender. "Here's your tip."

The bartender nodded and grinned. "Thanks," he said. "I'll be right back with your bill." He then walked away, showing off his tip to the other bartenders.

***

Iris, Rebecca, and Billie finished their drinks while they waited for the bartender to return with their bill. He did return a few minutes later. He walked over to Rebecca and handed her their bill.

Rebecca frowned. "This isn't that bad," she said. She looked over at the bartender. "Are you sure the total is right? Shouldn't it be more?"

The bartender chuckled. "I was told to give Billie the birthday discount since it's her birthday, and you two were given the friends discount," he said. The surprise was evident on their faces. "The owner told me to do it, so I did."

"Let me see that," Billie said, holding her hand out. "I've never heard of either a birthday discount or a friends discount."

Rebecca handed their bill to Billie. "I'm sure that between the three of us, we drank almost a hundred dollars in booze," she said. She chuckled and shook her head. "But not according to our bill."

Billie nodded. "The owner told you to do it," she said. She looked over at the bartender and smiled. "You can tell him that I appreciate it." She handed their bill back to Rebecca. "Pay our bill, Rebecca, so that we can leave."

They left Jackson's Jukebox, and Iris gave Rebecca, who had driven her and Billie there, her address. Irie smiled and nodded at Billie. She turned around and walked over to her car.

***

Iris drove away and returned to her apartment. She didn't know if Sadie would be home, but she would have been surprised if she wasn't, since Sadie had no other friends besides her.

Iris got to the apartment before Rebecca and Billie. She found Sadie at home, sitting in her bedroom, reading a book while smoking a cigarette.

"You're home early," Sadie said, not looking up from her book. "I expected you not to come home until after midnight."

Okay, this isn't going to be easy. "I invited Rebecca and Billie to join me here," Iris said. "Today's Billie's birthday."

Sadie closed her book and sighed. "Now, why would you invite those two back here?"

Here we go again. "I invited them because they're both charming, smart, funny women who I would like to get to know better," Iris said. She sighed and shook her head. "I'm not asking you to like or talk to them."

"What are you asking me to do, Iris?"

Iris shook her head and chuckled. "I'm asking you to behave yourself," she said. "If you want to, you can just stay in here." She went over to Sadie and sat next to her on her bed. "You don't have to hang out with us if you don't want to, Sadie."

"Well, good," Sadie said. "I'll stay in here if you don't mind."

There was a knock on the front door.

"Okay," Iris said. She pointed at Sadie. "You behave yourself." She left Sadie's bedroom and walked down the hallway to the front door.

Iris looked through the peephole and smiled. *Good, they made it.* She opened the front door after unlocking it. "Welcome to my apartment," she said, stepping back. "Come on in, Rebecca, Billie."

Rebecca walked in first, followed by Billie.

Billie looked around, smiling. "So, this is your place, Iris?"

"It is," Iris said, closing the front door and locking it. She pointed towards the living room. "Why don't y'all sit on the couch while I make us something to drink?" *I hope they like Jack Daniels because we don't have any vodka.*

"Okay," Billie said, smiling. "Let's sit down, Rebecca."

Rebecca and Billie went to the living room to sit on the couch while Iris went to the kitchen to make them something to drink.

Rebecca looked around, smiling. "I think this place is bigger than my apartment," she said. She chuckled and shook her head. "It feels Southern in here." She looked over at Billie, who had taken out a cigarette and lit it. "What do you think?"

"I like it," Billie said. She grinned and laughed. "It reminds me of a dorm room at Tulane."

Rebecca frowned. "I thought you said you didn't live on campus when you went there, that you lived at home with your family," she said. "Did I misunderstand you?"

Billie shook her head. "You didn't misunderstand me, Rebecca," she said. "I didn't live in a dorm room, but I did spend many nights in a few of them, if you know what I mean."

Rebecca nodded and grinned. "I don't know why, but for some reason, I thought you might have been a wallflower when you were a student at Tulane," she said. She shrugged her shoulders. "Maybe I did because I was one when I went to Colombia."

Iris returned from the kitchen, carrying three glasses. "Okay, ladies," she said, sitting on the couch beside Rebecca and Billie. "We don't have any vodka, so I couldn't make y'all your vodka tonics, but I was able to make something even better." *I hope they like what I made for them.*

Rebecca chuckled and shook her head. "I've tried many different cocktails, Iris, but there's a reason why I only drink vodka tonics," she said. "I'm not saying I won't try whatever you made us, but I'm warning you that I might not like it."

Well, at least Rebecca's honest. "I promise you, Rebecca, even if you don't like it, I'm sure that you've never had it before," Iris said. "What don't y'all take a sip and tell me what you think of it before I tell y'all what I made for us."

Billie smiled. "Fair enough," she said. She picked up her glass and took a small sip. She nodded in approval. "This is good." She looked over at Rebecca. "Try it, Rebecca. You might be surprised and find that you like it."

Rebecca took a sip and smiled. "Okay, this is different," she said. "What is it, Iris?"

"It's Johnny Walker with Dr. Pepper," Iris said. "I was a summer intern at Black Springs Press the summer before my senior year at Vanderbilt, and an editor named Raymond Walker taught me how to make it." *He was also the last man I had sex with.*

Chapter Thirteen

G eorgia called Billie a week after her birthday.

"I would like to have you over for dinner one night," Georgia said. "I don't care what night. You pick the date, and I'll be sure to have that night off work."

Georgia found out by asking Rebecca what some of Billie's favorite foods were and made sure she cooked them. Lucky for her, her mother had taught her how to cook.

Georgia finished cooking and waited for Billie.

***

Billie arrived at Georgia's apartment twenty minutes later.

Georgia opened her front door and smiled at Billie. "You're right on time," she said. "Come on in and make yourself at home." *Billie's always gorgeous, no matter what she wears: blue jeans, a T-shirt, or a summer dress.*

"Thanks," Billie said. "Which way is your living room?"

Oh, yeah, that's right. Billie hasn't ever been here before. Georgia pointed down the hallway. "The living room is down the hallway," she said. "Would you like something to drink?"

Billie nodded. "I sure would," she said. She chuckled. "Well, I'll see you in the living room." She turned around and walked away, going down the hallway to the living room.

Georgia went to the kitchen. *Okay, so what kind of drink should I make for us?* She glanced at her watch. *Well, it's too early to start drinking vodka.* She smiled. *There's that bottle of white wine Rebecca bought me. I haven't opened it yet but have been waiting for the right time and company.* She nodded. *It's both.* She pulled the bottle from the cabinet, opened it using her corkscrew, and filled two wine glasses.

***

Georgia joined Billie in the living room, sitting on the couch next to her.

"Here you go," Georgia said, handing Billie her wine glass. "I hope white wine is okay with you." She took a sip and smiled. "This might be the best-tasting wine I've ever had." *Thanks, Rebecca, for giving me this bottle.*

Billie took a sip and smiled. "I know this wine," she said. "It's German white wi̇fie." She held up her wine glass. "I think it's called Riesling."

Georgia nodded. "I think you're right," she said. She cleared her throat. "A former lover gave it to me, and tonight's the first time I've drunk any of it." *I don't have to tell Billie that Rebecca gave it to me.*

Billie looked around and smiled. "I like your apartment, Georgia," she said. "Your decor is warm and inviting."

Georgia grinned and chuckled. "You don't think it's too feminine?" *I don't know why I'm so defensive about my apartment, but I am.* "Other people have told me that it's too much."

Billie grinned. "Too much pink and purple?"

Georgia nodded. "Yeah, something like that," she said. She shrugged her shoulders. "I guess other people get this picture in their head of what my apartment will look like, and then when they get here, it doesn't match their expectations." *My mother raised me to be a Southern lady, and while I may be gay, most of her lessons have stuck.*

Billie nodded. "I can understand how that could happen," she said. She smiled. "I'll be honest; I didn't know what to expect."

Well, that's good, in a way. "So, you aren't disappointed?" *This is why I'm falling in love with her. Billie's so open and accepting.*

Billie shook her head. "Not at all, Georgia," she said. She reached out and took Georgia's free hand. "I know we haven't known each other that long, but I'm good at reading people."

Georgia frowned. "What do you mean, Billie?" *I know what she means. I'm just glad we're talking to each other. I was afraid it would be awkward between us because of what happened.*

"Your apartment reflects who you are on the inside," Billie said. She shook her head and chuckled. "You knew what I meant, Georgia. You just wanted to hear me say something nice about you."

Georgia blushed. "Maybe I did," she said. She sighed and shook her head. "I'll admit that I was afraid you wouldn't be able to say anything nice about me." She cleared her throat. *I hate to bring it up, but I feel compelled to mention it. We need to talk about what happened.*

Billie held up her hand. "I know what you're about to say," she said. "Let's not spoil the mood, okay?" She took a sip of her wine. "We should eat first."

Billie's right. Georgia nodded and stood up. "I'll go and get our food," she said. "Do you need any more wine?" *Well, Billie doesn't seem mad at me.* She sighed. *She does seem disappointed in me.*

Billie nodded and chuckled. "You might want to bring the bottle back with you," she said. She showed Georgia her empty wine glass. "I know I can drink some more."

Georgia left the living room and went to the kitchen, where she fixed a plate for Billie and herself. *I hope Rebecca was right about Billie's favorite foods. I hope Billie will still like what I cooked for her if Rebecca wasn't right.* She snapped her fingers. *Don't forget the wine.*

Georgia left the kitchen carrying two plates and a bottle of white wine. She placed the bottle of white wine on the coffee table and handed Billie her plate. "Here you go, Billie," she said. "I hope you like what I cooked for you." *I'm betting almost everything on this meal.*

Billie smiled. "Let's see, there's grilled chicken breast, green beans, mashed potatoes, and black-eyed peas," she said. "I love all of this." She chuckled and gave Georgia an amused look. "I would ask you how you knew some of my favorite foods, but I'm sure I know how."

Georgia chuckled. "Rebecca told me," she said. *I know she didn't ask me, but she had already guessed.* "I wanted you to enjoy having dinner with me."

Billie nodded. "Well, so far, I am enjoying it," she said. She grinned. "Okay, that's enough talking. Let's eat."

***

They started eating and didn't say anything, enjoying the food Georgia had cooked for them. She also liked grilled chicken breast, green beans, and mashed potatoes. She wasn't crazy about black-eyed peas but didn't hate them.

Georgia kept looking over at Billie. *She seemed to be enjoying what I had cooked for us. Billie hasn't said a word since we started eating.* She smiled. *However, neither have I. I should wait until after we're both done eating before I bring up what happened on the Fourth of July.* She sighed. *We have to talk about it.*

***

Billie and Georgia finished eating about twenty minutes later.

Billie looked over at Georgia and smiled. "That was good, Georgia," she said. She nodded and rubbed her stomach. "I'm as full as a tick."

Georgia nodded and grinned. "Me too, Billie," she said. "Well, I'm glad you enjoyed the dinner I made for us." *Once again, learning how to cook was one of the best things my mother taught me.* She looked at the empty plates sitting on the coffee table. She sighed and frowned. *I'd better wash these dishes now.* She leaned over, picked up the two plates, and stood up.

Billie chuckled. "Where are you going, Georgia?"

"I'm going to wash these dishes," Georgia said. She smiled. "My mother taught me the best time to wash dishes was right after you're done with them." *I also need some time to think. How will I bring up the one subject Billie doesn't want to discuss?*

Billie nodded. "Your mother's right," she said. "Do you need any help?"

Georgia shook her head. "You're my guest," she said. She pointed at the bottle of white wine. "Have another glass of white wine and smoke a cigarette." She grinned at Billie. "I'll be back before you know it."

Billie nodded and leaned back against the back of the couch. "Okay," she said. She filled her wine glass with white wine. "We might need to get another bottle."

Georgia shook her head and laughed. "We might, but let's finish this bottle first," she said. She shrugged her shoulders. "If we have to get another bottle, there's a liquor store only a few blocks from here."

"Okay," Billie said. She took a sip of her wine and smiled. "I'm not much of a wine drinker, but I like this wine."

Georgia nodded. "I like the aftertaste," she said. "It reminds me of biting into a crisp apple." *I would've opened the bottle sooner if I had known I would like this wine this much.*

Georgia left the living room, carrying their plates and forks. She entered the kitchen and went to the sink. She washed their plates and forks, frowning.

***

Georgia took twenty minutes to wash their plates, forks, and the pots and pans she used to cook their dinner. She rinsed them off and dried them with a towel.

You can't hide in this kitchen for much longer.

Georgia sighed and shook her head. I haven't lived with my mother for almost four years now, and I still hear her voice in my head whenever I'm stressed out.

Your friend is waiting for you.

Georgia shook her head. *She's not my friend, Mama. Billie's my girlfriend.*

Well, whatever she is, you're being rude right now, hiding here in the kitchen while she sits in your living room by herself. I thought I raised you better.

***

Georgia spent another ten minutes cleaning the kitchen, trying to drown out her mother's voice. She wasn't successful.

"Is everything okay in there?"

Oh, shit, how long have I been in here? Georgia glanced at her watch and shook her head. "Yeah, everything's fine," she said.

"I'll be right there." She grabbed the bottle of white wine and left the kitchen.

When Georgia left the kitchen, carrying the bottle of white wine, and returned to the living room, she found Billie walking around her apartment, smoking a cigarette and looking around with a smile.

Georgia held up the bottle of white wine. "I didn't forget the wine," she said. *Billie seems to be in a good mood. Do I want to ruin it by bringing up the one subject she doesn't want to discuss? Or do I just let it go and refill her glass with more wine?*

Billie turned around and nodded. "Good," she said. She picked up her wineglass from the coffee table and held it out to Georgia. "I could use a refill."

Georgia nodded. She refilled Billie's wine glass with white wine. "I'm sorry I was in the kitchen for so long," she said. "I had to wash our dishes and a few other things, too." *I hope Billie believes me.*

Billie chuckled. "You seem nervous, Georgia," she said. She took a sip of her wine. "Ever since I got here, you look like you want to say something to me, but you're afraid to say it."

Georgia sighed. *It's hard to keep anything from her.* She pointed at the couch. "Let's sit down, Billie," she said. She placed the bottle of white wine on the coffee table. "We've needed to talk about something for almost a month now." *Well, I hope she doesn't try to change the subject again. The sooner we discuss what happened on the Fourth, the sooner we can move past it.*

Billie nodded. "Yeah, I guess it's time we settle this issue," she said. She sat down on the couch and took a sip of her wine.

Georgia joined Billie on the couch, sitting beside her, but Billie surprised her by kissing her before she could say anything.

Billie smiled at Georgia and stroked her honey blonde hair. "I know you want to or feel like we have to talk about what happened on the Fourth, but we don't, Georgia," she said. "And before you ask me why, I'll tell you. I know you're crazy about me and that Bridget had been the one to instigate the kiss between you and her."

Georgia shook her head, confused. *I don't understand. Why hasn't Billie said something before now?* "Every time I've tried to talk to you about it, you've changed the subject," she said. "And now you say we don't have to talk about it?" *Why's Billie so understanding about Bridget kissing me now?*

Billie shook her head. "I couldn't talk about it before now," she said. "And I couldn't talk about it with you, even though I knew we would have to talk about it sooner rather than later."

Georgia nodded. "I planned this dinner because I felt we needed some time alone," she said. She shook her head. "I know we go out often, but I didn't think we could have an honest conversation about a difficult subject while drinking at a bar." *I also didn't want anyone else to overhear our conversation.* She reached out and took one of Billie's hands. "So, are we okay, Billie?"

Billie smiled and nodded. "Yeah, we're okay," she said. She took Georgia in her arms, her hands on Georgia's waist. "You can't stop worrying about us, Georgia."

Georgia sighed and nodded. "I'll try to stop worrying," she said. She took several long sips of her wine. She cleared her throat and shook her head. "I feel silly now, thinking this dinner was the only thing to save our relationship." *I wish Billie had told me sooner that we were okay.*

Billie patted Georgia's knee. "You don't have to feel silly," she said. "I'm sorry again for not telling you sooner that I wasn't going to let Bridget's kissing you change our relationship."

"Okay," Georgia said. *I'm not worried about our relationship for the first time in almost a month.* "So, what do you want to do now? Should we sit here, drink our wine, and hold hands?"

Billie held up her wine glass. "I say we finish our wine and then go out," she said. She smiled at Georgia. "We need to show the world that we're fine."

***

Thirty minutes later, Billie and Georgia arrived at Capote's.

Billie shook her head and chuckled. "Somehow, we always end up here," she said. She looked over at Georgia. "Are you sure you don't want to go to another bar? I mean, isn't there another gay bar in Boston?"

Georgia grinned and nodded. "There are a few of them," she said. *And I've been to all of them, but this one, Capote's, is the best.* "And sometimes, I don't mind going to one of them to drink."

"We can go to another bar," Billie said. She shrugged her shoulders. "It doesn't matter to me which bar we go to and drink in."

Georgia shook her head. "This isn't any bar to me," she said. "It's the only bar I feel at home in, even when I'm not working." *And Truman Capote is my favorite author. I cried for a week when he died.*

Billie smiled and nodded. "I know what you mean, Georgia," she said. "I feel the same way about Jackson's Jukebox."

Georgia looked around. "Where do you want to sit, Billie?" *There are a lot of people here on a Thursday night.*

Billie chuckled and grinned. "Why don't we sit where we always sit, in our favorite booth?" She pointed at it. "You see, there's no one sitting in it."

Georgia nodded and smiled. "You're right," she said. She reached out and took one of Billie's hands. "Let's grab it before someone else takes it away." *I'm glad that Billie doesn't mind coming here.*

Billie and Georgia walked over to their favorite booth and sat in it. They only had to wait a few minutes for a waitress.

"Well, look at this," the waitress said, walking up to their booth. "I would ask you, Georgia, if you were working tonight, but I already know you aren't."

Georgia chuckled and grinned. "Hey, Monica," she said. "How has your night been so far?" *She doesn't seem surprised to see us here.*

Monica shrugged her shoulders. "It has been okay for the most part," she said. She looked over at Billie and smiled. "Hey, Billie. I haven't seen you here lately."

Billie chuckled while glancing over at Georgia. "Well, I've got two part-time jobs now," she said. "So, I don't have much free time."

Monica shook her head. "Now, that's no excuse," she said. She took out her order book and chuckled. "I would ask you two what you would like to drink, but I'm going to guess that you two want your usual drinks."

Georgia nodded. "You know us too well, Monica," she said. *Somehow, I was like my father, always at a bar.* She looked over at Billie. "What about you, Billie? Do you want your usual drink, or are you feeling adventurous?"

"Yeah, I'll have my usual," Billie said. She sighed and took out a cigarette.

Something seemed to be bothering her. Georgia reached out and took Billie's free hand. "Are you okay, Billie? What's going on with you?"

Before Billie could answer, Rebecca joined them in the booth. "You haven't told Georgia what today means to you, Billie."

Billie shook her head. She looked at Georgia and told her about her summer romance with Michelle Connor.

***

You never forget your first love. "So, your relationship changed from friendship to romance on her birthday?" Georgia took out a cigarette and lit it. "How long had you known her by then?"

Why am I only hearing about this Michelle girl now? Why hasn't Billie told me about her before?

Billie chuckled. "Well, we had only been friends for less than a month," she said. "Michelle had been part of my life longer than that, though I didn't know it."

Georgia frowned. "I don't understand," she said. "What do you mean she had been part of your life, but you didn't know it?" *Billie's a closed book, and I haven't been able to open it yet.*

"Michelle was, and still is, my younger sister's best friend," Billie said. She shrugged her shoulders. "She knew me, but I didn't know her."

Rebecca nodded. "I get it," she said. "Go ahead and tell Georgia the rest of the story, Billie."

Georgia learned something about Billie when she told the story of her first love to her and Rebecca. However, Georgia realized later that Rebecca already knew about Billie's first love, Michelle Connor. She realized that she had fallen in love with Billie because the way Billie talked about Michelle was the same way Georgia felt about Billie.

"Do you still love her, Billie?"

Billie sighed and nodded. "I'm sure that I do," she said. She shrugged her shoulders. "I try to remind myself that our relationship was only a summer romance and nothing more."

Georgia reached out across the table and took one of Billie's hands. "Hey, don't do that," she said. "Don't downplay your relationship with her. There's nothing wrong with loving her and missing her." *I hadn't planned on falling in love with Billie, but I had fallen in love with her, and I'm not sure Billie feels the same way since she keeps her feelings hidden.*

Chapter Fourteen

B efore Jasmine knew it, the summer had gone by, and she
was still living at home, with no job or plans.

Where did the summer go?

Jasmine sighed and shook her head. She had given up trying
to get Billie's country club membership revoked. Instead, she
had been spending all her free time looking into the rule that
prohibited black people, called Negro in the rule book, from
becoming members. She wanted to know when the rule was
written and when the country club board stopped enforcing it.

***

Jasmine went to her mother a few days before the Fourth, hoping that her mother might know something about the racist
rule.

Jasmine went to her mother's bedroom and knocked on her
bedroom door while still standing in the hallway. "Hey, Mama,"
she said. "Can I talk to you about something?" *I don't know who
else to ask except for her.*

Her mother put down the book she was reading and smiled. "You know I'll always make time for you," she said. She patted her bed and showed Jasmine where to sit. "Come over here and sit with me," she said.

Jasmine entered her mother's bedroom, carrying the rule-book. She sat next to her mother on her mother's bed. She opened the rule book and pointed at the racist rule. "Do you know about this rule right here?" *I hope she didn't know about it.*

Her mother sighed and shook her head. "I didn't think it was still in the rule book," she said. She frowned and looked over at Jasmine. "What edition is this? Are you sure you didn't grab an old rule book?"

Jasmine sighed and shook her head. "No, Mama," she said. "This is the newest edition." She flipped through the rule book to the front, to the copyright page. She pointed out the year it was published to her mother. "It was published this year, Mama."

Her mother clicked her tongue. "Well, I'm sure it isn't enforced anymore," she said. She looked over at Jasmine and smiled. "After all, you're a member."

***

Jasmine soon discovered that the country club board hadn't stopped enforcing the rule, but instead enforced it or didn't, when they wanted to, using it to deny most black people who applied to become members.

Jasmine had convinced a clerk in the country club's records department to allow her to review all the applications from the past five years. The clerk, a young white guy in his early twenties, had a crush on Jasmine, and she used his feelings for her to get what she wanted from him.

Jasmine made copies of all the applications that had been denied and gave the files back to the clerk. "Thanks," she said, smiling at him. "I promise if I get caught with the copies, I won't tell anyone you helped me." *I'm not going to tell anyone he helped me. And I won't call him anytime soon, despite my promise to him.*

***

Jasmine looked through the copies she had made. She marked all the denied applications, separated them from the others, and examined them more closely.

All these people were denied membership for the same reason. Jasmine sighed and shook her head. *The bastards even mentioned the rule in the section about why the application was rejected.* She frowned. *Then why wasn't my membership application denied?* She went back through the applications (the copies she had made) and looked for her application. She also searched for Rebecca's application and Billie's application.

Jasmine found all three applications. *Okay, so why weren't these applications denied?* She took a closer look at them, reading every line. At the bottom, in the box where the reasons for accepting the applications were written, she read the same thing in Billie's, Rebecca's, and her application: "Old Money Family."

Jasmine chuckled and shook her head. *Well, it looks like I'm related to Billie. It seems that her grandmother, Josephine Carver, is also my grandaunt Josey. I don't know how to feel about what I've discovered. I wish I had a friend to talk to about all of this. Wait a minute. There's someone I can talk to about all this shit.* She frowned. *But will she even speak to me?* She shrugged her shoulders. *There's only one way to find out.*

Jasmine picked up her phone and called Rebecca. The phone rang three times before Rebecca answered it.

"Hello, who's calling me?"

"Hey, Rebecca," Jasmine said. She cleared her throat. "It's me, Jasmine." *Please, don't hang up on me. I need to talk to you.*

"Okay," Rebecca said. She chuckled. "You're the last person I thought would call me today."

"I'll get to the point," Jasmine said. *They were right about it.* "I'd like to talk to you and Billie more about it."

Rebecca chuckled. "I'm guessing that you've looked into that racist rule," she said. "Now, you want to share what you discovered with Billie and me."

"Yeah, that's right," Jasmine said.

"I'll tell you what, Jasmine," Rebecca said. "I'll call Billie and convince her to meet you at the country club in a few days. How's that sound to you?"

"Sounds good to me," Jasmine said. *I would've preferred to meet with them sooner, but I can't be picky now.* "Let's meet on the patio." *I need to bring copies of their applications to show them why they were approved.*

"We'll meet you there," Rebecca said. "Okay, we'll see you in a few days."

***

A few days later, it was Labor Day, and Jasmine was sitting at a table on the patio of the country club, waiting for Billie and Rebecca. She smoked a cigarette and sipped her coffee.

"Okay, Jasmine, we're here," Rebecca said. She glanced over at Billie and smiled. "I convinced Billie to meet you at the country club."

Jasmine nodded. "I see that," she said. She cleared her throat. *Okay, change your tone of voice. You're not here to challenge them but to inform them.* "Now, I only went back about five years, but I've found proof that the rule I told you two about, the racist one, is still being enforced."

Rebecca shook her head. "I want to say that I'm surprised and shocked, but I can't," she said. She sighed. "I've wondered why there aren't more black members."

Billie frowned. "Why didn't they enforce the rule with me?" She pointed at Rebecca. "Or with Rebecca?" She shook her head. "Or with you, Jasmine?"

Jasmine sighed. *I have to tell them everything I found out. I can't leave anything out.* "It seems that the rule wasn't enforced with any of us because of who our families are, Billie," she said. She pulled out the copies she had brought with her. She placed them on the table in front of Billie and Rebecca. "I made copies of our applications." She pointed out the remarks written in the small box at the bottom of the application to Billie and Rebecca. "The only reason why none of us were denied membership was because of our families."

Billie nodded. "And so it seems," she said. She frowned. "What about other people?"

I know what Billie's asking me. "Do you mean the other black people?"

Billie nodded. "Yeah, Jasmine," she said. "Why was their application denied?"

Jasmine sighed. "They used the rule to deny their membership," she said. She looked over at Rebecca. "I don't know how to feel about this, finding out about the rule and how they enforce it whenever they want to, using it to deny some people from becoming members and ignoring it whenever they don't want to piss off the wrong family."

Billie reached out and patted one of Jasmine's hands. "I understand how you feel," she said. "I don't know how to feel about it either."

Rebecca shook her head, scowling. "Well, I know how I feel about it," she said. She looked over at Billie and then at Jasmine. "I'm pissed off."

"We have to do something," Jasmine said. She shrugged her shoulders. "I just don't know what we can do about it." *I always knew I was their token black girl.*

Jasmine couldn't have predicted, only a year before, that she would find herself sitting on the patio of the country club with Billie and Rebecca.

Rebecca slammed her hand down on the table. "Well, we have to do something," she said. "We can't let them keep on excluding black people from here."

Jasmine sighed. "Do you think we can do anything, Rebecca?" *I've never thought of myself as a black woman, even though I've always been treated differently.* She held up her hands. "After all, none of us are even on the board."

Rebecca frowned. "You're right, Jasmine," she said. "None of us are on the board, but we're all members."

Jasmine shook her head. "Do you think anyone will listen to us, three black ladies? Young ladies, too," she said. She tapped the rule book sitting on the table in front of her. "They didn't even bother to remove the racist rule from the rule book." *They weren't trying to hide it.*

Rebecca smiled. "They didn't remove it because they didn't count on anyone finding it," she said. She reached out and patted Jasmine's hands. "They also didn't count on you coming along and reading the rule book."

Billie nodded. "That's right," she said. "And they didn't count on the three of us getting together either."

Jasmine frowned. *What does Billie mean?* "I don't understand," she said. "Are we friends now, Billie?" *Maybe I misunderstood what she said. I'm sure I did, because how can we be friends, considering I once tried to get her removed from the country club?*

Billie chuckled and grinned. "I'd say we're more allies than friends," she said. She shrugged her shoulders. "On the other hand, I'm not saying we can't be friends or won't become friends."

Rebecca held up her hands. "We can talk about you two becoming friends another time," she said. "Right now, we have to figure out how we're going to get rid of that racist rule."

Billie cleared her throat and shook her head. "We're going to need help if we want to get that rule removed from the rule book," she said. She looked over at Jasmine. "Jasmine's right about the board not listening to us."

Rebecca sighed. "So, what do we do now?"

Jasmine took out a cigarette and lit it. She took a drag off it, staring off in the distance. "We need to find someone who can help us and who the board will listen to at the same time," she said. She shrugged her shoulders. "I don't think my mother has any influence or pull here." *And I'm the reason she isn't a more significant part of the world we live in. It's one thing to be an unwed mother, but to have a mixed daughter, half white and half black, is even worse.*

Rebecca sighed and nodded. "Same thing with my mother," she said. She chuckled and glanced over at Jasmine. "You know that our mothers know each other, don't you, Jasmine?"

Jasmine nodded and grinned. "Yeah, I know," she said. *I've heard about you, Rebecca, from my mother since childhood.* She frowned. *Billie got quiet.* She looked over at Billie. "What about you, Billie? Do you know anyone who could help us?"

Billie smiled and nodded. "I think I do, Jasmine," she said. "We should ask my grandmother to help us."

Rebecca nodded. "That's a good idea," she said. She smiled and looked over at Jasmine. "Billie's grandmother has been a member here for a long time."

Oh, yeah, that's right. Billie lives with her grandmother. "Do you think your grandmother can help us?" Jasmine took a drag off her cigarette, waiting for Billie to answer her question. *If anyone can help us, it's going to be Aunt Josie.*

Billie nodded. "Yeah, I think she can help us," she said. She leaned back in her chair and grinned. "My grandmother's kind of a big deal."

Jasmine smiled back at Billie. "Is that right?" *I don't think Billie knows that we're related. If she does know, she's good at hiding it.*

Billie stood up, pushing her chair back. "We can either sit here and just talk about doing something about that racist rule, or we can go to my grandmother and ask her to help us," she said. "I say we go and ask her."

Rebecca stood up, pushing her chair back. "You heard Billie, Jasmine," she said. "Sitting here, talking to each other isn't going to do anything."

Jasmine nodded and smiled. "Okay," she said. She stood up, pushing her chair back. "Let's go." *What a strange turn of events.*

***

Jasmine, Billie, and Rebecca left the patio, walked through the country club, past the bar, and through the front entrance. They go to the parking lot, where they find out that Rebecca has parked next to Jasmine's car.

Billie turned around and looked over at Jasmine. "It just occurred to me that you will need directions to my grandmother's house," she said. "Do you want me to draw you a map?"

Jasmine grinned and shook her head. "I've lived here my whole life, Billie," she said. "I know how to get around." *I also already know your grandmother's address, but I'll let you give it to me anyway.*

Rebecca shook her head and chuckled. "You'd better give Jasmine your grandmother's address anyway," she said. She looked over at Jasmine. "I'll see you when we get there."

"Okay," Jasmine said. *Rebecca knows that I'm related to Billie.* She frowned. *I wonder why Rebecca hasn't told Billie.*

Billie handed Jasmine a small paper. "Here's my grandmother's address," she said. She frowned. "Are you sure that you don't need directions?"

Jasmine nodded. "I'm sure, Billie," she said. She held up the paper. "Your grandmother has been living there a long time, hasn't she?" *I feel I have an edge over Billie for the first time since we met. I know something that she doesn't know.*

Billie shrugged her shoulders. "I'm not sure, to be honest with you," she said. She shook her head and chuckled. "Well, I'm going to ride with Rebecca." She reached out and patted Jasmine's shoulder. "You're going to love my grandmother."

Jasmine nodded. "I'm sure you're right," she said. She turned around and walked over to her car.

Rebecca and Billie got into Rebecca's car. They then drove away, leaving the country club.

Jasmine sighed and shook her head. She had long suspected that she and Billie might be related in some way; they looked too alike not to be related in some way.

***

Billie and Rebecca were waiting outside Billie's grandmother's house when Jasmine pulled up in her car. She parked behind Rebecca's car and got out.

Rebecca poked Billie in the ribs. "I told you that she would find your grandmother's house," she said. She shook her head and chuckled. "Billie was worried that you would get lost."

Billie shook her head and grinned. "I didn't say that," she said. She cleared her throat. "I said that since Jasmine hasn't been here before, she might have difficulty finding it."

But I have been here before, Billie. Jasmine chuckled and shook her head. "I was able to find it with no problem," she said. She pointed at the front door. "So, we have to go inside the house to talk to Billie's grandmother."

Billie nodded. "That's right," she said. She turned around and went over to the front door. She looked over her shoulder at Rebecca and Jasmine. "Let's go, y'all."

Jasmine nodded and motioned for Rebecca to go ahead. "After you, Rebecca," she said. *This is going to be interesting.*

Jasmine followed Rebecca and Billie into Billie's grandmother's house. They entered the parlor first, and Billie turned around, stopping them with a wave of her hand.

"Y'all wait here," Billie said. "Since Josephine isn't here, she's either in her bedroom or the library."

Rebecca nodded. "Okay, Billie," she said. "We'll wait here while you go and find your grandmother."

Billie left the parlor and walked up the stairs.

***

Rebecca pointed at the couches. "Let's sit down and relax while we wait for Billie," she said. "I don't think we should just stand here."

Jasmine nodded. *I haven't been in this house since I was six or seven.* She smiled. *It still looks the same.*

Rebecca sat on one couch while Jasmine sat on the other.

Rebecca took out a cigarette and lit it. "I always feel like I'm in a museum whenever I'm here," she said. "Billie's grandmother sure does have many pictures hanging on the wall."

Jasmine nodded. "You're right, Rebecca," she said. "I like it here. There's a lot of history in this house." *This house might be called the Carver house, but it belonged to my family, the Carters.*

"They're waiting for us in here."

Jasmine stood up, getting off the couch. Rebecca did the same and turned to face the hallway.

Billie and her grandmother, Josephine, entered the parlor.

Billie smiled and pointed at Rebecca. "You remember my friend Rebecca, don't you, Josephine?"

Josephine nodded and smiled at Rebecca. "I do remember her, Billie," she said. "It is a pleasure to see you again, Rebecca."

Rebecca smiled back at Josephine. "Yeah, same here, Mrs. Carver," she said. "I don't think you've ever met our friend Jasmine here."

Josephine shook her head. "Hello, Jasmine," she said. She went over to Jasmine and hugged her. "I knew you would grow into a beautiful young lady."

Billie looked over at Rebecca, who shrugged her shoulders.

"You did say that many times, Aunt Josie," Jasmine said. She cleared her throat. "I just found out, Billie, that we're cousins." *I'm not sure yet how to feel about being cousins with Billie.*

Billie-frowned. "How are we cousins, Jasmine?"

"My grandfather, my mother's father, was Josephine's younger brother," Jasmine said. She cleared her throat. "We're here to see you, Aunt Josie, because we need your help. There's a racist rule that's still being used to deny black people membership at the country club."

Josephine sighed. "Yes, we must do something about it," she said.

Chapter Fifteen

S adie's aversion to Billie had intensified over the ten months since New Year's Eve. She couldn't help but notice Billie's increasing presence in her life- at the bookstore, her favorite bar, and even her home.

***

Sadie went to Capote's to look for Iris. She found Iris sitting at the bar.

Iris smiled at Sadie when she sat down beside her at the bar. "Hey, Sadie," she said. "I wasn't expecting to see you here."

Okay, I can either make small talk with Iris or get to the point and tell her what I have to say. "What are your plans for tonight, Iris?"

Iris chuckled. "Well, right now, I'm having a drink," she said. "What are your plans for tonight, Sadie?"

Sadie shook her head. *Don't try to turn the conversation around to me.* "I asked you first, Iris," she said. "Are you going to stay here and drink, or are you going bar hopping?" *Iris hadn't made any plans with me since she doesn't like to drink alone. I'm sure she has made plans to hang out with either Rebecca or Billie. I'm not sure how I feel about Rebecca, but I don't like Billie.*

Iris shrugged her shoulders. "I don't know yet if we're going to stay here and drink or if we're going to make the round of nearby bars," she said. She glanced at her watch. "I'm early, so I won't know what we'll do until they arrive."

"Who are you waiting for, Iris?" *I'd be surprised if she didn't tell me the truth. So far, we've always been honest with each other. I hope we never lie to each other.*

Iris chuckled and grinned. "You know who I'm talking about, Sadie," she said. "I told you a few days ago that I would celebrate Halloween with Rebecca and Billie."

Sadie nodded. "That's who I thought you were talking about," she said. She shrugged her shoulders. "So, you don't like hanging out with me anymore?"

Iris sighed. "We hang out all the time," she said. "I invited you to join us, remember?"

Sadie nodded and sighed. "Yeah, I remember," she said. *Iris only invited me because she knew I would say no. She knows that I don't like hanging out with anyone but her.* She crossed her arms over her chest. "You've been hanging out with Rebecca and Billie a lot lately."

Iris nodded. "You're right," she said. "I have been hanging out with them a lot. And do you want to know why, Sadie?"

"Yeah, I want to know why, Iris," Sadie said. *We've been friends for a long time; this is the first time Iris has tried to make other friends.*

"Billie and Rebecca have become my friends," Iris said. "I always have a good time when I hang out with them."

Sadie nodded and sighed. "I thought we were friends," she said. *So, this is how our friendship comes to an end. I knew one day it might end.*

Iris frowned and shook her head. She reached out and took one of Sadie's hands. "We are friends, Sadie," she said. "I know you don't like me having other friends, but I'm telling you, it hasn't changed anything between us."

Sadie sighed. "Are you sure about that, Iris?" She shook her head. "I don't understand how you can be friends with either Rebecca or Billie." *I know why they would want to be friends with her; Iris is charming, outgoing, and has a wicked sense of humor.*

Iris shook her head. "Well, if you bothered to try to get to know either of them, you would want to hang out with them too," she said. She shook her head. "But you haven't even given them a chance."

Sadie chuckled. "You're right, Iris," she said. "I haven't given them a chance, and I'll tell you why." *Iris may not like what I'm about to say about her new friends, but she knows that I won't lie to her or bullshit her in any way.* "They remind me, both of them, of the so-called mean girls who used to pick on us when we were growing up in Nashville."

Iris sighed. "Do you think I would be friends with mean girls, Sadie?" She took out a cigarette and lit it. "Sometimes, I don't think you think too much about what you say to me." She shook her head. "I would never be friends with mean girls."

Sadie shrugged her shoulders. "Well, you are, Iris," she said. "Rebecca and Billie stink of being mean girls." *I know mean girls when I see them, and they're mean girls.*

Iris shook her head and sighed. "You're wrong, Sadie," she said. "Billie and Rebecca aren't mean girls." She took a drag off her cigarette. "They are nothing like the girls who made our lives hell when we were younger."

Sadie shook her head. *Iris can't face the truth about her new friends.* "They're exactly like the mean girls who tormented us when we were kids," she said. "They're from Beacon Hill, the old money part of Boston." She held out her hands. "They were born mean girls, Iris."

Iris sighed and smiled. "You don't know anything about Rebecca or Billie, Sadie," she said. "Billie lives in Beacon Hill with her grandmother, but she's not from there."

Sadie frowned and squinted at Iris. "Well, where is she from then, Iris?" *I can't admit this to her, but Iris might know more about Rebecca and Billie than I do. All I know about Rebecca and Billie is that they live in Beacon Hill and are around our age, with Billie being younger than Rebecca, who is older than us.*

Iris frowned. "Billie's from New Orleans, Louisiana," she said. "Don't you remember me telling you that she's Southern like us?"

Sadie shook her head. "I don't remember you telling me that," she said. "And it doesn't matter that Billie's Southern like us. She still belongs to an old-money family." *Why can't Iris see the truth about Billie? Or about Rebecca?*

Iris shook her head. "You're letting your experience cloud your judgment," she said. She sighed and chuckled. "I just don't understand why you don't like Billie." She frowned and stared at Sadie. "Do you even know why you don't like her?"

Okay, I can't lie to her, even though explaining why I don't like Billie would be more straightforward. Sadie shrugged her shoulders. "I wish I knew why I don't like Billie," she said. "I didn't like her from the moment we met her."

Iris sighed. "I'm not asking you to like her or even become friends with her," she said. "I am asking you to let me be friends with Billie and Rebecca."

Sadie sighed and shook her head. "I can't stop you from being friends with them," she said. "You have to accept that I'm not becoming friends with either of them."

"We've been friends for most of our lives," Iris said. She reached out, took one of Sadie's hands, and squeezed it. "Nothing's going to change that, Sadie."

Sadie talked to Iris for another ten minutes. She had given up on stopping Iris from being friends with Rebecca and Billie.

Sadie finished her drink and stood up. "Well, I'll be going now," she said. She glanced at her watch. "I've got to work tonight." *I remember when I used to enjoy Halloween.* She sighed and shook her head.

"Okay," Iris said. She reached out and grabbed Sadie's elbow. "Why don't you take the night off from work and go out with us?"

Sadie shook her head. "I'm not hanging out with them," she said. "Just because you're friends with them doesn't mean I have to be friends with them too." *I don't think I'll ever understand how Iris can be friends with Rebecca and Billie. She refuses to see them for who they are, mean girls.*

Iris sighed. "Okay," she said. "Well, I hope you have a good night at work."

Sadie nodded. "Thanks," she said. She chuckled and punched Iris in the shoulder. "Try not to drink too much." *I always knew that one day, our friendship wouldn't be enough for Iris, and she would find new friends.*

***

Sadie left Capote's and drove to the bookstore. She didn't have to be there for another hour, her shift not starting until seven o'clock. *I don't feel like sitting at the apartment until it's time to go to work. I don't need to remind you that Iris is going out with Rebecca and Billie.*

Didn't you listen to anything I said?

Sadie shook her head. *I did, but you didn't listen to me. You've always been the most important person in my life, and I thought you felt the same way about me.*

I do feel the same way, Sadie.

Sadie sighed and shook her head, frowning. *That might have been true at one time, Iris, but not anymore.*

***

Sadie arrived at the bookstore and parked her car near the back door. She got out and walked around the building to the front door. She pushed the door open and stepped inside.

Sadie frowned and shook her head when she saw Billie standing near the cash register. *What's she still doing here?*

Billie looked up and smiled. "Hey, Sadie," she said, waving at Sadie.

I've got nothing to say to you. Sadie nodded and walked past Billie.

Sadie went to the office in the back, near the storage area. *I hope he's still here.*

The door was closed, and Sadie knocked on it.

"It's open," the owner said. "Come on in. Who's ever knocking on my door?"

Sadie opened the door and stepped into the owner's office. "Good evening, Mr. Armstrong," she said. "I was wondering if I could talk to you briefly." *For the most part, he's been a good boss. He might expect you to work hard, but he's not afraid of working hard himself.*

The owner chuckled and glanced at his watch. "You're an hour early, Miss Zimmerman," he said. "I know you often show up for work early, but this is even earlier than you usually show up for work."

Sadie shrugged her shoulders. *He doesn't need to know why I arrived at work an hour early.* "I didn't have anything better to do," she said. She cleared her throat. *I haven't been this nervous about talking to him since he interviewed me when I applied for the job here.*

The owner nodded and leaned back in his chair. "Okay," he said. "You wanted to talk to me about something?"

Sadie nodded. *Okay, try to be clear.* "I need to talk to you about Billie," she said. *This won't be my first time coming to him because I needed to talk to him about another employee.* She smiled. *I got that asshole fired.*

The owner sighed and shook his head. "I remember the last time you came to me to talk about a co-worker," he said. He pointed at the empty chair on the other side of his desk. "Why don't you take a seat, Miss Zimmerman?"

Sadie sat down in the chair. "You need to fire Billie, Mr. Armstrong," she said.

The owner shook his head. He took out a cigarette, lit it, and leaned back in his chair. "Miss Carver has been working here for almost ten months," he said. "You've been here long enough to know that most people don't last six months working here."

Sadie nodded and chuckled. *He's right. Most people don't last more than six months here. It's not a bad place to work, but the hours can be long, the customers can be irritating sometimes, and I sometimes wonder if I'm being paid enough.*

The owner took a drag off his cigarette. "Miss Carver's proving to be one of the best employees I've ever hired," he said. He held up one hand and started counting off. "Miss Carver shows up on time, hasn't missed a day or shift, and is willing to work extra shifts whenever I've asked her to."

Sadie sighed and shook her head. *I remember a time when he thought the same thing about me.* "I thought I was the best employee you've ever hired, Mr. Armstrong," she said. "I show up on time, do my job, and work every shift you've asked me to, just like Billie." *How does Billie do it? How does she manage to win over everyone she meets?*

The owner sighed. "It's not a competition, Miss Zimmerman," he said. "I know this is a small bookstore, but I think it's big enough to have two great employees."

Sadie shook her head. *Okay, this isn't going well.* "I'm not saying Billie isn't a great employee," she said. She sighed. "I need this job more than she does, Mr. Armstrong." *I have to be careful. I don't want to say anything to him that could give him a reason to fire me.*

The owner nodded and chuckled. "I'm sure you're referring to where Miss Carver lives," he said. He sat up straight. "I know that Miss Carver's from Beacon Hill." He took a drag off his cigarette. "I didn't hire her because she's from there but because she's the only person ever to ace my literary test."

Sadie frowned. "Billie aced your test?" *Okay, so she knows more about literature than I do. I'm still a better employee.*

"I don't know what your problem with Miss Carver is, Miss Zimmerman," the owner said. "And I don't care either."

Sadie sighed. *I wish I could tell him that Billie had done anything that would make him fire her, but I can't because she hasn't done anything to get fired by him.* "Well, you're the boss, Mr. Armstrong," she said. *There's no point in continuing this conversation.* "Is it okay with you that I go ahead and clock in?" *I could sit in my car until it's time to start my shift, but I'm not afraid of Billie and don't see any point in trying to avoid her.*

The owner gave Sadie a questioning look. "There's not much for you to do until Miss Carver finishes her shift," he said. "Are you sure you want to clock in an hour early, Miss Zimmerman?"

Sadie nodded. "I'm sure, Mr. Armstrong," she said. She sighed and shook her head. "My life's kind of crazy right now, and I need somewhere to hide from it." *I hope what I just told him is enough for him to let me clock in early.*

The owner nodded and chuckled. "I won't press you for more details, Miss Zimmerman," he said. He took one last drag off his cigarette and put it in the ashtray on his desk. "Miss Carver's taking care of the front, so why don't you take care of the back, Miss Zimmerman?"

"And do what, Mr. Armstrong?" Sadie shook her head and frowned. *Why did I ask him that? I bet Billie doesn't question him. Maybe that's why he considers her the best employee he's ever hired.*

The owner shrugged his shoulders. "I'm not sure, Miss Zimmerman," he said. "You're the one who wants to clock in early, not me."

Sadie nodded. "I see your point, Mr. Armstrong," she said. "Why don't I stock up the magazine rack?" *I'm sure he'll be okay with stocking the magazine rack.*

The owner nodded. "That's a good idea, Miss Zimmerman," he said. "Clock in and get to it."

Sadie nodded and left the owner's office. She went to the storage area, where the new magazines were kept. She grabbed a bundle and went to the magazine rack. She stopped when she saw Billie's name on a magazine cover.

***

An hour later, Billie left the bookstore, her shift over. She walked by Sadie, nodded at her, and gave her a polite smile.

Sadie shook her head and sighed. *I hope Mr. Armstrong didn't tell Billie about our conversation. I might need to ask him about it.* She glanced at the magazine with Billie's name on the front cover. She picked it up off the counter, a determined look in her eyes, and left the cash register.

Sadie found the owner sitting in his office, smoking a cigarette and reviewing some paperwork.

"Are you busy, Mr. Armstrong?"

The owner chuckled and shook his head. "I am, but I could use a break," he said. He leaned back in his chair and smiled at Sadie. "What's on your mind, Miss Zimmerman?"

Sadie placed the magazine on the owner's desk. "Did you know that Billie wrote short stories?" *I didn't know she did.* She sighed and shook her head. *Iris might be right that I know nothing about Billie.*

The owner picked up the magazine and took a closer look. "Miss Carver might have mentioned it when I interviewed her, but I'm not sure," he said. He handed the magazine back to Sadie. "It's kind of impressive, isn't it, Miss Zimmerman?"

Sadie frowned. "Yeah, I guess it is," she said, not wanting to admit that Billie had done anything impressive. "I know why now she could pass your little test."

The owner shook his head and chuckled. "You passed it, too," he said. He cleared his throat. "Is there anything else you want to show me, Miss Zimmerman?"

Okay, I know that tone of voice. He's lost his patience with me. Sadie shook her head. "I'll let you get back to your paperwork," she said. She turned around and went to the door. She glanced over her shoulder at the owner. "I hope you didn't tell Billie I asked you to fire her."

The owner smiled and nodded. "I didn't tell her, Miss Zimmerman," he said. He held up his hand. "I don't want you ever to mention it or come to me again if you have a problem with her."

Sadie nodded. "I understand, Mr. Armstrong," she said. "I'm going back to the front of the store." *Well, that's great. He knows that I don't like Billie and isn't going to listen to me anymore about her.* She sighed and shook her head, feeling the weight of her failed attempts. *So far, I've failed to end her friendship with Iris. And now, I've failed at getting her fired from here.*

***

Sadie closed the bookstore an hour later, at 10 p.m., and gave the owner the daily deposit. *I've worked at this bookstore for years, and it's become a part of my life. But lately, everything has changed, and I'm unsure if I can keep up.*

"Business was kind of slow today," Sadie said, handing the owner the deposit bag. "I doubt we did even close to a hundred dollars in sales today." *I don't know why the bookstore was open today, given it was Halloween.*

The owner nodded and chuckled. "I'm sure you're right about that, Miss Zimmerman," he said. He shrugged his shoulders. "It's still a hundred more than I had yesterday."

Sadie nodded and laughed. "That's a good way of looking at it, Mr. Armstrong," she said. "I'm going to lock all the doors. Do you need me to take care of the lights?" *I'm sure I know what he's about to say since we have the same conversation every time I close the store.*

"Just take care of the lights in the front, Miss Zimmerman," the owner said. "I'll take care of the lights back here."

Sadie nodded and chuckled. "Okay, Mr. Armstrong," she said. *He always says the same thing.* "I'll see you next time I work."

Sadie locked up the bookstore and turned off all the lights in the front of the store. She left the bookstore and went to her car. She got in her car and sighed. *I don't feel like going home since I know Iris won't be there.* She frowned. *Iris is out with her new friends and having fun with them.* She smiled. *Let's go to my favorite bar, where I always find solace. I know I won't have to deal with Rebecca or Billie since they're hanging out with Iris at Capote's.*

Sadie drove from the bookstore to Jackson's Jukebox. She found an empty parking space near the front door.

***

Sadie entered the bar a few minutes later and took a seat at the bar.

The bartender walked over to her and smiled. "Well, good evening, Sadie," he said. "I see you're not wearing a Halloween costume."

Sadie shook her head and chuckled. "I haven't worn a Halloween costume since I turned thirteen," she said. She grinned. "I stopped playing pretend after I discovered cocktails and whiskey." *For some reason, I find it easy to talk to him, to this bartender. I don't know why, but I do. Maybe it's because he doesn't flirt with me.*

"Speaking of whiskey, would you like your usual?"

Sadie nodded. "Of course I would," she said. She pulled out a twenty and handed it to the bartender. "Tell me when I owe you more money." *I'm good for at least three drinks.*

The bartender nodded. "I'll be right back with your drink, Sadie," he said.

Sadie turned around on the stool and sighed when she spotted Billie sitting alone in a booth. *What's she doing here? I thought she was hanging out with Iris and Rebecca.*

"Here you go, Sadie."

Sadie turned back around on the stool. She picked up her drink and smiled at the bartender. "Thanks," she said. She took a sip and licked her lips. "Whiskey has to be the best drink ever invented."

The bartender chuckled and grinned. "You always say that after taking that first sip," he said. He pointed over his shoulder. "I'll be over there if you need anything."

Sadie turned back on the stool and looked around while sipping her whiskey. *I'm so glad I found this bar.* She smiled. *I remember how I felt the first time I walked in here. I felt at home here. This place reminds me a little of my favorite bar in Nashville, Springwater Supper Club.*

Sadie shook her head. *I don't understand why Iris seems to like Capote's so much. I never felt at home there; it always felt like I was among the few black women there. I feel a little more at home here since most customers are black.* She sighed and shook her head. *The only thing I don't like about going here is that I have to pretend that I'm straight and have to flirt with men while I'm here.*

Sadie sighed and shook her head. *Okay, let's recap the day so far. I failed to end Iris's friendship with Billie and get Billie fired from the bookstore.* She looked around. *There's still one thing I might be able to do to remove Billie from one part of my life.*

What are you planning on doing, Sadie?

Sadie frowned. *I have only one option left, but I'm not sure how I will do it.*

What are you thinking, Sadie?

Sadie shook her head. *You'll find out soon enough, Iris.* She sipped her whiskey and looked around for the owner of Jackson's Jukebox. *I'm sure he's here since most of the time he's either walking around or sitting in his office.*

***

Sadie spotted the owner walking by the bar a few minutes later. She smiled at him and waved. "Hey, Drew," she said. "Come over here for a second."

Drew smiled and walked over to Sadie. "Hey, Sadie," he said. "I see you're not celebrating Halloween."

Sadie shook her head and chuckled. "Well, I'm an adult," she said. *Drew might be the only man I don't mind flirting with, even though I wouldn't ever go to bed with him.* "I need to talk to you." She frowned and looked around. "Can we go to your office? I would prefer to have a private conversation with you."

Drew nodded and chuckled. "Well, since you're one of my favorite customers and one of my favorite people in general, I'll grant your request for a private audience," he said. He pointed in the direction of his office.

Sadie left the bar and followed Drew back to his office. Once they entered his office, she didn't waste any time explaining why she wanted to talk to him.

"You need to fire Billie Carver," Sadie said. "She doesn't belong here with us, hard-working black folks." *This is a long shot at best. I know that Drew likes me, but I'm not sure if he likes me enough for me to convince him to fire Billie.*

Drew shook his head. "I'm not going to do that, Sadie," he said. He sighed. "Please leave my office now."

Sadie sighed and left Drew's office. She had failed again.

Chapter Sixteen

On Halloween, Drew surprised Willie by mentioning Thanksgiving.

"So, what are your plans for Thanksgiving, Willie?"

Willie chuckled. "It's funny you should mention it," he said. "My mother called me yesterday and reminded me that it would please her if I celebrated Thanksgiving with my sisters again." *I'm glad she called me because I hadn't realized it was almost time again for Thanksgiving.*

"I'd like to join you and your sisters for Thanksgiving again," Drew said. "I enjoyed myself last year and would like to do it again."

Willie chuckled. "I thought that the only reason you joined us last year was because of some family drama," he said. "Did you piss off your parents again?"

Drew chuckled. "No, I didn't piss them off again," he said. "I'm back on speaking terms with them." He cleared his throat. "They've already made plans to celebrate Thanksgiving with my mother's family, and I would rather spend Thanksgiving with you and your sisters than with my mother's family."

"Okay, I understand why you would want to spend Thanksgiving with us instead of your mother's family," Willie said. *I don't know how Billie or Nina feels about Drew joining us again for Thanksgiving.* He shook his head. *It doesn't matter because we're having it at my apartment, so I have a say in who's coming, not them.*

"So, will I join you and your sisters, Willie?"

Willie smiled. "Yeah, you sure are," he said. He shook his head and chuckled. "This is the first time you've called me and haven't asked me about Billie." *Of course, now that I've mentioned her name, he'll ask me about her.*

Drew chuckled. "Well, since you brought her up first, how's Billie doing?"

Willie shook his head and chuckled. "Can we not have one conversation without you bringing her up?" *Why did I mention her?*

Drew laughed. "You were the one who brought her up, not me," he said. "Anyway, are you going to answer my question, Willie?"

Willie sighed. "Well, I can only tell you the little I know," he said. "I've heard that Billie has two part-time jobs." *One of them is at a bookstore, which isn't surprising since Billie has been an avid reader her whole life, ever since she learned how to read. I also think the other part-time job is at a bar, although I don't know which one. If I had to guess, I'd say it was Capote's, since she loves going there.*

Drew chuckled. "Yeah, I know about her two part-time jobs," he said. "Well, I'll see you on Thanksgiving."

***

Nina didn't hear from Willie until the Halloween before Thanksgiving. She was having a Halloween party on her dorm floor when he called her.

Nina heard her phone ringing and went to her dorm room. She went to her phone and picked it up. "Happy Halloween," she said. "Who's calling?"

"It's me, your older brother."

Nina smiled and chuckled. "Oh, hi, Willie," she said. "And why are you calling me now, after not seeing or talking to me in almost a year?" *I won't let him get away with not calling or seeing me for almost a year.*

Willie sighed. "Yeah, I'm sorry about that," he said. "Listen, Thanksgiving is coming up, and you know that our mother would want us to celebrate it together."

Nina chuckled. "Yeah, I'm sure she's mentioned that to me once or twice," she said. "Is Billie going to be there?" *I recall that the last time, Willie wasn't sure if Billie would show up.*

Willie chuckled. "Yeah, Billie will be there," he said. He cleared his throat. "And my friend Drew will also be there."

Nina shook her head. "You invited him to join us again?" *I'm unsure how to feel about Willie's friend joining us and celebrating Thanksgiving.* "Why did you invite him to join us again, Willie?"

"Well, I didn't invite him again," Willie said. He chuckled. "Drew asked me if he could have Thanksgiving with us again. I know Billie seemed to like him, so I said yes." He cleared his throat. "Do you have a problem with him joining us, Nina?"

Nina sighed. "No, I don't," she said. *I'm not sure how I feel about Willie's friend joining us again and celebrating Thanksgiving with us.* She shook her head. *It doesn't matter that Willie's friend will be with us. I'm not looking forward to seeing him again, but Billie.* She cleared her throat. "I've got to get back to my party, Willie."

Willie chuckled. "Okay, I'll let you go," he said. "I'll see you in a few weeks, on Thanksgiving."

"Yeah, same here," Nina said. "Goodbye, Willie." *I wish I could say more to him, my older brother. I want to be closer to him and Billie as well. But so far, that hasn't happened.*

***

Drew waited a week before saying anything to Billie, which was also a week after he had spoken to Willie.

"Hey, Billie," Drew said. "How are you doing? Do you like working here?"

Billie's smile was warm as she responded, "I'm doing fine, Drew. And yes, I like working here." She chuckled softly. "I was wondering when you would talk to me."

Drew chuckled. "I didn't want to bother you," he said. He cleared his throat. "So, I'll celebrate Thanksgiving at Willie's apartment again." *Now, I'll find out how Billie feels about it.*

Billie nodded. "I'm not surprised," she said. She smiled. "You seem to enjoy hanging out with us."

"I enjoyed hanging out with you," Drew said. He frowned and scratched his chin. "Something kind of odd happened the other day." *I've been trying to think of why Sadie, one of the bar's regular customers, would ask me to fire Billie.*

"Oh, yeah, Drew?" Billie leaned back against the bar railing. "What happened?"

"One of our regulars asked me to fire you," Drew said. "I don't understand why she wanted me to do that. I didn't ask her." He shook his head, his concern growing. "Especially when I've seen you with her friend."

Billie sighed. "Okay, I'm going to take a wild guess and say that it was Sadie who came to you and asked you to fire me," she said. She shook her head. "First, she tries to get Iris to end her friendship with me, and then she tries to get me fired from the bookstore."

Drew chuckled. "I don't think Sadie likes you, Billie," he said. He grinned. "But Iris Mathews and Rebecca Dubois do seem to like you."

Billie nodded. "Yeah, they've become my friends," she said. She shrugged her shoulders. "I don't know why Sadie doesn't like me either."

Willie cleared his throat. "So, I've read a few of Iris's articles," he said. "I enjoyed them." *I did notice that most of the time, Iris wrote about issues facing gay people. I didn't have a problem with gay people, men or women. I also didn't care that Billie seemed to be that way. I had to get to know her better. I'm willing to accept if she won't go out with me because she isn't into men.*

Billie nodded and smiled. "Iris is a good journalist," she said. She shook her head. "Well, I'd better get back to work."

***

A few weeks later, it was Thanksgiving.

Drew left his apartment and was about to lock his front door when his phone rang. He sighed and shook his head. *I had better find out who was calling me.*

Drew went back into his apartment and reached for his phone. He picked it up. "Hello?"

"Hey, it's me."

Drew chuckled. "Hey, Willie," he said. "I was about to be on my way there." He frowned. "What's up? Do you need something?" *I hope everything is okay.*

Willie chuckled. "I just wanted to see if you were still coming over," he said. "I mean, I'm sure Billie's coming, so I thought I would just call you and make sure you were still coming."

Drew nodded. "Yeah, I'm still coming," he said. "Anyway, I'll be over there soon." *I don't think Willie's telling me the truth. I think he called me because he might have changed his mind about me celebrating Thanksgiving with him and his sisters.*

Drew hung up his phone and left his apartment. He got in his car. He drove away from his apartment building and drove to Willie's apartment.

***

Drew arrived at Willie's apartment a few minutes later. He parked his car near the front entrance and got out. He glanced at his watch. *I'm not ready to go in.* He took out a cigarette, lit it, and sat on the steps in front of the apartment building.

***

Billie arrived a few minutes later. She parked her car and got out.

Drew stood up and waved at her. "Hey, Billie," he said. He glanced at his watch and chuckled. "You're right on time." *No matter how she's dressed, Billie somehow manages to look gorgeous.*

Billie nodded and chuckled. "I've been getting better at arriving on time," she said. She pointed at the front door. "Have you been here long?"

Drew shook his head and held up his cigarette. "I wanted a quick smoke before I went in," he said. "I'm almost done with it." He took one last drag off his cigarette and threw it down. "Let's go, Billie."

***

Willie knew that Nina hadn't enjoyed doing most of the cooking, like she had done the previous year, so he decided to get most of the food from his favorite restaurant, Suzie's Soul Food.

The food arrived about an hour before anyone showed up. Willie was removing the food from the bags when Billie and Drew walked into his apartment.

Willie chuckled and shook his head. "Did y'all come togeth-er?" *Will they tell me the truth, or will they lie to me?*

Billie shook her head and grinned. "No, we didn't," she said. She looked over at Drew. "We ran into each other outside your apartment building."

Willie gave Billie a disbelieving look. "If you say so," he said. *Oh, yeah, I need to talk to Billie.* He pointed at the food. "As you can see, Nina didn't cook the food like she did last year, and I had to order our food from my favorite restaurant."

Billie shook her head. "You ordered our food for Thanksgiv-ing from your favorite restaurant?" She looked over at Drew and grinned. "Our mother didn't teach him how to cook."

Willie chuckled. "She taught me enough to cook my own meals," he said. He shook his head and grinned. "But she didn't teach me how to cook anything related to Thanksgiving."

Billie chuckled and nodded. "I'm not surprised," she said. She looked over at Drew and grinned. "He was our mother's baby boy, so she spoiled him."

Willie sighed. "No, she didn't," he said. "I was the oldest, remember? Nina was the only one who was spoiled." *Okay, enough small talk.* He cleared his throat. "Nina's on her way here, and we'll eat when she gets here."

"Okay," Drew said. He pointed to the small living room. "Let's wait for her in there."

Willie reached out and grabbed Billie's arm. "Hold on a minute," he said. He looked over at Drew. "You can wait in there, but I've got to talk to Billie." *I know Drew isn't going to like it, but I have to talk to her alone.*

"Okay," Billie said. She looked over at Drew and smiled. "Go ahead to the living room, Drew. Nina should be here any minute now."

Drew nodded and smiled. "Okay," he said. He turned around and left the kitchen, going to the living room, where he sat on the couch.

Billie turned to look over at Willie. "Let's go, Willie," she said.

***

Willie left the kitchen and walked down the hallway to his bedroom, with Billie following him. They entered his bedroom, and while Billie sat on his bed, Willie sat at his desk.

Billie took out a cigarette and lit it. "So, what's going on, Willie?" She took a drag off her cigarette. "What do you want to talk to me about?"

Willie shook his head and sighed. "I talk to our mother over the phone every two weeks, and she always asks me about you."

Billie frowned. "And what do you tell her, Willie?"

Willie shrugged his shoulders. "I don't tell her much because I don't know much about your life here or what you're up to, Billie," he said. "I'm not going to lie to our mother, Billie, though it would make talking to her about you easier." *I don't know why our mother seems more concerned about Billie than me or Nina.*

"Okay," Billie said. She sighed. "I'll try to talk to her more."

***

Nina left her dorm room. Most of her dorm mates had gone home for Thanksgiving, and Nina felt slightly unnerved by how empty and quiet the dorm building was. Its hallways, usually filled with her fellow students, were empty and abandoned.

Nina made a quick stop on her way from her dorm building to Willie's apartment. He had asked her to pick up a few things and had given her money. Lucky for Nina, the liquor store near Willie's apartment was open, and she could buy a bottle of whiskey, vodka, and three packs of cigarettes. She had to use her fake ID to buy the whiskey and the vodka, which made her nervous.

***

Nina arrived at Willie's apartment some twenty minutes later, and the first thing she saw after she parked her car was Billie's car, parked next to Willie's car.

Nina smiled. *Good, Billie's here. It won't be like last year, when we didn't know if Billie would show up.* She exited her car, retrieved the items she had bought at the liquor store, and entered the apartment building.

A few minutes later, Nina entered Willie's apartment. She ran into Drew in the kitchen.

"Hey, Drew," Nina said. "Willie said you'd be joining us again."

Drew nodded and pointed over his shoulder. "They're in his bedroom," he said. "They've been in there for the last ten minutes."

Nina nodded and walked down the hallway to Willie's bedroom. She opened the door and walked in without knocking. She went over to Billie and hugged her.

***

Drew's relationship with Billie changed after Thanksgiving, the second one they had celebrated together, along with Willie and Nina.

Before they parted ways, standing outside Willie's apartment building, Drew worked up his nerve and cleared his throat.

Billie smiled. "Do you want to tell me something, Drew?"

Drew grinned and nodded. "I do," he said. He reached into his shirt pocket and pulled out a small piece of paper. "I'd like you to call me sometime." He handed the paper to Billie. "That's my phone number."

Billie folded paper and stuck it underneath her bra. "I might call you, Drew," she said. She grinned. "Would you like to have my phone number?"

Drew nodded. "I would, Billie," he said. *It's a good sign that Billie's willing to give me her phone number. I don't know much about women, but I do know that if a woman willingly gives you her phone number without you asking for it, that means she likes you.*

Billie smiled and handed Drew a business card. He looked at it and chuckled. "Why do you have a business card, Billie?"

Billie cocked her head to one side and gave Drew an amused look. "I'm a professional writer, Drew," she said. She grinned. "I could show you some of my short stories."

Drew grinned back at Billie. "I would love to read them," he said. "Is your home number on here?" *I'm starting to grow on Billie. She's dropping her guard and getting comfortable with me. I won't mess this up by trying to get her into bed.*

Billie nodded. "I don't have an office, so the phone number on it is my home number," she said. She cleared her throat. "Anyway, I'd better get going."

"Okay," Drew said. He smiled at Billie. "I'll talk to you again soon." *I'll wait a few days before I call her. I don't want to come off as too eager.*

Chapter Seventeen

I t dawned on Bridget a few days later that Billie was too self-assured in her sexuality for Bridget to disrupt her equilibrium with any of her schemes.

Billie's maturity was a revelation to Bridget, and she couldn't help but feel a twinge of envy. Yet, this envy was overshadowed by a growing admiration for Billie. She yearned to delve deeper into Billie's life and understand the woman who had captivated her.

Bridget dedicated the next four months to relentlessly uncovering every detail about Billie's life. Her determination was unwavering, and she discovered that very few, if any, people knew anything about Billie's life before she arrived in Boston, except that she hailed from New Orleans and was a graduate of Tulane University.

***

Bridget set out to find everything she could about Billie's life in Boston. She realized that she only knew two people who also knew Billie: Rebecca and Jasmine. She approached Rebecca first, counting on their complicated and somewhat untrustworthy relationship, which held potential for valuable information. They met in the ladies' room at the country club.

Rebecca walked into the ladies' room. She nodded at Bridget. "You got any powder?"

Bridget nodded and pulled out a small baggie. "How much do you want?" *How do I begin this conversation?* She shook her head and cleared her throat. "So, have you seen or talked to Billie today?"

Rebecca shook her head. "I heard about what you did on the Fourth," she said. "Are you hatching a new plan to break up Billie and Georgia?"

Bridget shook her head. "I've given up on that," she said. She sighed. "I'm just curious about Billie. I want to know more about her." *I don't think Rebecca's going to help me. She doesn't trust me.*

Rebecca grinned. "Well, I'm not going to tell you anything about Billie," she said. She handed Bridget a handful of bills. "I'll take my usual."

***

Bridget approached Jasmine next, hoping that Jasmine would be more helpful than Rebecca had been. Bridget ran into Jasmine the week after Labor Day at the country club.

"Hey, Jasmine," Bridget said. "I haven't seen you in months." *Okay, Jasmine. Maybe you know something, anything, about Billie that I don't already know.*

Jasmine shrugged her shoulders. "I've been here or home," she said. She frowned. "Rebecca said that you've been asking about Billie. Why's that, Bridget?"

Bridget sighed. "I know it seems suspicious, me asking about Billie, but I'm just curious about her," she said. "I'm not plotting anything against her." *My reputation is worse than I thought it was.*

Jasmine chuckled. "I don't know why, but I believe you," she said. She shrugged her shoulders. "I can only tell you what I know about her."

Bridget smiled. "I just want to know about her life here," she said. "What does Billie do when she's not here?" *I can't escape the feeling that I've never known anyone like Billie.*

Jasmine nodded. "Well, Billie has two part-time jobs," she said. "She works part-time at a bookstore and has a waitress job at Jackson's Jukebox."

Bridget nodded. "Thanks, Jasmine," she said. *Jasmine proved to be more helpful than Rebecca.* "Anything else you can tell me?" *Wait a minute. I thought Jasmine was trying to get Billie kicked out of the country club.* "Are you still trying to get Billie kicked out of the country club?"

Jasmine shook her head and grinned. "No, I gave up on that, Bridget," she said. "I believe that when Billie isn't with Georgia, she's hanging out with Rebecca or some white woman named Iris Mathews."

***

Bridget started going to Jackson's Jukebox, where Billie worked part-time as a waitress. She always made sure to sit out of sight at the bar. The more Bridget watched Billie and learned about Billie's life in Boston, the more she found herself beginning to like Billie. This growing fondness was a mix of admiration and a hint of something more, something she couldn't quite put her finger on.

***

Bridget also went by the bookstore where Billie worked part-time. She went to the young black woman at the cash register. "Hi, I'm Bridget," she said. "Is the owner here? I want to talk to him."

"I'm Sadie," the young black woman said. "Yeah, the owner's here. If you wait right here, I'll get him for you."

"Hey, before you go, can I ask you something?" *Billie's popular at Jackson's Jukebox, so I'm sure she's made friends here, too.*

Sadie chuckled. "Okay," she said. "Go ahead and ask me."

"You work with a woman named Billie Carver, right?" *So far, I haven't met anyone who didn't have a high opinion of Billie. Will this Sadie be the first?*

Sadie nodded. "I do," she said. "What do you want to know about her?"

So, I'm not the first person to come around and ask about Billie. "What do you think of her?" Bridget cleared her throat. "I mean, is she a good co-worker?"

Sadie nodded. "Mr. Armstrong, the owner, thinks so," she said. She chuckled and shook her head. "I'm puzzled and intrigued by Billie."

Bridget nodded. "I know what you mean, Sadie," she said. "You can get the owner, Mr. Armstrong, now."

Bridget talked to the owner, Mr. Armstrong, for about fifteen minutes, and he had only positive things to say about Billie.

Bridget left the bookstore, satisfied with what she had learned about Billie from the bookstore owner and Billie's co-worker, Sadie.

***

Before Bridget knew it, it was Thanksgiving, which turned into a disaster.

"So, are you dating anyone, Bridget?"

Bridget sighed and shook her head. *My mother knows better than to ask me about my personal life, but my grandmother doesn't.* "No, I'm not dating anyone right now," she said. "I'm trying to enjoy being single."

Her grandmother shook her head and sighed. "I just don't understand how a pretty girl like you doesn't have a boyfriend," she said. She looked over at her daughter, Bridget's mother. "I told you not to send her to an all-girls private school."

Bridget sighed. *I'm so tired of hearing my grandmother complain to my mother that I don't have a boyfriend.* "The reason why I don't have a boyfriend isn't because I went to an all-girls private school, Grandmother," she said. *I can't believe that I'm about to say.* "The reason why I don't have a boyfriend is because I'm not straight, and I've always preferred other girls over guys." She stood up and left the dining room.

***

Bridget returned to the bookstore the next day, hoping to talk to Billie. She had to express her sincere apology to Billie for kissing Georgia.

Bridget sighed and shook her head. *Thanksgiving was yesterday, so the bookstore may not be open. I don't want to wait another day to talk to Billie. It's going to be hard enough for me to try to explain to her why I kissed her girlfriend. I can't claim ignorance since I knew Georgia was Billie's girlfriend.*

Most of the shops and stores Bridget drove by were closed, their parking lots empty, and all the lights were off.

Please be open. Bridget shook her head, trying to fight the uneasiness that was starting to overwhelm her.

***

Bridget arrived at the bookstore, and to her relief, it was open. She parked her car near the front entrance. *Okay, now here comes the hard part.* She chuckled and shook her head. *You survived your conversation with your mother yesterday, so you can go in there and talk to Billie.*

Bridget took out a cigarette and lit it. She took a drag off her cigarette and got out of her car. She walked over to the front entrance. *I have no idea what I'm going to say to Billie. The last time I saw or talked to her, I had just kissed her girlfriend.*

"I knew you would be back."

Bridget turned around to face the somewhat familiar voice. "Oh, hi, Sadie," she said. She chuckled and grinned. "Yeah, I'm back." She took a drag off her cigarette. *Billie may not be here, so I should ask Sadie about her.* "Is Billie here?"

Sadie chuckled and nodded. "Yeah, she's here," she said. She took out a cigarette and lit it. "So, you've worked up the nerve to talk to her, Bridget?"

Bridget frowned. *Did I tell her my name?* She clicked her tongue. *Of course, I told her my name.* "Yeah, I guess you could say that," she said. "Is Billie your friend?"

Sadie shook her head. "I wouldn't say I'm friends with Billie," she said. She sighed and took a drag off her cigarette. "Billie's friends with my best friend, Iris."

Bridget nodded. "I know about Billie's friends," she said. "Do you want to be friends with Billie?" *Why am I talking to Sadie? I should be inside, talking to Billie.*

Sadie chuckled. "Do you want to be friends with Billie?" She took one last drag off her cigarette and tossed it on the ground. "If you do, you might want to apologize to her for kissing her girlfriend, Georgia."

Bridget sighed. "You heard about that?" *I didn't think anyone knew about my kissing Georgia besides Billie.*

Sadie nodded. "Yeah, I did," she said. She pointed over her shoulder. "You've got a chance that Billie might forgive you if you're sincere with her."

Bridget frowned and shook her head. "Why do you think that I want Billie to forgive me?" She shrugged her shoulders. "Maybe I deserve Billie being mad at me."

Sadie smiled. "If you thought that, Bridget, you wouldn't be here," she said. She playfully punched Bridget's arm. "Good luck with talking to Billie." She turned to her left and walked away.

***

Bridget finished her cigarette, taking one last drag off it. She pushed the front door open and stepped inside the bookstore. She walked past the cash register, looking around for Billie.

Now, where in the world is she? Bridget frowned. *Did Sadie lie to me?* She sighed and shook her head. *I don't think she was lying to me. So, Billie's here, somewhere.*

Bridget walked around the bookstore, looking for Billie. She ran into Billie near the magazine rack, which Billie was stocking with new magazines.

Oh, shit, there she is. Bridget took a deep breath and walked over to Billie. "Hey, Billie," she said. "How have you been?" *It's not the best way to start what's going to be a tense conversation, but it's better than nothing.*

Billie looked over at Bridget and chuckled. "I was wondering when you would muster up the courage to say something to me," she said. "So, I guess you've had enough of watching me here and at Jackson's Jukebox."

Bridget sighed and shook her head. "I thought you didn't know I was watching you," she said. "I'd like to talk to you, Billie." *Okay, so how's she going to react? Will she talk to me, or will she tell me to go to hell?*

Billie tilted her head to her left and gave Bridget a disbelieving smile. "What do you want to talk about with me, Bridget?"

Okay, Billie hasn't rejected the idea of talking to me yet. "I'd rather have this conversation somewhere more private," Bridget said. "Is there somewhere we can talk in private?" *I'd rather not have to apologize to Billie in public.*

Billie carefully looked over at Bridget and then nodded. "Yeah, I know somewhere we can talk privately," she said. She pointed towards the back of the store. "The owner's office is that way, and he's not here right now, so we can talk in his office."

Bridget nodded. *I won't mention that I know where his office is since I spoke with him about Billie not too long ago.* "Well, let's go," she said. "You'll have to show me the way."

Billie chuckled and shook her head. "Oh, you know where it is, Bridget," she said. "Mr. Armstrong told me about your visit with him."

Bridget sighed. *Of course, he told her about us talking.* "I promise I'll explain why I've been watching you," she said. *I'm unsure how to explain why I've been watching her. I haven't thought about it.* She cleared her throat. "I'm ready if you are, Billie."

Billie nodded. "Okay, let's do this," she said.

Bridget followed Billie to the owner's office and stood by the door while Billie sat behind the owner's desk.

Bridget pointed over her shoulder towards the front of the bookstore. "Do you need to keep an eye on the front door?" *Where's the owner, Mr. Armstrong? Will he be mad if he returns and we're in his office?*

Billie shook her head. "It's been a slow day," she said. She shrugged her shoulders. "I don't know why we're open since all the other shops and stores are closed." She smiled. "The front door has a bell on it, so if anyone comes into the store, we'll know."

Bridget nodded. "Well, that's good," she said. She cleared her throat. "I'm sorry for what I did, Billie." *I can do better than that.*

Billie took out a cigarette and lit it. "Why don't you sit down, Bridget?"

Bridget patted her pockets and sighed. *I left my pack in my car.* "Can I get a smoke from you, Billie? I left mine in my car," she said. *This is going to be the hardest conversation I've ever had.* She sighed. *If you can tell your grandmother and mother the truth about your sexuality, then you can apologize to Billie.*

Billie pointed at the empty chair in front of the owner's desk. "You sit there, and I'll give you a cigarette," she said. She took a drag off her cigarette. "You're the one who wanted to talk, Bridget, not me."

She's right. Bridget sat down in the chair and held out her hand. "Okay, I sat down like you asked me to," she said. "Can I have a cigarette now?" *Watch the tone of your voice. Try not to get an attitude with Billie. You're not here to get into a fight with her or make her mad. You're here to apologize to her.*

Billie nodded. "Sure, you can," she said. She stood up, leaned over the desk, and handed a cigarette to Bridget. "Do you need a light, too?"

Bridget chuckled. "I'm afraid I do," she said. "My lighter is with my pack." *Okay, Billie's showing me that she's in control here.*

Billie grinned and chuckled. "I thought so," she said. "You'll have to stand up and get a little closer if you want me to light your cigarette."

Bridget nodded. She stood up and leaned across the desk.

Billie lit Bridget's cigarette and sat back down.

Bridget took a drag off her cigarette. "I want to apologize to you, Billie, for kissing your girlfriend on the Fourth," she said. "I shouldn't have done it, and I was wrong for doing it. It wasn't decent or polite to either you or Georgia." *I hope Billie accepts my apology because I don't know what to do if she doesn't.* "I hope you're still not mad at me for kissing Georgia."

Billie chuckled. "I'm not mad at you, Bridget," she said. "I wasn't mad at you when you did it."

Bridget frowned. "I don't understand," she said. "You know, or you should know, that I did it because I wanted to break you and Georgia up." *I still can't understand her.*

Billie nodded. "Yeah, I figured that out," she said. She shrugged her shoulders. "I don't know why you wanted to break up Georgia and me." She took a drag off her cigarette. "I could ask you, but I have another question for you."

"Okay," Bridget said. She took a drag off her cigarette. *I do not know what Billie will ask me, but I'm ready to be honest with her.* She sighed. *I'm so tired of lying, not just to other people, but most of all, I'm tired of lying to myself.* "You can ask me anything you want to, Billie."

Billie smiled, which made Bridget nervous. "Okay," she said. "I'm going to ask you an easy question, Bridget." She took a drag off her cigarette. "Why were you hanging out at the bar and here, not saying anything but watching me instead?"

Bridget chuckled. "I wouldn't call it an easy question," she said. She sighed. *I promised her I would be honest with her, so I will keep that promise.* "After I failed to break up you and Georgia, I decided I needed to know more about you."

Billie nodded. "Okay, I can understand why you would feel that way," she said. She grinned. "And I'll be honest with you, Bridget. You couldn't break up Georgia and me because our relationship isn't serious." She sighed and shook her head. "Well, I don't think it's serious."

Bridget nodded. *I know what Billie's saying. She might not think it's serious, but Georgia might.* "I hope you don't break her heart, Billie," she said. "Georgia's a good girl, and she doesn't deserve to get hurt."

Billie nodded. "I know," she said. She took a drag off her cigarette. "So, how was your Thanksgiving, Bridget?"

Bridget shook her head. "My grandmother kept asking me why I didn't have a boyfriend," she said. "And I told her the truth about my sexuality." She sighed. "My family didn't take it well at all."

Billie nodded. "Why did you do it?"

Bridget shrugged her shoulders. "I'm not sure," she said. "I think I was tired of lying to others and myself about who I am." She smiled. "I admire you, Billie, for living your life openly and honestly."

Chapter Eighteen

S adie suspended her campaign against Billie, realizing that whether she liked it or not, Billie had become an integral part of her world.

Later that night, Sadie had a long, heartfelt conversation with Iris about Billie.

When Iris returned to their apartment, she found Sadie waiting for her in the kitchen, sitting at the kitchen table, sipping coffee and smoking a cigarette.

Iris chuckled. "I didn't think I would see you again today," she said. She glanced at her watch and shook her head. "It's well past midnight."

Sadie nodded and grinned. "I know what time it is, Iris," she said. She sipped her coffee. "How was your night? Did you have fun with Rebecca and Billie?" *I would guess that she did have fun with them. I'm asking her about it only to tell her what I've been up to regarding Billie. It's time for me to tell Iris the truth.*

Iris grinned. "I had a blast with them," she said. She sat down at the kitchen table across from Sadie. "How was your night? What were you up to while I was hanging out with Rebecca and Billie?"

Sadie sighed and shook her head. *I know that tone of voice. Iris isn't happy with me, and I'm sure I understand why.* "I think you know what I was up to tonight," she said. She sipped her coffee and took a drag off her cigarette. "I'm guessing Billie told you about my conversation with her." *I shouldn't be surprised that Billie told Iris.*

Iris nodded. "She did," she said. She sighed and shook her head. "So, after you talked to me, asking me to end my friendship with Billie, you went on to try to get her fired from the bookstore and the bar?"

Well, I can't lie to her. Sadie nodded. "I did," she said. She shook her head. "I failed at getting her fired from the bookstore and the bar." She reached across the kitchen table and took one of Iris's hands. "I'm sorry, Iris."

Iris nodded. "I believe you, Sadie," she said. "And I think Billie forgives you, too."

Hearing that Billie forgives me for what I did makes me feel better, but I don't know why. Sadie nodded. "I'm glad to hear that," she said. She sipped her coffee. "I know I haven't been willing to listen to you about Billie before, but I'm ready now."

Iris frowned. "What do you mean, Sadie?"

"Tell me about her," Sadie said. "I want to understand why you're friends with her." *For the first time, I'm willing to listen to Iris's opinion about Billie. I realize that I had the wrong impression about Billie, and if Iris liked her, then Billie couldn't be the woman I thought she was.*

Iris shook her head and grinned. "You might know more about Billie than I do," she said. She shrugged her shoulders. "We met her at the same time, so I'm not sure why you aren't friends with her."

Sadie shrugged her shoulders. "I know we did," she said. "For some reason, Billie made a better impression on you than she did on me." She held up her hand to stop Iris from asking her why she didn't like Billie. "And before you ask, I don't know why I didn't like Billie."

Iris nodded. "Well, maybe you should find out," she said. She stood up. "It's late, and I'm going to bed now."

"Okay," Sadie said. "Good night, Iris." *She's right. I should find out why I didn't like Billie. Maybe then I'll understand why Iris is friends with her.*

***

Sadie spent the next three months reflecting on her feelings about Billie and observing Iris's friendship with Billie.

Iris would always invite Sadie to join her and Billie whenever Iris went out with Billie. The first time this happened was about a week after Sadie had failed to get Billie fired from the bookstore and the bar.

Iris poked her head into Sadie's bedroom. "Hey, I'm about to go out," she said. "I'm meeting Billie and Rebecca for drinks."

Sadie looked up from her book and smiled. "Okay," she said. "I hope y'all have a good time." *I'm sure Iris wants me to come with her, but I'm not ready to hang out with Billie.*

"Why don't you come with me?" Iris walked over to Sadie's bed and sat next to Sadie. "I'm sure you would love hanging out with Billie and Rebecca."

Sadie shook her head. "I'm sorry, but no," she said. She sighed and shook her head. "I don't dislike her anymore, but I'm not ready to become friends yet."

Iris nodded and left Sadie's bedroom. She would invite Sadie to join her whenever she went out with Rebecca and Billie. Sadie would decline because she wasn't ready to become Billie's friend or hang out with her.

Sadie knew she had to understand why she initially disliked Billie without bothering to talk to her. After much thought, she realized she had more in common with Billie than she had initially thought. She tried to see what Iris saw in Billie.

It was Iris who helped Sadie find common ground with Billie.

***

A few days after New Year's Day, Iris approached Sadie. "Hey, can I talk to you?"

Sadie nodded, closed her book, and gestured for Iris to enter her bedroom. "Sure," she said. "What's on your mind, Iris?" *I have no idea what Iris is going to tell me. We went out for New Year's Eve, and I thought we had a good time.*

"I realized something earlier," Iris said. She smiled. "You asked me a few months ago why I liked Billie and became friends with her."

Sadie nodded. "Yeah, I remember asking you that," she said. *One thing I've always admired about Iris is that she questions herself and is willing to change her mind.* "Have you figured out why you like Billie?"

Iris nodded. "I have, Sadie," she said. "One of the reasons why I became friends with Billie was that she reminded me of you in many ways."

Sadie chuckled. *If Iris had told me that before I failed at getting Billie fired from the bookstore and the bar, I wouldn't have listened, agreed with, or believed Iris.* "How does Billie remind you of me, Iris? I mean, besides that, we're both young black women from the South and are lesbians." *I know I have more in common with Billie than just those two facts, but I'm curious to hear more from Iris.*

Iris chuckled and shook her head. "Yeah, besides that," she said. "Now, I'm not sure this is going to make sense, but I realized a long time ago that one of the reasons why some people don't like you is because you remind them of something they don't like about themselves."

Sadie chuckled and grinned. "You're right, Iris," she said. "What you just said to me doesn't make any sense." *I've always known some people don't like me, but I've never worried about it, not caring what others, besides Iris, feel about me.*

Iris sighed. "Well, I'm sure you'll understand after you've thought about it," she said. She turned around and left Sadie's bedroom.

Sadie decided that it was worth getting to know Billie better. She also realized why she hadn't liked Billie at first. What Iris had said to her made sense, and she realized that Billie reminded her that she wasn't comfortable with either her sexuality or her black heritage.

***

Sadie went to Iris a few days later. She knocked on the open door of Iris's bedroom. "Hey, Iris," she said. "I'm sorry to bother you, but I need you to do me a favor." *I doubt she'll say no to what I'm about to ask her.*

Iris turned around in her chair and grinned at Sadie. "Did you figure out what I tried to tell you the other day?"

Sadie nodded. "I did, Iris, but that's not what I wanted to tell you," she said. *I'll tell her what I figured out another time.* "Could you arrange a meeting between me and Billie?"

Iris smiled. "I'm so happy you asked me that," she said. "Of course, I'll arrange a meeting between you and Billie."

I knew she would do it. "Good," Sadie said. "Billie can decide when and where we meet." *I'm counting on Iris to convince Billie to meet with me. I'm not sure Billie would say yes if I asked her.*

"Do you want me to be there with you, Sadie?"

Sadie shook her head. "No, I need to talk to Billie alone," she said.

***

Iris was able to convince Billie to meet with Sadie. She approached Sadie with the news a few days later.

"Hey, Sadie," Iris said, standing outside Sadie's bedroom in the hallway. "I talked to Billie, and she said she'll meet you at Jackson's Jukebox next week, on the 20th."

Sadie nodded and chuckled. "Okay," she said. *So, Billie agreed to meet me at my favorite bar, where she also works. Is she hoping to gain an advantage by meeting me there?* "You can tell her that I'll be there."

Iris nodded. "Okay, I will," she said. She walked over to Sadie and sat next to her on Sadie's bed. "Are you sure you don't want me to be there?"

Sadie nodded. "Yeah, I'm sure," she said. She reached out and grabbed one of Iris's hands. "I appreciate your offer, but I need to talk to Billie alone." *The conversation I'm going to have with Billie isn't going to be an easy one because I want it to be an honest one, and I don't think it will be if Iris is also there.*

***

Sadie arrived early at Jackson's Jukebox. She sat down in a booth within sight of the front entrance. She took out a cigarette and lit it after glancing at her watch. *Iris said Billie would be here at seven, and I'm ten minutes early.*

A waitress walked by, and Sadie got her attention by holding up her right hand and waving it.

"Hey, Sadie," the waitress said. "What can I get you?"

"I'll have a whiskey soda," Sadie said, her voice betraying her nerves. *I have to remember not to drink too much. I'm nervous and need a drink to settle my nerves, but I also don't want to get drunk.* "And can I also get a vodka tonic? Someone will join me soon, and I'd like to buy her a drink." *Buying Billie a drink is a good olive branch.*

"Okay," the waitress said, nodding. "Do you want me to wait until Billie gets here to bring her drink, or do you want it now?"

Sadie chuckled. *Of course, Billie told her co-workers about meeting me here.* "Let's wait until she gets here," she said.

The waitress chuckled and nodded. "Okay," she said. "I'll be right back with your drink, Sadie." She turned around and walked away.

Sadie took out her notebook and reviewed the questions she wanted to ask Billie. She shook her head and chuckled. *I'm not good at making new friends. Will she even want to be friends after this?*

***

The waitress returned a few minutes later with Sadie's drink. "Here you go, Sadie," she said, handing Sadie her drink. "Do you want to pay for it now, or would you like to start a tab?"

That's an easy question. "I'll start a tab," Sadie said. *It's easier than paying for drinks each time I order a new one.* "And put Billie's drink on my bill." *I'll buy her first drink, but that's it. After that, she can buy her own drinks.*

The waitress nodded and grinned. "Okay," she said. "Tell me when Billie arrives, and I'll bring her a drink."

Sadie took out a cigarette and lit it. She sipped her whiskey and went over her questions for Billie. *I hope Billie's willing to answer my questions. Iris said Billie doesn't talk about herself, but never hesitates to answer any question. She's both guarded and honest at the same time.*

***

Sadie had finished her whiskey and cigarette when Billie walked into the bar.

Sadie sat up straight and waved at Billie. "I'm over here, Billie," she said, standing up.

Billie nodded and walked over to the booth. She sat down across from Sadie. "I'll admit I was surprised when Iris told me you wanted to meet with me," she said. She took out a cigarette and lit it while giving Sadie a questioning look. "I never thought you would want to talk to me."

Sadie sighed and nodded. "I'm glad Iris was able to convince you to meet with me," she said. "I know we didn't get off on the right foot." *And that's my fault. I didn't even try to get to know her. Instead, I decided, without talking to her, that I didn't like her, even though I could tell that Iris did like her.* She cleared her throat. "Thank you for agreeing to meet with me." *I could ask her why she agreed, but I'm sure she'll tell me, even without me asking her.*

"You're welcome, Sadie," Billie said. "The only reason I agreed to meet and talk to you was because I know you're friends with Iris, who I adore."

The waitress approached them before Sadie could say anything and handed Billie a vodka tonic. "Here you go, Billie," she said. She then grinned and shook her head. "I just don't understand why you come here even when you have the night off."

Billie chuckled and smiled back at her. "Well, this bar reminds me of some of the bars I used to drink at back home in New Orleans," she said. "Thanks for the vodka tonic. How much do I owe you?"

The waitress shook her head. "You don't owe me anything, Billie," she said. She then pointed at Sadie. "She bought your drink."

Billie raised her drink up and nodded at Sadie. "Thanks for the drink, Sadie," she said. She turned her attention back to the waitress. "I don't know how long we'll be here, but I'd like to start a tab."

The waitress nodded. "Okay," she said. She smiled. "Well, if you need me, I'll return in a few minutes."

Billie nodded and smiled. "Okay," she said. She sipped her vodka tonic and waited until the waitress had walked away before she said anything to Sadie. "So, where were we?"

"You said the only reason you agreed to meet with me was because you knew I'm friends with Iris," Sadie said. *I know what she said is true.* "When we met, I'm afraid I misjudged you and decided I didn't like you."

Billie nodded. "Yeah, I got the feeling you weren't impressed by me," she said. She leaned towards Sadie, frowning. "Can you tell me why you tried to get me fired from the bookstore and this place?"

"Okay," Sadie said. She sighed and shook her head. *This won't be easy.* "I also tried to end your friendship with Iris." *We might as well put everything on the table and discuss everything I've tried to do.*

Billie shook her head. "I didn't forget that, Sadie," she said. "We'll talk about that too, but first, I'd like to know why you tried to get me fired from the bookstore and this place."

Sadie sighed and nodded. "I wanted to remove you from my life, Billie," she said. "In a short time, you became friends with Iris, my best friend, and started working at the same bookstore I did and at my favorite bar, this place." *Billie was a comet in my life, lighting and shaking it up.*

Before Billie could respond to what Sadie said, their waitress came by with another round of drinks.

Billie shook her head and chuckled. "We've barely drunk our drinks, and you're bringing us another round?"

The waitress nodded and grinned. "When I told the boss you were here, he told me to bring you and Sadie another round," she said. She looked over at Sadie. "And he said that this round is on the house."

Sadie smiled and nodded. "Okay," she said. *I guess Iris was right when she remarked that she thought the owner of this place, Jackson's Jukebox, had a crush of some sort on Billie.* "You can tell him that I said thanks."

The waitress chuckled. "I'll tell him," she said. She grinned and stepped closer to them. "I don't think he did it because of you, Sadie." She glanced over at Billie. "Everyone here knows he's got a soft spot for Billie."

Billie nodded and giggled. "I know it too," she said. She looked over at their waitress and grinned. "Tell Drew that I said thanks for the free drink."

Sadie chuckled and shook her head. *I'm amazed by how charming Billie can be. I don't know why I didn't see Billie's strengths before now.* "Well, now I know why he won't fire you," she said. "I wonder if Mr. Armstrong also has a crush on you, Billie?"

Billie shook her head. "Drew didn't fire me when you asked him to because he's got a crush on me," she said. "I happen to be a damn good waitress, Sadie."

Their waitress nodded. "Billie is a great waitress, Sadie," she said. She laughed and grinned. "The free drinks she gets all the time are because the boss has a crush on her; there's no doubt about that."

Billie shrugged her shoulders. "I can't do anything about that," she said. "I will say he wasn't the one who hired me."

Their waitress nodded. "Well, I'll leave you two alone," she said. "I'll be back soon to see if you need another drink."

When their waitress walked away, Billie looked over at Sadie. "Okay, now that we're alone again, let's recap what we've talked about so far," she said. She held up her right hand and started counting off using her fingers. "First, you tried to end my friendship with your best friend, Iris. And then, on the same day, you talked to our boss at the bookstore, Mr. Armstrong, and asked him to fire me. When he wouldn't do it, you came here and did the same thing with Drew." She sipped her vodka tonic. "You did all these because you wanted me out of your life. Did I leave anything out?"

Sadie shook her head. "You didn't leave anything out," she said. *When Billie says it, what I tried to do sounds so bad. It's something one of those mean girls back in Nashville would have done to me and Iris.*

Billie finished her vodka tonic and pushed the now-empty glass away from her. "So, now I'm wondering why you wanted to talk to me, Sadie," she said. "Why did you want to talk to me?"

Well, I wasn't ready for Billie to ask me that. Sadie shook her head and sighed. "I realized I didn't know anything about you," she said. "I also realized I had no reason to dislike you."

Billie nodded. "So, do you like me now, Sadie?" She crossed her arms over her chest and frowned. "Do you want us to be friends now, after everything you did?"

Okay, Billie's mad. Sadie shrugged her shoulders. "I don't know," she said. She sighed and shook her head. "I don't expect you to forgive me, Billie. I didn't ask you to talk to me because I wanted your forgiveness." *I thought Iris said that Billie had forgiven me. Maybe she only told Iris that because she knew Iris wanted to hear that from her.* "I was jealous of your friendship with Iris and worried I would lose my best friend." *There, I said it, Billie. That's the truth.*

Billie reached across the table and took one of Sadie's hands. "I understand how much your friendship with Iris means to you, Sadie," she said. "I also have a best friend who means the world to me."

Chapter Nineteen

Georgia talked to Rebecca a few months later, hoping that Rebecca might know how Billie felt about her. She had to wait for the rare night Rebecca came to Capote's without Billie or their new friend, Iris.

Georgia waved at Rebecca, her heart pounding with her unspoken feelings. "Hey, Rebecca," she said, her voice betraying her nerves. "Why don't you sit here at the bar?" *Here's my chance to talk to her.*

"Okay," Rebecca said. She walked over to the bar and sat down in front of Georgia. "I'll have my usual, please, Georgia."

Georgia nodded. "Okay," she said. "One vodka tonic coming right up." *How do I do this, then? Should I just come out and ask her, or should I engage in some small talk with her first?*

Georgia made Rebecca one vodka tonic and gave it to her. "There you go," she said. She picked up a towel and started wiping down the bar. "So, how have you been?"

Rebecca shrugged her shoulders. "I've been okay," she said. She sipped her vodka tonic and smiled. "You make the best vodka tonic in Boston, Georgia."

Georgia blushed. "Thanks, Rebecca," she said. She shook her head and cleared her throat. *Okay, I think that's enough small talk. It's time to ask her what I need to know.* "I was hoping that you would be able to help me."

Rebecca nodded. "Well, I'll try to help you if I can," she said. She took out a cigarette and 1lit it. "What do you need help with, Georgia?"

Okay, it's time to say this out loud to another person. "I'm sure I've fallen in love with Billie," she said. She sighed and shook her head. "The thing is, I'm not sure how Billie feels about me."

Rebecca frowned. "Have you asked her, Georgia?"

Georgia nodded. "I have asked her, Rebecca," she said. She sighed and frowned. "Well, that's not true. I haven't asked her directly. Instead, I've dropped a few hints." *I'm not used to asking my girlfriend how she feels about me. Most, if not all, of my other girlfriends told me how they felt about me. I didn't have to ask them.*

Rebecca shrugged her shoulders. "I don't know how Billie feels about you," she said.

Georgia sighed, feeling the weight of her past heartbreaks. Billie, much like herself, kept everyone at a distance. This was a defense mechanism Georgia had adopted after being hurt by those she loved, including her family and past girlfriends. She knew she had to confront Billie about her feelings, but the fear of rejection was paralyzing.

Georgia wrestled with her decision, her heart torn between hope and fear. She decided to ask Billie on New Year's Eve, believing it would be the best day to ask Billie about her feelings, whatever they were, about her.

***

A few weeks before New Year's Eve, with Christmas only eight days away, Georgia was hanging out with Billie at her apartment.

Georgia cleared her throat. "So, what are your plans for the holidays?" *I wish I could just come out and ask her, but I can't. I have to work my way up to it.*

"Oh, I'm going home to New Orleans for Christmas," Billie said. She sighed. "My parents want me to spend the holidays with them this year."

She's been living here for over a year and still thinks of New Orleans as her home, not here. "Oh, okay," Georgia said, trying to hide her disappointment. "That's too bad because I hoped you would go to my family's Christmas dinner with me." *Of course, if I did that, I would have to tell my family the truth about my romantic life, something I've been avoiding most of my life. I know how they'll react to learning that I'm gay. They won't like it and might even reject me.*

***

Georgia also went home for the holidays - to Arkansas, in her case. She found herself sitting on the porch of her parents' house, the same house she grew up in, by herself, feeling the weight of her solitude, smoking a cigarette, and sipping eggnog.

The front door opened, and Georgia's younger brother, Mason, walked out. He sat next to Georgia on the porch swing. "Hey, sis," he said. "I knew I would find you out here."

Georgia chuckled. "Where else would I be?" She looked over her shoulder and frowned. "The only good thing about spending Christmas here is that it reminds me why I left Arkansas in the first place." *Mason might be the only one to whom I could tell the truth.* She sighed and shook her head. *No, I won't do it to him.*

***

Georgia returned to Boston the next day. She arrived at her apartment and found a letter from Billie waiting for her. She went to her kitchen, sat at the kitchen table, and opened Billie's letter.

Dear Georgia,

I'm unsure if you'll be back in Boston after Christmas, as we didn't discuss our New Year's Eve plans. I would have called you if you had told me how to contact you while you were back home in Arkansas, so I'm writing you this letter instead.

I won't be back in Boston until after New Year's Eve. I'm not staying here in New Orleans. Instead, I will celebrate the end of this year with my best friend, Bobbie Lamont (I've told you about her, haven't I?). She lives in New York City now, and we've always celebrated New Year's Eve together (except last New Year's Eve, when we met).

I won't return to Boston until after New Year's Eve. I'll call you when I get back. I hope you enjoy the holidays with your family in Arkansas and go out to celebrate New Year's Eve (I'm sure Rebecca and Iris would join you if you call them).

Will see you again soon,
Billie

***

Georgia didn't go out on New Year's Eve, convinced that Billie had broken up with her, even though she hadn't said so in her letter. She didn't think to call Rebecca, but she didn't have to because Rebecca had called her.

"Hey, Georgia," Rebecca said. "Billie told me that she won't be back until after New Year's Eve, so she suggested I call you and invite you to join me and Iris."

Georgia sighed. "I don't feel like going out tonight," she said. "I appreciate you calling me, Rebecca, but I'm afraid I have to turn down your offer to go out and celebrate New Year's Eve."

***

Georgia only felt better when Billie returned to Boston a few days after New Year's Day. She called Georgia a few hours after she arrived at her grandmother's house.

The phone rang at Georgia's apartment. She stood up, got off her couch, and went to the kitchen, where her phone was. She went to it and picked it up.

"Hello?"

"Hey, Georgia, it's me. I'm back in Boston."

Georgia smiled. "Hey, Billie," she said. "I'm glad you're back." She kept her promise to call me when she got back. *Maybe now I'll stop worrying about her breaking up with me.* "Are you coming by?"

Billie chuckled. "Of course, I'm coming by," she said. "I'll be there soon."

***

Georgia cleaned up her apartment, not wanting Billie to see how messy it had become since the last time she had been there. She had just finished cleaning up when Billie arrived twenty minutes later.

Billie knocked on the door, which made Georgia chuckle and shake her head. *I've offered her the spare key so she wouldn't have to knock whenever she comes over, but she won't take it.*

Georgia opened her front door and smiled at Billie. "Come on in," she said. "Would you like something to drink, Billie?" *I'm so happy to see her again. I felt so lost without her.*

Billie smiled back at Georgia. "I'll take a glass of sweet tea, please," she said. She chuckled and grinned. "I know most of the time, I ask for something stronger, but I need to give my liver a break."

Georgia nodded. "I understand," she said. "It's a good thing for you that I drink sweet tea." *Billie must've done a lot of drinking while she was gone.*

Billie went to the living room and sat on the couch while Georgia went to the kitchen. She made Billie a glass of sweet tea and grabbed a beer out of the refrigerator for herself.

Georgia entered the living room, sat beside Billie on the couch, and handed her a glass of sweet tea. "Here's your sweet tea," she said. "How were your holidays?" *Billie seems different.*

Billie smiled. "They were good," she said. "I spent some time with my family and celebrated New Year's Eve with my best friend."

Georgia nodded. "I'm glad to hear that," she said. She sighed and shook her head. "I wish I could say the same about my holidays." *We've never talked about our families, and now I know why. Billie comes from a happy one, while I don't, though I can say not all of them are backward, white trash. My younger brother, Mason, isn't, despite his strong accent.*

Billie frowned. "I'm sorry to hear that," she said. "You're still in the closet, aren't you?"

Georgia nodded and sighed. "I don't think they would accept me," she said. She shrugged her shoulders. "I think my younger brother might, and I almost told him." *If we had a better relationship, I would have told him, but we don't, so I didn't.*

Billie nodded. "You should tell him," she said. She sighed. "I understand being afraid that your family might not accept you. My stepfather still doesn't know."

Okay, let's talk about something else. "So, tell me about New Year's Eve," Georgia said. "Did you have fun with your best friend? What did y'all do to celebrate New Year's Eve?" *Billie doesn't talk about her best friend. All I know about her best friend is her name, Bobbie Lamont. I don't know anything else.*

Billie shrugged her shoulders. "We drank a little and did all the usual things," she said. "I talked to Rebecca, and she told me she invited you to join her on New Year's Eve." She shook her head. "And you turned her down."

***

Georgia got the message and didn't bring up the subject again. She went to Rebecca again and asked her for advice.

Once again, Georgia had to wait for the rare night when Rebecca came to Capote's alone. She waved at Rebecca as soon as she stepped inside.

"Hey, Rebecca," Georgia said. She pointed at an empty stool. "Why don't you sit here?" *Okay, this time, I won't even attempt to make small talk with her. I'll get right to the point.*

"Okay," Rebecca said. She sat on the stool and placed her hands on the bar. "You look like you want to ask me something."

Georgia nodded. "I do," she said. "Have you talked to Billie recently?" *I'm sure she has talked to Billie, but I want to know if Billie also keeps Rebecca at a distance.* "Did she tell you anything about her trip back home or celebrating New Year's Eve with her best friend in New York City?"

Rebecca chuckled and shook her head. "I'm not surprised you asked me about that," she said. "I'm guessing you asked her, and she didn't tell you anything besides that she had fun."

Georgia sighed and nodded. "She then changed the subject," she said. She shrugged her shoulders. "So, I haven't brought it up again." She frowned. "I was hoping Billie told you more than she had told me." *Why is Billie so guarded? Why does she keep everyone at a distance?*

"Well, she didn't," Rebecca said. She shrugged her shoulders. "For whatever reason, Billie doesn't want to talk about it, whether it's her trip home to New Orleans or her stay in New York City with her best friend. If you want my advice, Georgia, drop the subject and don't ask Billie again."

Georgia sighed and nodded. "You might be right," she said. She frowned. "Is it just me, or does Billie seem different?"

***

Georgia followed Rebecca's advice and didn't ask Billie about it again. She was still troubled by the change in Billie's attitude, but decided to trust her feelings and tell Billie that she wanted them to become exclusive. She also wanted to celebrate Valentine's Day with Billie, something they hadn't done before.

Billie surprised Georgia a few days later when she asked Georgia to meet her at Capote's. Georgia said she would, though she was nervous.

***

Two days before Valentine's Day, Georgia sat in a booth near the front entrance of Capote's. She sipped her drink and took a drag off her cigarette. She reviewed the events of the past month in her mind, going over what had happened between herself and Billie since Billie returned to Boston.

Georgia had been waiting for almost twenty minutes when Billie arrived. She walked in, saw Georgia, smiled, and waved at Georgia.

Billie walked over to the booth and sat down across from Georgia. "Hey, Georgia," she said. "I hope you haven't been waiting long." She chuckled and shook her head. "I'm sorry I'm late. I was on my way here when I realized I had to make a quick stop to get gas and some smokes."

Georgia nodded. "I haven't been waiting long," she said. "How have you been? It's been a few days since we spent time together." *I hope I didn't sound bitchy. I wasn't complaining about us not spending any time together.*

Billie took out a cigarette and lit it. "I've been busy," she said. "Trying to find time to write isn't easy when you've got two part-time jobs like I do."

Why do I feel that Billie just rebuked me? Georgia cleared her throat. "Well, you could always quit one of your part-time jobs," she said. "You were the one who wanted to have two part-time jobs." She shook her head. "I don't know why you even have those part-time jobs. It isn't like you need the money."

Billie frowned and squinted at Georgia. "I know I don't need the money," she said. She sighed and shook her head. "I have to spend time around other people to write about them. You're not a writer, Georgia, so you won't understand."

Georgia shook her head. "That's not fair, Billie," she said. "I could understand if you just talked to me." *Billie's starting to remind me of those silly boys I tried to date when I was younger, just a teenager before I realized I was gay. She's willing to accept my love but refuses to give me any love in return.*

A waitress walked over to them and smiled. "Hey, girls," she said. "I'm so glad to see you two." She looked over at Georgia. "Are you ready for another drink, Georgia?"

Georgia nodded. "I am ready," she said. She looked over at Billie. "I'm sorry, I forgot to order you a drink." *I was too nervous and couldn't remember what Billie liked to drink. So afraid I might order the wrong drink, I didn't bother to order her a drink.*

"I'll have my usual," Billie said. She waited until their waitress had walked away and cleared her throat. "We need to talk about our relationship, Georgia."

Most of the time, when my past girlfriends said that to me, I would know they either wanted to end our relationship or make us exclusive. Georgia reached across the table, separating her from Billie, and grabbed one of Billie's hands. "I also want to talk about our relationship, Billie," she said. *Before I tell her what I want to change about our relationship, specifically our becoming exclusive, I should remind her of what our relationship means to her and me.* "I know things have been kind of brittle between us lately, but I'm not willing to give up on us yet."

Billie frowned. "Brittle? What do you mean by that, Georgia?"

Georgia sighed. "You know what I mean, Billie," she said. "Things have been different between us. You've been different since you came back to Boston." *Does she not see how our relationship has changed, or does she not want to see it?*

Billie nodded. "Okay, I think I understand what you're trying to say to me," she said. She shrugged her shoulders. "I'm sorry we haven't been spending as much time together as we used to, Georgia."

This conversation isn't going the way I want it to go. Georgia shook her head. "I believe you, Billie," she said. "I don't want to fight or argue with you." *Okay, I need to take control of this conversation and steer it in the right direction.* "You mean the world to me, Billie."

Billie smiled and shook her head. "I know that," she said. She sighed and frowned. "I know I don't make it easy, dating or getting to know me, but I appreciate you being patient with me."

Georgia smiled. "I also know it's not easy to date me," she said. She sighed. "I know I'm too often needy and unsure, but I hope you know that I don't mean to be that way, to be that needy, clingy girlfriend." She took a deep breath and slowly exhaled. "I want us to be exclusive, Billie. You're the only woman I want to be with."

Billie sighed and shook her head. "I wish I felt the same way, Georgia," she said. "I'm afraid you've always taken our relationship more seriously than mine."

Georgia frowned. "What are you trying to say to me, Billie?"

Billie stood up. "I'm saying it's over between us," she said. She turned around and walked away.

Chapter Twenty

I n the seven months since Billie's birthday, Iris had become one of Billie's few friends in Boston. Rebecca was Billie's other friend. She read some of Billie's short stories and was impressed by them.

***

The next day, Iris went to her editor. She knocked on his office door and stepped inside. "Are you busy? Do you have a moment?"

Her editor leaned back in his chair. "I'm busy, but I can spare a moment or two," he said. He took off his glasses and wiped his forehead. "What do you need, Iris?"

Iris shook her head and grinned. "I don't need anything," she said. She cleared her throat. "Do you still want to publish fiction written by local writers?" *I've never done this before, so I'm suggesting he consider publishing a short story written by someone I know and consider a friend.*

Her editor nodded. "I do," he said. "Do you have someone in mind?"

Iris nodded and handed her editor the magazine where she had read one of Billie's short stories. "Read the story titled Moonshine Tastes Better," she said. "The author lives here in Boston." *I should tell him the whole truth and not leave anything out.* "And I know her, too."

"Okay, I will," her editor said. He threw the magazine on his desk. "I'll let you know what I've decided."

***

Billie's story was a hit with the readers, and letters poured in, requesting more stories and an interview with Billie. Her editor, beaming with pride, showed Iris the letters.

"Do you think you could talk your friend into giving you an interview?"

Iris nodded. "I know I can talk her into giving one," she said. She smiled. "Billie may not like talking about herself, but she loves to talk about her stories."

***

A few hours later, Iris went out to drink with Rebecca and Billie. They went to Capote's and sat in their favorite booth.

Iris cleared her throat. "So, our readers loved your story, Billie," she said. She smiled. "We got a ton of letters about it. Our readers want us to publish more of your stories." *Should I tell her the rest of it?* "They also want to know more about you. They want an interview, Billie."

Billie nodded and chuckled. "And who did your editor assign to interview me?" She grinned. "It's you, isn't it, Iris?"

Iris nodded. "Yeah, it's me," she said. She reached out and took one of Billie's hands. "If you think about it, it wouldn't be the first time I've interviewed you." She chuckled. "Do you remember the night we met, Billie? The first time we talked was kind of an interview, with me asking you questions."

Billie giggled and grinned. "You're right," she said. "So, yeah, I'll let you interview me for your newspaper."

***

Billie sat down with Iris a few weeks before she left Boston to go home to New Orleans for the holidays.

The interview went well, with Billie answering all of Iris's questions without avoiding them.

Iris: When did you start writing stories?

Billie: I started writing stories after I turned thirteen, in the summer of 1981.

Iris: Why did you start writing stories?

Billie (smiles): I did it because my best friend loved reading them.

Iris learned a great deal about Billie through the interview, and what she learned only made her like Billie even more.

Iris took notes during the interview and wrote a summary of the interview. Her editor was pleased with the interview and made only a few suggestions, pointing out that the interview was lengthy and they didn't have room in the paper to publish the entire thing.

After much persuasion, Iris convinced her editor to publish the interview in three parts. It was a resounding success with their readers, leaving both Iris and her editor satisfied and content.

***

Almost two months later and two days before Valentine's Day, Iris had just finished writing an article when her office phone rang.

"Hello, you've reached Iris Mathews' desk. How may I help you?" Iris glanced at her watch and frowned. *I have no idea who could be calling me right now.*

"Oh, good, I'm so glad you gave me your office number."

Iris smiled. *I know that voice.* "Hey, Rebecca," she said. "The only reason I gave you my office number is because I thought you might need it in case you had to get a hold of me." *And I'm here more than I'm at home.*

"It's a good thing you did," Rebecca said. She sighed. "Billie just called me, and I had to calm her down before I found out why she called me."

Oh, no, something's wrong. "So, why did Billie call you, Rebecca?" Iris reached into her desk and pulled out her cigarettes and lighter. She took one out and lit it. "What's going on with her?" *The last time I talked to Billie was just before she left Boston. She seemed excited about going home for Christmas and nervous about it at the same time. She told me she knew she should tell her parents the truth about her, but didn't know if she could handle them reacting badly.*

"Billie broke up with Georgia not even an hour ago," Rebecca said. She sighed. "She's a mess, Iris. I've never seen her this upset before."

Iris shook her head. "I don't understand," she said. *I thought Billie was happy with Georgia.* She frowned. *Something must've happened while Billie was gone. Did Georgia cheat on Billie?* "I was under the impression that Billie was happy. What changed?"

Rebecca sighed. "I don't know, Iris," she said. "The only thing I know for sure is that we need to take Billie out so she doesn't sit around and brood about breaking up with Georgia."

Iris nodded. "You're right, Rebecca," she said. She leaned back in her chair. "I don't think we should take her to Capote's since Georgia works there." *Rebecca knows that.* "Of course, you already know that. Why don't we go to that other bar Billie likes?"

Rebecca chuckled. "It's called Jackson's Jukebox, Iris," she said. "We've taken you there a few times."

Iris shrugged her shoulders. "Yeah, only a few times," she said. "So, when should we take her out? Tonight? I'm free for the rest of the night." *If I go out, I'll have to call Sadie and tell her what's happening. She won't be happy about me not coming home, especially after I promised her we would spend time together.*

"I offered to take her out tonight, but Billie said no," Rebecca said. She sighed. "She's spending some time with her grand-mother."

Iris nodded. "Well, that's good," she said. *Besides her best friend in New York City, her grandmother is one of the few people Billie is close to and confides in. I wish I could say I was also one of those few people, but not yet, though I'm becoming close to Billie.* "When do you want to take her out? Tomorrow night?"

"Let's take her out on Valentine's Day," Rebecca said. "Billie doesn't need to be alone on that holiday." She sighed. "What do you think, Iris?"

"You're right, Rebecca," Iris said. *I know from experience that Valentine's Day is only a good holiday when you're with someone. It's a lousy holiday if you're single, and if you've just broken up with your partner, either by your choice or by their choice, it can be the worst day in your life.* "What do you think of my suggestion, Rebecca? Instead of going to Capote's, let's take Billie to Jackson's Jukebox."

"That's a great suggestion, Iris," Rebecca said. "Why don't you meet us there around seven?"

Iris nodded. "I'll be there," she said. "I'll see you in a few days, Rebecca." She hung up her office phone and sighed.

***

Two days later, Valentine's Day. Iris sat in a booth at Jackson's Jukebox and sipped her drink, a Scotch soda, while she waited for Rebecca and Billie to get there. She glanced at her watch and frowned. Rebecca said to meet her here at seven, and it's now ten past seven.

Iris smiled when Rebecca and Billie walked into the bar. She stood up and waved at them.

Billie and Rebecca walked over to Iris. They sat down across from her in the booth.

Billie's smile was warm as she greeted Iris. "Rebecca told me that she had invited you to join us," she said, reaching across the table to Iris's. "I'm glad she did, and you're here, Iris."

Rebecca shook her head and chuckled. "I knew Iris would want to hang out with us tonight," she said. She looked over at Billie. "And I was confident you would enjoy her hanging out with us."

Before Iris could say anything, a waitress spotted Billie and walked to their booth. She went over to Billie and smiled at her. "I thought I saw you walk in," she said. She shook her head and grinned. "I think you're here more than anyone else, including the owner, Billie."

Billie smiled and laughed. "You might be right," she said. "And I'm not here all the time. I do have another part-time job, you know?"

Their waitress nodded. "Oh, I know," she said. She looked over at Iris. "I see y'all brought your white friend again."

Iris shook her head and chuckled. "They didn't bring me," she said. "I meet them here." *I think this is the same waitress who served us the last time I came here with them.* She grinned. "Are you surprised to see me again?" *One of the many things I've learned from my friendship with Sadie is how to interact with black people.*

The waitress shrugged. "Well, I'm not surprised to see these two again," she said, glancing over at Billie and Rebecca. She chuckled. "But to be honest with you, I'm a little surprised to see you again." She leaned forward towards Iris on the table. "You see, sugar, most of the time, when white people come here, it ain't because they want to drink with black folks, but because they've heard about this place and want to see it for themselves."

Iris nodded. "I know what you're saying," she said. She smiled. "I ain't like most white people. You see, all my friends, including these two and my best friend, are black." *What do you think about that, sassy black waitress?*

Billie nodded and chuckled. "It's true," she said. "I don't know why Rebecca likes coming here, but I do know why I do, even when I don't have to and have the night off from work."

Their waitress grinned and laughed. "I'm sure you do, Billie," she said. She cleared her throat. "So, do y'all know what y'all want to drink?"

Billie nodded. "I do," she said. She smiled. "I'll have my usual vodka tonic."

Rebecca smiled and nodded. "I'll have the same," she said. She looked over at Iris. "What about you, Iris? Are you ready for another drink?"

Iris glanced at her glass. *It's almost empty.* She nodded and smiled. "I will be ready for another drink in a few minutes," she said. She looked over at their waitress. "I'd like another scotch soda, please."

Their waitress nodded. "Okay, I'll be right back," she said. She turned around and walked away.

Billie sighed, took out a cigarette, and lit it.

Iris looked over at Rebecca, who shrugged.

Iris shook her head and cleared her throat. "I heard what happened with Georgia two days ago," she said. "I'm sorry your relationship with Georgia is over, Billie." *I hope Billie ended her relationship with Georgia for the right reasons.* She reached across the table and took one of Billie's hands. "How are you handling it, Billie? How are you doing?"

"So, you told her." Billie shook her head. "I shouldn't be surprised. I don't think you know how to keep anything to yourself."

Rebecca held up her hands. "I told her because she's your friend, Billie," she said. She sighed and shook her head. "And I told her because I'm worried about you." She glanced over at Iris. "So is Iris."

"I'm fine," Billie said. She took a drag off her cigarette while giving Rebecca and Iris a wary look. "I don't want to talk about me ending my relationship with Georgia."

"I don't think you're fine, Billie," Iris said. She held up her hands. "We don't have to talk about what happened with Georgia if you don't want to talk about it."

Their waitress returned with their drinks. "Here's your scotch soda," she said, handing Iris her drink. "And here's y'all's drinks." She placed Billie's and Rebecca's vodka tonics on the table before them.

Billie smiled. "Thanks," she said. "How has your night been so far?"

The waitress's question was casual. "Would you bring your girlfriend here?" she asked Iris, a playful smile on her lips.

Iris smiled. "I would if she wanted to come here," she said. *I won't ask her why she thinks I would have a girlfriend instead of a boyfriend.* "Why do you think I shouldn't?" *This bar doesn't seem anti-couple to me.*

Their waitress grinned. "You shouldn't bring your girlfriend here because we don't play love songs here," she said. She pointed over her shoulder at the jukebox. "Have you ever looked at the songs on the jukebox? There ain't no love songs on it." She sighed and shook her head. "No, this bar is where you go when you're heartbroken and want to drink your sadness away."

Billie smiled. "And that's why I love this bar," she said. She sipped her vodka tonic and sighed. She pulled out a twenty and handed it to their waitress. "Be sure to keep us happy."

Their waitress nodded and smiled. "Oh, you don't have to worry about that, Billie," she said. "I'm going to give y'all some time to enjoy your drinks." She turned around and walked away.

Iris leaned forward. "Are you friends with her, Billie?"

Billie smiled. "I wouldn't say that we're friends," she said. "I enjoy working with her, and she's easy for me to talk to, even though she's older than us."

Iris nodded. "I've noticed that you seem popular wherever we go," she said. "You seem to get along with your co-workers." *I know only a few people who don't seem to like Billie.*

Billie nodded. "Well, I try to get along with my co-workers," she said. "Both here, at this bar, and in the bookstore."

I'm glad Billie mentioned the bookstore. I have a reason now to ask her about Sadie. Iris cleared her throat. "What about Sadie, Billie? Do y'all get along when y'all are working at the bookstore together?"

"We might work at the same bookstore, but we don't work together," Billie said. "Why don't you ask me what you want to know, Iris?"

Iris chuckled. *I sometimes forget that Billie's a direct person and doesn't like to tiptoe around a subject.* "I want to know if y'all are getting along at the bookstore," she said. She sighed. "I know Sadie can be difficult to deal with sometimes."

Billie frowned. "I thought you knew, Iris," she said. She looked over at Rebecca. "Why doesn't Iris know?"

Rebecca shrugged her shoulders. "I thought she did, too, Billie," she said. She frowned and looked over at Iris. "Sadie didn't tell you, Iris?"

Iris shook her head. "No, she didn't," she said. She looked over at Billie. "I hope you and Sadie are getting along better than y'all have in the past." *When did Sadie start keeping things from me?*

Billie chuckled. "We're getting along fine, Iris," she said. "Sadie's no longer hostile towards me."

Iris smiled. "I'm glad to hear that," she said. "If I had known that, I would have brought her." *It took a year, but Billie's charm worked again. She found a way to get past the wall that Sadie put around herself.*

Billie shook her head. "I didn't say I'm friends with Sadie," she said. "I don't think we'll become friends anytime soon, Iris. I'm sorry to say."

Iris chuckled and grinned. "I hope you're wrong, Billie," she said. "I would love for you and Sadie to become friends." *They would be great friends if they gave each other a chance. Maybe they're too much alike to be friends.* She shook her head. *No, I don't believe that.*

***

A few hours later, the three of them, Rebecca, Billie, and Iris, were having a good time.

Iris cleared her throat. "So, will you tell me what happened between you and Sadie?" *I don't like this feeling, not knowing something about Sadie. Why didn't she tell me?*

Billie grinned. "Sure, Iris," she said. She cleared her throat. "I met her here and talked to her."

Iris frowned. "Don't spare any details, Billie," she said. "I know you talked to Sadie because I'm the one who set up the meeting between y'all." *Well, this isn't exactly true.*

Billie nodded. "That's true," she said. She smiled. "Sadie admitted to me that she disliked me so much because she feared losing her friendship with you."

Iris nodded. "Yeah, that sounds like something she would say," she said. *I'm glad that Sadie admitted to Billie why she didn't like her, although I'm sure there were other reasons. Sadie doesn't dislike someone for only one reason. She has many reasons why she doesn't like someone.*

Billie shrugged her shoulders. "I'm not sure that was the only reason she didn't like me, but I didn't press her," she said. "Anyway, I'd say my rivalry with Sadie has ended." She shook her head and laughed. "All of my rivalries have ended in the last six months."

Billie never saw either Jasmine or Bridget as her rivals. Iris nodded and grinned. "I'm pleased to hear that, Billie," she said. She grinned. "I never doubted for a second that your charm would win them over."

Billie chuckled and shrugged her shoulders. "I don't think it was my charm," she said. "To be honest with you, Iris, I don't know why any of them disliked me, but I also didn't care either."

Chapter Twenty-One

The day after Valentine's Day, Drew overheard a conversation between two of Billie's fellow waitresses.

"Did you hear what happened last night with Billie?"

"If you mean Billie broke up with her white girlfriend, that didn't happen last night. Last night, Billie came here with her friends, the mixed girl and the white girl."

"So, when did Billie break up with her white girlfriend, if she didn't do it last night?"

"She did it three days ago, two days before Valentine's Day."

Understanding the sensitivity of the situation, Drew decided to wait before asking Billie out. He knew she needed time to readjust to being single again and didn't want to rush her. He also made sure not to ask her about her breakup, respecting her privacy.

***

Before Drew knew it, it was Memorial Day, and six weeks had passed. The bar was open, but business was slow. Drew had given most of his employees the day off.

Only three other people were working besides Drew. They were Billie, another waitress, and the bartender.

Drew was sitting in his office, going over that week's payroll, when his office phone rang. He shook his head and sighed. He reached out and picked up his office phone.

"Hello?"

"Hey, Drew, it's me."

"Hey, Willie," Drew said, smiling. He leaned back in his chair. "I don't think you've ever called me here before, so there must be a good reason for you to do it today." *Willie must want something from me. Or he wants to ask me something.* He chuckled. *He might ask me to leave Billie alone.*

Willie chuckled. "I'm surprised you're at work," he said. "Don't you know it's Memorial Day, Drew? It's a holiday."

"Yeah, I know it's a holiday," Drew said. "Sometimes, we're busy on this particular holiday." He sighed. "But not this time."

"You should take the day off," Willie said. "I'm having a party later on tonight. You should come."

Drew shrugged his shoulders. "I might come by," he said. *How do I ask him if Billie's invited to his party without saying her name?* "Is it going to be a big party?"

Someone knocked on Drew's office door.

Drew sighed and shook his head. "I've got to go, Willie," he said. "Someone just knocked on my office door." *I'll call him back when I finish this payroll.*

Willie chuckled. "Okay, boss man," he said. "Well, I hope you come by." He then hung up the phone.

"Whoever is knocking on my door, you can come in," Drew said, putting his office phone back on its cradle. *I don't like it when Willie calls me boss man.* He looked up when the door opened and smiled.

"Hey, Drew," Billie said, walking into his office. "Can I talk to you?"

Drew nodded. "Sure," he said, sitting up straight in his chair. "Is everything okay?" *Billie never bothers me when I'm in my office. She knows I don't like to be bothered when I'm in here, especially when I'm going over paperwork.*

Billie nodded. "Everything's okay," she said. She pointed at the empty chair on the other side of Drew's desk. "Do you mind if I sit?"

Drew shook his head. "I don't mind, Billie," he said. *Whatever Billie wants to talk to me about, it must be serious if she has to sit instead of standing.* He took his pack of cigarettes off his desk and took one out. *Billie might want one, too.* "Would you like a smoke, Billie?"

Billie smiled. "I sure would, Drew," she said. She leaned forward and accepted the cigarette from Drew. She pulled out her lighter and lit it, giving Drew a questioning look. "It's slow, Drew. How much longer are you going to keep it open?"

Drew shrugged his shoulders. *Billie's right; it has been slow. The bar isn't making any money today.* "Do you have somewhere better to be, Billie?" He took out a cigarette for himself and lit it. He took a drag off it and chuckled. "Is that why you're asking me how much longer the bar will be open?"

Billie grinned and shook her head. "I do have plans, but that's not why I'm asking," she said. "What about you, Drew? Do you have any plans for today?" She took a drag off her cigarette. "I'm sure Willie has invited you to his party."

Drew chuckled. "How do you know Willie is having a party, Billie?" *I still haven't figured out their relationship. They live separate lives, only seeing each other during the holidays.*

Billie grinned. "Willie might think I don't know what's going on with him, but I do," she said. "And Nina told me about Willie throwing a party last night." She took a drag off her cigarette. "You didn't answer my question, Drew."

Drew chuckled and nodded. "No, I didn't, Billie," he said. He leaned back in his chair and took a drag off his cigarette. "I don't have any plans." *I won't tell her the bar wouldn't be open if I had plans for today.*

Billie nodded. "I didn't think you did," she said. She gave him a questioning look. "What about Willie's party? Are you going to it?"

"I might," Drew said. He grinned and shrugged his shoulders. "But then again, I might not." *I don't know if I'm in the mood to hang out with Willie. My interest in Billie has put a strain on our friendship.* He shook his head and sighed. *I'm unsure if Willie is against me being with Billie because he's afraid I'll break her heart or because he thinks she'll break mine. Either way, it's not his place to say who I can be interested in, even though we're friends. And even though he's her older brother, he also can't say who Billie can talk to over the phone or spend time with, which drives him crazy.*

Billie nodded. "So, I guess you haven't decided yet," she said. She took a drag off her cigarette and smiled at Drew. "I'm going to convince you to close the bar and let everyone go home."

Drew grinned. *If anyone else had said that to me, I would have just shaken my head and wished them the best of luck. But Billie isn't anyone else.* "And how in the world will you do that, Billie?" *I noticed she didn't say she would ask me to close the bar and let everyone go home. She's going to convince me.*

Billie grinned. "Oh, I'll find a way," she said. She shook her head and cleared her throat. "So, what's the latest gossip about me?"

Drew cleared his throat. "Why do you think there's gossip about you floating around here?" *I try not to pay attention to the gossip spread around here, but I sometimes overhear conversations.*

Billie smiled. "I've been the center of gossip for most of my life," she said. "Back home, it was because my best friend was white."

Drew leaned forward, his elbows on his desk. "What about here, in Boston? Why are you the cause of gossip here?" Billie was a puzzle, a mystery that intrigued him. She was engaging and didn't fit into the usual boxes people like to put others in.

Billie nodded. "I am, Drew," she said. She took one last drag off her cigarette and put it out in the ashtray on Drew's desk. "I'm a member of three different communities, which is enough to make many people uncomfortable with me."

***

Drew and Billie talked for another ten minutes. Drew waited for Billie to convince him to close the bar and let everyone go home.

So far, we've discussed how challenging it has been for Billie to adjust to her new life in Boston and how she misses her best friend. Billie's been open and honest with me for the first time since we met almost two years ago, not holding anything back. I wonder if she's told anyone what she's telling me right now. I know she has friends and gets along with all her co-workers here.

Billie finished another cigarette, took one last drag off it, and put it in the ashtray on Drew's desk. She stood up, sighing. "Well, I guess I'll get back to work," she said. She grinned. "And I'll let you get back to reviewing the payroll."

Billie turned around and was about to leave Drew's office when he stopped her.

"Hey, Billie," Drew said, standing up. "You told me you would convince me to close the bar and let everyone go home." He smiled at Billie. "Did you forget to do that, or did you change your mind?"

Billie shook her head and grinned. "I didn't forget, Drew," she said. "And I didn't change my mind either."

Drew chuckled. "Okay," he said. *Billie's either waiting for the right time to convince me to close the bar and send everyone home, or she hasn't figured out how she will convince me to close the bar, which she knows I don't want to do.* "I'm ready, Billie. Try to convince me."

Billie nodded and grinned at Drew. "Okay, I will," she said. "My friend Rebecca's throwing a party at her apartment, and if you close the bar, I'll let you come with me to it."

Drew smiled. *So, Billie invited me to her friend's party, but only if I close the bar and send everyone home.* "Are you inviting me to a party, Billie?" *Since the day I met her, I've wanted to either ask her out or ask her to ask me out. I've always been drawn to her, but our friendship and Willie's disapproval have kept me from making a move.*

Billie smiled at Drew and nodded. "In a way, I am, Drew," she said. "I also want to leave here before the party starts."

Drew chuckled and nodded. "So, you're offering me something you think I want," he said. He leaned back in his chair and put his hands behind his head. "You seem confident that your invitation to your friend's party will be enough to make me close the bar and let everyone else go home." *Billie sometimes comes off more cocky than confident.*

Billie walked back over to his desk, placed her hands on it, and leaned forward, her face almost within Drew's arm's reach. "I'm inviting you to a party, Drew," she said. "I'm not asking you out, though I know you want me to and have wanted to ask me out since we met."

Drew chuckled and shook his head. "I think you're splitting hairs, Billie," he said. "Inviting someone to a party is the same as asking them out." *Come on, Billie. It's okay that you asked me out. Willie won't like it, but when has his disapproval stopped you from doing anything?*

Billie shrugged her shoulders. "Maybe," she said. She grinned. "It doesn't matter because I know you want to say yes."

Drew shook his head. "And how do you know that, Billie?" He stood up and leaned forward, their faces almost touching. "Are you a mind reader now?"

Billie giggled. "No, I'm not a mind reader," she said. "Everyone who works here knows you've got a crush on me." She smiled. "So do I."

Drew shook his head and chuckled. *Billie's right.* "Okay," he said. He sat back down in his chair. "You've convinced me, Billie. Tell everyone to start cleaning up because the bar's closing for the day."

Billie nodded and grinned mischievously. "I told you I'd find a way," she said, her eyes sparkling with amusement. "I'll tell them." She turned around and walked out of Drew's office.

Drew shook his head and laughed. *Billie did convince me. She knew it would be hard for me to say no to going to a party with her. And maybe she doesn't consider inviting me to a party the same thing as asking me out, but it is the same thing.*

Drew finished the weekly payroll while Billie and her two co-workers cleaned the bar.

***

Thirty minutes later, Drew emerged from his office, the sound of the closing door echoing through the empty bar.

Billie and her two coworkers waited for him outside the bar, smoking cigarettes and chatting among themselves.

"How in the world were you able to talk him into closing the bar, Billie?"

Billie grinned. "It doesn't matter," she said. "I did, and you're welcome."

The waitress turned to the bartender and grinned. "I told you he had a crush on Billie and would find it hard to say no to her," she said. She looked over at Billie. "He didn't believe me when I told him about the boss's crush on you."

The bartender nodded and chuckled. "She did tell me," he said. He shrugged his shoulders. "In my defense, I was sure the boss wasn't capable of having a crush on anyone."

Drew locked the front door, glancing over his shoulder at Billie.

Billie grinned at him and held up her hand.

Drew waited until the other two had left before walking Billie to her car.

Drew looked over at Billie and chuckled. "So, why didn't you want the others to see me walk you to your car?"

Billie grinned and shook her head. "I'm sure you already know why, Drew," she said. She shrugged her shoulders. "I think there's enough gossip about you and me anyway, so why give them more things to talk about behind our backs?"

Go ahead and ask her. Drew cleared his throat and tried to gather up his courage. "So, since I closed the bar like you wanted me to, I hope your invitation to your friend's party is still good," he said. *I don't know what it is about her, but I turn into a tongue-tied teenager whenever I try to talk to Billie.*

Billie nodded and smiled. "Yeah, it's still good," she said. "Unless you'd rather go to Willie's party."

Drew shook his head. "I've been to enough of his parties," he said. He smiled. "I won't risk hurting your feelings by dismissing your invitation to your friend's party." *Well, she either will accept my explanation or won't, but it doesn't matter. I'm going to the same party she's going to, so I'll have some alone time with her. Or at least, I hope so.*

Billie grinned. "And you won't want to do that, would you?" She wrote down the address of Rebecca's apartment and gave it to Drew. "Here's Rebecca's address," she said. "I'll see you there, Drew."

Drew nodded. "Yeah, you will," he said. He took a step back. "I'll see you at your friend's apartment." *Today's turning out better than I thought it would.*

Billie smiled, nodded, and got into her car.

Drew watched Billie drive away. He glanced at the address, written by Billie on a small slip of paper, and smiled. *Stop standing there like an idiot.* He went to his car, which was parked down the street. He unlocked it and slipped inside it. He took out a cigarette and lit it.

Drew considered it a good sign that Billie had invited him to a party. He couldn't tell if she liked him or not.

***

Drew drove to Rebecca's apartment in the upper-crust neighborhood of Beacon Hill, his heart racing with anticipation. He parked his car near Billie's, down the street from the apartment building. He exited his car and started walking to the building, smiling when he saw Billie smoking a cigarette by her car.

"Hey, Billie," Drew said, waving at her. *It's only been a few minutes since we parted ways, but every time I see her, it's like seeing her for the first time again.*

Billie turned around to face Drew and smiled. "You found it," she said. She waved back at him. "I'm glad you came."

"I'm glad you invited me, Billie," Drew said, walking up to Billie. He looked away, afraid she might see the eagerness in his eyes, took one last drag off his cigarette, and tossed it away.

Billie nodded. "Well, let's go," she said. "Just follow me, okay, Drew?"

Drew nodded and followed Billie from her car to the apartment building.

Billie looked over her shoulder at Drew and smiled. "You're about to meet my two friends, Iris and Rebecca," she said. "You've seen them before, I'm sure."

Drew nodded and chuckled. "Yeah, I've seen them around," he said. "How long have you been friends with them?" *I learned long ago that when a woman wants to talk about her friends with you, you should listen to her.*

Billie grinned. "I've been friends with Rebecca for almost two years now," she said. "And Iris has been my friend since last New Year's Eve."

Drew nodded and chuckled. "I've read some of the articles you told me about, the ones your friend wrote," he said. "I enjoyed them. Your friend is a good writer." *I won't tell her I won't have read them if she hadn't told me about them.*

Billie and Drew entered the apartment building and took the elevator to the fourth floor.

Billie looked over at Drew and grinned. "You're lucky that the elevator's working today," she said. "Most of the time, it's not working."

The elevator ride was brief. Billie and Drew stepped out of the elevator, and Drew followed Billie down the hallway to apartment 412.

Billie knocked on the door and glanced at Drew, who smiled at her. She smiled back at him.

The door opened. Billie and Drew walked into the apartment.

Billie stood by the young woman who had opened the door and looked at Drew. "Drew, this is my friend Rebecca," she said. "Rebecca, this is Drew. He's one of my older brother's friends and my boss at Jackson's Jukebox."

Drew chuckled. "We kind of know each other, Billie," he said. He shook his head and cleared his throat. "How have you been, Rebecca?" *Has she told Billie how we know each other?*

Rebecca shrugged her shoulders. "I'm okay," she said. She grinned and looked over at Billie, standing next to her. "You know, when you called earlier and told me you were bringing someone, I didn't think you meant him."

Billie laughed. "Who did you think I was going to bring with me?" She shook her head. "It doesn't matter now." She reached out and took Drew's hand. "Come on, Drew. Let's get a drink."

It was a small party, with only about ten people there. Drew walked around, keeping Billie in his sight, and tried to talk to everyone there. He knew some of them, besides Rebecca, having seen them at his bar, but there were also people there he didn't know. He enjoyed talking to them the most and discovering how they knew Billie.

***

A few hours later, the party died, with most of the people gone. Drew sat with Billie in the living room while Rebecca cleaned up.

"Well, I had fun," Billie said. She smiled at Drew. "Did you enjoy yourself?"

Drew nodded. "I did," he said. *I haven't been alone with Billie all night, but that's okay.* He grinned and shook his head. "I think you have more than two friends. Everyone I talked to seems to like you."

Billie chuckled and grinned. "They didn't always like me," she said. She shrugged her shoulders. "I'm just glad they don't dislike me anymore."

***

Drew and Billie talked for a few more minutes, and then Billie surprised Drew by sitting in his lap and kissing him.

"In case you haven't figured it out, Drew, I like you," Billie said, smiling. "I'm sure you've been waiting a long time for me to tell you that."

Drew smiled back at Billie. "I have been waiting," he said. "And in case you haven't figured it out, I like you, too."

Chapter Twenty-Two

A little over three weeks later, Rebecca sat in the living room of her apartment and smoked a cigarette while sipping coffee. It was Friday, but not just any Friday. It was Juneteenth, and Rebecca felt she had to do something to celebrate this special day. She decided to call Billie and find out if Billie had to work.

Rebecca left her living room and went to her phone, which was hanging on the wall in the kitchen. She picked it up and dialed Billie's number.

The phone rang four times before Billie answered it.

"Hey, Billie, it's me," Rebecca said. "I'm glad I caught you at home." *Hopefully, she doesn't have to work today.*

Billie sighed. "Hey, Rebecca," she said. "I'm glad you called because I need someone to talk to right now."

Okay, something's bothering her. "What's on your mind, Billie?" Rebecca sat down at her kitchen table. "What's bothering you?" *I'll wait until I find out what's bothering her to invite her to celebrate today with me.*

"I know you saw me kiss Drew," Billie said. She sighed. "Well, we've been dating almost three weeks now, and I'm having a hard time dealing with my feelings about it."

Wow, this is the first time Billie has admitted having difficulty with anything. "Go on, Billie, I'm listening," Rebecca said. "I'm your friend and I'd like to help you, if I can."

"Honestly, it's kind of embarrassing," Billie said. "I mean, I'm almost twenty-four and I've had plenty of boyfriends before Drew, but I feel like I'm a love-struck teenager."

Rebecca suppressed a chuckle. "Please continue, Billie," she said. "Why do you feel like a love-struck teenager?" *I wasn't surprised when she told me Drew had a crush on her. Maybe she also had a crush on him?*

Billie sighed. "I didn't kiss Drew out of some impulse," she said. "I knew he wanted to date me, starting from the day we met." She chuckled. "I did enjoy him having a crush on me."

Rebecca took out a cigarette and lit it. "So, what's the problem?" *It sounds like Billie's enjoying dating Drew. I hope he's a better boyfriend to her than he was to me.*

"Well, it's not a problem," Billie said. "I only wanted a casual relationship with Drew and didn't think I would catch feelings for him." She sighed. "But I now believe that I was wrong."

Okay, this kind of thing calls for an in-person conversation. "I want to hear more, Billie, but I think it would be better if we have this conversation face to face instead of over the phone," Rebecca said. "Why don't you come over here? We'll try to figure out what you should do about your feelings for Drew."

"Good idea," Billie said. She sighed. "I'm going to throw some clothes on and be on my way there." She then hung up the phone.

Rebecca knew it would take Billie about fifteen minutes to arrive at her apartment. She straightened up her apartment, swept up her kitchen, and threw out all the trash that had been sitting on her coffee table. She also put on a pot of coffee and cooked some grits. She smiled. *I know how much Billie loves grits.*

***

Rebecca was wrong about how long it would take Billie to drive from her house, where she lived with her grandmother, to Rebecca's apartment. Instead of taking fifteen minutes, it took Billie almost twenty minutes.

Rebecca was in the kitchen when Billie knocked on her front door. She smiled and left the kitchen. She walked through her small living room to the front door.

"Hey, Rebecca, it's me," Billie said, behind the front door. "Are you going to let me in or what?"

"Hold on, I'm coming," Rebecca said, chuckling. She glanced through the peephole to confirm Billie had knocked on her front door. She opened the door and stepped back, gesturing for Billie to enter. "Come on in, Billie. I've got a pot of coffee made for us and two bowls of grits ready for us to enjoy."

Billie smiled and nodded. "One day, you'll explain to me who taught you to cook grits," she said. "Whoever they were, I'm glad they did." She shook her head and chuckled. "I never thought I would miss grits, but it only took me a few months of not having it for me to realize that I did."

"Do you want some coffee first, here in the living room, or do you want to sit in the kitchen and enjoy some grits?" *I'll let Billie decide where we'll be sitting. After all, she's the one who needs some help.*

"Let's sit here and have coffee first," Billie said. "It's always better to eat grits after they've cooled down a little."

Rebecca nodded. "Okay, go ahead and take a seat," she said. "I'll get the coffee." *Okay, so I will let Billie decide how this conversation will proceed.*

Billie sat down on the couch in the living room while Rebecca fetched their coffee from the kitchen. She returned to the living room a few minutes later, carrying two cups of coffee. She sat on the couch beside Billie and handed her a cup of coffee.

Billie flashed a smile at Rebecca. "Thanks," she said. She sipped her coffee. "Now, that's good coffee."

Rebecca nodded and took out a cigarette. *Okay, so now I'll let Billie start.*

Billie took another sip of her coffee and sighed. She cleared her throat and shook her head.

Rebecca reached out and took one of Billie's hands. She squeezed it and smiled at Billie. "You start whenever you want to, Billie," she said. "I'm here for you." *Now, this is my chance to show Billie how good a friend I am to her.*

Billie cleared her throat and started talking. "I've liked Drew from the first time I met him, my first Thanksgiving here, in Boston," she said. She grinned and chuckled. "It's been a long time since a black guy has liked me."

Rebecca nodded, not surprised. She knew from her own experience with Drew how charming he could be, even when she first met him. He, for the most part, made a good first impression. *There's a reason why his bar is so popular.* "I've a feeling that Drew isn't the first black guy to like you or have a crush on you, Billie," she said. She chuckled. "I'd be willing to bet on it."

"I wasn't surprised when I found out Drew had a crush on me," Billie said. "I was surprised when I realized that I also liked him." She shook her head. "I didn't think I liked guys in that way anymore, and so I was so confused by my attraction to him."

Rebecca chuckled and nodded in understanding. *I know what Billie means. I felt the same way when I realized that I was bisexual.* "Sometimes, we didn't know ourselves as well as we think we do," she said. She grinned. "And sometimes another person can make us feel things we thought we couldn't feel anymore."

"I was able to keep away from Drew until I became a waitress at his bar," Billie said. She shook her head and grinned. "I didn't know he was the owner until after I started working there."

Okay, I've got a question. "I need to ask you something," Rebecca said. "What about your relationship with Georgia? I know you were attracted to her. Why did you act on your attraction to her but resist your attraction to Drew?"

Billie sighed. "I was more comfortable with my attraction to Georgia than I was with my attraction to Drew," she said. "Most of my former boyfriends have been white guys, not black guys."

Rebecca gave Billie a questioning look. "You mostly dated white guys, Billie? In Louisiana?" *She's braver than I thought she was. It has been the opposite for me. When I date guys, it's usually black guys, not white ones, though I haven't dated a guy since I broke up with Drew.*

Billie shrugged her shoulders. "I don't think it's easy anywhere," she said. "Now, I'll admit I had to be careful when it came to dating white guys, but I could tell which ones liked me and which ones wanted to date me for the wrong reasons."

Rebecca nodded. "I know what you mean," she said. *I've had to do the same thing with black guys. Let's get back to what we were talking about.* "What changed your mind about Drew?"

Billie smiled. "I started talking to Drew after last Thanksgiving," she said. She shrugged her shoulders. "He seemed to be okay with just being friends with me."

Rebecca chuckled. "I find that hard to believe," she said. *I believe Drew can only be friends with a woman, but I'm not sure he can do it with a woman he has feelings for.*

"I found it easy to talk to him," Billie said. "He seemed to accept me for who I was and didn't flirt with me."

Rebecca nodded and sipped her coffee. *I'm glad that Billie is confiding in me and sharing what has been happening in her life.* "So, what changed? Why did you decide to act on your attraction to Drew?"

Billie frowned. "Well, I acted because my feelings for him changed," she said. She shrugged her shoulders. "I'm not sure when they changed, but I know they did."

Okay, I might suggest something here. "I'd like to suggest something, Billie," Rebecca said. "Maybe your history with black guys stopped you from acting on your attraction to Drew."

Billie nodded. "You're right, my history with black men did stop me from acting on my attraction to Drew," she said. She shrugged her shoulders. "And they also confused me because I didn't think I could be attracted to or have feelings for a man."

Rebecca nodded. "Okay, we think we've already gone over that part," she said. "Tell me more about your experience with black guys." *It seems to me that it would have been easier for Billie to date black guys, especially in the South.*

Billie sighed. "Well, I learned that while black guys liked me, they didn't understand me," she said. "They didn't like or understand why my best friend was a white girl." She frowned. "And when they found out that I'm mixed, having a white father, they stopped seeing me as a black girl."

Rebecca nodded. "I know what you mean," she said. She sighed. "I've gone through the same thing when a black guy I liked found out my mother's a white woman." *Of course, I'm sure most, if not all, of the black guys I've dated knew I had a white mother before they started dating me.*

Billie smiled. "Yeah, I'm sure you did," she said. She sighed. "Black guys made me feel like I wasn't black enough." She chuckled. "White guys were different. They always made me feel like a black girl, even after they found out I was mixed." She cleared her throat. "I'm nervous about my feelings for Drew and confused about them, too."

"It's okay to be nervous about your feelings for Drew," Rebecca said. "And it's okay to be confused about them, too." *I'm guessing this is the first time Billie didn't understand why she had feelings for someone.*

Billie smiled at Rebecca. "Thanks for listening to me," she said. She sighed and shook her head. "I feel like I'm too old to be confused about my feelings for another person."

Rebecca smiled back at Billie. "We're friends," she said. "I'm always here for you if you need me." *It feels good to have a friend. It has been too long since I've had a friend.*

Billie nodded and took out a cigarette. She lit it and leaned back in the couch, her back resting against the back of the couch.

I hope Billie's feeling better now. Maybe she's talked enough about what's bothering her and is ready to do something. "Do you feel any better, Billie?"

Billie shrugged her shoulders. "Well, I still feel confused about my feelings for Drew," she said. She grinned. "But I do feel better about deciding to date Drew." She took a drag off her cigarette. "I know you made grits for us, and I do want to eat them, but I don't want to sit here. I want to do something."

"Let's go out and have a few drinks," Rebecca said. "After all, it has been too long since we've gone out." *I'm exaggerating a little bit. I'm sure Billie knows I'm only kidding.*

Billie chuckled. "I know that's not true," she said. "But you're right, we should go out and have a few drinks."

Rebecca smiled and stood up. "Okay, it's settled," she said. "I'm not going to let those grits go to waste, so we'll have a small bowl each and then go out." *It's better to have a full stomach before going out for a few drinks.*

Billie stood up. "Good idea," she said. "Let's eat in the kitchen."

***

Rebecca and Billie left the living room and went to the kitchen, where Billie sat down at the kitchen table while Rebecca prepared a bowl of grits for both of them.

"So, where should we go to have a few drinks?"

"Why don't we go to Jackson's Jukebox?" Rebecca grabbed the two bowls of grits and sat at the kitchen table, across from Billie. She handed Billie a bowl of grits. "We always have a good time whenever we go there." *And it's one of my favorite bars.*

Billie sighed and shook her head. "I don't know if I want to go there," she said. "I need some time away from Drew."

Rebecca shook her head, frustrated. "Well, the only other bar we like going to is Capote's," she said. "And I don't think you want to go there, because of Georgia." *I don't need to remind Billie that we haven't been to Capote's since she broke up with Georgia. Well, I've been there a few times, but not with Billie.*

Billie nodded. "Yeah, you're right," she said. "If we go to Capote's, there's a chance we would run into Georgia."

Rebecca chuckled. "I'm not worried about running into her," she said. "I'm more worried about her watching us, making us uncomfortable." *I'm still not sure why Billie ended it with Georgia, but I'm sure Georgia feels the same way.*

Billie sighed. "Yeah, I think she's having a hard time," she said. "I didn't want to hurt her, but I did."

Rebecca went over to Billie and embraced her. "I know you didn't want to hurt her," she said. "And I also know that you did what you thought was best for you both." *From what I saw and from what Billie told me, I think Georgia took their relationship more seriously than Billie did.*

Billie chuckled. "You don't seem worried about Drew either watching us or bothering us," she said. "Why's that, Rebecca?"

Rebecca smiled. *Okay, now Billie's teasing me back.* "We both know Drew will leave us alone, too busy in his office even to notice we're there."

***

Billie and Rebecca left her apartment twenty minutes later. Instead of taking one of their cars, they got a taxi. They arrived at Jackson's Jukebox some ten minutes later, and they made their way in and sat down in their favorite booth.

Billie cleared her throat and shook her head. "Why don't you tell me about your relationship with Drew?"

Rebecca sighed. "Okay, just remember you asked me," she said. She told Billie about her relationship with Drew.

Chapter Twenty-Three

When Nina's sophomore year at Harvard ended in June 1992, instead of leaving Boston and returning to New Orleans, she decided to get an off-campus apartment and stay in Boston for the summer. Billie helped her get a job at the same bookstore where Billie worked part-time.

Nina had grown accustomed to the academic rigor and the vibrant campus life at Harvard and was looking forward to her junior year.

So, Nina spent her summer in Boston working at the bookstore, either sitting in her small studio apartment reading or walking around Boston, visiting all the tourist sights. She eagerly counted the days until her third year, her junior year, at Harvard started.

***

On the morning of Nina's twentieth birthday, August 10, Nina was sipping coffee and sitting on her bed when her phone rang. She looked over at the ringing phone and frowned.

I'm not expecting anyone to be calling me right now. Nina glanced at her watch and shook her head. *It's too early for Mama or Father to be calling me.* She reached over and picked up her phone.

"Hello," she said.

"Hey, Nina, it's me," a familiar voice said. "I wanted to tell you happy birthday."

Nina smiled. "Hey, Billie," she said. "Thanks." She shook her head and chuckled. "I'm glad you remember my birthday." *I'm only teasing her. She's always remembered my birthday.*

"Now, you know good well that I've always remembered your birthday," Billie said. "I'm not Willie."

Nina chuckled. "Okay, you're right," she said. "The only birthday he could ever remember was his own." *Maybe I should stop doing this, bashing him behind his back. It's not fair to him or nice.*

Billie chuckled. "Oh, I'm sure he knew when our birthdays were," she said. "He just didn't care because those days weren't about him."

Nina nodded. "You might be right," she said. She cleared her throat. "So, it was good talking to you, Billie." *I wouldn't want to keep her from hanging out with her friends or new boyfriend.*

"I'm not done talking to you yet," Billie said. "So, do you have any plans to celebrate your birthday?"

Nina chuckled and shook her head. "I don't have any plans to celebrate my birthday," she said.

"You don't have any plans?" Billie chuckled. "I can't believe you don't want to celebrate your birthday."

Nina shook her head and laughed. "I didn't say I didn't want to celebrate my birthday," she said. *Sometimes, Billie takes what I say to her and goes beyond, assuming she knows what I feel.* "I just didn't make any plans." She sighed. "I'm only turning twenty, so it isn't a milestone or a big deal."

"Turning twenty is a big deal," Billie said. "So, I'm coming over and we're going to celebrate your birthday."

Nina smiled. "Okay," she said. "I'll be sure to have coffee ready for us." *So, my big sister does want to spend time with me.*

***

Twenty minutes later, Billie arrived at Nina's apartment. Nina invited her in, and Billie sat on Nina's bed while Nina made her a cup of coffee. She returned to her bedroom and sat next to Billie on the bed. She handed Billie's coffee to her.

Nina wanted to ask Billie about her life, having heard a few things while working at the bookstore, but she knew better than to ask Billie any personal questions.

Billie sipped her coffee and smiled. "Now, this is some good coffee," she said. She reached out and took one of Nina's hands. "I know we haven't seen each other since last Thanksgiving, and I'm sorry about that."

Nina shrugged her shoulders and gave Billie what she hoped was an understanding smile. "I understand you've been busy," she said. *Why am I doing this again? Why do I make excuses for her?* "I've been kind of busy too."

Billie sighed and shook her head. "Mom called me the other day and she wasn't happy that I didn't know what was going on with you," she said. She chuckled and grinned. "I'm sure she also called Willie and gave him the same speech."

Nina nodded. "I'm sure you're right," she said. She chuckled and grinned. "Unlike you and Willie, I know how to stay out of trouble." *It helps that my best friend doesn't live here, in Boston.*

Billie laughed. "I've been staying out of trouble," she said. "I'm not a rebellious teenager anymore." She sipped her coffee and gave Nina a questioning look. "You seem like you want to ask me something, Nina." She smiled. "What's on your mind?"

Nina cleared her throat and shook her head. "I do have something I want to ask you," she said. *Okay, I have to tell her that I've been talking to Michelle.* "I know, because Michelle told me in a letter that you spent your birthday in New York City, hanging out with your best friend Bobbie and her."

Billie chuckled and nodded. "Michelle tells you everything, doesn't she?"

Nina shook her head. "I don't think she does," she said. She sighed. "Michelle's a closed book, even with me sometimes." *I sometimes wonder if I should try to convince Michelle to leave New York City and move up here so she can be part of my life again. I don't because I'm not sure she would leave New York City, especially when she's dating Bobbie.*

Billie squeezed Nina's hand. "You miss her, don't you?"

Nina nodded, not saying anything. *Of course, I miss my best friend.*

Billie took out a cigarette and was about to light it when she stopped herself. She looked over at Nina, giving her a questioning look while holding up her cigarette.

Nina chuckled and shook her head. "Sorry, but there's no smoking in this building," she said. She held out her hands. "I don't know, they didn't allow smoking here until after I moved in." *But on the bright side, since I have to go outside to smoke a cigarette, I've cut down on my smoking, going from smoking almost a pack a day to only half a pack a day.*

Billie shrugged her shoulders and put her cigarettes back in her pocket. She sipped her coffee. "Would you like to go out and celebrate your birthday, Nina?"

Nina smiled and nodded. *If anyone else had asked me, I would've said no, but I'm not going to turn down Billie.* "I'd love to celebrate my birthday with you, Billie," she said. "I don't remember the last time I celebrated my birthday with you."

Billie nodded. "Yeah, it's been a long time, hasn't it?" She sipped her coffee, her eyes closed. "So, where should we go?"

Nina sipped her coffee. "I hate to remind you of something you already know, but I'm only twenty, so we can't go to a bar or nightclub," she said. *I know Billie loves to go out to drink, whether it's at a bar or a nightclub.* She smiled. *The only thing Billie loves to drink more than alcohol is coffee.*

Billie nodded and chuckled. "I haven't forgotten how old you are, Nina," she said. "I know you're four years younger than me."

Nina laughed. "Well, I'm glad you haven't forgotten," she said. "I know how much you love to go out and drink, so I just felt I needed to remind you that I'm not old enough to go to either a bar or a nightclub." *I won't tell her that I used to go out with Michelle before I moved here, and Michelle always found a way for us to get into bars or nightclubs despite being underage. Of course, Michelle may have already told her, but I doubt it.*

Billie chuckled. "I always found a way to go to a bar or a nightclub to drink when I was younger than you are now," she said. "Now, don't tell anyone this, especially either Mom or Willie, but I had fake IDs made for me and Bobbie."

Nina nodded while grinning at Billie. "I'm not surprised to find this out," she said. *So, I followed her example despite not knowing Billie had done the same thing.*

Billie grinned. "I know where we can go," she said. "There's one bar where we can go to celebrate your birthday."

Nina frowned. "I'm going to need you to explain yourself," she said. *I don't know of any bars or nightclubs that would let someone my age inside, not without a fake ID.* "I don't have a fake ID, and unless you can get one for me, I don't see how we can go to a bar."

Billie chuckled and grinned. "I'm guessing you must not be talking to Willie," she said. "I'm sure that you have talked to Willie lately, you would either already know or be able to guess what I'm about to tell you."

Nina shook her head and gestured for Billie to continue. *And I'm reminded again of how little I know about either Billie's or Willie's life. I had hoped that they had outgrown keeping things secret from me.*

Billie clicked her tongue, grinning. "Okay, what I'm about to tell you is going to surprise you, and I'm sure you're going to have many questions," she said. "Here's the thing. I have a boyfriend and he's the owner of a bar." She leaned back against the headboard of Nina's bed and sipped her coffee.

Nina shook her head and giggled. *So, what I've heard about her is true. I wouldn't have ever believed that she had a boyfriend.* "I didn't think you would ever have a boyfriend again," she said. "Is he a white guy?" *Given what I saw when I was younger, I would be surprised if he weren't. Mama also used to worry about it, telling my father that she worried about Billie, not wanting her to date a white guy.*

Billie shook her head. "I didn't think I would date a guy again," she said. "And no, he's a black guy."

Nina shook her head and chuckled. "A black guy, uh?" *I'm not sure what to say to her. I never thought I would see the day my older sister would date a black guy again.* "I thought you didn't like black guys."

Billie shook her head and grinned. "Oh, I like them, but most of the time, they don't like me," she said. She shrugged her shoulders. "Believe it or not, it has always been easier for me to date white guys."

Nina nodded. "I believe you, though I still don't understand why it was easier for you to date white guys instead of black guys," she said. She chuckled. "But then again, I'm not worried about understanding why." *I'm being honest with her. I'm just glad she's opening up to me.*

***

Nina and Billie left Nina's apartment thirty minutes later. Nina followed Billie to her car, which was parked in the parking lot near Nina's apartment. She stopped Billie by grabbing her elbow.

"So, how are we doing this?" Nina pointed at Billie's car. "Are we driving separately or are we riding together?" *If we drive in our own cars, there's no guarantee that we'll spend some time together.*

Billie smiled. "Let's ride together," she said. She chuckled. "It would be easier for me to give you directions to the bar we're going to."

Nina smiled and nodded. "Okay," she said.

They hopped into Billie's car, and she drove them to the only bar in Boston she was sure would let Nina in, even though Nina was only twenty.

"I'm sure you're curious about how I got a boyfriend," Billie said, glancing over at Nina. She shook her head and grinned. "I knew he liked me and wanted to date me after meeting him at Willie's apartment."

Oh, Billie can't be talking about Drew. Nina squinted at Billie. "Are you saying your new boyfriend is Drew, one of Willie's friends?" *I never thought Willie would let his friends date me or Billie.*

Billie nodded. "Yeah, that's what I'm saying," she said. She giggled and shook her head. "I promise I will tell you the whole story, but first, I want to know about your dating life." She looked over at Nina. "So, are you dating anyone?"

Nina shook her head and chuckled. "I've dated a few guys in the two years I've been a student at Harvard, but nothing serious," she said. She shrugged her shoulders. "To be honest with you, Billie, I've been more focused on my studies, not worrying about my dating life." *There's another reason, one I won't tell her. Unlike her, I've always preferred to date black guys, and there aren't a lot of them at Harvard.* She sighed. *Or other black girls, either.*

***

Nina and Billie arrived at Jackson's Jukebox.

Nina smiled. *I've heard about this place from some of my fellow students.*

Billie looked over at Nina and grinned. "Well, here we are," she said. "This bar is named after our grandfather, Jackson Baldwin."

Nina chuckled and nodded. "I knew that," she said. *I haven't told anyone this bar is named after our grandfather because I don't think any of my classmates would believe me.*

Billie and Nina left Billie's car and walked to the front entrance. Nina followed Billie into the bar and to a booth nearby. They sat down, and Billie looked around for a waitress.

Nina cleared her throat. "So, what are we going to do when a waitress asks me to show her some ID, Billie?"

Billie grinned. "We don't have to worry about that," she said. "Drew's the owner."

***

A waitress came over to their booth a few minutes later. She nodded at Nina and smiled at Billie. "Hey, girl," she said. She grinned. "I would ask why you're here since you're not scheduled to work today, but I know better."

"I'll tell you why I'm here, Millie. I'm here because of her," Billie said, pointing at Nina. "This is my younger sister, Nina, and today is her twentieth birthday."

Millie frowned. "You know she can't be here, Billie," she said. "No one under the age of twenty-one is allowed to be even in here."

"Why don't you go and get the owner," Billie said. She smiled. "I'm sure I can talk him into letting her stay."

Millie laughed and grinned. "I know you're his girlfriend now, Billie, but don't overestimate your power over him," she said. She shrugged her shoulders. "If it were up to me, I would ask you and her to leave, but I'm not the owner." She sighed. "I'll go and get him." She then walked away.

***

A few minutes later, the owner, Billie's boyfriend, walked to their booth.

Billie stood up and hugged him. "Hey, Drew," she said. She pointed at Nina. "You remember my younger sister, Nina, don't you? Today is her twentieth birthday."

Drew sighed. "She can't be in here, Billie," he said.

Billie smiled. "I'm not going to let her drink," she said. "I want her to have a great birthday, and I think this is the best place for us to celebrate her birthday."

Drew chuckled. "Okay," he said. "I'll be right back."

Drew left their booth and went back to his office. When he returned to their booth a few minutes later, he held out his hand. "Can I see your right hand, Nina?"

Nina looked over at Billie, who smiled and nodded. She gave Drew her right hand.

Drew stamped her wrist and smiled at Billie.

Nina looked at what he had stamped on her wrist. It was the number 21 in a circle, and it was marked out. She chuckled and nodded, understanding what Drew had stamped on her. "Thanks," she said.

Drew smiled at Nina and nodded. He looked over at Millie, who was standing nearby. "I want you to make sure that Nina has a good time, but no alcohol for her."

Millie walked away to get Nina and Billie something to drink.

Chapter Twenty-Four

When Truman left his grandmother's house the next day, the day after Christmas, she stopped him before he walked out the front door.

"Hey, Josephine," Truman said, remembering not to call her grandmother or anything like that. "Do you need something?" *I hope she won't give me a hard time for saying goodbye to Billie.*

Josephine nodded. "I need you to do something for me," she said. She stepped closer. "I want you to keep an eye on Billie for me."

Truman frowned. "What do you mean, keep an eye on Billie?" He shook his head and sighed. "Billie's grown up, Josephine. I can't keep her out of trouble even if I weren't always working." *And from what Willie has mentioned a few times, whenever I could get him to talk about Billie, Billie doesn't listen to anyone except for her best friend, Bobbie.*

Josephine chuckled. "I know you can't keep her out of trouble," she said. She sighed. "I am worried about her having problems with the other members of the Upper Crust world."

"Okay," Truman said. "What do you want me to do about that, Josephine?" *Billie will have problems, and I can do nothing to stop that. The world we live in, the Upper Crust, isn't accepting of anyone like Billie.*

"I would like you to keep an eye on Billie," Josephine said. "Do whatever you can to make it easier for her." She reached out and took his arms. "I need you to promise me you will do that for me."

Truman nodded. "I promise I will," he said. He turned around and left his grandmother's house.

***

Truman did his best to keep his promise to his grandmother and kept his eye on Billie. Their grandmother knew it wouldn't be easy for Billie to be accepted by the other families of the Upper Crust.

Truman was pleased to see that Billie had become friends with Rebecca Dubois, whom he felt would be Billie's best ally and guide. He kept in touch with Billie, calling or spending time with her once a week. He watched as she handled her two rivals, Jasmine Carter and Bridget Jackson. Somehow, she had charmed them into ending their rivalry with her. Or so he thought.

***

Truman sat in his small studio apartment in South Boston, the Friday before Labor Day. He had just returned home, tired from a long day at the law firm where he had been working since graduating from law school two years before.

His phone rang, and Truman frowned. *I'm not expecting anyone to call me. Maybe I shouldn't answer it and just let it ring.*

He sighed and shook his head. *I'd better answer it.* He leaned over and picked up his phone, answering it.

"Hello, you've reached Truman Carver's residence," Truman said. "This is Truman speaking. How may I help you?"

"Hey, Truman, it's me," a familiar voice said. "So, you do go home sometimes."

Truman smiled. "Hey, Billie," he said. He glanced at the calendar hanging on the wall in the kitchen. "We've already talked this week, so what's going on with you? Why did you call me?" *Please, don't tell me any bad news about Josephine, Billie.*

Billie chuckled. "Don't worry, I don't have any bad news," she said. "I just wanted to chat with you."

***

Truman and Billie chatted for a few minutes, catching up.

Billie cleared her throat. "I'd like to see you, Truman," she said. She laughed. "What do you think? Would you mind spending some time with your little sister?"

"I wouldn't mind at all," Truman said. Billie must have something on her mind. "So, where do you want to meet?"

"Why don't I just come to your apartment, Truman?" Billie chuckled. "Or are you embarrassed to show your bachelor pad to me?"

Truman shook his head and grinned. "It's a bit messy, but I try to keep it clean," he said. He glanced at his watch. "I'll see you when you get here." *I should have enough time to clean up this place before she arrives.*

***

Twenty minutes later, Truman opened his front door and smiled at Billie.

"You were right on time," he said, stepping back. "This is the first time you've ever been here, isn't it?" *I don't remember Billie coming by before now.*

Billie nodded. "It is my first time here," she said. She smiled at Truman and walked in, going past him. She went to his small living room/bedroom and sat on his couch.

Truman closed his front door and joined Billie, sitting beside her on his couch with a pull-out bed.

Billie took out a cigarette and lit it. "So, how have you been, Truman?" She grinned. "How's your dating life? Are you seeing anyone?"

Truman grinned back at Billie. "I've been busy at work," he said. He sighed and shook his head. "My dating life is an entirely different story." He chuckled. "No, I'm not seeing anyone." He shrugged his shoulders. "I work seventy to eighty hours a week, which doesn't leave any time for a relationship or even to date." He smiled. "I've heard that your dating life is going well." *I'm lucky that Willie works in the same building as me, even if we don't work at the same law firm. And I'm fortunate that he keeps me updated on what's going on with Billie whenever we have lunch together. He sometimes tells me things that I know Billie may not tell me.*

Billie grinned and laughed. "I would ask you who told you, but I think I can guess who told you," she said. She shook her head. "I thought that Josephine knew better than to tell you about my dating life."

Truman shook his head. "She didn't tell me," he said. He smiled and chuckled. "I have lunch with Willie almost every day, Monday to Friday, and he's the one who keeps me updated on your life." *So, Billie tells Josephine about her dating life.*

Billie shook her head. "I didn't know he knew anything about my dating life," she said. She sighed. "I'm dating one of his best friends." She cleared her throat. "I found out that Jasmine's our cousin."

Truman nodded. "I wanted to tell you, but I didn't want to stick my nose into your life," he said. *So, Billie didn't know.*

Billie chuckled and shook her head. "Now, you're trying not to stick your nose into my life?" She took out a cigarette and lit it. She grinned at Truman and took a drag off her cigarette. "I know that Josephine asked you to keep an eye on me."

Well, I don't think there's any point in lying to her. Truman nodded and grinned back at Billie. "She did," he said. He shrugged his shoulders. "I was worried about you, too."

Billie reached out and slapped Truman on his chest. "You didn't have to worry about me," she said. "I'll admit that I had some trouble with a couple of other ladies, but they were nothing I couldn't handle."

Truman nodded. "Yeah, I know," he said. *Okay, I shouldn't say anything else. Billie may not be mad that I was watching her for Josephine, but she might not like how much I know about what has been going on in her life.* He stood up. "Let's get out of here."

Billie nodded. "That sounds like a good idea," she said. She stood up, chuckling. "Come on, let's go. I'm ready."

Truman stood up. "I'm going to use the bathroom," he said. He rubbed his chin. "I need to shave and wash my face." *I wonder where Billie wants to go.*

Truman went to the bathroom and freshened up. He washed his face and shaved while Billie waited near the front door.

Truman left the bathroom and joined Billie by his front door. "Okay, I'm ready," he said. "Let's go."

Billie held up one hand. "I need to make a phone call before we go," she said. She chuckled and grinned. "Don't worry, I won't take long."

Truman smiled. "I'm not worried," he said. "I'll wait for you in the hallway so that you can have some privacy." *Now, who in the world would Billie be calling right now?*

***

Truman waited in the hallway while Billie made her quick phone call. He waited five minutes, and Billie joined him in the hallway, closing his front door behind her.

"Okay, we can go now," Billie said, smiling. "Thanks for letting me use your phone."

"You're welcome," Truman said. He smiled. "Now, will you tell me who you called, Billie?" *I have a feeling that she's up to something.*

Billie grinned and shook her head. "I've a surprise for you," she said. "I'm not going to tell you what it is, so don't even ask."

Truman shook his head and laughed. "Okay, I wouldn't ask," he said. "I never thought you would ever try to surprise me." *Billie has a stubborn side; when she says she won't answer a question, she means it. I may not know her as well as Willie, but I do know this much about her.*

***

Truman and Billie arrived at the Harvard Club thirty minutes later. They walked in, and Billie followed Truman to a booth in the back.

Billie waited until they sat in the booth. Then, she looked over at Truman and smiled. "Why are we sitting in the back, Truman?" She took out a cigarette and lit it. "Are you worried about being seen with me?"

Okay, Billie's teasing me. Truman grinned and shook his head. "I'll sit here whenever I come here," he said. "So, no matter who's with me, when I bring them here, this is where we sit."

Billie nodded. "Okay," she said. She took a drag off her cigarette. "Why haven't you told me about this place or brought me
here before now?"

Truman shrugged his shoulders. *I'm not sure why I didn't tell
Billie about this place.* "I don't know why I haven't told you
about this place or why I haven't brought you here," he said.
He sighed. "I know we're becoming friends, but you're still my
younger sister."

Billie gave Truman a long, hard look, deciding, it seemed
to Truman, if he was telling her the truth. She laughed and
grinned. "Okay, I believe you," she said.

A waitress came over to them and smiled at Truman. "Good
evening, Mister Carver," she said. She glanced over at Billie. "I
see you have a guest."

Truman nodded. "This is my younger sister, Billie," he said.
"Can you bring us a vodka tonic for her and a scotch soda for
me?" *No, young lady, I'm not on a date. So, you can stop giving
Billie that look, like she doesn't belong here.*

The waitress nodded. "I'll be right back with your drinks."
She then walked away.

Billie waved at the waitress and held up three fingers. She then
looked over at Truman and smiled. "So, here you are, Mister
Carver," she said. "You must come here often if a waitress knows
who you are."

Truman nodded. "Most of the time, when I come here, I'm
with clients," he said. He chuckled. "I'm trying to impress them
by bringing them here." *And most of the time, it works.* He
frowned. *Billie just glanced at her watch and looked towards the
front door.* "What's going on, Billie? Why did you glance at your
watch and the front door?"

Billie smiled and shook her head. "You'll find out soon
enough," she said.

The waitress returned with their drinks. She placed Truman's
drink, his scotch soda, in front of him and put the other two
drinks, both vodka tonics, in front of Billie.

Truman frowned. *Why did she bring us three drinks instead of the two I asked her to get us?*

"Thank you," Billie said, standing up. "Okay, are you ready for your surprise?"

Truman looked over his shoulder and saw Rebecca Dubois walking towards them. He shook his head and chuckled. "I should've known that you called her," he said. "You won't give up, will you?" *Billie seems determined to fix me up with her friend Rebecca.*

Rebecca joined them in the booth, sitting beside Billie and across from Truman. She smiled. "Billie invited me to join you two," she said. "I hope you don't mind, Truman."

Truman chuckled and shook his head. *The more I resist, the harder Billie pushes.* "I don't mind you joining us, Rebecca," he said. "I don't know why I'm surprised, Billie. You seem determined to play matchmaker with me and Rebecca."

Billie grinned. "I don't know what you're talking about," she said. She looked over at Rebecca. "I made sure to order a drink for you."

Rebecca flashed a quick smile at Billie. "Thanks," she said. She sat down across from Billie. "So, how have you been, Truman?"

Truman chuckled, picked up his drink, and sipped it. "I've been okay," he said. He leaned back and grinned. "I'm sure you two ladies have better things to discuss besides me."

Billie sighed and shook her head. "Sorry, Rebecca," she said. "I guess Truman's in one of his moods when he doesn't want to talk."

Truman nodded and took another sip of his drink.

Rebecca shrugged her shoulders. She turned her attention to Billie. "So, Billie, are you having any more problems with either Jasmine or Bridget?"

Billie shook her head. "Both of them seemed to have realized that they can't push me around," she said. She chuckled. "I still don't understand why either of them didn't like me when they first met me."

Rebecca nodded. "What about your co-worker at the bookstore?" She frowned. "I don't remember her name."

Billie shook her head. "You should remember her name, Rebecca," she said. "After all, Sadie is Iris's best friend."

Rebecca smiled. "So, you've found your place in the three different worlds we live in," she said. "And you did it in less than two years."

Billie sighed and shook her head. "I did, but what are we going to do about that stupid racist rule?" She reached out and grabbed one of Truman's hands. "What do you think, Truman?"

Truman frowned and looked over at Billie. "I'm sorry, Billie," he said. "I wasn't paying attention. Did you ask me a question?" *I'm pleased that Billie seems to have found a place in all the worlds she's part of, the Upper Crust, the black, and the gay world.*

Billie sighed and shook her head. "Do you remember Jasmine coming over with me to talk to Josephine the previous Labor Day?"

Truman chuckled and nodded. "Yeah, I remember," he said. "Wasn't that when you discovered she's our cousin?" *Maybe I shouldn't remind Billie that I kept something from her.*

Billie pointed at Truman and grinned. "You don't need to remind me about that," she said. She shook her head and chuckled. "The only thing that makes me feel better about not knowing is that Jasmine didn't know either." She frowned and looked over at Truman. "Why didn't Josephine tell me?"

Truman shrugged his shoulders. "I could take a guess, but I won't because I've given up a long time ago trying to figure out why Josephine does or doesn't do things," he said. *Hasn't Billie figured out yet that Josephine is the black sheep of her family and our family?*

Rebecca smiled. "If I don't know better, I'd say you two are acting like you've known each other all your lives," she said.

"You two tease each other like any older brother and younger sister I've ever known or met."

Billie smiled and nodded, pleased, while Truman laughed. "I don't know how to be a big brother, since I was raised as an only child," he said. He looked over at Billie and smiled. "I didn't even know I had a younger sister until Josephine told me about you, Billie."

Billie reached out and patted Truman's hand. "Well, I think you've been doing a great job of being my older brother," she said. She chuckled and shook her head. "Willie could learn a few things about being an older brother from you."

Truman cleared his throat. "I think we get along so well, Billie, because we didn't grow up together," he said. He shrugged his shoulders. "I'm sure we would've gotten on each other's nerves if we had grown up together." *Willie might not want me and him to be brothers, but we are friends, and I wouldn't be a good friend if I didn't try to defend him when someone was talking bad about him, even if it's Billie doing it.*

"Okay, that's enough of that," Rebecca said. She smiled at Billie and turned her attention to Truman. "I'm sure you've already figured this out, but I will say it anyway." She chuckled and grinned. "We both know why Billie invited me to join you two. It's because she's trying to hook us up."

Truman grinned and nodded while glancing over at Billie, who, though blushing, didn't look away. "Why do you think, Rebecca, that Billie wants us to get together?" *I might get Billie to be honest if I ask Rebecca instead of asking her.*

Billie shook her head. "You can't tell me that you're not attracted to Rebecca, Truman," she said. "I've seen the way you look at her."

Rebecca blushed. "And just how has Truman looked at me?" She shook her head and cleared her throat. "I didn't think you liked me, Truman."

Truman chuckled and grinned. "I've always liked you, Rebecca," he said. He frowned. "I thought you knew that." He looked over at Billie. "Billie figured out after spending some time around us."

Rebecca nodded. "I'm surprised," she said. She shook her head. "You were always so polite and friendly with me." She reached out and took Truman's hand. "Why didn't you tell me you like me, Truman?"

Truman shook his head. "I didn't see the point," he said. *I noticed that you used the present tense, Rebecca. And if I don't correct you, you'll know, and so will Billie, that I still like you.* He held up his hands, grinning. "You never stay single long, Rebecca, so when would I be able to tell you how I feel about you?"

Billie frowned. She looked over at Rebecca and gave her a questioning look. "Do you know what Truman means, Rebecca?"

Rebecca chuckled and nodded. "Truman's right," she said. "I've never gone without a date if I wanted one."

Billie smiled and nodded. "I believe that," she said. She cleared her throat. "So, now the question that I need to ask is this one, Rebecca. Do you like Truman, Rebecca?"

Truman blushed and shook his head in disbelief. "I could have asked her, Billie," he said. "I don't need your help getting a date or asking a young lady out." He sighed and smiled. "I've always been good at finding dates when I want one."

Billie shook her head. "I don't believe you, Truman," she said. She pointed at Rebecca. "There she is, an attractive young woman sitting before you. Are you going to ask her out or not?"

Truman nodded and chuckled. "I'll ask Rebecca out when I'm ready," he said. He sighed and shrugged his shoulders. "You don't seem to understand that I don't have much free time. Not with the long hours I work."

Chapter Twenty-Five

Three days later, Rebecca sat in her bedroom apartment. She couldn't believe Billie had attempted to set her up with her older half-brother, Truman. The real shock, however, was Truman's silence about their past acquaintance. She frowned, trying to make sense of it. Billie must have known that Truman knew her, as he was the one who introduced them.

The sudden ring of the phone jolted Rebecca out of her thoughts. She glanced at her watch, puzzled. *Who could be calling me today?* She sighed and stood up.

Rebecca left her bedroom and went to her kitchen, where her phone was hanging on the wall by the sink. She picked up the phone and cleared her throat.

"Hello?"

"Hey, Rebecca," a familiar voice said. "I was wondering if you would celebrate Labor Day at the country club."

Rebecca chuckled in disbelief. "I hadn't decided yet, Jasmine," she said. "I'm not sure how you got my number, but I have a feeling I know." *Jasmine was the last person I expected to hear from.*

Jasmine cleared her throat. "So, have you been to the country club lately?"

Rebecca sat down at her kitchen table and pulled out a cigarette from the pack sitting on the table. "I was there a few days ago, with Billie and Truman," she said. She grinned. "You won't believe this, but I think Billie tried to set me up with him."

"I thought you and he dated long ago," Jasmine said. "I mean, there's a spark between you two, isn't there?"

Rebecca nodded. "You might be right about that," she said. *Which is why I sometimes flirt with him.* She smiled. *And sometimes, he'll flirt back with me, though not when he's around Drew or Willie.*

"I've had that feeling too," Jasmine said. She sighed. "The real reason I called you is because I need your help and Billie's help, too."

Rebecca lit her cigarette. "You're still trying to get rid of that racist rule, aren't you?" *Jasmine is the last person I would ever have thought would become a crusader.* She frowned. "What about Billie's grandmother and your grandaunt, Josephine? I was under the impression that she would help you."

Jasmine sighed. "She is helping me," she said. "The board is proving to be more stubborn than even she thought they would be."

Rebecca shrugged her shoulders. "I'll help you in any way I can, Jasmine," she said. "And I'm sure Billie feels the same way." *I'm proud of Jasmine for not giving up and for wanting to make a change at the country club.*

"Thanks, Rebecca," Jasmine said. She sighed. "Well, I'll let you go. I hope to see you again soon at the country club."

"Okay, Jasmine," Rebecca said. "Keep your chin up." She hung up the phone and took a drag off her cigarette.

The phone rang again, startling Rebecca.

Now, who's calling me? Rebecca took a drag off her cigarette and picked up her phone.

"Hello?"

"Hey, Rebecca, it's me, Billie," she said. "How are you?"

Rebecca grinned. "Hey, Billie," she said. "I'm okay." *I'll tell her about the conversation I just had with Jasmine.* "I just got off the phone with Jasmine."

Billie laughed. "Oh, yeah? And what did she want?"

"She's still trying to get rid of that racist rule," Rebecca said. She took a drag off her cigarette. "It seems that even with your grandmother's help, the board is dragging its feet on changing the rule."

"That's not surprising," Billie said. She cleared her throat. "Has Truman called you yet?"

Rebecca giggled. *So, that's why Billie called me.* "No, Billie, Truman hasn't called me yet," she said. "Did you think he would call me?" *I didn't think he would, not because he doesn't like me, but because maybe he didn't feel comfortable dating or asking out a woman one of his friends had dated.*

Billie sighed. "Well, I hoped he would," she said. "All he does is work his ass off."

"Yeah, from what I've heard, the law firm he works at keeps him busy," Rebecca said. *It's time to change the subject.* "So, how have you been?"

"Oh, I'm okay," Billie said. "Say, do you have any plans for today?"

Rebecca chuckled. "Jasmine asked me the same thing," she said. "No, I hadn't made any plans for today."

***

Rebecca spoke with Billie for another twenty minutes, and Billie persuaded her to meet at the country club. She wasn't in the mood to attend Capote's or Jackson's.

When their conversation ended, Rebecca hung up her phone, chuckled, and shook her head while grinning. She glanced at her watch. *Well, since Billie wants us to meet at the country club in about an hour, I have plenty of time to decide what to wear.*

***

Ten minutes later, Rebecca was still sitting in her kitchen, sipping coffee and smoking a cigarette, when someone knocked on her front door.

Rebecca shook her head and chuckled. She didn't get many visitors, so she felt she knew who was knocking on her door. She stood up and left the kitchen, going to the front door.

Rebecca looked through the peephole and smiled. She opened the door.

"Hey, Billie," she said. "I thought we were going to meet at the country club." *Oh, no, Billie's got that look in her eyes again. Something must be on her mind.*

"I changed my mind," Billie said. "I knew you would wait until the last minute to leave." She smiled and walked past Rebecca, entering her apartment. She went to the kitchen and made herself a cup of coffee. She then sat down at the kitchen table.

Rebecca shook her head and grinned. "Come on in, Billie," she said. "I insist on your making yourself right at home." *I think living here is starting to erode Billie's polite ways.* She closed the front door and went to the kitchen.

Rebecca joined Billie in the kitchen, sitting at the table across from her. She picked up her cup of coffee and sipped it. "So, why did you come by when we planned on meeting at the country club?" *One thing I've learned about Billie is that while she isn't always open about herself, she isn't afraid to be truthful when asked a question, even though she doesn't always enjoy being questioned.*

Billie grinned. "I wanted to make sure you would attend the country club," she said. "I've noticed you don't seem to like going there like before, when Truman introduced us to each other."

Rebecca sighed and nodded. "You're right," she said. She sipped her coffee, deep in thought. "I'll be honest with you, Billie, after Jasmine told us about that stupid racist rule, I don't feel like I belong there anymore." *That's not entirely true. I'm not sure if I ever truly felt like I belonged there. I might come from one of the Upper Crust families of Boston, but until I met Billie, I didn't have any real friends.* She shook her head and laughed. "I think the only reason you wanted to make sure I showed up there is because you have also asked Truman to meet us there."

Billie held up her hands and grinned. "Okay, you're right," she said. "I did call him before I came over here."

So, Billie's determined to set me up with Truman. Rebecca chuckled and shook her head. "Why are you so determined for him to date me?" She sipped her coffee. "How do you know we haven't dated before?" *We haven't, though we've known each other for a long time.*

Billie shook her head and smiled. "I know y'all haven't dated before," she said. "And before you ask me how I know that, I'll tell you. I already asked Truman."

"Did he tell you why he's never asked me out?" Rebecca grinned and sipped her coffee. *I can make a good guess. Truman may not be best friends with Drew, but he's friends with Willie, who is also friends with Drew. It's part of the bro code that friends don't date or ask out their friends' ex-girlfriends.*

Billie shook her head. "He didn't have to tell me why," she said. "After discovering that he's friends with both Willie and Drew, I figured out why he hasn't ever asked you out." She sipped her coffee. "Though that doesn't stop him from flirting with you or you with him."

Rebecca shrugged her shoulders. "I won't deny that we sometimes flirt with each other," she said. *Okay, it's time to change the subject.* "Have you always been a matchmaker, Billie? Did you try to set up your best friend Bobbie with anyone?"

Billie grinned and shook her head. "No, I never did," she said. "Believe it or not, despite her shy ways, Bobbie never had trouble getting a boyfriend." She sipped her coffee. "One time, I did help a guy run into her at the swimming pool of the country club, back home, in New Orleans."

Rebecca nodded. "Go on, Billie," she said. She took out a cigarette and lit it. "I'm all ears." *I've noticed that Billie doesn't seem to like talking about her best friend or her old life when she lived in New Orleans. I wonder why.*

Billie shook her head. "It's a long story," she said. "And we don't have time for me to tell it."

Rebecca reached out and took one of Billie's hands. "Is there something bothering you, Billie?" *I'm starting to learn how to read her. When something's bothering her, she doesn't always want to talk about it, preferring to brood about it or write about it.*

Billie nodded and sighed. "Are you sure it won't bother you, me talking about her?"

Rebecca shook her head. "You're my friend, Billie," she said. "And if something is bothering you, I want you to tell me what it is." *Billie has listened to me when I needed someone to talk to, and I want to be there for her.*

Billie tried to smile. "Okay," she said. She sighed and shook her head. "I'm worried about Bobbie."

Rebecca frowned. "Why are you worried about her, Billie?" *I don't know why Billie would be worried about her because from the little she's told me about Bobbie and their friendship, it seems Billie was always the one who got them into trouble.*

"Well, I'm worried about her because I know that she hasn't gotten over losing her boyfriend from Arkansas," Billie said. She sighed. "And I'm sure she's snorting too much cocaine."

Rebecca nodded and gave Billie an understanding smile. "It sounds like Bobbie is going through a wild phase," she said. *So, I guess what I've heard about Catholic girls is true. They all go through a wild phase in their lives, especially when they move away from home.*

Billie nodded and chuckled. "Bobbie's been going through a wild phase for the last few years," she said. She sighed and shook her head, frowning. "I'm worried that she's going to go too far."

Rebecca shrugged her shoulders. "Well, from what you've told me about her, she's got some good sense," she said. "I'm sure she'll stop before she does anything that could ruin her life." *I hope what I just said to Billie is true. I'm unsure, since I don't know Bobbie and haven't met or spoken to her.*

Billie sighed. "I hope you're right," she said. She shook her head and chuckled. "I haven't gone through a wild phase yet." She looked over at Rebecca and took a sip of her coffee. "What about you, Rebecca? Did you ever go through a wild phase?"

Rebecca nodded and grinned. "Oh, yeah, I did," she said. "I'm sure you're surprised, but I wasn't always this well put together." *I don't know if Billie could have handled me a few years ago. I was out of control back then, while I was dating Drew.*

Billie smiled. "What happened? Why did you stop?"

Rebecca shrugged her shoulders. "I'm not sure why," she said. She sighed. "I think I became tired of how messy my life had become." She stood up. "Okay, we're going to the country club after I get dressed."

Billie nodded. "Okay," she said. She grinned. "Do you need any help in picking what to wear?"

Rebecca shook her head and grinned back at Billie. "No, I don't need any help," she said. "I've been dressing myself for a long time now." *Sometimes, I can't help but feel that Billie flirts with me. She's subtle about it, so I don't know if I should flirt back with her or ignore her tone and how she sometimes looks at me.*

***

Rebecca and Billie left her apartment twenty minutes later. Billie drove them from Rebecca's apartment to the country club in her car.

Billie looked over at Rebecca and smiled. "I like your outfit, Rebecca," she said. "It suits you."

Rebecca chuckled and smiled back at Billie. "Well, like I told you earlier, I've been dressing myself for a long time now," she said. "And I've been a member of the country club ever since my sixteenth birthday party." *What a disaster that party was. The only people I knew at that party were my mother and her family, who, most of them, didn't even want to be there.*

***

When they arrived at the country club, Rebecca saw Truman's car. She shook her head and chuckled while grinning at Billie. "Well, look over there," she said. "I know that car and so do you, Billie."

Rebecca and Billie left Billie's car and went into the country club. They went to the back patio, where Truman was waiting for them.

Rebecca went over to him and hugged him. "Billie seems determined to set us up," she said, almost whispering. "I think she wants us to become a couple."

Truman smiled and nodded.

Chapter Twenty-Six

Willie visited his parents for Christmas. He enjoyed himself for the most part, glad to be home and not in Boston, if only for a few days. His mother cornered him before he left the following morning, the day after Christmas.

"I need to talk to you before you go," she said, stepping before him.

Willie sighed and shook his head. "I thought I would be able to get out of here before you could corner me like this," he said. *Why is she doing this now?* "Okay, what's going on, Mama?"

"I need you to keep an eye on your sisters," she said. She held up her hands and chuckled. "I know they're both young ladies now, not little girls, but I still worry about them."

Willie nodded. "I know you do," he said. He shrugged his shoulders. "I don't know what you expect me to do. Nina's in college, and Billie lives with her white grandmother."

His mother sighed and frowned. "I wish you wouldn't call Josephine, who happens to be your grandmother too, Billie's white grandmother," she said. She reached out and placed her hands on his shoulders. "I appreciate you spending Thanksgiving with them, Willie."

Willie smiled. "I enjoyed having Thanksgiving with them," he said. *It's crazy that I get along with them better now that we all live in Boston than we ever did when we all lived in New Orleans.* "Okay, Mama, I'll do my best to keep an eye on them."

His mother smiled. "Thank you, Willie," she said. "Now, I want you to promise me that's what you will do."

Willie sighed and nodded. *She's not going to let me leave until I promise her.* "Okay, Mama," he said. "I promise I will keep an eye on Nina and Billie."

***

Willie did his best to keep his promise to his mother and kept an eye on Billie and Nina. Nina was, he found out, too busy at school to get into any trouble. On the other hand, Billie had plenty of time to get into trouble. She was making waves in her three worlds: the Upper Crust, the African-American, and the LGBT.

Willie wasn't surprised because Billie had always been one to make waves wherever she went. He couldn't help her find acceptance in either the Upper Crust or the LGBT world, but he could in the only world he shared with her, the African-American one.

Willie knew that Billie wouldn't come to him for help and would be furious at him if she found out he had involved himself in her life.

So, Willie had to be discreet in helping her whenever he could and keeping an eye on her. He tried to keep his friend Drew away from Billie, unsure if he liked that Drew was interested in her. He wasn't happy when he found out that Billie got a job as a waitress at the bar Drew owned, Jackson's Jukebox. He sometimes wondered if Drew had become his friend because Jackson Baldwin was his grandfather.

***

The day before his birthday, Willie had just gotten home from work when his phone rang. He sighed and shook his head. *Now, who in the world is calling me?* He picked up his phone. "Hello, this is William Baldwin speaking," he said. "How may I help you?"

"Hey, Willie, it's me, your baby sister."

Willie grinned. "Hey, Nina," he said. He glanced at his watch. "Is everything okay?" *This might be the first time she's ever called me.*

Nina chuckled. "Yeah, everything's okay," she said. "I just wanted to call you and tell you that I plan on celebrating your birthday tomorrow."

Willie shook his head and grinned. "I appreciate you wanting to do that, Nina," he said. "I don't plan on going out tomorrow or doing anything to celebrate my birthday." *My life isn't going to change just because I'm twenty-eight.* He sighed and shrugged his shoulders. *Here I am, still in my twenties, but I don't feel young.*

"I'm sorry," Nina said, sighing. "I didn't ask you if you wanted to go out and celebrate your birthday, Willie." She took a deep breath and slowly let it out. "I'm telling you I'm taking you out to celebrate your birthday."

Willie grinned and laughed. "Oh, you're telling me, Nina?" *She's starting to remind me of Billie, hard-headed as a mule.* "Are you trying to tell me that you're going to force me to go out and celebrate my birthday?"

"If I have to force you, I will, Willie," Nina said. She chuckled. "Come on, be nice to your baby sister."

Willie closed his eyes and rubbed them. "You're not going to change your mind, are you, Nina?" *I guess there are worse things in the world than having a younger sister who insists on taking you out to celebrate your birthday, even if you don't feel like celebrating.*

"No, I'm not," Nina said. "Soon, I'll come by tomorrow evening, say around seven? Does that work for you, Willie?"

Willie smiled. "Yeah, that works for me," he said. He cleared his throat. "So, I'll see you tomorrow, Nina." *She didn't say anything about Billie coming along, but I'd be surprised if Nina didn't make her come out with us. Nina's determined to become closer to me and Billie.*

***

The following day, Willie sat at his desk in his home office, reviewing some paperwork. He was trying to finish up some legal briefs before Nina showed up to take him out to celebrate his birthday.

Willie heard a knock on his front door. He glanced at his watch and nodded. *If that's Nina, she's right on time.*

Willie stood up and left his home office, which was also his bedroom. He went to his front door and opened it after glancing through the peephole.

"Hey, Willie," Nina said, walking into Willie's apartment. "As you can see, I talked Billie into coming out with us to celebrate your birthday."

Willie nodded and chuckled. "I see that," he said. He looked over at Billie and grinned. "How have you been, troublemaker?" *I knew Nina would talk Billie into going out with us.*

Billie grinned back at Willie. "I've been making waves wherever I go," she said. She went to him and hugged him. "Happy birthday, bubba."

She hasn't called me that in a long time. "Thanks," Willie said. He shrugged his shoulders. "Don't ask me if I feel any older."

Billie chuckled and grinned. "Okay, I won't ask," she said. She slapped his shoulder. "I know what you mean. I still don't feel like I'm twenty-four."

Nina laughed. "So, are we just going to stand here, or are we going to sit down and maybe visit?"

Willie pointed over his shoulder. "The living room is that way," he said. He chuckled. *I don't think I've ever had this many people in my apartment.* "Why don't y'all sit on the couch while I get us something to drink?" *I could try to talk to them out of taking me out to celebrate my birthday, but I doubt they'll listen to me.*

Nina nodded and smiled. "Sounds good to me," she said. She looked over at Billie. "What do you think, Billie?"

"Yeah, sounds good to me too," Billie said, nodding. She reached out and grabbed Nina's arm. "Come on, let's go and sit down."

***

Willie went to his kitchen to get them something to drink while Nina and Billie went to his living room. They sat on the couch together.

Willie pulled out three glasses from the cabinet near the refrigerator. *Okay, so Nina hasn't said what she wants to do to celebrate my birthday.* He grinned and shook his head. *I might get lucky, and they'll let me decide what we're doing or where to celebrate my birthday.*

Willie left his kitchen and went to his small living room. He handed Billie and Nina their drinks, a glass of sweet tea, and sat on the battered chair he had gotten from the nearby thrift store. He sipped his sweet tea with his eyes on Nina.

"So, what do you have planned for us today, Nina?"

Nina chuckled and shook her head. "I hadn't decided what we're going to do, Willie," she said. She shrugged her shoulders and grinned. "Hell, I wasn't sure I could talk you into doing anything to celebrate your birthday." She looked over at Billie. "I talked to Billie before I called you, and she didn't think I could talk you into going out."

Billie nodded. "Nina's right," she said. She chuckled. "I'm surprised you would even want to go out with us."

I know why they would think that about me. "Well, I know I haven't been the most approachable person when we were growing up," Willie said, frowning. He shrugged his shoulders. "I'm sorry about that." He cleared his throat. "I didn't know how to be a good older brother."

Billie nodded. "And you resented us, too," she said. "You thought our father only married our mother because of me, and you envied Nina for having a father."

Now, how in the hell did Billie know that? Willie nodded. "You're right, Billie, on both counts," he said. *Okay, time to change the subject.* "I'm not sure I want to go out to celebrate my birthday." He shrugged his shoulders. "I don't feel like turning twenty-eight is any kind of milestone like turning twenty-one or eighteen or even nineteen."

Billie nodded. "I know what you mean, Willie," she said. She chuckled and glanced over at Nina. "You'll know what we're talking about in a few years."

Nina shook her head. "I'm always going to want to celebrate my birthday," she said. "So, we're not going anywhere until we decide where to go to celebrate Willie's birthday."

Willie chuckled and pointed at Nina while looking over at Billie. "She's starting to remind me of our mother," he said. He shook his head. "I didn't know that she could be this pushy."

"Don't you know, Willie, that the women in our family are pushy?" Billie chuckled and shook her head, grinning. "Why don't we go to a bar?"

Willie shook his head and chuckled. "Okay, we may be old enough to drink at a bar, but Nina isn't old enough," he said.

"After all, she only recently turned twenty." *I shouldn't have to remind Billie about Nina's age.*

Nina and Billie laughed while grinning at each other.

Willie frowned. *Okay, why are they laughing so much?* "Is there something I don't know about?" *When did they start getting along so well?*

Nina held up her hand. "I'll tell him, Billie," she said. She turned her attention to Willie. "Billie took me out for my birthday, and we went to Jackson's Jukebox."

Willie nodded. *Okay, that's the one bar in Boston that Billie could get away with bringing Nina.* "You didn't drink, did you, Nina?" He shook his head. "Never mind, you don't have to answer. I'm sure that Drew made sure that you didn't get served alcohol."

Nina nodded. "He did," she said. She grinned and shook her head. "He marked my wrist and told Billie not to let me drink."

Willie grinned. "You're lucky, Nina," he said. "Most of the time, Drew doesn't let anyone under twenty-one enter his bar." He looked over at Billie and smirked. "She's the only reason why he did. I don't think that Drew can say no to our sister." *Yeah, Billie, I noticed. And so far, you haven't been taking advantage of his inability to deny you anything.*

Billie giggled and smiled. "Well, he hasn't told me no so far," she said. She shrugged her shoulders. "I can't help that he's crazy about me and wants to give me the world."

Nina cleared her throat. "So, anyway, let's get back on track," she said. She looked over at Willie. "Is there anywhere you want to go to celebrate your birthday, Willie?"

Willie sighed and shook his head. "Like I said earlier, I don't want to celebrate my birthday," he said. *But I won't be that guy who refuses to go out when his sisters want to take him out.*

Billie sighed and shook her head. She looked over at Nina. "I had a feeling that he wouldn't be in the mood to celebrate his birthday," she said.

Nina sighed and nodded. "I enjoyed celebrating my birthday with Billie," she said. "I felt like we had become closer." She looked over at Willie. "I want the same thing with you, Willie." She glanced over at Billie. "I want us all to be closer."

Willie chuckled and scratched his chin. "That isn't going to be easy," he said. He shook his head and grinned. "We might be from the same family and have the same mother, but we have nothing else in common." *Hell, we don't even have the same last name.*

Billie shook her head. "We have more in common than that, Willie," she said. She reached out and playfully punched him in the shoulder. "Now, we want to take you out to celebrate your birthday, and nothing you can say will change our minds."

***

Billie and Nina argued with Willie for another twenty minutes, determined to take him out and celebrate his birthday.

Willie sighed and shook his head. *Billie was right. They won't give up; nothing I can say will change their minds.* He held up his hands, smiling at them. "Okay, I get it," he said. "I'm crying uncle."

Nina grinned. "I thought you would argue with us for another ten minutes," she said. She giggled and glanced over at Billie. "I told you we would be able to convince him."

Billie nodded and smiled back at Nina. "Yeah, you were right," she said. She turned her attention back to Willie. "Okay, so where do you want to go, Willie?"

Willie grinned. *I'm glad I have some say in what we're about to do.* He cleared his throat. "How about, instead of going to a bar, which y'all seem to want to go to, we get something to eat?" *The only time we ever got along when we were kids was when our parents would take us out to eat. We knew we had to be on our best behavior.*

Nina nodded. "Sounds like a good idea to me," she said. She looked over at Billie. "What do you think, Billie?"

Billie smiled and nodded. "It's been a long time since the three of us have gone out to eat together," she said. She grabbed her pack of cigarettes off the coffee table and stood up. "Let's go."

Willie grinned and laughed. "So, we're not going to talk about where we're going to eat?" *I guess it doesn't matter to either of them where we're going, just as long as they get to take me out to celebrate my birthday.* He stood up. "Give me five minutes to change clothes."

***

Willie, Nina, and Billie left his apartment ten minutes later, after Willie had changed clothes and gotten out of his work attire. Billie and Nina almost got into Billie's car, but Willie stopped them, stepping in front of them.

Willie grinned. "I know the best place for us to celebrate my birthday," he said. "And it's close enough that we don't have to drive there, but can walk there instead." *I could tell them where we're going, but I'd rather surprise them.*

Billie frowned and squinted at Willie. "We'd better not be walking to some kind of gentleman's club," she said. "I swear to God, Willie, you better not be messing with us."

Nina rolled her eyes. "I'm sure Willie knows better than to mess with us, Billie," she said. "And I'm sure he knows better than to try to take us with him to a place with strippers."

Willie grinned. *Okay, so note to myself. I shouldn't try to take either of them to a gentleman's club.*

Nina and Billie followed Willie from his apartment building. They walked three blocks south. Willie and Billie smoked cigarettes while Nina told them about her new class schedule.

***

Billie smiled when they arrived at the restaurant, a small hole-in-the-wall kind of restaurant. "I should've known you would want to come here," she said. She looked over at Nina. "He's mentioned this place to me a few times."

Nina looked at the sign hanging near the front entrance. "This is where you want to eat, Willie?"

Willie nodded. "Yeah, this is the place," he said. He walked up to the front door and pulled it open. "Trust me, y'all are going to love this place." *The other thing we three have in common is that we're Southerners and love being from the South, even if Billie was born in Boston.*

The owner was cleaning one of the tables when Nina, Billie, and Willie walked in. She smiled at Willie. "Well, hey there, stranger," she said. "I haven't seen you in a few days." She walked over to him and hugged him. "I was afraid you had found a new favorite restaurant."

Willie laughed and shook his head. "I've been busy," he said. He stepped back and pointed at Billie and Nina. "Today's my birthday, and these two young ladies with me are my younger sisters, Billie and Nina." He turned his attention back to them. "Billie and Nina, this is the owner of this fine establishment, Miss Suzie." *I'm sure Nina will have some questions about this place.*

Miss Suzie smiled and nodded. "So, you finally decided to bring your sisters here," she said. She went over to Billie and Nina. She smiled at them and hugged them. "I've heard so much about y'all."

Billie chuckled. "Oh, you've heard about us, uh?" She glanced over at Nina. "Did you hear that, Nina? Willie likes to talk about us."

Miss Suzie laughed. "He does more than just talk about y'all to me," she said. She reached out and took their hands. "He brags about y'all to me all the time." She glanced over at Willie. "He's very proud of y'all, with you, Nina, going to Harvard, and you, Billie, working two part-time jobs while writing short stories." She shook her head. "Now, where are my manners? Y'all didn't come here to listen to me rattle on." She stepped back. "Just follow me now. I'll show y'all to Willie's favorite booth."

***

Willie, Nina, and Billie followed Miss Suzie to Willie's favorite booth. "I'll be right back with something for y'all to drink," she said, smiling at them. She turned around and walked away.

Nina cleared her throat. "Okay, I've got a few questions for you, Willie," she said. "How long have you been coming here, and why have you been talking about us to the owner, Miss Suzie?"

Willie grinned. *I knew it.* "I've been coming here ever since I moved here, after I graduated from Tulane," he said. He chuckled and shook his head. "I never thought I would miss New Orleans, but after I found this place, I realized I did miss it." *And I was tired of clam chowder.*

Nina nodded in understanding. "I know what you mean, Willie," she said. She glanced over at Billie and cleared her throat. "What about us? Did you miss us, too?"

I could be a jerk and say something that will hurt her feelings, but I won't do that. Willie smiled. "Yeah, I did miss y'all," he said. He shrugged his shoulders. "I didn't expect to miss you or Billie, since we didn't get along, and I thought y'all only irritated me." He reached out and took their hands. "Much to my surprise, I'm enjoying having y'all around and in my life."

Chapter Twenty-Seven

B illie and Drew started dating after they went to Rebecca's party. Drew was happy and enjoyed being Billie's boyfriend. He tried to spend time with her and kept their relationship private, not wanting the other waitresses to know about his relationship with Billie.

***

Two weeks after they started dating, Drew went to Billie after she had clocked out, but before she left the bar.

"Hey, Billie," he said, nervous. "I think it would be better for both of us if we kept our relationship private by not telling anyone else who works here about it." *I hope she knows it isn't because I'm ashamed of dating her.*

Billie shook her head and giggled. "We could try to keep it private and not tell anyone here about it," she said. She shrugged her shoulders. "I think they already know, even if they haven't said anything."

Drew frowned. "I haven't told anyone about us," he said. *I didn't think Billie gossiped with the other waitresses. Was I wrong?* "Have you, Billie?"

Billie shook her head. "I know how to keep things to myself," she said, grinning. "They knew about your crush on me, and I didn't tell them." She reached out and patted his face. "Don't worry about it, Drew. We know how to work together, so whether we're dating doesn't matter."

Billie has a point. Drew sighed and shook his head. "I'll try not to worry about it, but I don't like my employees knowing about my dating life," he said. He took her hand and kissed it. "We'll just have to remember to behave ourselves when we're here." *I will have a tough time being her boyfriend and boss, but she's worth it. She's the most amazing woman I've ever known or met.*

***

Drew noticed the other waitresses always stopped talking whenever he walked by. He would give them a look and tell them to get back to work. They would shake their heads, grin, and giggle when he walked away.

Drew's friendship with Willie became tense because he was dating Billie. Drew knew he would have to talk about it with Willie and waited for the right time when Willie confronted him, about two weeks after he started dating Billie.

Drew was in his office, reviewing some paperwork, when his phone rang. He frowned, shrugged his shoulders, and picked it up. "I'm kind of busy right now," he said. "So, I don't know why you called, but you can make it quick?"

"I'll be quick, Drew."

Drew sighed and shook his head. *I was waiting for him to call me.* "Hey, Willie," he said. "How have you been? What have you been up to lately?"

"Were you ever going to tell me you're dating Billie?" Willie sighed. "I was sure I told you to leave my younger sister alone."

"Billie's a grown woman," Drew said. "She's the only one who can say who she dates, Willie." *I hoped that he would be happy that I'm dating Billie.*

"I know that, Drew," Willie said. He sighed. "You better not be playing around with her."

***

Drew and Willie had a long talk about it, and Drew promised Willie that he was serious about Billie. Willie seemed to believe him and accepted their relationship.

Drew took Billie out two or three times a week, showing her the Boston he knew. He even told his parents about Billie, and they were eager to meet her, relieved to learn that she was black, not white, like his last two girlfriends.

***

A little over seven weeks later, Rebecca was sitting on the elegant patio of the country club, the late afternoon sun casting a warm glow. She was smoking a cigarette, the smoke curling into the air. Jasmine was sitting across from her, fidgeting with her napkin.

"Are you sure she's coming?"

Rebecca chuckled and nodded. "Yeah, I'm sure, Jasmine," she said. She took a drag off her cigarette. "When was the last time you talked to her?" *I don't think I've ever seen her this nervous before. Remember that time at the charity event? She was a wreck then, but she managed to pull through. She's not even trying to hide her anxiety.*

Jasmine sighed. "It's been almost a year," she said. She glanced at her watch and shook her head. "I wish I had better news to share with her."

Rebecca reached out with her free hand and placed it on Jasmine's left hand. "One thing, among many, I've learned about Billie is that she values honesty," she said. She leaned back in her chair and smiled at Jasmine. "Are you trying to change things around here because it's the right thing to do, or are you doing it because you want to be friends with Billie?" *She's changed a lot in only two years. I wonder if Billie knows how much she's changed the people she's met since moving here? I'm not sure how she's changed me, but I'm sure she has, in some ways.*

"I'm doing it because it's the right thing to do," Jasmine said. She sighed and shook her head. "And if I become friends with Billie at the same time...well, I don't see anything wrong in that."

Rebecca smiled. "No, there's nothing wrong with that," she said. "I consider myself to be one of her few friends, and I always enjoy myself when I spend time with her." *I also learn things about her and sometimes learn things about myself, too.*

Before Jasmine could say anything, they heard the back door open. Billie stepped out on the patio, and Truman followed behind her. She looked around and smiled when she made eye contact with Rebecca.

Billie and Truman walked over to them and joined them at the table.

"Hey, Rebecca," Billie said. "You didn't tell me Jasmine would be having lunch with us." She looked over at Jasmine. "Hey, Jasmine. How are you? I haven't seen you in almost a year now."

"I'm okay," Jasmine said. She cleared her throat and shook her head. "I wanted to update you about my efforts regarding that rule we discussed the last time we saw each other."

Billie nodded. "I've been wondering how you were doing with that," she said. She lit a cigarette; her eyes did not leave Jasmine. "And so has Josephine."

Jasmine sighed and frowned. "I've run into more resistance than I thought I would," she said. "Even with Aunt Josie's support, most of the board isn't willing to address the issue of that rule." She shook her head. "They won't even admit it's in the rule book."

Truman nodded. "They know what could happen if they do," he said. He looked over at Billie. "A few years ago, a country club in Birmingham, Alabama, lost a PGA tournament because they wouldn't allow black people to become members."

Jasmine frowned. "So, if they know what can happen if anyone else finds out about it, why won't they get rid of the rule?"

Rebecca shook her head and frowned. "They don't want to get rid of that rule," she said. She sighed. *I'm sometimes amazed by Jasmine's naivety.* "They want to keep it because, I'm sure, they're afraid if they don't have it, they won't be able to keep black people from becoming members here."

Jasmine frowned. "So, what do we do now? What's the next step?"

"I say we use their precious rules against them."

The four of them, Billie, Rebecca, Jasmine, and Truman, turned in their chairs. Bridget walked up to them, smiling, though she also looked nervous. She went to the only empty chair and pulled out. "Can I sit here?"

Billie nodded and smiled. "Sure, you can join us, Bridget," she said. "How have you been?"

Bridget sighed and shrugged her shoulders. "Well, I've been better, but I've also been worse," she said. She looked over at Jasmine. "So, I've heard the board is giving you a hard time."

Jasmine nodded. "They are, Bridget," she said. She bent over, opened her gym bag, and pulled out the country club's rule book. "What do you mean, we should use their precious rules against them?" She placed the country club's rule book on the table and pointed at it. "I've read this thing I don't know how many times now, and the only rule that I think needs to be changed is the one about not allowing so-called Negros to become members."

Bridget smiled and shook her head. "Yeah, I saw that rule," she said. She reached over and tapped the rule book. "There's another rule in there that I know many members have broken."

Jasmine frowned. "Which rule are you talking about, Bridget?" She opened the rule book and started flipping through it. "All the other rules seem okay, as far as I can tell."

Bridget chuckled and grinned. "I didn't see it either until after I read the rule book three or four times," she said. She pointed at the rule book. "I can show it to you if you'll let me see that stupid rule book."

Jasmine frowned and looked over at Billie, who grinned and nodded. "Okay," she said, pushing the rule book across the table to Bridget. "Show me what you're talking about, Bridget."

Bridget opened up the rule book and flipped through the pages until she found what she was looking for, the rule that could be used against the board. "Now, where is it?" She smiled and turned the rule book around so Jasmine could read it. "It says here that all members are forbidden from engaging in so-called immoral activities."

Billie chuckled and grinned. "And do they define what they consider an immoral activity?"

Bridget grinned and nodded. "Lucky for us, they did," she said. She flipped a few pages. "And right here, the immoral activities are defined."

Jasmine leaned forward and read. "So, whenever they wrote this, they considered gambling, drinking to excess, taking drugs, and having sex outside of marriage as immoral activities," she said. She shook her head and chuckled, grinning. "Did they forget about this rule?"

Bridget shook her head. "I don't think they forgot about it," she said. She grinned. "It's more likely that they know that if they tried to enforce the rule, most members would be kicked out."

Jasmine cleared her throat. "So, how do we use this rule about immoral activity to our advantage?" She sighed and shook her head. "I mean, the board wouldn't even admit that the racist rule is still in the rule book, so why should they care about this rule?"

Bridget grinned. "I thought you might say something like that," she said. She pulled out a small notebook from her purse and opened it. "After I found that rule about immoral activity, I decided to start noting how many members have broken this rule." She flipped through the pages, pointing out the names she had written down. "Everyone on the board has engaged in what their rule book calls immoral activities."

Truman cleared his throat. "Are you saying that you spied on them?"

Bridget shook her head. "I didn't have to, Truman," she said. She grinned and glanced over at Rebecca. "You may not know this, but I sometimes sell cocaine to many members of this country club." She chuckled and grinned. "And I've seen the other ones drink, either here or at the few bars I go to, when I don't drink here myself."

Billie nodded. "Do you have any proof, Bridget?" She sipped her coffee and then took a drag off her cigarette. "They're going to deny that they've done anything wrong."

"Billie's right," Jasmine said, sighing. "We'll need proof because otherwise, they wouldn't flinch."

Bridget shook her head and chuckled. "We don't need proof," she said. She pointed at the rule book, at the paragraph at the bottom of the page. "It says here that the suspicion of engaging in immoral activity is enough for anyone to lose their membership."

Truman frowned. "Are you suggesting, Bridget, that Jasmine should use blackmail to get the board to do something about the racist rule?" He shook his head. "I think there's a better way to handle this situation."

Bridget sighed and shook her head. "I sometimes forget you're a lawyer, Truman," she said. "There are other ways to handle people like the board besides using the law."

"Yes, I know about them," Truman said, standing up. "I can't be involved with those things because they're illegal and I'm an officer of the court." He looked over at Billie. "Come on, I don't want you to be part of anything Bridget has in mind."

Billie glanced at her watch and nodded. "I'll go if you'll drop me off at Drew's apartment," she said. She reached out and patted Jasmine on the shoulder. "Be careful, Jasmine. I'll help you in any way I can, but there are some lines that you shouldn't cross."

Jasmine stood up. "I'd like to talk to you some more, Truman," she said. "I need to know what the options are to make the board get rid of that racist rule...the legal ones."

Truman nodded. "Come on then," he said. "I need to drop Billie off, and then we can get some coffee and discuss your options."

Truman, Jasmine, and Billie walked away.

***

Bridget sighed and shook her head. "I was just trying to help," she said. She frowned and looked over at Rebecca. "I don't understand why Truman doesn't want me to help Jasmine."

Rebecca shook her head and chuckled. "Can I ask you something, Bridget?"

Bridget sighed and took out a cigarette. "Sure, go ahead," she said. "I didn't know being a good person would be this hard."

Rebecca leaned forward and rested her elbows on the table. "Jasmine came to me and Billie about this racist rule almost a year ago," she said. "And I know Jasmine looked into the rule book because she wanted to find a way to get Billie kicked out of the country club."

Bridget nodded. "Yeah, that's what she told me," she said. She sighed and shook her head. "And I wanted to get Billie kicked out, too."

Rebecca nodded. "Yeah, you didn't like Billie when you first met her, did you?" She sipped her coffee. "So, when you couldn't find a way to get Billie kicked out of here, was that when you decided to try to break her and Georgia up?"

Bridget nodded. "Yeah, something like that," she said. She lit her cigarette and took a drag off it. "I've apologized to Billie about that already, Rebecca."

"I've known you a long time, Bridget," Rebecca said. "Why are you trying to be a good person now?" She smiled and nodded. "It's because of Billie, isn't it?"

Bridget stared at Rebecca, not breaking eye contact. "Yeah, in a way, you could say it's because of Billie," she said. "Billie showed me that I didn't have to pretend to be someone else."

Rebecca nodded. "So, who are you trying to be now, Bridget?"

Bridget sighed. "I'm trying to be myself, Rebecca," she said. She frowned and shrugged her shoulders. "I'm not sure who that is, but I'm working on it."

Rebecca nodded. "If you want other people to like you, Bridget, and be your friend, the best way is to be yourself," she said. "I can't speak for Billie, but I'd like to be your friend." She smiled. "What do you think about that, Bridget?"

Bridget smiled back at Rebecca. "I'd like that," she said. "I would enjoy having you as a friend." She chuckled. "And Billie, too."

***

Drew sat in his apartment, waiting for Billie. It was Halloween, and Drew wanted them to go out. He had just finished talking to his parents over the phone. He had told them about Billie and promised them they would meet her.

His phone rang. Drew chuckled and picked it up. "Like I said, I promise I will introduce Billie to you, Mom," he said. "I think the best time to do it is Thanksgiving." *I haven't celebrated Thanksgiving with them for almost two years now.*

"It's me, your friend," Willie said. He chuckled. "So, you told your folks about Billie, uh?"

Drew shook his head. "Yes, I told them about Billie," he said. "I know they will love her, Willie." *He should know if I'm willing to introduce her to my parents, which means I'm serious about Billie.*

"I don't know if you should do that," Willie said. "You don't want to rush things with her."

Drew sighed. *He's right.* "No, I don't," he said. He glanced at his watch. "Listen, I'm expecting Billie to show up any minute now, so I will have to let you go." *I know that two of them are getting along better than ever, but I'm not sure Billie would like to know that I am talking about our relationship with him.*

"Okay," Willie said. "I'll talk to you again soon." He then hung up the phone, ending their conversation.

Drew shook his head and sighed. *I don't know if Billie's ready to meet my parents or wants to meet them.*

There was a knock on his front door. Drew grinned and glanced at his watch. *That has to be Billie who just knocked. She's right on time.*

Drew stood up and went to his front door. He looked through the peephole and opened the front door. "Hey, Billie," he said. "You're right on time." *Every time I see her, it's like the first time. How can she be so gorgeous?*

Billie walked in, smiled at Drew, and went past him. She went to his small living room and sat down on his couch.

Drew joined Billie in his small living room and sat beside her on the couch. "I love your costume," he said. "Remind me again, Billie. Who are you dressed up as?" *I didn't think she would dress up, but I'm glad she did.*

"One of my favorite authors," Billie said. "I've told you all about her, and her name is Millie Harlow."

Drew smiled. *I now understand why my mom would tell me that the best kind of girls are bookworms.* "I remember you telling me about her," he said. "Have you always been a fan?"

Billie chuckled and shook her head. "I've heard about her, but it wasn't until I read some of her short stories that I became a fan," she said. She grinned. "And after reading a few of her interviews, I became an even bigger fan."

***

Drew and Billie left his apartment ten minutes later. They walked to his car, holding hands.

Drew smiled. *I can't believe that we're still in the holding hands phase. I feel like I'm a teenager in love for the first time.* "I can't believe you talked me into having a Halloween party at my bar," he said. "Do you know how many people have tried before you?"

Billie grinned. "I do know," she said. "I mentioned it the other day, and everyone told me there was no way you would approve of having a Halloween party at the bar."

Drew chuckled. "Well, I guess they were wrong," he said. He frowned. "So, are you saying this was your idea, right?" *I won't put it past any of my waitresses or other employees to use my affection for Billie against me.*

Billie nodded. "It was my idea," she said. She chuckled and grinned. "Everyone else had long given up on trying to convince you," she said. She shook her head. "They didn't believe me when I told them I had changed your mind."

***

Drew drove them from his apartment to his bar. They arrived at the bar twenty minutes later, laughter and music spilling onto the street. Drew parked his car in his designated spot, and they made their way inside, the familiar scent of beer and fried food greeting them.

Billie sat down in her favorite booth while Drew talked to his manager, wanting to know how the evening was going.

Drew cleared his throat. "So, did everyone scheduled to be here show up?" *The first thing I had to learn about owning and running a bar was that not everyone always showed up for work. I had to learn to be flexible and go with the flow.*

His manager smiled and nodded. "I know it's hard to believe, but everyone did show up," he said. He chuckled and shook his head. "I think we might be overstaffed."

Drew shrugged his shoulders. "We might be," he said. "Let's see how busy we get before we start sending people home." He looked over his shoulder and smiled at Billie. "I won't be sitting in my office tonight, but if you need anything, I'll be nearby."

His manager nodded. "I'll try not to bother you while you're with Billie," he said. He grinned. "I want to know how she convinced you to let us have a Halloween party here."

Drew shrugged his shoulders. "She talked me into it," he said. He grinned. "But I won't tell you how she did."

***

Drew joined Billie in the booth a few minutes later.

Billie smiled. "Is everything okay?"

Drew nodded. "So far, so good," he said. He looked around, smiling. "It's starting to get crowded." *I'm glad that Billie talked me into having a Halloween party here.*

Drew and Billie were talking when he noticed that Billie kept glancing at her watch while looking at the front door.

Drew frowned. "Are you expecting someone, Billie?" *She's up to something; I know it.*

Billie nodded and smiled. "I invited Truman and his new girlfriend to join us," she said. She reached out and took Drew's hand. "I hope you don't mind if they join us."

Drew sighed. *Well, there goes having a romantic dinner with Billie.* "I don't mind," he said. He cleared his throat. "When did you invite Truman and his new girlfriend to join us?" *It's always awkward between me and him whenever Willie's not around. He's the only thing we have in common.*

"Earlier today," Billie said. She took out a cigarette and lit it. "Did I tell you about the racist rule the country club still has in their rulebook?"

Drew nodded. "Yeah, you did," he said. He chuckled and shook his head. "My parents wanted me to apply for membership there, but I had to tell them I didn't want to be a member." *I also didn't think they would accept me there. I've gone there a few times with Truman and seen how many members were black, not many at all.*

***

Fifteen minutes later, Billie's friend Rebecca walked in with Truman.

Drew chuckled and shook his head. *I always knew that Truman had a crush on her.* He looked over at Billie. *She seems pleased with them being together.*

Rebecca and Truman walked over to them and sat in the booth with them.

Rebecca smiled. "Hey, Drew," she said. "I appreciate you letting Billie talk you into having a Halloween party here and inviting us to join you and Billie."

Drew smiled back at Rebecca. "You're welcome," he said. He glanced over at Truman. *I suppose I should say something to him, too.* He cleared his throat. "Hey, Truman. Haven't seen you in a while. How have you been?"

Truman shrugged his shoulders. "I'm okay," he said. He glanced over at Rebecca. "Okay, I'm better than that." He chuckled. "I have been keeping myself busy at the law firm, and now, thanks to Billie and Rebecca, I'm looking into the country club and their outdated thinking about black people."

So, I noticed he didn't mention Rebecca or how long they'd been dating. Drew chuckled and shrugged his shoulders. *If I want to know, I should ask.* "So, let's stop pretending there isn't an elephant in the room." He cleared his throat. "How long have you been dating Rebecca, Truman?"

Truman chuckled and grinned while looking over at Billie. "We haven't been dating that long," he said. He pointed at Billie. "She's the one who encouraged us to be together."

Billie did? Why would she want her best friend to date her older half-brother? Drew turned his attention to Billie. "Why did you do it? Encourage them to date each other?"

Billie smiled. "I thought they would make a good couple," she said. She chuckled and nodded. "And I also picked up on the fact they were attracted to each other."

Rebecca smiled at Billie. "Thanks, Billie," she said. "I'll admit I didn't like how pushy you were, but I'm glad you did it." She reached out and took one of Truman's hands. "I also thought that we would make a good couple."

Billie leaned forward, her eyes on Drew. "What do you think? Do you agree with me and Rebecca? Do you also think that she and Truman make a good couple?"

Drew sighed and shrugged his shoulders. "I'm her ex-boyfriend," he said. "Why does what I think matter?" *I don't know how to feel about this. I knew Rebecca would date again, but I was sure it wouldn't be with another guy. I had been under the impression that she had given up on guys and was only dating other women now.* He glanced over at Truman. "Does it matter to you, Truman? Do you need my blessing or approval?"

Truman shook his head. "No, Drew, I don't need either one," he said. He glanced over at Billie and then at Rebecca. "But I'm sure they want both from you."

"I hope you two are happy together," Drew said. *That's about as close as I'm going to get to offer either my blessing or my approval.* He cleared his throat. "So, am I the only one looking forward to Thanksgiving?"

Rebecca glanced over at Billie. "It's still Halloween, Drew," she said. "But since you mentioned it, will you spend Thanksgiving with Willie and his sisters again this year?"

Drew shook his head and glanced over at Billie. "No, not this year," he said. "This year, I'm going home to spend it with my parents." *I want to invite Billie to join me, but I don't want to put her on the spot.*

Billie reached out and grabbed one of Drew's hands. "We'll miss having you, Drew," she said. She smiled at him. "I hope you enjoy having Thanksgiving at home, with your parents."

Chapter Twenty-Eight

T he conversation between Truman and Jasmine was a short one. Jasmine showed Truman the proof she had of the racist rule and how the board only enforced it when they wanted to, letting Billie, Rebecca, and Jasmine join the country club because of who their families were.

Truman promised Jasmine that he would investigate it. The next time they would meet to talk, a week later, he wouldn't have good news to tell her.

***

When Truman arrived at the coffee shop, he found Jasmine waiting for him, sitting at a table near the front entrance. She smiled and waved at him.

Truman sighed and shook his head. *This isn't going to be easy to tell her.* He walked over to the table and sat down across from Jasmine. "Hello," he said, glancing at his watch. "I hope you haven't been waiting long."

Jasmine shook her head. "I've only been here for about five minutes," she said. She cleared her throat. "I hope you have good news."

Do I have good news for her? "Yes, and no," he said. "I looked into it, like I said I would, and found out two things." He sighed and shook his head. "I've got good and bad news to tell you."

"Okay," Jasmine said, frowning. "What's the bad news?"

"I can't help you," Truman said, shaking his head. "I found out that my law firm is the official attorney of the country club." He reached out and took Jasmine's hand. "Do you understand what that means, Jasmine?" *I hope she does, because I don't want to explain it to her.*

Jasmine sighed and nodded. "It means you can't help me," she said. She shrugged her shoulders. "I didn't want to go with Bridget's suggestion, but I might have to follow her advice, even if I disagree."

Now, I can give her the good news. "Don't forget, I also have good news to tell you," Truman said. He reached into his jacket pocket and pulled out a business card. "I do know who can help you, Jasmine." He handed her the business card. "This lawyer can help you."

Jasmine read the business card and smiled. "This name sounds familiar," she said. "Why does this lawyer's name, William Baldwin, sound so familiar to me, Truman?"

Truman smiled. "Well, maybe you know him better by his nickname," he said. "Billie has known him all her life." He glanced at his watch. *I hope Willie shows up. He might be able to convince Jasmine that he can help her better than I can.*

Jasmine smiled. "I remember Aunt Josey telling me that Billie's older brother, Willie, was a lawyer, just like you," she said. "Are you saying that he can help me?"

"Yes, that's exactly what he's saying, Miss Carter."

Truman stood up and turned around, smiling. *I know that voice.* He glanced at his watch and nodded. *And he's right on time.* "Jasmine, this is my friend and fellow attorney, William Baldwin," he said. "I asked him to join us."

Willie walked up to their table and sat across from Jasmine and beside Truman. "Good afternoon, Miss Carter," he said, offering his hand. "It's a pleasure to meet you."

Jasmine shook his hand. "There's no need to be so formal," she said, smiling. "After all, we're cousins."

Willie chuckled and nodded. "So, Billie has told me," he said. He cleared his throat. "Now, Truman has filled me in on the situation you find yourself in, regarding the country club's racist rule and how the board enforces the rule when they're sure they can get away with it."

Jasmine chuckled. "You certainly talk like a lawyer," she said. "My question is a simple one, Mister Baldwin. Can you help me or not?"

Willie smiled. "You can call me Willie, Miss Carter," he said. "I do have a few questions." He leaned back in his chair. "Why are you doing this? What do you want to accomplish?"

Jasmine looked down at the table, at her hands, and sighed. "I've been a member of that country club for most of my life, and I never felt like I belonged there," she said. "The only reason why they let me join is because of who my family is, and I know that's not right."

Willie nodded. "You're right," he said. "Are you ready for all the trouble that will come your way, Miss Carter?" He glanced over at Truman. "Hey, would you mind giving Miss Carter and me some privacy?" He shook his head and grinned. "I don't want to put you in any kind of dilemma, so you don't want to hear what we're going to do about that racist rule, Truman."

Truman nodded and stood up. "You're right, Willie, I don't want to know," he said. He looked over at Jasmine and smiled. "I'm sorry I couldn't help you, Jasmine, but I'm sure Willie can help you." *I hope I don't get assigned to defend the country club if there's any legal action. I don't want to have to go to court and have to argue against Willie.*

Jasmine nodded. "Thanks, Truman," she said. She stood up and walked over to him. "If it's okay with you, I'd like to hug you, since we're cousins."

Truman smiled and nodded. "Okay," he said. *I think Billie's starting to rub off on Jasmine. She isn't afraid to be affectionate anymore.*

Jasmine hugged Truman and kissed him on the cheek. "Don't be a stranger," she said. "And if you see Billie anytime soon, ask her to call me."

Truman nodded. "Okay, I will," he said. He untangled himself from Jasmine and stepped back. He looked over at Willie and grinned. "I hope the next time I see you won't be in court, Willie."

Willie chuckled and grinned. "Yeah, same here," he said. He shook hands with Truman. "Tell Billie that she needs to remember to call Nina and me sometime."

***

Almost two months later, and a few days after Christmas, Bridget parked her car near the front entrance of Jackson's Jukebox. She sighed and took out a cigarette. *Why am I here?* She lit it and got out of her car.

Bridget had only been there a few times and always felt out of place, knowing everyone wanted to know why she was there. *Why couldn't we have met at Capote's instead?* She took a drag off her cigarette and shook her head. *I know why, and it's because of me. Ever since I kissed Georgia when Billie walked away, I haven't felt comfortable there.*

Bridget finished her cigarette, throwing it away, and walked away from her car. She entered the front entrance, opened the door, and stepped inside. She stood by the front door for a minute and waited for her eyes to adjust to the darkness.

Bridget glanced at her watch and frowned. *So, they're not here and I'm early.* She walked up to the bar and was about to sit down when a waitress came by, waving at her.

"I'm going to take a wild guess and say you're Bridget," the waitress said. "The rest of your party isn't here yet, but you can go ahead and sit at the reserved booth."

Bridget nodded. "Okay, thanks," she said. She cleared her throat. *Remember what Billie told you the last time you were rude to a waitress?* "Could you please show me where this booth is, miss?"

The waitress nodded and smiled. "I sure can, Miss Bridget," she said. She turned around and walked away.

Bridget followed her, ignoring the looks she was getting from the other patrons there. *I should ask Rebecca why she wanted us to meet here, but does it matter?*

The waitress came to the booth and pointed at it. "There you go, Miss Bridget," she said. "Do you want something to drink while you wait for the rest of your party?"

Bridget nodded. "I would love a drink, miss," she said. *Oh, yeah, this isn't Capote's or the bar at the country club. I'll have to tell her what I want to drink.* "I'll have a scotch soda, please."

The waitress nodded. "I'll be right back with it," she said.

***

A few minutes later, Bridget was enjoying her scotch soda when Rebecca and another young black woman, whom Bridget realized she had seen before, walked into the bar.

Bridget stood up and waved at Rebecca. "Hey, Rebecca," she said. "I'm over here." *I think the black lady with Rebecca works with Billie at the bookstore.* She frowned. *I think Sadie's her name.*

Rebecca grinned. "I know where you're sitting, Bridget," she said. "After all, I'm the one who reserved the booth." She looked over at her companion. "Go ahead and sit down." She smiled. "Don't worry about Bridget, she might look mean, but she's a sweetheart deep down inside."

Bridget chuckled. *I never thought Rebecca would ever call me a sweetheart.* She offered her hand to Rebecca's friend. "It's a pleasure to see you again, Sadie," she said. "I didn't know that you knew Rebecca." *Is Sadie a friend, or is she one of Rebecca's many fans?*

Sadie glanced over at Rebecca. "Yeah, I do," she said. "She's friends with my best friend, Iris Mathews."

Rebecca and Sadie sat down in the booth across from Bridget. The waitress saw them and nodded. "I'll bring your drinks, Miss Rebecca," she said. "I'll just be a minute."

Bridget cleared her throat. "Did you say your best friend is Iris Mathews?" *Why did Rebecca bring Sadie with her instead of Billie or even Jasmine?* "Is she the same Iris Mathews I've heard about, one of the best journalists in this city?" *Rebecca's the one who told me about Iris Mathews and introduced me to her essays, book reviews, and articles.*

Sadie grinned and nodded. "Yeah, that's her," she said. "Rebecca has told me that you're a fan, Bridget." She leaned closer to Bridget, her elbows resting on the table. "Is that true?"

Bridget nodded. "Yes, it's true," she said. She cleared her throat. "I've been reading her work for almost two years now." *She's helped me understand myself, though I don't think I'll ever tell anyone that, not wanting to be that vulnerable with anyone.*

The waitress returned with their drinks. "Here you go, Miss Rebecca," she said, handing Rebecca her vodka tonic. She gave Sadie's drink to her. "And here you go, Miss Sadie."

Bridget waited until the waitress walked away. She shook her head and cleared her throat, frowning. "Okay, Rebecca," she said. "So, why did you want to talk to me?" She glanced over at Sadie. "And while I'm asking, why did you bring Sadie?" *The more I've gotten to know Rebecca, the more I realize there's more to her than I thought.*

Rebecca nodded. "Okay, I'll tell you," she said. "The last time we talked, you said you wanted to be friends with Billie and me." She took out a cigarette and lit it. "Do you remember saying that, Bridget?"

Bridget frowned. *She knows that I remember saying that.* "Yeah, I remember," she said. "And I meant what I said." *I don't blame Billie for hesitating to become my friend, not after what I tried to do to her, and I understand why Rebecca doesn't believe that I've changed.*

Rebecca nodded. "I believe you," she said. She looked over at Sadie and smiled. "Sadie said something similar to me about a week ago, didn't you, Sadie?"

Sadie sighed and nodded. "I did," she said. She shook her head and cleared her throat. "Iris has become friends with Rebecca and Billie, which is why I want to be friends with them."

Rebecca nodded. "You see, Bridget, you and Sadie here are in the same boat," she said. "Both of you have been hostile towards Billie before, but now, you have changed your mind about Billie and want to be friends with her." She leaned back and sipped her vodka tonic. "So, I thought the two of you should meet each other."

Bridget sighed. "I think I know what you're trying to do, Rebecca," she said. She frowned. *Let's be honest now.* "I'm not easy to get along with or get to know." She shook her head. "I don't want to be difficult anymore." She looked over at Sadie. "I'm willing to try to become friends with you, Sadie, if you're willing to try to get to know me and put up with me."

***

Willie became closer to Nina and Billie. He mentioned it to his best friend, Malcolm, while talking over the phone.

"I'm telling you it's strange to get along so well with them," he said, smiling. "I never thought it would happen." *The three of us getting along was something our mother always wanted for us.*

"I told you a thousand times that your sisters weren't as bad as you said they were," Malcolm said, chuckling. He cleared his throat. "I haven't earned Bobbie's trust yet, but I'm working on it."

Willie sighed and shook his head. "You still trying to get back with her?" *I'll never understand what he sees in her.* "Listen, I've got to go, so I'll talk to you later."

***

Willie made it a point to spend time with Billie and Nina, having dinner together once a week. He talked to their mother over the phone weekly, and she was pleased that her children were getting along, which he knew she would be.

Willie's life was going well, and then his best friend, Malcolm, was killed when the World Trade Center building was bombed on February 26, 1993. Billie was the one who told him, calling him.

"Hey, Billie," Willie said. He frowned and glanced at his watch. "Why are you calling me?"

"I'm sure you've heard the news," Billie said, her voice trembling. "Malcolm was at the World Trade Center."

Willie sighed. "Just because he lives in New York City doesn't mean he was there," he said. "I'm sure he's fine." *I'll call him when I get done talking to Billie.*

Billie sighed. "He was there," she said. "Bobbie told me that he was there to get an interview."

Billie turned out to be right.

***

Willie left Boston and went to Malcolm's funeral a week later. Billie and Nina went with him. He didn't ask them to go or even think of asking them to come with him. They showed up at the airport and got on the same flight.

Willie, Billie, and Nina went to Malcolm's funeral. While Nina sat beside Willie, Billie sat with Bobbie, who was also there.

Nina leaned closer to Willie. "I told you she would be here," she said. "You may not have understood what he saw in her, but she saw something in him."

Willie nodded. "I know she did," he said. He looked over at Billie. "I told him a million times that she was nothing but trouble." *He wouldn't listen to me, not when it came to her. He didn't even want to break up with her the first time, when we left New Orleans. I told him she was only a summer romance, but he disagreed.*

***

Willie didn't see Billie again until the next day, when Willie and Nina caught an early flight back to Boston. They sat next to each other on the flight back.

Willie shook his head and frowned. "I just can't believe it," he said. "I knew being a journalist could be dangerous, but I never thought Malcolm would get killed because of it."

Nina nodded and squeezed his hand, but she didn't say anything.

Billie sat on his left side, on his other side. She seemed to want to say something to him several times, but she would stop herself.

Willie sighed. *I don't think she knows what to say to me. She wants to say something, but doesn't want to say the wrong thing.* He looked over at Billie. "So, how was Bobbie? How's she dealing with it?"

Billie turned her attention to Willie, met his eyes, and sighed. "She loved Malcolm and is devastated by his death," she said. "He meant the world to her."

Willie nodded. "I know how she feels," he said. "I'm devastated too." *Malcolm might have been Bobbie's first love, but he was my best friend long before she knew him.* "He was my best friend." He shook his head. "We didn't always get along, but we could always talk to each other."

Billie reached out and took Willie's free hand. "I know you're taking Malcolm's death hard," she said. "And I know he was your best friend." She looked out the window, frowning. "I know that one day, I might have to deal with Bobbie dying." She shook her head. "Or she might have to deal with my death."

Willie nodded. "I don't know how to do anything without him around," he said. "Malcolm has been part of my life since we were just kids." *He never cared that I had a white father.* He smiled. *The only thing he cared about when we first became friends was that I played ball with him.* He sighed and shook his head. "I wasn't on good terms with him, and we argued the last time we talked over the phone."

Billie frowned. "What did y'all argue about, Willie?"

Nina leaned over, frowning. "Hey, Willie," she said. "If you don't want to talk about Malcolm or why y'all argued the last time y'all talked over the phone, you don't have to."

Willie sighed and shook his head. *Nina must see how uncomfortable I am with Billie's question. I never thought that Nina would be the one to come to my defense.* "It's okay, Nina," he said. "I want to talk about the last time I talked to Malcolm over the phone."

Nina frowned. "Are you sure, Willie?" She looked over at Billie. "Maybe we should leave him alone, Billie." She sighed and shook her head. "We both know he isn't as open about his feelings as we are."

Billie frowned and squinted at Nina. "He isn't a moody teenager anymore, Nina," she said. "Willie knows how to share his feelings with us." She sipped her drink, a vodka tonic. "I know I'm not the only one who believes that three of us have become closer over these past months, ever since his birthday."

Willie patted Billie's hand. "It's okay," he said. He sighed and shook his head. "I argued with Malcolm about your best friend, Bobbie." He shrugged his shoulders. "I tried to talk him out of trying to get back with her."

Billie frowned. "Why were you so against Malcolm dating Bobbie, Willie?" She shook her head. "You never liked the idea of them being a couple, did you?"

Willie shook his head. "It wasn't that I didn't like the idea of them being a couple," he said. "It's more like I didn't understand what he saw in her." He sighed. "I don't remember why I felt that way, and now, I wish I had been a better friend to him."

Billie sighed and shook her head. "You were the best friend you could be, Willie," she said. "Malcolm may not have always liked how you shared your opinions, but I'm sure he appreciated how honest you were with him."

Willie sighed. "I hope you're right," he said. He looked over at Billie and frowned. "When did you become such an expert on my friendship with Malcolm?" *Why am I being hostile to her? She's only trying to help.*

Billie chuckled. "I know enough, Willie," she said. "You forget that I've been around and have seen how much your friendship with Malcolm meant to you."

***

Willie, Billie, and Nina arrived at Logan Airport. Their plane made its way to the gate, and the other passengers started to depart after it reached a complete stop.

Nina stood up, but Billie stopped her, reaching over Willie to grab Nina's elbow. "Hold on a minute," she said. "There's no point in standing up right now." She glanced over at the other passengers. "It might be better to wait until everyone else departs first."

Nina nodded. "You're right," she said. She sat back down. She chuckled and shrugged her shoulders. "I'm just ready to get off this plane." She looked out the window. "It feels good to be back home."

Willie nodded. *Nina's right. This is our home now.*

They waited for the other passengers to depart the plane and stood up. They grabbed their carry-on luggage and left the plane.

***

Billie and Nina followed Willie from the gate to the baggage claim, where they retrieved their other luggage.

Willie turned around to face Billie and Nina. "Well, I guess this is where we part ways," he said. He glanced at his watch. "It's going to be fun trying to catch a taxi." *Rush hour traffic started ten minutes ago. And it's never easy for me to catch a taxi.*

Nina frowned and shook her head. "I'm not ready for us to part ways," she said. "I'd like to spend some more time with y'all both."

Billie held up her hands. "I've got an idea," she said, smiling. "Why don't we go to the airport bar and have a few drinks?"

Nina frowned and looked over at Willie. "I'd rather not hang out in the airport bar," she said. She sighed and shrugged her shoulders. "But I don't have a better idea."

Willie chuckled and nodded. "I could use a drink," he said. He grinned and shook his head. "I don't think we've ever sat in a bar and had a few drinks together, Billie." *And I know why we haven't ever had a drink together. It wasn't until recently that the two of us got along. For most of my life, I resented Billie, believing that our father cared more about her than he did about me. After all, our parents were married when she was born, but not with me.*

Nina shrugged her shoulders. "Okay, let's go to the bar," she said. She sighed. "I hate to remind y'all that I'm still not twenty-one yet."

Billie grinned. "You don't have to drink, Nina," she said. She picked up her luggage. "Come on, let's go."

Billie knew where the airport bar was, so Willie and Nina followed her.

Nina walked closer to Willie. "How does she know where the bar is?"

Willie laughed and grinned. "Billie has flown out of here before," he said. "I would've been more surprised if she didn't know where it was, Nina." *I don't think Nina knows how much Billie drinks.*

***

They arrived at the airport bar a few minutes later. They sat in a booth with Billie and Willie on one side, while Nina sat on the other side, across from them.

A waitress came by a few minutes later. "Good evening," she said, nodding at them. "What are we drinking this evening?"

Billie raised her hand. "I'll have a vodka tonic," she said. She pointed at Willie. "And he'll have a gin screwdriver."

Willie smiled and chuckled. *So, Billie knows what I like to drink. I wonder who told her?*

The waitress nodded and wrote down their order. She turned her attention to Nina. "What about you, miss? What would you like to drink?"

Nina shook her head and grinned. "I'll take a club soda," she said. She cleared her throat. "I'm the designated driver."

The waitress nodded. "Okay," she said. "I'll be right back with your drinks." She then walked away.

Billie took out a cigarette and lit it. "Oh, you're the designated driver now, Nina?" She grinned and shook her head. "You just didn't want to tell her you're not old enough to drink."

Nina frowned and waved her hand in front of her face. "Do you have to do that, Billie?" She cleared her throat. "Smoking is a bad habit."

Billie chuckled and shook her head. "I know it's a bad habit," she said. "I do want to quit, Nina." She sighed and frowned. "I sometimes wish that I hadn't ever started smoking."

Willie hadn't said anything since they sat down in the booth. He was staring down at the table, lost in his thoughts.

Nina reached out and took one of his hands. "Hey, Willie," she said. "I just want to tell you I'm here for you if you want to talk."

Willie sighed and shook his head. "I don't think talking will help me feel better," he said. He looked around, frowning. "Everything looks the same, but I know it isn't the same." *It's a different world now, one without Malcolm in it.*

Billie put her arm around Willie's shoulders and held him, pulling him closer to her. "I'm here for you, too," she said. "I can't imagine how you feel right now." She sighed. "I just want to remind you that you're not alone." She glanced over at Nina. "We're both here for you."

Willie tried to smile but failed. "Thanks," he said. "I think I need to take a few days off from work." *Speaking of work, Billie may want to be updated on Jasmine's case.* "I don't know if you've talked to Jasmine lately, but I'm still finding other people who were denied membership at the country club because they're black."

Billie patted Willie's back. "We don't have to talk about it right now," she said. "I'm glad you took her case, Willie."

Willie chuckled. "Are you kidding me, Billie? This case is shaping up to be one that could be the biggest one I've ever done," he said. He sighed. "The only thing that worries me is that I might have to face Truman in court." *I'll never admit this to him, but I know he's a fine lawyer.*

***

Willie, Billie, and Nina sat in the airport bar for two hours. While Nina only drank club soda, Willie drank gin, and Billie drank vodka.

Billie sipped her vodka tonic and grinned at Willie. "Okay, so I know why I left New Orleans," she said. "But what about you, Willie? Why did you leave?"

Willie sipped his gin screwdriver and grinned back. "I left because I wanted to see more of the world," he said. He shook his head and chuckled. "I didn't want to be one of those people who never leave their hometown." *I also wanted to leave the South.*

Billie nodded. "Okay, I can relate to that," she said. She chuckled and shook her head. "If anyone had asked me a few years ago where I would go after graduating from Tulane, I would have told them I was on my way to Los Angeles."

***

Willie and Billie talked about their childhood in New Orleans, adjusting to living in Boston, and dating. Nina had to convince them it was time for them to go home. They left the bar and caught a taxi outside the airport. Willie was dropped off first.

Willie smiled at Billie and Nina. "Hey, thanks for coming with me," he said. *Mama has often told me that the people who care about you will be there for you. It looks like my sisters do care about me.*

Chapter Twenty-Nine

Nina's relationship with Billie had become closer, which pleased her. She no longer felt invisible around Billie or Willie. She was glad that she had been able to be there for him, grieving over his friend's death.

Nina's junior year at Harvard came to an end. She decided to stay in Boston for the summer instead of going back home to New Orleans. She told their mother it was because she wanted to take some summer classes, but that wasn't the whole truth, and their mother knew it, though she didn't say anything.

***

June turned into July. Nina was sitting on her bed in her off-campus apartment when her phone rang. She reached out and picked it up.

"Hello?"

"Hey, Nina, it's me," her older brother said.

Nina smiled. "Hey, Willie," she said. She looked over at the calendar hanging on the wall near her bed. "We've already talked this week, so why are you calling me?" *I wonder if Mama asked him to call me, to check up on me.*

Willie chuckled. "Can't I just call you? Do I need a reason to call you, Nina?"

Nina laughed. "No, I guess you don't need a reason to call me," she said. "Have you talked to Billie lately?" *I figure she was spending the summer, or at least some of it, in Alabama with her best friend, Bobbie.*

"I have talked to her," Willie said. He sighed. "She isn't having a good summer."

Nina frowned. "And why's that, Willie?" *He knows something about Billie that I don't know.* "Isn't she in Alabama, spending some time with Bobbie?"

Willie sighed. "No, she isn't," he said. "I'm sure she wanted to spend some time with her best friend, but she's still here, not wanting to leave her white grandmother's side."

Nina sighed. "I know you know her name, Willie," she said. She frowned. "What's wrong with Josephine?" *Whatever's wrong with her must be serious if Billie refuses to leave her side.*

"I don't know all the details," Willie said. "All I know for sure is that she's in poor health and Billie's scared."

Why didn't Billie tell me what was going on with her the last time we talked over the phone? "Okay," Nina said. She sighed and shook her head. "Thanks for telling me, Willie." *I need to go and see Billie.* She smiled. *I know, I'll spend her birthday, which is coming up soon, with her.*

***

Billie's birthday arrived a few weeks later. Nina left her off-campus apartment and drove to Josephine's house in Beacon Hill.

Nina shook her head and frowned. *I wonder why Billie still lives with Josephine and hasn't gotten an apartment of her own?* She sighed. *I may not understand why Billie's close to Josephine, but I know Josephine's important to Billie. And I know that she's having a tough time dealing with Josephine's poor health, though she hasn't said anything to me about it.*

***

Nina arrived at the Carver house and parked behind Billie's car. *Well, since her car is here, Billie should be here too.*

Nina left her car and approached the front door. She knocked on it. When no one came to the door, she knocked a little harder.

Nina kept knocking on the front door for another five minutes.

"I hear you knocking, and I'm coming."

Nina smiled. *Good, Billie is home.* She giggled and knocked again, hitting the door with the flat of her hand, almost banging on it.

"Would you please just calm down with the knocking?"

The front door opened with Billie frowning. "Oh, it's you," she said, her face softening. "Hey, Nina."

"Hey, Billie," Nina said, smiling at Billie. "You seem surprised to see me." *I bet she didn't think I knew where she lived.*

Billie nodded. "I am surprised to see you," she said. "Why are you here?" She glanced over her shoulder, back into the house. "This isn't a good time."

Nina shook her head and frowned. "It's your birthday, Billie," she said. "And I want to spend it with you." *I know she's worried about Josephine, but that doesn't mean she can't enjoy her birthday.*

Billie shook her head. "I know it's my birthday," she said. She sighed. "I don't feel like going out and celebrating my birthday."

Nina stepped closer, bridging the distance between her and Billie. "Willie called me the other day," she said. "He told me that Josephine isn't doing well." *Let me help you, Billie. I want to be there for you the way we were for Willie. You're not alone and don't have to face this mess alone.*

Billie sighed and nodded. "He's right," she said. "Josephine isn't doing well." She shook her head. "I'm afraid that she could die any day now. I'm scared, Nina. I don't know how to deal with this."

Nina nodded. "I understand why you're not in the mood to celebrate your birthday," she said. She reached out and took one of Billie's hands. "I don't think you should be alone on your birthday." *I'm here, Billie. I understand your pain and am here to share it with you.*

Billie sighed and shook her head. "I could try to tell you to go away and leave me alone," she said. She chuckled and grinned. "But I have a feeling that you're not going away and aren't going to take no for an answer."

Nina smiled and nodded. "You're right," she said. "I'm not going away, no matter what you say to me." *You're not the only one who's hardheaded in our family. I'm here for you, Billie.*

Billie shook her head and laughed. "Sometimes, you sound just like our mother," she said. She shrugged her shoulders. "But then again, sometimes I sound like her, too."

Nina grinned and giggled. "Well, it would be strange if we didn't sound like her sometimes," she said. "After all, she's our mother." *I've always considered Willie and Billie my siblings, not caring that we didn't have the same father. As I see it, all three of us came out of the same womb, and that's good enough.*

Billie stepped aside and smiled at Nina. "Since you're not leaving, come on in," she said.

Nina stepped inside, and Billie closed the door.

Nina turned around to face Billie. "Do you think it would be okay with you if I saw Josephine?" *It's past time that I met her.*

Billie nodded. "She's been wanting to meet you," she said. She smiled at Nina. "Josephine feels that our mother's children are her grandchildren."

Nina smiled. "Well, I'm sure Mama would be pleased to know that Josephine feels that way about her children," she said. *The more I've learned about Josephine, the more I realize she wasn't in our lives before now because of her husband.* She shook her head and cleared her throat. "I've never been here before, Billie, so you'll have to show me the way."

Billie nodded. "Of course," she said. She turned around and glanced over her shoulder at Nina, grinning. "Okay, just follow me."

Nina followed Billie from the front door, up the stairs to the second floor, and down the hallway to Josephine's bedroom. The door was closed.

Billie sighed and shook her head. She looked over at Nina. "I hope she isn't sleeping," she said. "If she is, I'm not waking her up."

Nina nodded. "I understand," she said. "Why don't you knock on the door and find out?" *I hope Josephine isn't sleeping. I want to talk to her and maybe even get to know her a little before it's too late.*

Billie knocked on the door. "Josephine, are you awake?" She glanced over at Nina. "You've got a visitor."

"Yes, I am awake," Josephine said. "Please, come on in."

Billie held up her hand and opened the door.

Josephine sat up in her bed and smiled when she saw Nina standing in the hallway, behind Billie. "Well, hello, Miss Carson," she said. She looked over at Billie and smiled. "She looks so much like your mother, Billie."

Billie smiled back and nodded. "Yeah, I've always thought so too," she said. "Nina would like to visit with you, if that's okay with you, Josephine."

Josephine nodded. "I would love that," she said. "Please, come on in and sit here, Miss Carson." She pointed at the chair near her bed.

Nina nodded. "Okay, Josephine," she said. "And you can call me Nina." *I hope that she doesn't mind that I called her by her first name instead of Mrs. Carver. Billie has said that Josephine believes in good manners.*

Billie and Nina entered Josephine's bedroom, and while Billie stood by, Nina sat close to Josephine, in the chair near her bed.

"So, Nina, what would you like to discuss with me?" Josephine glanced over at Billie. "Billie, dear, are you sure you want to stand there? You would be more comfortable if you found a chair and sat in it."

Billie chuckled and shook her head. "I need to stand, Josephine," she said. She glanced over at Nina, who was frowning at her. "I've been writing since I woke up this morning, around seven-thirty."

***

Nina's questions to Josephine were direct and to the point, reflecting her determination and curiosity. She asked all the questions she wanted answers to, not holding back. Josephine answered all Nina's questions, not hesitating, and being honest with her.

Nina smiled at Josephine. "I enjoyed talking to you," she said. *Okay, now I should spend some time with Billie.* She cleared her throat. "If you don't mind, I'd like to spend some time with Billie." She glanced over at Billie. "After all, it's her birthday." She turned her attention back to Josephine. "It would mean a lot to me because Billie celebrated my birthday with me last year."

Josephine smiled and nodded. She looked over at Billie, still standing at the foot of her bed. "It would be okay with me if you celebrate your birthday with Nina," she said. She sighed and shook her head. "I am not going to die today."

Billie chuckled. "You better not die today, Josephine," she said. She cleared her throat. "But if you need anything, we'll be across the hallway, in my bedroom."

Nina smiled and nodded. "Thanks, Josephine," she said. She stood up and went to the door. She glanced over at Billie, still standing by Josephine's bed. "Come on, Billie. You heard Josephine say it's okay with her." *I understand now why Billie has gotten so attached to Josephine. She's an amazing woman.*

Billie nodded, chuckling. She walked over to Josephine and gave her a quick kiss on her cheek. "We'll be in my bedroom," she said. "So, if you need anything, just let me know, okay?"

Josephine nodded. "I do not foresee myself needing anything from you," she said. She pointed at the nightstand table near her bed. "I have got all the things I need right there."

Billie looked at the nightstand table and shook her head. She walked over to it and removed the pack of cigarettes. "You don't need to smoke, Josephine," she said. "You need to give your lungs a break."

Josephine sighed. "I am sorry, Billie," she said. "I know my doctor has told you to stop me from smoking, but what is the point? I am already dying."

Billie sighed and shook her head. "Yeah, I know," she said. "But why make it worse?"

Nina cleared her throat. "Come on, Billie," she said. "Josephine can't smoke because you took her cigarettes." *I won't point out that Billie has no reason to get on any soapbox, since she's also a smoker.*

Billie nodded. "You're right, Nina," she said. She patted Josephine on the shoulder. "Remember, Josephine, if you need anything, I'm just down the hallway, in my bedroom."

Nina and Billie then left Josephine's bedroom. Nina followed Billie down the hallway to her bedroom.

***

Billie and Nina walked into Billie's bedroom. Billie sat at her desk while Nina sat on Billie's bed.

Nina pointed at the pile of pages sitting by Billie's typewriter. "What have you been writing, Billie?" *I haven't read all her short stories, but I loved the ones I have read.* "Willie says that your short stories are being published."

Billie nodded. "More and more of them are being published every day," she said. She sighed and took out a cigarette. She lit it while looking over at Nina. "I appreciate you coming over and wanting to celebrate my birthday with me, but I'm not in the mood to celebrate my birthday."

Nina reached out and took one of Billie's hands. "I understand," she said. "I know it has been rough for you, dealing with Josephine's poor health." She smiled at Billie and squeezed her hand. "I want to remind you that I'm here for you." *Billie looks so scared. I've never seen her this scared before in my life.*

Billie sighed and took a drag off her cigarette. "I am having a rough time," she said. She chuckled and shook her head. "All the bullshit I've been through these last few years, having to deal with other people's issues is nothing compared to watching someone I love die and knowing there's nothing I can do about it." She wiped the tears off her face. "I'm afraid I won't be fun to be around today, Nina."

Nina shook her head. "It's okay, Billie," she said. "I didn't come here to have fun with you." She stood up and went over to Billie. "I came here because I didn't want you to be alone." *There's no reason Billie has to deal with this, losing Josephine alone. I'm here for her. How much more do I have to do to show her how much I love and care about her?*

Billie tried to smile. "Thanks," she said. She looked over at the phone on the nightstand table near her bed. "I'd call Bobbie, but she's going through her own kind of grief right now."

Nina nodded. "Yeah, I know," she said. She shook her head. "I didn't realize how much Willie's friend Malcolm meant to her." *I remember how her face lit up when she talked about him to Billie. He was her first love.*

Billie shrugged her shoulders. "I don't think she realized either until he died," she said. She sighed and shook her head. "Every day, I wake up and I wonder, will this be the day she dies?"

Nina shook her head. "You can't think like that," she said. She hugged Billie. "Instead, try to remember that every day you spend with her is another memory you can hang on to and always have."

Billie nodded. "You're right, Nina," she said. She wiped some more tears off her face. "I never knew my father, but because of Josephine, I've gotten to know him, in a way."

Nina frowned. "What do you mean, Billie?" *Billie and Willie had the same father, but different feelings about losing him. Willie pretends he didn't lose a father and that my father is his father. But with Billie, it's the opposite. She searches for him, wanting to know everything about him.*

"He wrote in a journal," Billie said. "And Josephine kept them all." She pointed at the pile of notebooks near her desk. "I've read them all, I don't know how many times." She smiled at Nina. "It's the closest I can get to knowing him."

Nina nodded. "Okay, I can see why you would feel that way," she said. She grinned. "It's a good thing Josephine kept all his journals." *Something tells me Josephine knew what she was doing by keeping all his journals. She knew one day, one of his children, maybe even all of them, including Billie's other brother, Truman, would want to read them.*

"Yeah, it is," Billie said. She took a drag off her cigarette. "I used to wonder where I got my talent for writing." She looked over at Nina and smiled. "I know where I got it now." She glanced through the open door and down the hallway to Josephine's bedroom. "I got it from Josephine, Nina."

Nina smiled back at Billie. "Yeah, I think so too," she said. She chuckled. "Which is a good thing since you're named after her." *Not her first name, but her middle name.*

Chapter Thirty

Josephine's health took a turn for the worse two weeks after Billie's birthday. She lingered in the hospital for another three weeks, with Billie never leaving her side, falling asleep sitting in the chair next to Josephine's bed. Truman would come by every day and sit with Billie a few hours after work.

***

A few days after Josephine died, Truman found himself sitting in the first pew at Trinity Church, attending Josephine's funeral. Billie sat next to him, on his left side, while Billie's other siblings sat next to him on his right.

Truman looked over at Willie and Nina. "Hey, I appreciate you two coming," he said. "Thank you." *I know why they're here, and it isn't because they were close with Josephine. They're here for Billie, their sister.*

Willie nodded. "You're welcome, Truman," he said. He cleared his throat. "I wish I could say this is the first funeral I've been to, but it isn't."

Truman nodded. "Yeah, I know," he said. *Willie's thinking about Malcolm's funeral.* He cleared his throat and turned his attention to Nina. "Josephine enjoyed talking to you the other day."

Nina nodded with a sad smile. "I enjoyed talking to her too," she said. She sighed and shook her head. "I wish I had talked to her sooner and more often."

We all wish we had talked to her more often. Truman nodded but didn't say anything.

Billie reached out and took one of his hands. "How are you holding up?"

Truman sighed. "I don't know how I am holding up," he said. He looked around and noted who was there. "There are many more people here than I thought there would be." *How many people are here because they're sorry to hear that Josephine died? And how many people are here because they're glad she's dead?*

Billie nodded. "You're right," she said. She shrugged her shoulders. "Most of the people here I've never seen before." She frowned. "If Josephine meant so much to them, why is it only now that they're showing up?" She shook her head. "None of these people, besides the few I know, were Josephine's friends."

Truman sighed. *Billie's right.* "Josephine had many friends, but none are here," he said. "She outlived them all." *Josephine's last friend died only a few weeks before, while Josephine was in the hospital. I hesitated to tell her, but Billie convinced me to tell her. Josephine just sighed and nodded, not saying anything. I don't think she was surprised.*

Billie shuddered. "I don't want to outlive my friends," she said. She leaned closer to Truman. "Josephine's friends may not be here, but my friends are here, if that means anything to you."

Truman nodded. "Yeah, I see them," he said. He looked around and tried to remember their names. *Sitting in the pew behind us, the second one, are Iris Mathews, the journalist, her friend Sadie Zimmerman, and Rebecca, who might be my girl-friend, though I won't call her that, and she hasn't asked me to call her that. Willie's friend Drew, who also might be Billie's boyfriend, is sitting in the same pew as me and Billie. And I can't forget Jasmine, sitting two pews behind Willie.* "I think most of the Upper Crust showed up."

Billie nodded. "You might be right," she said. "Josephine wasn't popular among the other families or even in her own, but they all respected her."

Truman leaned over and whispered to Billie. "Most people here didn't even know Josephine," he said. "They might have heard of her and maybe even respected her, like you said, but they didn't know or care about her."

Billie shook her head. "You're wrong about that," she said. "Josephine meant a lot to many people, even if they didn't know or have a relationship with her."

Truman shrugged his shoulders. *I know what Billie means, even if I don't understand why or how Josephine meant so much to so many people.* "This isn't my first funeral either," he said, glancing over at Willie. He sighed and shook his head. "How I feel right now reminds me of the first funeral I went to."

Billie frowned. "What was the first funeral you went to, Truman?" She shook her head and sighed. "I'm sorry I asked you that. You don't have to talk about it if you don't want to talk about it."

Truman nodded. "It's okay," he said. "I do want to talk about it." He closed his eyes. "It was our father's funeral." *I don't remember much about it, only a few flashes.* "I remember Josephine crying while my mother didn't cry." He looked over at Billie. "The way she saw it, she had already lost him."

***

Willie shifted around, not able to sit comfortably.

Nina looked over at him and frowned. "Would you please stay still?" She glanced over at Billie and Truman sitting on her other side. *Poor Billie and Truman. They both look so sad. Josephine's death is hitting them hard.*

Willie sighed. "I can't believe you talked me into coming," he said. He frowned. "I don't feel like I belong here." He looked around and shook his head. "Everyone else here knew her better than I did." *I don't know what I'm doing here. I didn't know her at all.*

Nina sighed. "You do belong here, Willie," she said. "You know that funerals aren't for the dead." She glanced over at Billie and Truman. "They're for the living, the people who are dealing with the death of their loved one or friend." *I heard Mama say that to my father when they argued about whether or not I should go to Delilah's funeral. It was hard to see her in her casket, but Mama knew I had to see her, if only to face her death.*

Willie nodded. *Nina's right.* "Yeah, so we're here for Billie," he said. He looked over at Billie and sighed. "I don't know what to say to her, Nina." He shook his head. "Nothing I can say will make her forget what happened." *I don't know why I'm being so weird. I should know how Billie feels right now.* He sighed and shook his head. *You're her big brother. Start acting like it.*

Nina shook her head. "Billie isn't expecting you to say or do anything," she said. "She just needs us to be here, if only for her." *This is the second funeral I've been to in only six months. I don't know which one is worse, losing your best friend because he was killed in a terrorist attack, or your grandmother dying of old age. Death, no matter how it comes, either suddenly or slowly, still stings.*

"This is the same church where they had our father's funeral," Willie said. He looked over at Truman. "Truman doesn't remember, but that's the first time we met, not years later, at college." *I wanted him to be my brother then, but after that day, not after the way his mother looked at us.*

***

Drew was also there, sitting next to Willie at the right end of the pew. He sighed and shook his head. "I wish I were sitting next to Billie," he said, frowning. "After all, I'm her boyfriend and should be comforting her." *If Josephine weren't Billie's grandmother or I weren't her boyfriend, I wouldn't be here. I've heard of Josephine Carver but never met her.*

Rebecca shook her head and frowned at Drew. She reached out and slapped his shoulder. "Billie is exactly where she needs to be sitting," she said. "Of all the people here, Billie and Truman are the ones who are feeling the loss of their grandmother the most." *Almost half of the people here couldn't stand Josephine, and the other half, besides those here for Billie and Truman, feared Josephine.*

Drew sighed and nodded. "You're right," he said. He glanced over at Billie, who was leaning against Truman and crying. "I just wish I could take away all of her sadness." *Funerals are strange. It's the only time men are allowed to cry, but we can't cry too much. No, we have to stand there, with tears streaming down our faces, but our faces have to be like stone, not emotions showing.*

Rebecca reached out and touched Drew's shoulder. "I know you want to do that," she said. She sighed and shook her head. "But you also know you can't do that. Billie has to be sad today. She just lost one of the most important people in her life." *I hope Billie doesn't do anything foolish or rash, like leave Boston. I don't know how, but she has become one of the most important people in my life, and I don't know what I would do if she moved away.*

Drew nodded, frowning. "Yeah, I know," he said. He looked around, seeing many familiar faces and many he didn't know or recognize. "This is quite an interesting mix of people." *Most of the so-called Upper Crust families are here. I know a few of them, if only by reputation.*

Rebecca shrugged her shoulders. "If you say so, Drew," she said. "Most people here only showed up because it's expected of them." *The only people who matter are the few here for the right reasons, because they care about Billie or Truman.* She smiled.

Billie has impacted many people's lives, and I wonder if she realizes how important she has become and how much she has changed things around here.

***

Jasmine sat in the pew behind Rebecca. She noticed her talking to Drew, sitting in the first pew. She frowned. "They both need to be quiet," she said, shaking her head. "This is a funeral, not a party." *I'm glad that my mother understood why I had to come here. The rest of my family may not have liked or cared about Aunt Josie, but I did, and that's why I'm here.*

Bridget chuckled. "They know it's a funeral," she said, poking Jasmine in the ribs. "Don't worry about them." She shrugged her shoulders. "People deal with death in many different ways." *I'm lucky that Jasmine called me and told me about this funeral.* She looked over at the front pew, where her family was sitting. *My family has been giving me the silent treatment ever since I told my grandmother that I wasn't straight.* She sighed and shook her head. *They don't want to be seen with me in public.*

Jasmine shrugged her shoulders. "You might be right," she said. She sighed and shook her head. "Still, I think it's disrespectful to be gossiping at a funeral." *It's also disrespectful, which is the reason why most are here. They're not here because they're mourning Aunt Josie's death. No, they're here because it would look bad if they didn't show up. It's only when you die that you get the respect you deserve.*

Bridget shook her head and softly chuckled. "They're not gossiping, Jasmine," she said. "You remember that they used to date." *Now, Drew is dating Billie while Rebecca is dating Truman.* She frowned. *Or at least, that's what I've heard.* She shook her head and giggled. *They're dating members of the same family. If that's not messed up and weird, I don't know what is.*

Jasmine looked over at Bridget and scowled at her. "There's nothing funny going on here," she said. "This is a funeral, for Christ's sake." *Why did Bridget have to sit next to me? Why isn't she sitting with the rest of her family?* She reached out and pinched Bridget's arm. "Behave yourself, Bridget."

Bridget rubbed her arm, frowning. "Okay, I will," she said. *Why is Jasmine being so bitchy? Oh, yeah, that's right. Billie's grandmother was also her grandaunt.* "I'm sorry, Jasmine. I wasn't trying to be disrespectful." She reached out and took Jasmine's hand. "I'm sorry for your loss."

Jasmine sighed. "Thanks, Bridget," she said. "Billie isn't the only one who is heartbroken."

***

Iris and Sadie sat together in the second pew, next to Rebecca.

Iris shifted around, frowning. "I wish we were sitting closer to Billie," she said. "She needs to be with everyone who cares about her." *Funerals are strange. It's the only time it doesn't matter who your friends are, because it's all about your family.*

Sadie shook her head. "You know how funerals work," she said. "The family of the departed sit together while their friends sit somewhere else." *I don't know how Iris talked me into coming here. I'm not sure I belong here.* She shook her head and sighed. *I may not be Billie's rival anymore, but I can't say that we're friends. I don't know if we'll ever be friends, despite Iris being friends with Billie.*

Iris nodded. "Yeah, I know," she said. She looked towards Billie, who was sitting with her family. "Poor Billie, I know she's going through hell right now." *Her face would light up whenever she talked about her grandmother. They got along so well, despite their different backgrounds and the age difference.*

Sadie nodded. "Yeah, of course she is," she said. She leaned closer to Iris. "I may not be friends with her, like you or Rebecca, but even I know how important her grandmother was to Billie." *After I found out that her grandmother used to be a famous writer, I realized where Billie got her talent for writing.* She smiled. *And when Iris found out that her grandmother was Josephine Carter, her journalist role model, she wanted to talk about her all the time with Billie.*

Iris nodded. "Her grandmother was important to me, too," she said. She sighed and shook her head. "I'm lucky that I got to talk to her a few times before she died." *I'm glad that Sadie wasn't there. She wouldn't ever let me forget how I acted the first time I met Billie's grandmother.* She chuckled and smiled. *I've met a few famous writers before and was able to maintain my cool and be professional, but not with Josephine Carver.*

Sadie gave Iris a dirty look, frowning. "Don't forget that we're at a funeral," she said. "I don't think Billie would appreciate you chuckling at her grandmother's funeral." *I hope Billie appreciates me coming. I don't like funerals, they're so creepy.*

"You're right," Iris said. She looked over at Sadie. "I appreciate you coming here with me."

***

The church was packed, with almost every pew occupied. Only the last two pews, the back ones, were practically empty, with four women sitting in the next to last pew and a woman sitting in the back pew by herself.

Three of the women were sitting together while the other one, the fourth, sat by herself at the end of the pew. The three women were softly talking to each other while the other women, sitting in the same pew and the other sitting in the pew behind them, listened.

"This is the second funeral we've been to in the last six months, Bobbie," the auburn-haired woman said, looking over at the dark-haired woman sitting beside her. She shook her head and frowned. "I thought the only funeral I would ever have to go to would be my parents' funeral."

Bobbie sighed and nodded. "Yeah, I know," she said. She looked down at her hands, which were clenched together. "The first funeral I remember going to was my little sister's, over ten years ago." She looked over at the woman sitting beside her, on her right. "Thanks for coming with me to this thing, Natalie." She reached out and took Natalie's hand. "I appreciate it, and I'm sure Billie also appreciates it."

Natalie nodded. "I'm here because I know you need me to be," she said. She sighed and shook her head. "I'm not here for Billie, though she has my condolences."

At the end of the pew, the woman sitting away from them turned and looked at them. "Well, I'm here for Billie," she said. She sighed and shook her head. "I don't know what I will say to Billie or even if I'll get to speak to her."

Bobbie frowned and looked over at the woman. "You don't have to sit there, Michelle," she said. "You can sit with us, if you want to."

Michelle shook her head. "No, that's okay," she said. "I should be sitting up there, next to Nina." She sighed. "Billie doesn't know I'm here." She looked over at Bobbie. "Nina's the one who told me about the funeral."

***

The woman sitting in the back pew by herself shook her head and frowned. *Why am I here? Should I be here?* She looked towards Billie and sighed. *I haven't even talked to Billie in almost nineteen months, since she broke up with me.*

You're here because it's the right thing to do, Georgia.

Georgia rolled her eyes. *Oh, great, it's bad enough that I'm crashing Billie's grandmother's funeral, but I also have to listen to my mother's voice in my head, too?*

Wait a minute. You weren't invited to attend this funeral?

Georgia shook her head. *No, Mom, I wasn't invited.* She sighed and patted the pack of cigarettes sitting in the breast pocket of her jacket. *I'm dying for a smoke. If I knew I wouldn't cause a scene, getting up and leaving while everyone else was listening to the preacher, I would stand up, leave this pew, walk outside, and light a cigarette.*

You will do no such thing, Georgia Ann Grace.

Georgia sighed. *I didn't say I was going to do it, Mom.* She clenched her hands together and stared at them. *I made a mistake in coming here. I shouldn't be here.*

Yes, you should be here. You're not here because you want to be here, but because you care about Billie.

Georgia nodded. *I do care about her, Mom. The truth is, I haven't stopped caring about her or loving her either.* She stared at the four women sitting in the pew before her. *Okay, let's see if I can figure out who those women are. I've heard them say their names, and their names sound familiar. Oh, yeah, I remember now. Billie's first love was Michelle, and her best friend was Bobbie. Okay, so who are the other two?* She snapped her fingers. *That Natalie has to be Bobbie's roommate, and Jordan is Billie's other friend from New Orleans.*

Are you going to say anything to Billie?

Georgia shook her head. *No, Mom, I'm not going to say anything to Billie. When the service ends, I will leave; hopefully, no one will see me.*

***

The minister walked up to the podium, looked at Truman, and nodded.

Truman nodded. "It's time, Billie," he said. He cleared his throat. "Are you sure you want to do this?" *I'm glad Billie offered to give Josephine's eulogy. I don't think I could do it.*

Billie nodded. "I'm sure," she said. "Wish me luck."

Billie stood up, left the pew, and walked to the podium. She cleared her throat and took out some papers. "Good afternoon, I'm Billie Carver, and I'm here to give Josephine's eulogy," she said. "I'll admit that I had a hard time writing this eulogy for Josephine, not knowing if I could put what Josephine meant to me into words."

Willie leaned closer to Truman. "I'm surprised she's giving the eulogy instead of you," he said. He shrugged his shoulders. "You knew Josephine longer than Billie did."

Truman nodded. "You're right, Willie," he said. "I did know Josephine longer than Billie, but she also lived with Josephine." *In less than three years, Billie became close to Josephine. They bonded so quickly, finding in each other something they were both missing in their life.*

Billie unfolded the papers and placed them in front of her. She started reading what she had written. "I met Josephine a little over three years ago," she said. "I received a letter from her and learned that my father's mother was alive and wanted to meet me."

Billie told the story of how Josephine came into her life and how Josephine had changed her life. "She taught me how to be brave and never to let anyone tell me who I was or who I could be," she said. "I also gained a brother because of Josephine."

***

Josephine's funeral ended an hour later. Billie and Truman stood outside near the front door.

Truman looked over at Billie. "So, how many people are coming to the house, now that this is over?" *Billie wrote a beautiful eulogy for Josephine. I'm surprised she was able to read it without crying. Everyone else was crying by the time she finished reading it.*

"Only the people who matter," Billie said. She cleared her throat. "Okay, Truman. It's time to accept everyone's condolences."

The crowd of mourners exited the church and gave Billie and Truman their condolences for the next ten minutes. When the last person left the church, the minister went to Truman and shook his hand.

Billie and Truman went to Truman's car, which was parked at the back of the church. They got in and then they drove away.

***

They arrived at Josephine's house ten minutes later. Truman parked his car behind Billie's car.

"Are you sure your friends are coming?" *I'm glad that no one else is coming over. I'm not comfortable with most of the people at the funeral being at Josephine's house.*

Billie nodded. "I'm sure," she said. She glanced at her watch. "They probably waited for us to leave before they left the church."

***

Billie turned out to be right. Billie's friends showed up about five minutes later. Billie greeted them at the door while Truman sat in the parlor, sitting on the couch and smoking a cigarette. They followed Billie into the parlor and sat down on the other couch.

Truman frowned and looked over at Billie's friends. *Okay, let's try to remember their names. Billie introduced me to them just before Josephine's funeral started.*

Billie sat next to Truman on the couch and leaned towards him. "I know what you're doing," she said. She shook her head and grinned. "You're trying to remember their names, aren't you?"

Truman nodded and chuckled. "You're right," he said. He sighed and shrugged his shoulders. "I'm usually good at remembering names, but not today." He looked over at Billie. "Tell me again." *I wonder why the friends Billie made here didn't come over. They showed up to Josephine's funeral, which I know meant a lot to Billie. It also meant a lot to me.*

Billie nodded. "Okay, I will," she said. She pointed at one of her friends, an attractive woman with dark hair who was nervously smoking a cigarette. "That one is my best friend, Bobbie Lamont." She smiled. "We've been best friends for almost twenty years."

Truman nodded. "You've mentioned her a few times," he said, smiling. "She seems nice." *She barely spoke to me when Billie introduced her to me. I almost got offended until Billie explained to me that she's shy.*

Billie nodded. "Bobbie is nice," she said. She then pointed at the red-haired woman sitting on the other end of the couch. "That's Jordan McCullers sitting over there." She smiled. "We've been friends for the last three years."

Truman nodded. "So, she's your newest friend, uh?" *I remember Billie telling me all about Jordan and how they became friends after they graduated from Tulane, before Billie left New Orleans.*

Billie nodded. "She is," she said. She shrugged her shoulders. "I sometimes regret that we didn't become friends before, when we were students at Tulane."

Truman smiled. "It doesn't matter now," he said. "Bobbie and Jordan must be good friends, traveling all the way here, just to be here for you in your time of need." *Jordan flew in from Birmingham while Bobbie drove here from New York City.*

Billie nodded. "They are good friends, both of them," she said. She sighed. "Now, I wouldn't call the one sitting between Bobbie and Jordan my friend, but I appreciate her being here."

Okay, let's see if I can remember her name. "She must be Natalie Adams, Bobbie's roommate," Truman said. He frowned. "Why don't you consider her a friend, Billie?" *I remember Billie telling me that she and Natalie had clashed when they first met three years ago, when Billie spent a few days in New York City while on her way here. Billie seemed to believe that Natalie was jealous of her friendship with Bobbie.*

Billie sighed and shook her head. "We just didn't click," she said. "I don't know why, since we're both friends with Bobbie, you would think we would find something in common, but we haven't."

Truman frowned. "If she isn't your friend, why is she here?" *Maybe Natalie wants to be your friend, Billie, but you don't want to be her friend.*

Billie shrugged her shoulders. "I don't know why she's here," she said. She looked around and sighed. "What are we going to do now, Truman?"

Truman sighed and shrugged his shoulders. "I don't know," he said. "I can't think right now about anything besides how much I'm going to miss having Josephine around." *There's a massive hole in my heart where my love for Josephine used to be.*

Billie gestured at the house they were in. "What's going to happen with this house?" She frowned and sighed. "Do I need to start looking for another place to live?"

Truman reached out and took one of Billie's hands. "You don't have to worry about having to move, Billie," he said. "I don't know for sure, but I would be willing to bet Josephine left this house to either you or me."

Billie nodded. "You're probably right," she said. She wiped the tears off her face. "I've known this day was coming for a long time." She sighed. "I used to have nightmares about it. They used to be so bad that when I woke up from them, I would have to leave my bedroom and go to Josephine's bedroom, to make sure she was still alive."

Truman sighed and nodded. "I remember you telling me about those nightmares," he said. "I didn't start having nightmares about Josephine dying until the last time we had to check her into the hospital." *And then I had to face the fact that Josephine was dying, that she wasn't going to get better.* "Can I ask you something, Billie?"

Billie nodded. "Sure, go ahead," she said. She took out a cigarette and lit it. "What's on your mind, Truman?"

"Why didn't your Boston friends join us?" *I tried to talk to Rebecca, but she left the church before I could.*

Billie took a drag off her cigarette. "I'm having breakfast with them tomorrow morning," she said. She looked back over at her friends sitting on the couch. "They wanted to come over, but I felt I needed to spend time with Bobbie and Jordan." She sighed. "They're leaving tomorrow and I don't know when I'll see them again."

Truman nodded. "Okay, I get it now," he said. He took out a cigarette and lit it. "Here we are, sitting in the parlor and smoking, after always giving Josephine a hard time about her smoking." *Both of us need to quit smoking, especially after giving Josephine a hard time for doing the same thing.*

Billie nodded. "Yeah, I know," she said. She cleared her throat. "I'm surprised that everyone who knows me, even if I wouldn't consider them my friends, showed up for Josephine's funeral."

I know who Billie is talking about. "Well, Jasmine was there because Josephine was her grandaunt," Truman said. He shrugged his shoulders. "I couldn't tell you why those other two ladies were there."

Billie nodded. "I thought the same thing," she said. "And then I asked Rebecca." She took a drag off her cigarette. "Rebecca told me that Bridget and Sadie wanted to show me support in my time of need." She chuckled and shook her head. "Both of them couldn't stand me when they met me, and they both tried, in different ways, to wreck my life or hurt me in some way."

Truman nodded. "They were your rivals," he said. "Rebecca told me all about the mess you went through with them." *I knew Billie was having some trouble, but I didn't realize how much shit she had been through because of Sadie, Bridget, and even Jasmine.*

"Yeah, I've been through the ringer because of them," Billie said. She chuckled and shook her head. "And now, they want to be friends with me." She took a drag off her cigarette. "I can't believe it."

Truman chuckled and grinned. "The more I get to know you, Billie, the more you start to remind me of Josephine," he said. He looked around at the pictures hanging on the walls in the parlor. "She made many friends in her life." *Maybe that's why Josephine and Billie clicked so quickly. Josephine must have seen something in Billie that reminded her of herself.*

***

Thirty minutes later, Billie's friends left. They sat in the parlor, smoking cigarettes and sipping whiskey.

"I'm sure Josephine told you about her marriage to our grandfather," Truman said. "She was so pleased when you accepted her offer." He reached out and took one of her hands. "You're the reason why she didn't give up. You brought her back to life, Billie."

Billie tried to smile but failed. "When will I stop missing her?" She sipped her whiskey and wiped the tears off her face.

Truman touched her forehead and her chest, just above her heart. "Josephine will always be with you, Billie."

***

Billie moved to Boston to learn about her father and get to know Josephine better. She accomplished both and realized that, despite being born there, she didn't belong there.

Billie never believed the profound impact she had made on the lives of the people she had met in Boston. She helped Jasmine come to terms with her mixed heritage, helped Bridget live her life honestly, and helped Sadie let go of her fears of losing Iris. And although she would eventually end it with Drew, she never regretted dating him or Georgia. She stayed friends with Rebecca and Iris for the rest of her life, even when she left Boston two years after Josephine's death. And she remained close to Willie and Nina, which made her mother happy. And after Truman stopped dating Rebecca, she introduced him to Bobbie, whom he married less than two years later.

Billie would later realize that Truman was right. The lessons she learned and the stories Josephine told her would help her for the rest of her life. She would hear Josephine's voice whenever she was unsure what to do, whether it was about her life or what to write next. She would become the woman she was always meant to be because of her relationship with Josephine.

About the author

Zelmer Wilson was born in Fort Collins, Colorado, in July 1975. During the summer of 1990, while visiting his mother and sisters in Birmingham, Alabama, he discovered his calling in life; he wanted to be a writer. He has been writing ever since that summer. He is the author of nine novels. He resides in Nashville, Tennessee, with his wife, Suzie Rae and their four cats. He's writing his tenth novel, Heritage Road.

Afterword

Dear Reader,

Thanks for buying The New Girl. I hope you enjoyed it. As an independent author, I don't have a marketing department or the exposure of being on bookshelves. If you enjoyed The New Girl, please spread the word and support writing more books by writing an Amazon review or telling a few friends about this book.

- Write a review on Amazon
- Buy my next book, Heritage Road
- Check out my other books, In the Middle, Bobbie Lamont, The Distance Between, Nothing but Trouble, Billie Carver, Next Best Thing, A Real Southern Lady, and The Company She Keeps
- If you'd like to Fnd out when my next book, Heritage Road, will be published, go to my Zacebook page, Zelmer Wilson the Author, www. facebook.com/Wilson.zelmer or my website, www.zelmerwilson.com

Thanks again,
Zelmer Wilson